NEIGHBOR Feud

ANNIKA CHAMPENOIS

Sunny Laughs Press

Published by Sunny Laughs Press

Paperback ISBN: 979-8-9861083-6-0

Praise for Neighbor Feud

"What happens when feuding turns to flirting and judgment turns to understanding? Annika Champenois has written an engaging enemies-to-lovers story with a strong couple at the center and an interesting secondary cast. Both Jordan and Keisha are well-rounded, complete with struggling families, emotional baggage, strengths and weaknesses, failings and foibles, and some lovely, endearing traits. As I read, I became part of their story, sharing their sorrows, hopes, fears, and dreams. When what was meant to be the coup d'etat on their feud turned into a blessing, I followed them there as well. I thoroughly enjoyed their story."
—Susan Aylworth, author of the *Rainbow Rock Romance* series

"This story is thoughtful, real, heart-tugging, and beautiful. I feel that I am a better person after reading it."
—Tiffany Fletcher, inspirational speaker and author of *Mother Had a Secret*

"No review can truly capture the magic of this book; you just have to read it yourself. *Neighbor Feud* is funny, chaotic, and unexpectedly deep. ... A suburban romantic comedy that takes neighborhood tension into a full-blown, laugh-out-loud war."
—Readers' Favorite five-star review

Praise for Walter Times Two

"Annika is a talented writer who has given readers a creative and clever romp around BYU campus and Provo. ... Sparkling and witty dialogue fills the book and moves the story along at a crisp pace."
—Brad Wilcox, popular youth speaker and author of *The Continuous Atonement*

"With a delightfully sweet tone and loads of laughs, Champenois (author of *Artfully Annoying*) immerses readers in a faith-based romance that packs serious heart. ... [T]he novel's innocence and sense of wonder will appeal to readers who enjoy tender, satisfying love stories."
—BookLife

"Annika Champenois has crafted a unique love story that's hard to put down. The plot will grab readers' attention, and the story will keep them turning the pages."
—Readers' Favorite five-star review

CHAPTER 1

Army-crawling across Jordan Taylor's carpeted living room floor, Keisha listened to the sound of him stoking the grill in the backyard while his youngest children played. One voice grew louder, and she tensed. If he sent someone in for something, she was in trouble. Two minutes was all she needed. Two minutes of distraction.

The loud voice grew distant, letting her breathe a sigh of relief.

She edged around the corner and looked up at the slingshot that hung from the kitchen ceiling. "Target acquired," she whispered.

He had no right to confiscate her children's toys, even if she *had* used this one to fling a few pebbles at his wall. For the last few days, the slingshot had been displayed where she could see it through the window, taunting her. His kitchen, like hers next door, was as far removed from the backyard as it could be and faced the driveway.

She moved all the way into the room before she stood, out of sight of her barbecuing neighbor. Putting her bottle on the counter, she reached for the slingshot and tried to untie it from the light fixture.

The knot tangled. She pursed her lips, trying again and again to loosen it. At last she freed her quarry, along with a piece of paper that had been crumpled up inside it. Curious in spite of the ticking clock, she unfolded the paper and felt her expression darken.

It was a photo of a snowman. He had built it in his yard last winter, complete with a red wig reminiscent of her hair and a sign that said "Abominable Snowwoman." Apparently he had taken a picture of it too. Her scowl deepened.

"Caught you."

Her head whipped up. Jordan stood in the opening to the kitchen, his bulky frame imposing and his slate-gray eyes narrowed as he pointed a water blaster at her.

She shrieked, grabbed her bottle of cherry-scented detergent, and threw it at him. It was supposed to have gone into a foam explosion she would leave in his home, but time was up. Jordan threw his arms in front of his face, and she ran past him as the aroma of cherry—a scent he hated—soaked his shirt.

"What the—Ew!" His voice sounded behind her as her feet pounded the floor. "Keisha!" he roared while she sprinted outside and toward her house. Heavy steps followed. A stream of water hit her back, and she yelped and looked over her shoulder. Jordan was working the water gun with one hand and covering his nose with the other as he ran. Keisha looked ahead and sprang up the steps to her home. She slammed the door behind her, hearing a spray of water against the wood.

Panting, she dropped the slingshot and the mocking photo on the floor. With a hand on her chest, she struggled to regain her breath. Another spray hit the door and another yell sounded outside, but it didn't matter. The corners of her lips lifted. She had won this round.

***

KEISHA JOHANSEN WAS, OF course, a perfectly responsible and mature mom. She enjoyed the faint scent of cherry drifting into the kitchen as she prepared school lunches the next morning. Bread and jam filled the granite counter between the kitchen and the white-walled, somewhat messy, living room. Sunlight streamed in through the windows, and she grinned. She could just imagine it lighting up the message she had left on Jordan's roof last week. Not that she had time to savor her victory.

"June, would you get the mail?" she called out as she unscrewed the peanut butter jar and flipped slices of bread onto the cutting board.

"Mommy." One of the twins tugged at her sleeve and spoke through a hole in his teeth. "Make it with loth and loth of peanut butter, okay?"

"Mom, I don't feel ready for the spelling test. What if I fail?" Lizzie asked, leaning her arms on the countertop and giving Keisha a clear view of her anxious brown eyes.

"Do I *have* to go to school?" Frayden whined with all the pre-teenage reluctance a ten-year-old could muster. He stood opposite Lizzie on the dining and living room side, leaning away from the counter as though it, or the people around it, were a source of contamination. His russet hair needed another haircut, but the ornery set of his face showed the stubbornness of a boy who wouldn't let his mom get close with a pair of scissors.

Keisha dropped the peanut butter knife between the sandwiches and dipped a hopefully clean knife into the glass of jelly, her hands flying. She shook back her red-brown mane to keep it out of the food. There had been no time to comb her hair yet.

"Lizzie, I prepped you for the test last night," she said. "You'll do great. You always do. Thank you, June Bug, just put the mail right there on the table." Away from the crumbs. And the cereal spill.

"Mo-om, I'm thirteen years old. You can't call me June Bug anymore." The reproachful look on her oldest daughter's face was priceless. If only Keisha didn't fear she would see it every day for the next seven years.

June was Keisha's first teenager, and as far as Keisha was concerned, she would also be the last. If only scientists would hurry up creating time machines, then Keisha could make the four others skip their teens. Man, she would use such a machine right now on Frayden if she could.

She felt a tug on her other sleeve.

"Loth and loth of jelly, pleathe."

"Has everyone brushed their teeth?" she asked, smearing on extra strawberry preserves in response to her second gap-toothed son's request.

"Frayden hasn't," Lizzie volunteered, distracted from her upcoming test. "He says he's going to breathe on everyone at school, and then they'll fall over."

"Eww," June exclaimed.

"Cool," Carl and Kale said at the same time, tearing their gazes away from their lunch sandwiches.

"Would they, Mom? Would they fall over if he breathed on them long enough?" Lizzie asked, all eight years of her life seemingly concentrated on that question and her readiness to believe whatever her mom told her.

"Depends on what he ate, I guess." Keisha wrapped the last sandwich and threw it into Kale's Spiderman lunch box. "Everybody, out to the car."

Her five children scrambled for the bathroom.

"I said the *car*." She waved her keys at the deserted room, which paid as much attention to her as did her children. "If you needed to use the bathroom, you should have done it five minutes ago."

Five minutes later, she snatched up Kale by his open red backpack as he ran toward the front door. Shoving his lunchbox into his backpack, she zipped it shut and let him go.

Carl received the same treatment. Freed, he ran after his brother, closely followed by Lizzie and Frayden. Next came June, who slammed the door in Keisha's face. Before Keisha could open it, it flew open, and June stuck her head in and yelled, "Mom, we're gonna be late!"

June's mouth rounded as she found herself face to face with Keisha. "Oh."

"Yes. 'Oh,'" Keisha agreed, brushing away the hair that had blown into her face at June's yell—or maybe at the abrupt movement of the door, the less dramatic part of her reasoned.

"My bad," June yelled over her shoulder as she rushed to the car.

The Missouri morning air was crisp and crowded with voices. Keisha strode to her dark red van. Beside her, in the shared driveway, the Taylors' truck was on and running.

"Dad, why can't I sit in the front?" one of the Taylors called out.

"Just get in, kid. I'm sick and tired of this argument," Jordan answered from the driver's seat.

"We're ready, Mom. Start the car," Lizzie sang out.

Keisha turned it on, but just then, the truck beside her shot backward and stopped, crooked and blocking her path.

Her eyes widened at the sudden obstacle. She put her head out the window. "Jordan Taylor, get your car out of my way! And next time, remember that ladies go first!"

"Oh, really?" he yelled back. "I'll be sure to let her go first when I see one!"

Laughter rang out from his oldest daughter in the passenger seat while June groaned. Jordan revved his engine as though preparing for a race, making Keisha's blood pressure rise in tandem with the noise. Finally he backed out of the driveway and sped off down the street.

"Come on, Mom, we can beat him." Carl bounced in his seat.

Shaking her head, she turned in the opposite direction—after all, there was more than one way out of their neighborhood block—and pushed the van to the exact speed limit. Maybe she could catch him at the intersection. "We don't want to play games in traffic, Carl." Although it wouldn't hurt if she *could* get there first.

"But Mom, his kids will be awful about it if we lose," June told her.

"You never talk to them anyway," Frayden scoffed from the back seat.

June glared at him. "So what? Don't forget, Selima's in some of my classes, even if she does keep skipping school."

The poor fifteen-year-old was retaking eighth grade for the second time. Keisha worried about Jordan's daughter sometimes. She was a quiet sweet girl with large hazel eyes and hair as chestnut brown as her dad's and most of her siblings'.

They reached the intersection, but there was no catching up to Jordan. Not then, nor at the next crossing. It was probably better that way anyway. She focused on safe driving as she continued through the suburban streets the ten minutes to school.

"E-X-P-U-N-G-E," Lizzie spelled as they pulled up to the curb in front of the elementary school, a bright red car separating them from the Taylors' silver truck. "Mom, what does 'expunge' mean?"

Keisha gave her an encouraging smile. "It means you're going to get a hundred percent again." She blew Lizzie a kiss while everyone except for June unbuckled and jumped out.

"You know I'm proud of you, Lizzie," she called, leaning toward the window that faced the school.

Lizzie smiled and skipped to the building.

"I'm proud of all of you," Keisha yelled, in case one of them felt left out when she complimented Lizzie.

"Sheesh, Mom, if you're trying to get me back for yelling in your face at home, you got me," June complained in her shotgun seat between Keisha and the window.

In the rearview mirror, Keisha saw Jordan's car pull away. "Okay, let's go."

June pulled a pair of sunglasses from her backpack and put them on, looking like a celebrity as the wind played with her short hair through the open window. Keisha shook her head at her daughter's confidence. *She* had probably never looked half as cool at that age.

This time, they made it before the Taylors.

She put the car in park in front of the middle school and leaned over to ruffle June's blond hair. "You're my cool girl, you know that?"

"Hey, watch the hair."

"I'm just making sure it keeps that windblown look," she said helpfully.

June laughed and got out. Swaggering toward the school, she ran her fingers through her hair, making it crazier than ever. Girls from her class ran over to join her, their group growing as they reached the front doors. June was popular, all right.

Keisha smiled and turned on the radio as she drove. When a spirited fighting song came on, she scrolled the car windows shut and sang along.

She was feeling good about her voice twangs and fancy undulations, belting out songs of revenge, until she turned onto her home street and saw Jordan's car parked in the exact middle of the driveway, leaving no space for any respectably sized car on either side.

Turning off the radio, she cursed under her breath.

The curb was empty. On her side, a strip of grass she would have to ask June or Frayden to mow soon divided the sidewalk from the road. On the other side, a well-tended bed of flowers reflected the pride of a man who wanted passersby to think that his was a well-kept house and yard.

Should she?

Movement caught her eye. Jordan stood on the other side of his ever-open kitchen window, a broad grin on his smug face. He tipped his head back to drink something. When his gaze returned to her, he raised his eyebrows in a challenge.

That sealed her decision. No way could she let him have the upper hand twice in one morning.

Keisha's car came on sideways, the wheels on the right side coming up on the edge of the driveway ramp before going off into the bed of petunias—or begonias, or whatever they were—and stopping on top of them.

She looked up at Jordan's window, but it was abandoned. Seconds later, the man barged out of his house, red-faced and yelling and waving a can of beer.

Of course it was beer. Her heart sped up at the sight of the can, but she forced a steely calm as she turned off the ignition.

She wasn't afraid of Jordan. That was her strength. From the very first time they had yelled at each other, she had never allowed an ounce of fear to color her interactions with him. And boy, had they done a lot of yelling since then.

Of course, yelling was only the beginning. When he planted cactuses in her garden, she blew her leaves into his yard. When he destroyed the sheets she had hung to dry, she painted his rooftop. She never feared his reactions. In fact, she welcomed the anger without any real repercussions. Pranks she could deal with.

She smoothed her hair, opened the door, and stepped out. "What were you saying? I couldn't hear you with the door closed."

"Get that car out of my flowerbed," he raged. "We've spent hours and hours on that!"

Keisha rolled her eyes. "And I've spent dollars and dollars on my sheets, but I don't see you volunteering to pay me back. Besides, it's hypocritical to have a messy backyard and a perfect front yard. I should think you'd appreciate my effort to help people know how to judge you correctly when they see your place."

"Move that wreck out of there or I'll call the police."

She walked to her house, willing her heartbeat to stay normal. "You're drunk. Get back in your house, or *I'll* call the police." She sent him a strict glance and shut the door.

***

Jordan threw his can on the ground and immediately regretted it as the liquid spilled onto the front porch. What a waste of good beer. Gnashing his teeth, he strode to the offending car.

That woman! How did she come up with ways to get back at him so quickly? He wanted to kick her vehicle, but Keisha's warning about the police restrained him. Instead, he knelt and held up a pink begonia that had been flattened into the soil.

In all honesty, he rarely touched those flowerbeds. It was Selima who spent her time here. If only he had thought to mention that before. Keisha might have chosen to back her car out.

Poor Selima. His graceful, withdrawn oldest daughter tended to her plants with more interest than she showed in most things. Jordan indulged her in anything that helped her. He couldn't bring back her mom, but he could let her tinker with the garden.

For four years his wife had been gone. For four years he had stumbled alone, trying to be everything his family needed, calling on his oldest son to help, wishing he could turn back time.

He made a noise deep in his throat, cutting off the sorrow that threatened to come out. Selima's flowers were killed, and the murder instrument still stood on top of them.

His blood boiling, he swung his gaze up at the Dodge Grand Caravan. Never mind Keisha's warning. It was rare for either of them to call the police on each other, and the woman deserved a comeuppance that—

The gas door. Did his eyes deceive him? Was it loose?

He reached up and took hold of the edge. The gas door popped open on its spring.

His mouth spread in a grin, and he sprang up and ran to his garage.

How perfect. Taking her gas would be easy. He grabbed a hose and a couple of buckets, knocking over a bicycle in his hurry and wincing at the crash. Making his way back to the garage door, he stole a look at Keisha's intrusive kitchen window. It was always open when the weather allowed it so she could keep an eye on him. At the moment, however, it appeared to be empty. He lowered himself to the ground and crawled back to her van.

Hopefully she wouldn't notice the sudden drop in the gas tank volume until it was too late. He chuckled as he removed the cap and inserted the hose, leaving the other end of the hose in the bucket. Using his finger, he added pressure and sped up the process, then did the same thing into the other bucket. Just imagine her car stalling on a deserted road. Or better yet, what if it were near a gas station? Near enough to taunt her, but too far away for her to make it. How would she look when it happened? The image of her mad face popped into his mind, familiar and hilarious, eyebrows pinched above raging blue eyes.

Several other images showed up beside it, slowing his thoughts and bringing with them a twinge of regret. Sometimes he did wish—well, that things were different. When she moved in three years ago—but no, it was too late to change it.

He shook himself and removed the hose. Things being unchangeable and all that, he might as well have his fun. The corner of his mouth moving upward again, he dripped a little bit of gas back into the tank, replaced the cap, and closed the door securely.

Chapter 2

Keisha huffed her way from her workplace's parking lot, skipping her building and proceeding down the street. She needed to calm herself before she could go to work.

When she had started her car after breakfast, the van had given her a 'Low fuel' warning, and the gauge had pointed to empty. That was impossible though. She had filled it two weeks ago. The car must be mistaken. Once, she drove that van for three weeks with a 'Check engine' warning, and when she finally got it to the mechanic, it turned out the engine was fine.

It wasn't until the car sputtered that the truth hit her. It wasn't a mistake. It was Jordan.

When she poured in her emergency gallon of gasoline, the car worked again. When she got it to the gas station and filled it partway up, there was plenty of room for the gas.

Jordan must be laughing at home. The mere thought was infuriating. That was why she headed to the art boutique two blocks from work. It was a tiny place, squished between a Mexican restaurant and a used bookstore. The moment she saw it, her body relaxed.

At the entrance, she took a balancing breath. Then another. A smile lightened her face. She pushed the door open.

Cramped though it was, the store had a liberating effect on her. A flowery smell filled the air, and the white walls were covered with appealing art. The Computer Graphic pieces drew her in, and she approached them as she might approach a treasure. Some of the CGs looked so real, like photographs. In others, the digital element made them look like they had been painted or sketched.

There was a new black-and-white graphic of a little boy with his mouth open. He stared at her as though she had done something surprising. The picture looked so alive she nearly laughed out loud. How amazing that someone could create that effect on their computer.

The digital landscapes were stunning as well, but somehow, she always ended up gazing at the portraits. Once upon a time, she had enjoyed people-watching, just looking at those around her and silently admiring them. Even now, art like this grabbed her attention. She had several pieces at home, and one of these days, when she felt the need, she would buy more.

Tearing her gaze from the boy with the surprised expression, she left the store and went to her office building.

"Look who's here," Shawna greeted her with her usual friendly teasing as Keisha entered the row of cubicles they shared.

"Good to see you too, Shawna." Keisha sat down at her workstation. "As for you, George," she nodded at the stuffed giraffe on Shawna's desk, "you look a little droopy."

"You know, most of us would love to be able to eat breakfast at whatever time we'd like and then amble down to the office whenever we felt like it," Shawna continued the faux insults, not taking the bait. She just shook her wiry blond curls and rolled her eyes. Her walls were decorated with photos of her favorite African animal, but she was especially fond of the stuffed animal, which had been given her by a nephew. Shawna had a soft spot for children.

"And most of you would love to be a single mom with five children, isn't that right?" Keisha logged in on her computer and opened a priority file. She was beyond lucky to have gotten this job. The manager who hired her had been flexible, allowing her to work only during school hours. The next manager had let the arrangement stay but wasn't as quick to give that privilege to others.

"Well, I'd sure love to be a mom," Shawna said significantly.

Keisha sighed. "I know." She looked at her friend. "I'm sorry."

"Don't be." A light glinted in her eyes. "Troy and I decided to stop waiting for all my fertility treatments to miraculously work out, if they ever will. We're looking into foster care."

Keisha's eyes widened. "Really? As of when?"

"As of yesterday. I mean, we got in touch with the program some time ago and started taking classes, but yesterday, they contacted us about meeting with one of the children."

Shawna's face was mostly expressionless, but someone who knew her well could see she was holding back a smile while she waited for a reaction.

Keisha focused on her bright eyes and made herself exclaim, "That's exciting. I'm happy for you."

Sure enough, the smile broke out like the first flash of sunlight at dawn.

Keisha smiled too, but she felt as though her smile, in comparison, was only like a lightbulb turning on in a dusty room.

Shawna would be a wonderful parent, but what about her husband? Something in Keisha wanted to warn her that things might change, but she swallowed back the words. She couldn't make assumptions about Shawna's husband based on her own dismal experience.

It went like a bad fairy tale. Man marries woman. They have children. Man turns mean.

Or did he merely show his true colors once they started having children?

Keisha didn't trust men.

"Now, how's the famous Jordan Taylor?" Shawna asked, changing the subject and moving her chair closer in anticipation.

Keisha straightened. "*In*famous, if you please. He's stealing my gas."

"*No.* What is *with* this guy? Just last week—wasn't that last week, the sheets? He has *zero* respect for your private property." Shawna loved news about Keisha's battles the way some people loved soap operas.

"I know, right?" Keisha said, quickly warming to the conversation and launching into a description of Jordan's automobile sins from that morning.

When Shawna's phone rang, Keisha leaned back and thought of the incident Shawna had referred to. It evoked the usual feelings of annoyance, triumph, and exasperation. A couple of weeks ago, Jordan had decided to complain about the fact that she hung her bedsheets out to dry outdoors. The more he complained, the closer she moved them to his yard. When she moved them *into* his yard, they were promptly returned to her own property, the clothing rack upside down and pinning the sheets into the dirt.

Jordan must have thought that was the end of that. Then one day he walked into his kitchen only to find his window—the one he always rudely kept open in order to eavesdrop or yell at her—obscured by a layer of white fabric.

Due to his wonderfully loud reaction, Keisha got to watch as he tore out of his house, where he yelled again at the sight of the innocent sheet covering the wall outside his kitchen. From her window, Keisha raised her eyebrows as he tore down "that blasted bedsheet," along with another couple of "blasted sheets" which lay peacefully sunning themselves, slung across his truck and his lawn and never hurting a soul.

Of course, she had no expectations of having the bedding returned neatly folded and clean, but she did figure she would get them back eventually, in some sort of condition.

When she found one of her front-yard trees draped in toilet paper last week, she had a moment of disappointment. As she slowly ascended the ladder, she sulked. Something about it seemed so unworthy of his usual extensive warfare. After three years of enmity and rather creative ways of showing it, was he running out of ideas, resorting to more traditional shenanigans? Maybe he wasn't worth sparring with anymore. Maybe—She reached for the first strip of toilet paper. It was thick to the touch, the edges frayed, the paper one continuous strip.

Frowning, she touched the strip beside it. Then she touched the first one. Fabric. Toilet paper. Fabric.

Fabric?

Her sheets! He had ripped up her sheets and hung them in her tree among branches and toilet paper! What kind of madman would do that?

"The man is crazy," she yelled and flew down the ladder.

She didn't stop to think as she raced down the stairs to her basement, returned with the red paint left over from decorating some of her children's rooms, and pushed her screechy ladder in place so she could gain access to Jordan's rooftop. In loud, red block letters, she graffitied a section of his roof with the word GOTCHA. It was perhaps the most childish prank she had yet played on him, but it felt good.

By the time he came home from some errand or other, she was back in her house with a smirk and complete satisfaction at the thought of her message on his rooftop declaring her victory, with him none the wiser. She would laugh behind his back for as long as it lasted.

Smiling to herself, she put in her earbuds and returned to the work at hand.

Her favorite songs kept her company while she worked. Back in community college, she had kept a balance between art and math, enjoying stimulating humanities classes in between the practical accounting work. Now she mixed spreadsheets with music, and if she wanted art, well, there were always the pictures of giraffes staring at her from Shawna's cubicle.

Two hours after lunch break, Carrie Underwood's "Good Girl" made her pull out her cell phone. She frowned at the caller ID and accepted the call. "June Bug, what's up?"

"Mom, I forgot my jiujitsu uniform at home. I think it's on my bed. Could you get it for me? Like, right now?"

She looked down at her watch. June's practice session was starting in twenty minutes. "I'll be right there. I'll bring it to the dojo, okay?"

"Thanks, Mom." June hung up.

With a sigh, Keisha saved her spreadsheet. June couldn't be late for her class. She grabbed her brown leather purse.

Outside, her walk turned into a hobble as she dug around in her purse for the car keys.

"Ma'am, you dropped this."

She turned. On the sidewalk stood two young men, surely just out of their teenage years, in white collared shirts, black slacks, and nice ties. One of them held out her wallet.

"Thanks." She took it.

"I'm Elder Sørensen," said the first man and held out his hand. She shook it, her eyes moving to the shiny nametag that confirmed his name, complete with a strange letter that matched his accent.

"And I'm Elder Johnson," said the other young man, offering his hand as well.

"We're missionaries of The Church of Jesus Christ of Latter-day Saints," Elder Sørensen told her. "We're sharing a message from God about the restored church of Jesus Christ."

Was he for real?

"I know this message is of value to you and your family. It—"

"Sorry, but I'm busy," Keisha interrupted. "I have to go."

"Oh, we could meet you later if—"

"No thanks, I'm not interested." Their persistence and uncharacteristic confidence annoyed her. Men were supposed to leave when she told them to. Why did men never do what they were supposed to?

Even now, he of the strange letter stepped forward instead of away. "This message really is important. Who do you know that might be interested?"

She prepared to give him *the glare,* but something stopped her short. Not her conscience. An idea that curled her lips. "Actually, there *is* someone."

Thousand-watt lights came on in the boys' eyes, and one of them whipped out his cell phone. Oh yes, they were serious about sharing their message. She hoped they were every bit as persistent as they seemed.

"His name is Jordan Taylor." She clenched her hands on top of her purse in anticipation. "He lives on 1230 Quail Drive. I think he might like to hear what you have to say. He's been looking for God in his life."

Was it bad to lie about such a thing? She bit her lip, then shrugged. No need to worry about a supreme being who didn't know her. All that mattered were her children, and she lived life honestly enough for them.

Besides, she could just picture Jordan's gray eyes wide with confusion—then narrowed in annoyance—and finally filling with understanding and murderous intent, his square jaw tensing, once he realized whose fault it was that these missionaries were pestering him.

She would judge his annoyance by the level of his next prank. It had better be good.

Elder Sørensen was eagerly typing on his phone. "Can you give us his phone number, as well?"

She smiled and rattled off the digits.

"Sounds like you're great friends with him. You know his number by heart," Elder Johnson said while his companion put away the phone.

"Oh, I call him at least three times a week." To make complaints. She absolutely refused to have him on her contact list or even to use her cell phone on him, so she had to punch in the entire number on the landline every time. It had been a shock to move in and find something as ancient as a landline phone in the house, but she had soon found a use for it.

"Thank you so much. We promise this will help your friend. Have a great day, and if you have any questions about the church, please check out the website or call the number on this card."

Realizing it was the easiest way to get rid of them, she took the card he pressed on her and looked down at a picture of a woman in old-fashioned clothes holding a baby. Virgin Mary and Baby Jesus?

She put it in her pocket without a second glance, found herself shaking hands with the missionaries again, and then turned and headed for the parking garage. She had wasted enough time already. June would be waiting for her uniform, and Keisha knew how much the jiujitsu lessons meant to her.

Chapter 3

June paced inside the entrance of the martial arts club, or the dojo, as Mom liked to call it to prove she knew something about June's favorite sport. She stayed within sight of her teacher so he would see she was on time even if she couldn't begin exercises with the others. This class mattered, and she couldn't let him think she was slacking off. Especially not with those letters.

Her jaw clenched at the reminder of the envelope she had seen this morning. She had torn it up, like the others. He had no business writing to Mom.

The door pushed open, and Mom stepped inside with a white gi in her hands, her red hair shining under the ceiling light.

"Thanks, Mom. I owe you." June snatched the gi and rushed for the dressing room.

"Can I stay and watch?" Mom called behind her. "I can only stay for fifteen minutes anyway, and then I have to go pick up the others."

"Whatever," June yelled back and entered the locker room.

One minute left. She hurried to get dressed. Mom was probably out there with a cheesy grin right now, just because June had let her stay.

A smile tugged at her mouth. It didn't hurt to make Mom happy.

With her gi fastened, June ran back to the gym just as warm-ups began.

"Everyone, shrimp," *Mestre* Benicio called out, his Brazilian accent colorful.

June sprawled on her back along with her classmates and shrimped her way from one wall to the other, moving herself forward with her hips and shoulders, holding out her hands and feet in defense of each position. Her core tightened, and her back got sore on the ground, but it was a kind of sore she was used to. If she fell in a fight, she would know how to move against the floor to minimize injuries. An opponent who didn't know martial arts might not be so lucky.

In between bear crawls and crab walks, she caught sight of Mom on the bleacher. From a distance, she looked small and innocent. Up close, of course, she was warm and larger than life—but still fragile.

June's determination firmed as *Mestre* called out a kick for everyone to practice. She got up and got started, keeping her fists tight and her legwork accurate. Every move made her better. They gave her muscle memory and strength and confidence. She breathed hard through the shoulder locks and smiled when they got to the triangle choke. She wasn't the helpless girl she had once been. She was strong, and she could defend others.

***

Keisha's heart swelled with pride for June as her daughter practiced kicks and punches that would have looked great in any spy movie. She was beautiful and strong, accepting the teacher's corrections and improving quickly in her skills.

Unfortunately, the clock was ticking. With one last look at the wall clock, Keisha slipped out of the dojo, back into the hot streets and cloudy day. Her car awaited.

She sure spent a lot of time in that old Dodge. Moms ought to have their pick of Lamborghinis to make all their driving worth it.

When she arrived at the elementary school, Carl and Kale jumped up and down as though the sidewalk were a trampoline. Both let go of Lizzie's hands and scrambled toward the still-moving van.

Keisha braked hard, stopping five feet from the curb, her heart in her throat nearly choking her.

"Mom, I wanna do cowboy!" Kale's yell reached her through the open window while he grabbed the door handle and pulled.

"Me too, Mom. Me too." Carl put his hand over Kale's and tugged on the handle.

"*I* thaid it first."

"But I wanna do cowboy more."

"Hold it, hold it." Keisha held up both hands and refused to unlock the doors until the twins looked up and stopped arguing.

"*Never* go near a car while it's moving, boys," she said in her most dreadful voice. "That means our car too."

Kale's lip quivered. "I'm thorry, Mom."

Keisha's heart melted. It still beat fast at the thought of what could have happened, but she unlocked the doors and reached over to touch Kale's cheek when he climbed in.

"Can I do cowboy since I said I'm thorry first?" he blurted out.

She shook her head, laughing. "Get in, all of you. Lizzie, how'd it go?"

"I got a hundred percent." Lizzie smiled happily, holding up the paper. Her hair was half in and half out of a funky little braid that hadn't been there that morning. Maybe one of her friends at school was experimenting with hairdos.

"That's my smart girl." Keisha reached back and gave her shoulder a squeeze while Frayden came in and took a back seat. The twins started buckling up. "Okay, what's this about cowboys?"

The two of them broke out like Chaos from Pandora's box, yelling at the same time.

Pulling away from the curb, Keisha tuned out Kale and focused on Carl's words.

"We have to learn a . . ."

"A TIME PERIOD . . ." Kale was shouting.

". . . dress up . . ."

"AND PRESENT . . ."

". . . present on it," Carl finished, and Kale shouted for another two seconds before he completed his own sentence.

We have to learn about a time period and dress up and present on it, Keisha pieced together the words in her mind. Bingo. Message received.

"And I wanna be a cowboy," Carl repeated.

"Me too."

"Okay, boys. What day do you have to present?"

"Um." They looked at each other. "Really thoon?" Carl said.

"I think it's tomorrow," Kale said.

Of course it was. "Do you have a paper that describes the assignment?" she asked, rolling her shoulders to counter the stress that built in her at the thought of that deadline.

The boys rummaged through their backpacks and each produced a paper, flapping them at her between the front seats.

"Hold on to those for now. I'll look at them as soon as we're home."

"Mom, where'th June?" Carl asked, looking around in the car as though she might pop out behind Frayden.

"She has jutsu, of courthe," Kale told him scornfully.

"Mom, why don't you pick her up when she has jutsu?" Carl asked. Suddenly he gasped. "Will you thtop picking me up when I'm thirteen?"

"Only if you insist on it, and you'll have to beg hard. I don't like to let June walk home alone, but it's a short walk, and she knows how to defend herself, so I don't argue." *Anymore,* she added in her mind. She and June saw eye to eye on most things, but when June got an idea in her head, she could be remarkably stubborn.

"Tho you'll keep driving us?" Kale sounded relieved, but Keisha looked over in time to see him frown at a new thought. "You don't have to drive me if you'll let me be a cowboy," he offered.

Carl's mouth dropped open. "You snake," he yelled, throwing himself at Kale as far as his seatbelt allowed.

"Carl, don't," Lizzie squealed, trying to pull him away.

"Stop that right now, Carl. Kale, don't hit him back. Stop, or neither of you will be cowboys," Keisha scolded, her last warning finally getting to them.

"Now," she said when they faced forward obediently. "Is there no way both of you can be cowboys?"

"I don't want to be the thame as him," they whined at the same time, pointing at each other.

"If I can't be a cowboy, I want to be a thief." Kale folded his arms across his chest.

"Sheesh, you guys are a pain," Frayden said as they came to a stop at the house, Keisha parking neatly on her side of the double-driveway.

He was out of the car before Keisha unbuckled herself. She sighed. If only he wouldn't act so arrogant around his family all the time. He *had* to grow up nicer than his dad. He couldn't seriously be annoyed with his siblings that often. Some of it had to be for show.

She turned back to Kale while Lizzie slipped outside as well. "Thieves don't come in a specific time period."

"But I wanna be a thief now."

"Yeah, persuade the teacher to let him be a thief," Carl piped up. His little face held complete confidence in Keisha's ability to change the teacher's mind. It was both flattering and exasperating the way her youngest children believed Super-Mom could do anything.

Her heart gave a painful tic as she thought of June and Frayden. They had grown up in a home where it was painfully clear she wasn't all-powerful or in control. No one should ever have to see their mom get knocked around. She quickly pulled her mind back to the twins. "Was that a nice way to ask?"

"Thorry, I mean, will you please persuade the teacher to let him be a thief?" Carl rephrased his request and stared at her with large, beseeching eyes that opened up wider and wider, making it a strain for her not to laugh.

"Wait a minute." Keisha put a hand to her head a moment after the idea occurred to her, moving her fingers around and making an otherworldly humming noise.

"Ssh, she'th thinking Great." Kale poked his twin in the side and put a small hand over his own mouth, waiting in silence.

Keisha gave an inner sigh of satisfaction and reveled in the moment. She didn't remember when "thinking Great," as the twins called it, had started, but it always earned her a moment of complete admiration, so she gladly did it whenever the opportunity arose.

She looked down at the boys, whose eyes reflected near worship, and snapped her fingers. Their eyes grew huge.

"Robin Hood," she said.

Carl's mouth opened, but no words followed. He didn't seem to know what she meant.

Kale understood. "Robin Hood," he exclaimed. "I'll be Robin Hood. He's the betht thief ever. Ith he from a time period?"

"He is, and we'll learn all about his time period so you can present it." She opened her door and climbed out of the car.

"Yaaaaay," Kale screamed as though he were cheering at a football game.

"Can't you quiet your kid?" Jordan's spiteful voice yelled from his open window next door.

"Can't you shut your window?" Keisha shouted back, anger rippling down her back. Her ex had always been annoyed with the children, his outbursts triggered by their noise and their mess. The difference was that now she didn't have to take it. "Come on." The twins followed her inside, still excited. "Now let me see those papers."

The boys thrust their assignments at her, then turned and ran to the backyard, yelling and screaming.

"I said we have to research your time periods," she called as the glass door closed behind them. With a shake of her head, she looked down at the papers and found the due date. "That's in a month." She shouldn't have trusted the twins when they guessed at the deadline. "That's okay, then. I guess we don't have to get started just yet."

She dropped the pages on the dining table and went to the kitchen to prepare dinner.

***

JORDAN SAT IN FRONT of his computer in the study, eager to get more work done. Though the kids were now home, the house was mostly quiet, and he wouldn't hear much noise from Keisha's family through the wall.

His fingers tapped the furnished desk table. He probably shouldn't have yelled about her kids. He was so used to complaining about anything she did that bothered him that sometimes it spilled over onto others. Keisha could take it though. She could take it and dish out even more in return.

He grinned and opened a file. His newest client needed a draft by the end of the week, and Jordan was ready to put the rest of his ideas to paper.

He enjoyed architectural design. Switching from a company to free-lance a few years ago had been risky, but it had soon paid off, and working from home had its perks. He twisted to look at the rug behind him, where two pink stuffed bears and railroad tracks lay scattered. This was both a workroom and a playroom.

"Wait! I want to play too. Wait!" Imogene's six-year-old voice shouted somewhere in the living room. Little feet pattered across the floor, followed by the rolling noise of the glass door to the backyard.

She must have run after Solomon. At nine, he was the closest in age to her. Samuel and Selima were too old to play.

It sounded like she forgot to shut the door.

Stretching, Jordan got up and left the office. He wandered through the living room and stopped in the open doorway to the backyard.

Solomon was out there inspecting the hedge. Imogene turned and saw Jordan. "Daddy, I wanna play with the dog," she said.

She looked so cute with her blond curls and round face. With two dark-haired parents, she was the only child with light hair, probably inherited from Jordan's dad's side of the family. Jordan leaned against the doorframe and asked, "What dog?"

"The Johansens have a dog," she announced.

"Really?" That was news to him, and it made him tense. If Keisha had gotten a dog, would she find even more ways to annoy him?

"We saw them playing," Solomon said.

"In our yard." Imogene stomped her foot. "The twins played with him in our yard, so I should get to play with them too."

Jordan straightened. "They were in here? Did they go through the hole?" He started toward the hole in the juniper hedge Keisha still hadn't patched up. Not that he had volunteered to do it. It was useful for some of the pranks he played, but it wasn't meant for little boys to crawl through.

"I don't know. We saw them through the window," Solomon said.

Jordan turned to his children. "If Keisha's gotten a dog, she needs to keep it on her side. I won't—" He took a step, felt something squish, and looked down.

Dog poop oozed out on both sides of his sneaker.

"Uh, Dad," Solomon began in his placating tone.

Jordan pulled his shoe free and stormed across the lawn, trying to wipe his shoe on the way. "And she needs to know it right now!" he yelled.

Not wanting to get his floor dirty, he ran along the side of his house to the front, where he made a beeline for Keisha's door. Leaping onto the porch, he started pounding on the door.

Keisha always called him when she had complaints to make. Jordan always took the bull by the horns and faced her in person.

"Keisha! I know you're in there," he yelled and punched the doorbell.

The door swung open so hard he stumbled backward and narrowly missed getting hit in the face.

Keisha's blue eyes glowered at him. The smell of chicken gravy wafted out from behind her. "*Now* what's the matter?"

"'What's the matter?'" he repeated. "My kids tell me yours have been letting your dog run around all over in my backyard. It's even done its business in there."

Keisha rolled her eyes. "We don't have a dog."

He stiffened. "Oh, yeah? Are you calling my kids liars?"

"Oh, I wouldn't blame them for making things up. No doubt they're craving attention from you since you're always working from home doing whatever it is you do." She shut the door in his face, leaving Jordan open-mouthed with the things he still wanted to say.

He caught his breath on a curse and whirled around. On the sidewalk stood George from across the street, cane in hand while he stared at Jordan.

"You inventin' pets now?" asked the older man.

Jordan shook his head and raised his foot. "It's real. I stepped in its poop. It was there."

"I don't need to know." George shuffled along, using his cane to speed up his progress.

Jordan suppressed a groan. George was nice enough. He probably wasn't even one of the neighbors who reported him and Keisha the night they aimed megaphones at each other's house in a yelling war. Of course, they should have realized they were keeping others awake besides themselves. That had been an embarrassing night at the police station.

He went to his garage, keyed in the code, and ducked inside as soon as he could. Picking his way along the utility shelves, he rubbed the back of his neck.

Since Keisha had moved in, neighborhood block parties had grown awkward. Some of the neighbors told Jordan he ought to be nicer to Keisha. Some of them told Keisha to be nicer to him. Though he had been here longer, he didn't want to guess which of their two families would win a popularity contest. The neighbors had probably seen Samuel come home drunk and worse.

He raised his chin. Samuel was a good kid. Every family had problems. Each of Jordan's children were a dream, plus some baggage. Anyway, when Jordan and Keisha were in fight mode, most of the neighbors kept their distance.

His gaze settled on the utility buckets with Keisha's gas under a table. Fight mode took up most of his time. He may have stolen her gas, but he wanted this space for something else. What would be a good way to return the gas without nicely handing it over?

***

KEISHA HAD LOOKED IN the backyard and the living room. Finally she opened the door to the twins' room and put her hands on her hips. "Well, well, well, what have we here?"

Carl and Kale looked up with a start. Between them, a beautiful spotted spaniel stuck its nose into a basket full of Legos. The rainbow painted on the white wall behind it formed a perfect halo above its head.

"Mom!" Carl threw his arms around the poor thing, and it pulled its head back and tried to shake him off. "Can we keep him?"

She shook her head and came over, kneeling to look at the tags on his collar. "I'm sorry, Carl. I think he—*she*—already has an owner. I'm sure her owner misses her. Don't you think so?"

Kale put his hand on her arm. "I think his owner wath mean to him," he whispered, "and doesn't want him back. Someone who'th mean doesn't deserve to have their dog back."

"I think the owner's very nice to *her,* Kale, and is very sad right now because he or she doesn't know what happened to the dog. But you two can play with her until the owner comes and picks her up, okay?" Getting out her cell phone, she watched their expressions brighten.

"Yaaay," they cheered. Their shouts drew Lizzie, June, and even Frayden to the room. By the time Keisha finished her phone call, the spaniel was panting with excitement, running from person to person while still taking time off to explore the furniture and sniff at a plastic triceratops on the floor.

"Mrs. McDougal will pick her up in a bit," said Keisha.

"Can we play with her until then?" Lizzie asked.

"Yes, but don't feed her anything during dinner."

"Oh, she's so cute." June rubbed the furry sides with gusto.

Frayden was on his hands and knees in front of the dog, moving from side to side and making her more and more playful. Keisha got down to pet the spaniel too. It did her heart good to see Frayden enjoying himself with the others. His preteen disdain was gone, and it didn't return even when they went downstairs to eat.

Everyone's excitement was palpable throughout dinner. Keisha enjoyed it until Mrs. McDougal arrived and took her dog home, leaving the twins in tears.

Carl threw himself on the floor and refused to move.

"Guys, come on." Keisha tried to raise Carl, but he moved away and lay at a different angle. She crossed her arms and looked at Kale's tear-stained face turned toward the door. "I thought we agreed that it's best for the dog to be with her owner. Didn't you see how happy she was to see Mrs. McDougal? It's obvious her owner treats her very well and isn't mean at all."

"No, she wasn't happy," Carl said stubbornly. At least he had finally accepted the gender of the dog.

"Are you kidding?" Keisha exclaimed in exaggeration. "Did you see how crazy her tail went? I know you saw it. The dog was whapping you in the face with her tail, like this."

She swooped down and brought a soft fist repeatedly to his cheek, then grabbed him and tickled him until he screamed with laughter.

"Me too, Mom, me too! She wagged me in the face too," Kale yelled.

Keisha turned to him and gave him the same treatment. Lizzie laughed, and June rolled her eyes but looked amused as the twins ran laughing and screaming from the room.

Children got over hard things so quickly. With a smile, Keisha followed the boys to get started on their bedtime routine.

Once the children were all in bed, she settled on the worn dark green couch with a book and a deep yawn. Hopefully reading would keep her awake while the Taylors settled down next door. It was time to make a comeback, just as soon as his family had gone to sleep.

Most of the Taylor kids were older than hers, so their bedtimes were later. If that man imposed any kind of bedtime on them, that was. She wasn't sure if he cared enough to keep order among them.

She closed her eyes instead of rolling them, meaning to show disgust to an imaginary audience. She hadn't meant to fall asleep, but the next time she opened her eyes, her surroundings were midnight silent, and the crickets outside were faintly going at their fiddles.

She shook her head, waking herself up further. Putting the book down, she padded outside, barefoot and silent.

A glare of headlights made her draw back and crouch on her own doorstep.

Samuel Taylor's shining, dented blue sports car pulled up in front of his house—or rather, in front of the partially ruined flower-bed, although Keisha couldn't see the damage in the starlight. The engine turned off, and the seventeen-year-old stumbled outside, muttering something under his breath.

Keisha looked down at her hands and realized they had curled into fists. "You're letting your kids grow up to be troublemakers, Mr. Taylor," she hissed. Worry for Samuel pricked her, mingled with worry for her own children. She had seen Samuel drunk before, and at least twice she was certain he had been on drugs.

The front door slammed behind the boy. No lights went on, no voices sounded. Jordan Taylor, as usual, wasn't sitting up for his son like a good parent, ready to interrogate him about what he had been doing. She wished he would.

Keisha took a deep breath and expelled the unsettling image of Samuel from her mind. She had a mission to complete.

She walked around her car and stumbled, sucking in her breath and barely catching herself from falling over a large utility bucket that scraped her shin.

"Ouch." She pulled out her cell phone and turned on the flashlight.

There were two buckets. One had a note on top, written in scrawly handwriting: *Found this. You really should watch your stuff.*

Cautious, she pried off the lid. The inside was full of liquid, and it smelled like gas.

"Har, har." He thought he was so funny, stealing her gas and pretending he'd found it sitting around. He'd have cried tears of laughter if he'd seen her fall over it. Keisha lugged the buckets to her front porch, grunting with the effort. They were big, but she wasn't so sure they held all the gas he'd siphoned from her car.

She walked back down the driveway, stretching her ribs and trying to catch her breath as she looked for something, anything, to get back at Jordan.

Two gas cans lay in the open back of her neighbor's truck, begging to be exchanged with her empty jugs.

She picked up the first one and shook her head. Sometimes the Taylors made things too easy.

Chapter 4

Jordan got out and slammed the door of his truck. How he hoped Imogene and Selima would both stay put at school today. It was hard to care for a family that was always running away.

He sent a long look at the empty curb in front of his house. Where was Samuel and his car? At school, or with his so-called friends?

Shaking his head, he made his way to the truck-bed, ready to bring his new furniture inside. At least he could put his house in order today. His family of five had accumulated enough books that they needed another bookcase, because he had no intention of clearing the shelves that held his late wife's novels.

He gazed at the new bookcase. It was dark wood like most of his furniture and would help his living room better match the front yard in orderliness, as Keisha might say.

"Do you need a hand with that?"

He turned. Two young men in suits and ties approached from the direction of his house as though they had just been over to knock. Salespeople?

Never mind that. He could use the help. "Sure." He clapped the truck bed. "It's awkward for one person to carry."

It took the three of them some maneuvering to get the bookcase inside without scraping any of the doorways. After that, they brought in the shelves and a chair of matching mahogany wood.

"Right there's good. As you can see, we've been piling things on the floor." Jordan waved a hand at the scattered books on the living room rug.

The man with darker hair looked around, his cheeks dimpling. "I know how that goes. I come from a family of nine. We always have things lying around."

Jordan's eyes popped open. "Really?" He and his wife had been chewed out a couple of times for having "a large family," and that was before Imogene and prior to a scary miscarriage. People really should mind their own business. He, for one, would happily support and defend someone with a large family from others' judgment. That included the Johansens, no matter his war with Keisha.

Curious, he turned to the other man. "What about you?"

The blond young man grinned. "I'm an only child. Denmark isn't known for big families."

"Denmark?"

"That's where I'm from. I'm Elder Sørensen, by the way."

"Uh, Jordan."

"Elder Johnson," said the dark-haired man.

They shook hands while Jordan narrowed his eyes at their nametags, which confirmed their names as Elder. Another name that sprang out from the tags was "Jesus Christ."

"Elder's a church title," Elder Johnson explained. "We're missionaries of The Church of Jesus Christ of Latter-day Saints. We have a message to share about the restored gospel of Jesus Christ and how it blesses and strengthens families."

That sounded too good to be true, like ever so many sales pitches, yet Jordan couldn't help but look at these put-together, polite young men and wish that Samuel might look like this. Not that Jordan didn't love him with his shirt untucked and his hair uncombed, but when Samuel's eyes were glazed over and his expression wild, Jordan feared for him. Something was different about these two. He couldn't imagine they'd go off somewhere and take drugs like his son did.

"God has a plan of happiness for each of us and our families." Elder Sørensen picked up the conversation, his eyes bright. "It began before this life and continues into the next."

Before? Next? "You mean, reincarnation?" Jordan asked.

The blond missionary shook his head. "Resurrection through Jesus Christ."

"Okay, that's not new, but you said something about before this life."

"Yes. Before this life, we lived with God. He's literally our father, the father of our spirits." He pulled a pamphlet from his bag and opened it to a page of pictures and text. "That was when he presented to us his plan for our progression. Do you mind if we sit?"

Jordan chewed on his lip but beckoned to the couch and took a seat as well so they could go through their pamphlet. He wasn't sure why he let them talk. The idea of a religious fix was strange. Still, it couldn't be denied that his family needed *something*, and these boys with their different backgrounds and family sizes seemed to have something that worked for them.

His thoughts drifted to Imogene. His youngest daughter repeatedly wandered off, putting him into a panic until he found her. He couldn't get her to stop. She had been only three years old when Alicia died, yet her now seven-year-old mind knew she was missing out on an essential part of her upbringing. One of his biggest fears was that she would get lost and never come home, and then what would he and the rest of the family do? What would Alicia think, if she still existed like he hoped she did?

One thing was for certain: Alicia wouldn't be happy to see what Samuel did. She wouldn't approve of his friends or their marijuana.

And then there was Selima. Sweet Selima. He hated to see his teenage daughter suffer from the loss of her mom, but he struggled to know how to connect with her.

Only Solomon appeared to do all right. He was an angel, often attending to Imogene but also, somehow, to his older siblings.

"Will you pray to know if this is true?" Elder Johnson asked after going over a story of prayer and the beginning—no, restoration—of this church that believed in life before and after death.

Jordan shifted in his seat. "I don't know. It seems a bit much." He wasn't so much interested in finding out about this church as he was in having something help his family. He also hadn't tried praying before.

Elder Sørensen opened his mouth but stopped. There was silence for a bit as they all looked at each other.

Elder Johnson gave Jordan a piercing look. "You can try praying about something else. Ask God for help with something. He answers when you pray in faith or even just want to believe."

"I suppose I could do that," Jordan said carefully.

Elder Sørensen held up the dark blue book they had said was translated by the power of God. "And will you read this?" He grinned. "Don't just put it on that new bookshelf, but open it up and read it?"

Jordan shrugged. "Sure, I'll read." He would read a page anyway. If it wasn't interesting, he could stop.

"I think you'll feel something special as you read it." Elder Johnson stood, looking at once both young and impressively mature, although he was probably only a year or two older than Samuel. "Try praying, and we promise you'll get an answer. Can we come again next week? How about on Wednesday?"

"Oh. I guess." Jordan was taken aback. He hadn't realized they would come again, but the thought made him smile. As he picked up his phone to check his calendar, a flame of hope rose inside him. Could his children gain some of the confidence these young men had? Even if he had to deal with homework like reading this book and saying unnatural prayers, it just might be worth it.

"Come tomorrow," he said. "You can meet my kids."

The missionaries blinked. "Sure," said the elder from Denmark and pulled out his phone.

They set the appointment, and Jordan walked the missionaries to the door. They waved goodbye and got on a pair of bikes he hadn't noticed before.

"See you tomorrow," they called.

"See you then." He took a whiff of the bright, sunny day.

Maybe this Jesus-resurrection-missionary thing wouldn't be half bad to invite into his home for a time.

He returned to his living room, his steps slow. The new bookcase was still empty. He should get started organizing the books that had taken up floor space for the last month.

First though, he opened up a window, letting in sunshine and the sound of music—no, of defiance. He frowned. Keisha knelt in her garden outside, accompanied by one of her usual angry songs. Did she have to be so loud in her opinions?

His feeling of lightness slipped away, and he started to groan but then stopped short. How about he give her something else to listen to?

***

Keisha took a deep breath of grass-scented air and hummed along to Gloria Gaynor's "I Will Survive." June called her songs her Hate Song playlist, but Keisha was quick to defend them as fight songs. There was no hate in this one, only a woman of strength and confidence.

Today was too wonderful to spend at the office. She would work from home, but not until after she got some yardwork done out here. The air was not too hot, and the skies were blue and stretched forever and ever in all directions.

Her coffee cup sat abandoned at the table in front of the wobbly lawn chair Kale had decapitated with his wooden sword last year. With her rough work gloves as a shield, she unwound a long piece of bindweed from one of the pea plants. It was wonderful to immerse herself in the outdoors rather than to stew in front of a computer. Today was a perfect day.

"—in the northern parts of Alaska, moose are continuing to impede traffic," an unfamiliar voice interrupted Gloria Gaynor's powerful lyrics.

Well, it *was* perfect until the sound of the Taylors' TV next door crashed across the soft outdoor noises.

She pulled a little harder on the next weed and glared at the house next door. "Oh, for the love." Why didn't Jordan close his glass door? For that matter, why didn't he turn off the lights? His children had left them on in their bedrooms and bathrooms, as usual. He would leave them on all day, also as usual. It was an utter and total waste of electricity when he was the only one at home.

She shook her head and continued weeding, trying to ignore the sound of the TV until a thought occurred to her: Jordan never turned on the television in the morning.

The noise next door cranked up several notches.

"Ugh." She brushed a gloved hand across her chin and got dirt on her face. She didn't feel like fighting him this morning. She wanted her idyllic day back, and yelling at him wouldn't give her that.

Instead, she turned up the sound at the tail-end of "I Will Survive." Of course, her choice of music wasn't idyllic, but at least it was more entertaining than Jordan's rude box.

It didn't take long. Carrie Underwood was halfway through the song, "Undo It," when Keisha noticed the volume next door getting louder. She rolled her eyes and rolled her shoulders and turned up the volume again.

Not long after, the words of someone narrating the scavenging habits of a coyote intruded on Carrie Underwood's warnings to a "Good Girl."

"—everything from deer to vegetables and fruits," droned the TV.

"Nature channel? Seriously?" Keisha muttered. "You have no interest in the nature channel, Mr. Taylor, and neither do I." She turned up the volume of her song the last two digits.

Then she hacked at two large weeds among the tomatoes.

"—attacks *from the* FRONT—"

Each word was louder than the one before. Keisha huffed and ran to get her Bluetooth speakers from the house. She quickly connected them to her phone. Carrie Underwood's song and the ecologist's voice rose louder, and she felt the competition raise her blood pressure. Oh, but it would be unbearable if Jordan's loudest was louder than hers. She hoped for the life of her that her speakers had a greater range of volume than his TV and also that she wouldn't go deaf today.

The loud but hitherto calm, scientific voice abruptly turned into the crashing yells of thousands of people. She nearly jumped out of her own skin. One excited voice spoke over the crowd: "—steals the ball and shoots it! *Two* baskets within *five* sec—"

Keisha ripped her gloves off her hands and dunked the last of the weeds in the trash can. She was so done.

Stomping inside, she slammed the glass door behind her, threw down her now silenced cell phone and speakers, and turned on her company laptop. She would relinquish her claim on the backyard for now. The basketball game and spectator's voice continued to carry through her open window and Jordan's, but after a minute, her archenemy lowered the volume enough that she could tune it out.

This wasn't retreat. She would get back at him later. She was just taking a break from being annoyed.

Her cell phone buzzed against the table, sounding like it wanted to drill a hole through the defenseless piece of furniture.

Dubiously she looked down at her phone and eyed the caller ID. On the fourth ring, she picked up.

"Keisha, what are you up to these days?" Mom asked without preamble, giving her no time to say hi.

Keisha cleared her throat. "Oh, the usual. Watching the children. Working." Looking for a more or less legal way to dispose of the neighbor.

"Are Carl and Kale close by? I don't hear them. Shouldn't they be loud enough to hear?"

"Mom, they're both in school. Kindergarten."

"Oh, that's right." Mom tittered. "They do grow so fast. Isn't that what I was saying to your father the other day? I said, 'the grandkids grow so fast.'" She laughed at her own joke. "I still wonder how you could have had that many. Children, that is. We had only you, and goodness knows I didn't have any free time on my hands for twenty years. But I do like children. There's an especially nice eleven-year-old across the street—"

She makes him sound like a pet, not a child, Keisha thought dryly.

"I've invited him over a couple of times to see some of our trinkets and hear the stories behind them. He's such a good boy that I don't worry he'll break them."

Those "trinkets" were valuable, fragile souvenirs from exotic countries Keisha's parents had traveled to. She felt a flicker of interest at the memory, along with a dose of anxiety. She had always been ordered not to touch them or even slam the door to the room where they reigned.

"Mom, I'm glad to hear you're doing well," she said, even though her mom hadn't said as much. "What about Dad? Is he around?"

If she could move things along, she wouldn't have to be on the phone much longer.

"He's outside, but you know him."

Keisha breathed out. Yes, she knew him: busy, uninterested. Though she hadn't planned to talk to him, she did wish he wanted to talk to her. Evidently Mom didn't think there was a chance of that.

"Always another project, always something to work on," Mom said. "You two are alike in that way."

Not even close. At least, Keisha hoped not. Yes, she was always busy, but unlike her dad, who had to continue on with what he was doing before he could take time to chat—if he even remembered to chat later and hadn't gotten started on something else in the meantime—she usually put aside what she was doing to attend to *her* children's needs. Hadn't she postponed her accounting work to answer the phone just now? Dad would never have done that. He focused on one thing at a time and allowed nothing to interrupt his schedule.

"Well, Keisha, I can only hope your twins will be as well-behaved as our little neighbor boy when they turn eleven," Mom said, as though people magically changed on their birthday, "but I seriously doubt it. That's not your fault though. I'm sure you're doing the best you can, but I know you can't devote enough time to make that happen. But truly, you're doing fine work for a single mom."

"Thanks, Mom," Keisha mumbled.

"And I hope you have some adult friends by now. I know you're busy with work and the children, but you've got to spend time with other grownups too."

Keisha shut her eyes in exasperation. She already had Shawna at work and far too much interaction with Jordan. Sure, it might be nice to see Shawna outside of work sometime, but inviting her over felt—weird, somehow. Besides, the children kept her busy and far from bored. If there was a void in her life for adult company, surely her ongoing feud with Jordan filled it. Ha. What else did she need?

Mom ended the conversation in just a few more sentences. Keisha put down her phone and massaged her forehead.

If Mom had delivered nothing but straight criticism about Keisha as a mom, it would be easier to forget the conversation, but the thin compliments she mixed in with those thoughtless jabs about her children's upbringing made her hope and long for more positive approval. It was terribly frustrating.

Keisha looked up at the ceiling and groaned.

She loved Mom. She just didn't feel like Mom understood her.

For a moment she fingered her laptop. The weatherman's voice sounded through her window as he dictated next week's weather. Her mood soured. Jordan's TV was still on, and it was an annoying reminder that he had bested her.

Well, not for much longer. The day wasn't so perfect anymore, and she no longer felt like working from home, but at least she could get back at Jordan before she left.

She walked briskly outside while the weatherman announced a ten percent chance of precipitation. Reaching the Taylors' garage, she remembered the time she had figured out their garage door code. She had opened the door twenty times that week, forcing Jordan to go out and close it again and again, often in the middle of the night. He had changed his code after figuring out she was the problem, but she still had access to the garage itself. It was just too easy to pick the lock on the little side door.

From there, she went straight to the little box on the left wall. She had noticed it on one of her earlier—ah, excursions.

The circuit breakers looked terribly bored in the electrical panel. They moved willingly and with a gratifying, loud snap under her fingers.

The weatherman stopped midsentence. Keisha returned outside. There were no longer any lights on in the Taylors' home. No electricity was being wasted.

From Jordan's house came a livid shout and loud cursing. He must have realized there was more to this than a power outage. Keisha retrieved her purse and got in her car, backing out of the driveway and pausing to look up at the Taylors' home. Jordan ran through one of the bedrooms, and—now he was out of sight. Ooh, there he was in another room, trying to turn on the light. Giggles overtook Keisha while Jordan thundered on to another room, the windows giving her glimpses of his frustration.

The day ended up pretty perfect after all.

***

June shut the car door behind her while the others walked up the driveway.

The letter had burned a hole in her backpack all day. Was he seriously going to write every day? She hadn't had time to hide it in her room before school, but at least she had managed to keep it secret again. No way would she let Mom see any of those letters.

A clanking sound made her look over. Jordan appeared from the side of his house, carrying a ladder. When he saw Mom, his face turned thunderous, and he looked straight ahead.

Oh-ho. June looked at Mom. She was walking to the house, the corners of her mouth lifting in a sly smile. June lengthened her stride and caught up at the door. "What'd you do to Jordan today, Mom?"

"Taught him a lesson about electricity." Mom's eyes sparkled. "I don't know how long it took him to realize the circuit breaker was off."

June snorted and took off her sneakers. The Taylors were all right. Jordan yelled too much, like Dad used to, only Dad had done more than that. Jordan just played pranks that made Mom mad and June laugh. She wanted Mom to best him, but that was all. Jordan wasn't a bad egg.

Neither was Selima. June never knew what to say to her beyond "hi" when they saw each other, but at least she seemed nice even if she did skip school.

Anyway, she had other things to think about. Like whether to read Dad's letter before she tore it up.

***

"Yaaay!" Carl and Kale danced around yelling as soon as Keisha gave in to their requests for a fire that evening.

"But only for tonight," she warned, tempering her own smile. "There's no need to use the fireplace when it's still early fall. No one here is cold."

"Can I start the fire?" Kale beamed with hope.

Keisha started to shake her head but changed her mind. "Two matches. I'll let you have two matches." She crumpled up the pages of a newspaper to add to the fire.

"Me too, Mom, me too," Carl said, and of course she had to give him equal treatment.

June and Lizzie carried firewood in from the garden shed, both of them grinning from ear to ear. If Frayden hadn't gone to his room already, he probably would have found this fun too. Then again, maybe not. It was hard to tell with preteens.

Kale grabbed his first match, and Keisha hurried to speak up. "Be careful. Try to hold it diagonally, like—"

His match broke on the matchbox before she could finish her sentence.

She shook her head. "Okay, try the second one."

His second match fared no better, and neither did Carl's matches. Finally June took a match and lit the fire. As it grabbed hold of the wood, Lizzie sat down and let the warm flickering glow light up her happy face.

Carl climbed onto the couch with one of his favorite picture books. "Now you read, Mom."

Keisha settled down with a six-year-old boy on either side and began reading *Green Eggs and Ham*. Once she finished it, the twins had another book ready for her. The ceiling creaked above them, reminding her of when they used to have deer get on the roof in their previous home.

There was a time Dad had read bedtime stories to her. She shifted in surprise at the memory. Those had been wonderful days. He had read to her for a year before he decided that now that she could read herself, he could stop.

Then she had married a man who never read to his children.

Never mind that. She burrowed deeper into the couch while Kale snuggled against her left side. Life was beautiful now.

A wet slap and a shriek from Lizzie made Keisha jump.

The fireplace had gone dark. The logs sizzled, and a bit of smoke rose from them. A few dark orange sparks still glowed.

"What on earth—"

A rushing sound was followed by another wet slap. Lizzie sprang back as the water hit the logs and put out the rest of the fire.

"Huh?" June asked, but Keisha was already jumping to her feet and running to the fireplace, a combination of excitement and frustration mounting inside her.

She stuck her head in and looked up into the darkness. "Get out of my chimney, you lunatic!" Her yell echoed up and down the walls.

For a moment there was no answer. Then a strange whistling noise echoed through the dense space.

"Ooh, Mom, it'th a ghost," Kale exclaimed, appearing on his hands and knees beside her as he looked up the chimney. She pulled back just as he did, and they turned to face each other. Kale was beaming. Keisha looked to her left and wasn't surprised to find Carl mirroring Kale's expression on her other side.

She put her head up the chimney again. "I said, get out!"

Waaawoaooo.

She pulled her head back to say something to Carl—just in time. Another splash of water whirled down and hit the logs, sending soggy ashes flying. She sprang back, knowing just how mad she would be right now if the water had hit her.

Laughter echoed down toward her.

"OUT," she yelled.

"I'm not *in* your chimney," Jordan yelled back.

"You're so busted!"

"What, you gonna put me in timeout?"

"Get off my roof!"

"Are you done polluting the air?"

"Are you done polluting my life?" she countered while June tugged on her sleeve. "What?" she asked impatiently.

"Mom. The ladder," June whispered.

Keisha stilled. "You're a genius," she praised June. Then she pushed to a stand and rushed outside while Jordan shouted something else at her.

She stopped between her house and the Taylors' and looked around frantically. Where had he put the ladder? Surely—

She looked up, and her shoulders fell. A ladder hung suspended above her, one end on the flat part of Jordan's roof and one end on hers. As she watched, Jordan's large silhouette appeared and crawled across the ladder toward his own roof, chuckling like the maniac he was.

"The man is crazy," she mumbled, mildly concerned.

He didn't even fall off.

"Ugh." If only he had leaned the ladder against the house. She could have moved it, and he would have been stuck up there all night.

She straightened as something else occurred to her. He had pranked her from the roof. He had *been* on his roof.

That meant he would have found the message she had painted up there. Her shoulders drooped lower still. She had hoped to laugh behind his back for weeks and weeks, if not longer.

"Double ugh," she muttered and returned inside.

Carl and Kale looked up eagerly when she entered.

"Did you get it?" June asked. "Did you move the ladder?"

Keisha shook her head.

Lizzie let out a breath that sounded both disappointed and relieved.

"What ladder?" Kale asked.

Keisha stared into the sodden fireplace while Lizzie explained June's idea to the twins. What a gloomy way to end the day, bested by Jordan right before bedtime. If it had at least been a few hours earlier, she would have had time to get over it and hatch a plan for revenge.

"Now what are you gonna do, Mom? What are you gonna do back to him?" Carl asked, bouncing on his toes.

"Yeah, now what?" Kale asked, bouncing even more.

With her gaze still fixed on the damp mess in front of her, Keisha brought a hand ever so slowly to the side of her head. Her mind had lit up with a new idea, but she closed her eyes to hide it and began to hum and move her fingers.

Carl and Kale grew quiet. When Keisha opened her eyes, the twins were predictably staring at her in awe. Lizzie watched with a curious expression, and June stood with her arms crossed and a smirk on her face.

Instead of speaking, Keisha knelt and picked up a blackened log. Ashes crumbled off it onto the ground. She raised it and drew it across a newspaper page she hadn't burned, looking critically at the streak the log left behind. It worked like chalk. Black chalk.

She stood and smiled angelically at the twins. "I'll make a drawing for Jordan. How about on his car?"

June burst out laughing, and Lizzie clapped a hand to her mouth.

CHAPTER 5

"CHECK OUT THE TOP, will you? You're nimbler than me," Jordan said to Samuel while he bent and ran his hand over the metal above the rear wheels. The silver truck shone from the car wash he had taken it to this morning after finding Keisha's cartoons.

Samuel climbed into the truck bed and steadied himself. In the middle of a growth spurt, his slight frame was beginning to fill out. His dark brown hair, matching Jordan's, waved in the wind. "Yeah, who cares if I fall?" he grumbled.

Jordan squinted at the paint, looking for any scratches Keisha might have made. The inside of his car might be comfortably worn and faded, but he did his best to keep the outside nice. "That's what you get for laughing when you saw the car this morning. Whose side are you on anyway?"

Samuel scoffed as he inspected the car. "Don't you ever think you should stop fighting her?"

Jordan shook his head. "Nah, it's too late to stop. We're in too deep." He kept his voice light and hopefully free of regret. "What I *do* wonder is what you think of me meeting with these missionaries."

"Don't change the subject." Samuel's knee slipped on his way back down to the ground. "I swear, even if she didn't scratch the paint, *I* will if you keep making me climb around like a monkey."

"You'll be there today when they come?"

Samuel rolled his eyes. "Sure." Then he laughed. "Watch out. If you let them keep coming, they might teach you to love your neighbor."

Love. Jordan froze. Samuel knew what he thought of Keisha. All his children did, due to his confounded computer. The attraction he had felt the day Keisha moved in had been a breath of fresh air. But only for a moment. Then it had felt like a betrayal to his dear wife, so he covered it up with brashness and unwittingly set the scene for their current relationship—a never-ending war.

It *was* too late to change things. Wasn't it? It did no good to fantasize about an alternate universe. Instead, he should be thinking of a way to get back at her.

What would Jesus do? The question popped into his mind, and Jordan frowned. That sounded like something the missionaries would ask. If he continued to have them over, they might start to get to him, but they didn't have him in their net yet, so he pushed the thought aside and tapped his chin. What was something Keisha hated?

***

STICKY FINGERS AND LOUD mouths. That had been her morning, and yet by the time they were all at school, Keisha missed the children.

Shaking her head, she took a bowl and a box of cereal into the small backyard. She lived a good life. As busy as the children kept her, they were what she wanted. At times they left her at her wits' end, but she was living her dream in this home where she was in charge and had the power to let laughter and fun rule.

She was sitting at the plastic lawn table trying not to read the back of the Lucky Charms box for the fifth time when a smell she truly hated made her raise her head and look around.

Jordan Taylor couldn't possibly be on the other side of the hedge spying on her. That wasn't something he did. Even if he *was* there, he couldn't have had enough beer to give off such a strong smell this early in the morning.

If he had drunk that much, he would get an earful from her. She got to her feet and started down the length of the yard, looking over the hedge. The smell grew stronger—behind her.

Slowly she turned around and looked in the direction of the stink.

Three cans of beer lay in her backyard, as out of place as a snake in a cage of paradise birds.

In *her* yard.

At *her* place.

She felt the blood leave her face. Blindly, she put a hand on the hedge behind her and sank into it, nearly falling when it didn't hold her up the way a stone wall would have. Alcohol at her place meant—but he couldn't be here! But he was!

She looked around wildly and made to dash into the house—no, away from it. He might be in there. The children! Where were they? School. She'd pick them up and—She'd sneak through her neighbor's yard to get to the driveway—

She stopped with both hands in the hole of the hedge, crouching and ready to crawl through.

The neighbor's yard.

The neighbor.

Thoughts of the man next door returned bit by bit, along with pieces of her mind. She had almost forgotten about him in her distress.

Jordan. Rude, exasperating Jordan.

Rude, exasperating Jordan who always played tricks on her.

This was his doing. It was his revenge for whatever she had last done—oh yes, for using last night's sodden, ashy logs to draw on his car.

The realization washed over her, bringing with it the taste of relief. There was only Jordan next door and beer cans in her yard. She turned to look at them.

Seconds ticked by while she distrustfully eyed the smelly mess. Finally she stepped over to the odious cans and bent down, picking them up with shaking fingers. She expelled a breathy laugh, banishing her fears. One of the cans was empty and crushed, but the other two were still full—or nearly full. They were open and leaking. Leaking their awful stink into her children's playground.

Rage crashed over her. In three long strides she was at the glass door, sliding it open so hard that it bumped the wall and rebounded three inches. She sprinted through the house trying hard not to spill any liquid on the way, ran out front, and dumped the offensive objects into the Taylors' black garbage can. Then she stormed back inside, scrubbed her hands under hot water for a full minute, and picked up the home phone.

"Jordan Taylor," she yelled as soon as he picked up. "You dirty swine! You keep your alcohol out of my place, you understand me?"

"So long as you keep your dog out of mine," he chuckled. "I thought you might appreciate me making your backyard match your junky front yard."

"Why don't you grow up and get yourself and your son off that stuff? And get him off his drugs too!" she screeched.

"Don't you—"

She slammed the phone on his threatening tone, then slammed it again, and then she slammed it just one more time for good measure. If only she could do it hard enough to break it. All of a sudden, she understood Jordan's habit of attacking the door instead of calling. Hanging up on him hardly gave her any satisfaction.

The floor creaked as she began to pace, back and forth, huffing. "You think you can raise my hackles, Mr. Taylor?" she ground out, feeling the hairs on the back of her neck stand on end. "You think you can go in my backyard and mess up my place? This is it. I'm coming after you to mend that hole in the hedge. You should have done it ages ago. Barbarian. Monster. You—" Her breath caught and held. She kept moving, but the words stuck in her dry throat. At last she came to a halt, and her breath released itself.

In a rare display of weakness, she covered her face with her hands, her life spinning around her in a fit of nausea. The living room was dead silent, the echo of her steps only a memory. The house appeared to witness her distress but didn't understand it because she had never experienced in this home what she had before she came here.

And she had vowed she never would.

***

Jordan stared at the little bit of Keisha he could see. Oh, she hated the stuff all right. He had watched her pick up the cans and run into her home. How many times had she berated him for drinking? How mad had he made her?

When she called, he had rushed out front and was soon rewarded. Through her kitchen window, he saw her pace in her living room, appearing and reappearing on the other side of the doorway. At first it was fun. Then his sense of satisfaction faded. He wasn't sure why. Something seemed different than usual, until all of a sudden she stopped moving.

There she stood, a sliver of her visible through the doorway, so still in comparison to her pacing from before. Was she crying? But why? What was wrong?

He stood still, as though her lack of movement had spread to him. She could be dealing with any number of things. He'd never know. She'd never confide in him. Maybe his latest prank was too much on top of everything else.

His heart plummeted, making him feel sick. Maybe a number of his pranks were too much. He'd never seen her cry, but that didn't mean he'd never made it happen.

Finally Keisha moved out of sight. Jordan let out his breath, and his heart resumed a tentative beat.

***

June hated it when Mom needed help but wouldn't ask for it.

The lines around Mom's eyes and mouth stretched tight, and her jaw clenched as though she held something in. Yet all she'd done since June came home was say hi and tell her dinner would be ready in an hour.

"How was your day?" June asked, feeling weird. Usually Mom was the one to ask her and not the other way around.

"Fine." Mom gave Lizzie back her homework. "Everything looks good."

"Thanks, Mom!" Lizzie scrambled away to the living room and put her assignment in her backpack.

June edged closer to Mom. "What did Jordan do?" It was the easiest way to ask about her day. He always did something. *Mom* always did something, and June gloried in Mom's confidence when she went after him. It was so different from how she used to shrink and let Dad rail at her. No one stepped on Mom these days. No one.

The lines only pulled tighter. "More pranks."

That was it? No details, no lively stories of how she got the better of him? Mom's shoulders were hunched, the way they used to be when Dad was around.

"Mom, are you okay?"

Mom looked at her in surprise but got distracted when Kale ran over and climbed onto the chair beside her. "I have homework too, but you can't do it for me," he said, putting a coloring book and a marker on the counter. "Carl, come on," he called, and Carl came running over.

Mom stroked Kale's hair and then June's. "Everything's fine," she said, waving a hand and turning to the kitchen.

June wished she could put someone in a loop choke. Preferably the invisible enemy that had stressed out Mom today, whoever it was.

"June, my rainbow'th orange." Kale moved his hand aside so she could see the page. "Ithn't it cool? Other rainbows are red and yellow and blue, but not mine."

She forced herself to smile. "It's very cool." She played with his hair, but unlike Mom, she mussed it up. It was more fun that way.

She looked around to make sure everyone was in their place. Lizzie was reading on the couch, and the twins were busy with their coloring books. Frayden was nowhere in sight, but that was normal. June pursed her lips. Sometimes she didn't know what to do with him. Still, all appeared to be well, so she picked up her backpack and sneaked off to her room.

Mom was upset, and June was getting letters. Or rather, taking them. Had Mom seen one of them? Recently June was always first to get the mail, but maybe something had showed up while she was at school.

She pulled the shoebox from under her bed, took off the lid, and stared at the small stack of letters: some unopened and most ripped to pieces.

If he had upset her, June would tear up his latest letter just like the others.

The problem was that it didn't do any good. The letters didn't stop coming. Maybe they wouldn't stop.

It was time for her to take control. She tugged a notebook from her backpack, ripped out a sheet of paper, and slammed it on her desk. Raising her pen, she let it hover above the paper. The anger she had felt when she read that last letter simmered, but she couldn't let it affect her.

Think logically, she told herself. *Cool and collected.*

How could she make him stop? What should she write?

Don't write to Mom.

She could write that.

You hurt her.

No, that would make Mom sound vulnerable. One should never expose their weaknesses to the opponent.

She chewed on the end of her pen and finally lowered it to the paper.

`What do you want?`

***

WHAT WOULD JESUS DO?

The question followed Jordan like a pesky firefly as he walked along the fields at the edge of town with Samuel that Saturday. It had become sort of a habit for him to walk with Samuel, letting him be a sounding board and someone to counsel with about the family now that he no longer had Alicia. Today it wasn't his family who concerned him most though.

He pressed his lips together. The glimpse of Keisha standing still after the beer prank plagued his mind. What was he doing messing with a busy single mom?

What would Jesus do?

He kicked a protruding tree root. It was *her* fault. At least, it was partly her fault. As for Jesus, Jordan had great respect for the man—or God?—but there was no way he could ever be like him. Jordan was just an imperfect man with an infuriating neighbor.

Yet the question kept popping into his mind. It ruined the feud he had never meant to start but nonetheless had a lot of fun with. Sure, there were times his pranks had probably really messed with Keisha, as well as times she had truly made him mad, but it was invigorating. Did he have to stop now?

He cleared his throat and turned to Samuel, ready to leave his sudden conscience behind and focus on other things. "What did you think of the missionaries today?"

Samuel shrugged. "What *should* I think?"

That didn't sound like whole-hearted approval, but Samuel wasn't one to yell out his interest.

"You gonna be there for their next visit?"

"I guess I have to. Selima seemed to like them. I have to make sure they don't lead her astray somehow."

Jordan's spirit hummed with excitement. If Samuel was with the missionaries, he wouldn't be out with his friends.

Samuel shortened his stride and gave him a sideways look. "I haven't seen Keisha leave her house much recently. Did something happen? Or do you think she's thinking up something big to hit you with?"

Keisha's irate voice when she yelled at him about the beer came to mind. Jordan cringed. Her anger had made him think it was one of his better pranks, but her face, when he had seen it since then, had been guarded and closed off. Not the way she usually looked after he upset her.

Still, she likely *was* thinking up a way to get back at him. She always did.

"Probably both," he answered, keeping his voice steady. "She didn't like my latest prank, but when does she ever?"

It wasn't the missionaries who were changing his mind. He stepped around a gopher mound in the soil. It was just that he was beginning to think about things a little differently, and with that, his conscience seemed to have bounced back into his life.

He wasn't the only one either. Jordan had felt Samuel's interest during the lesson he attended. It was what he had prayed for. He blinked and nearly missed a step. Had his prayer been answered, like the elders promised?

Maybe he'd just been lucky. He did want the children to pay attention to those lessons. If his children were influenced by those missionaries, maybe they would get that blessing the elders had mentioned. His thoughts strayed to Keisha. She could probably use a bit of that influence too. She and her family weren't without their problems.

What would Jesus do?

He took a deep breath of fresh air and let it out. So it came down to this, did it? It was time he stopped regretting their unintended war and instead tried to change things. He would no longer engage in battle with her. He wouldn't, not if he could help it.

She would push him into something though. She would try.

He set his jaw. He might not be able to end the whole feud, but he would end his side of it.

CHAPTER 6

"WOULD YOU GET THE mail, June?" Keisha hurried to spread the usual sandwich fixings on the kitchen counter. It had been two weeks since the beer incident, and she had worked from home all that time, keeping an eye on her property just in case. Today, though, she was ready to return to the office. "Frayden, do you have your soccer uniform?"

"*Yes*, Mom." Frayden rolled his eyes.

"More peanut butter. More," Carl cried, emphasizing his words with a hop on the floor.

"And jelly. I want more jelly on mine." Kale stood tall to keep his little fingers on the edge of the counter while he tried to see what she was doing.

"'Please,'" Keisha told them.

"Please," they chorused. The long-awaited front tooth was starting to make its appearance in each boy's mouth. Their lisps would soon be a thing of the past.

"Got your lunch, Lizzie? All ready for your math quiz?"

"Yeah. I'm going to do great," Lizzie spouted off as though quoting Keisha.

Keisha smiled while June came back with a pile of junk mail. "And don't you forget it. Thank you, June."

"Mom, the Taylors are already gone," Lizzie said, looking out the window.

"That's all right. We won't have to look at their sorry faces this morning," Keisha said, making the twins and Lizzie giggle, Frayden snicker, and June snort while Keisha's hands continued to fly. She couldn't care less about seeing the neighbors. Jordan and his beer and his door-pounding habits. *Humph!*

"I might see Selima," June reminded her. "She's been skipping classes less. Maybe she won't have to repeat eighth grade for the third time after all."

By the time everyone had used the restroom and been rushed outside, Keisha feared they wouldn't make it to school on time.

"Are you buying your *cowsthume* today?" Carl stumbled over the word as Keisha drove down the street.

"Costumes." She corrected his pronunciation and made it plural. "I have to be a cowgirl for your presentation and then a twelfth century lady for Kale's." Parents were allowed to join the presentations to help keep them going in the right direction, and she had opted to do just that. She braked and bit her tongue as she waited for someone to back out of their driveway.

"Don't buy them without us."

"You'll be there when we look for clothes for the two of you," she assured them, pressing the gas pedal and speeding up.

"Don't buy your own without us either."

"You really want to see your mom try on different costumes?" she asked, amused.

"We have to make sure it's the right stuff," Carl said.

"Of course it'll be the right stuff," June said suddenly. "Don't you remember back when we all dressed as pirates, and Mom was, like, Elizabeth Swann? The day we moved in here? Mom's a genius at this kind of thing."

"Yeah." Lizzie stared ahead, her mouth rounded as though she tasted something delicious. "We should do something like that again."

"We should, huh?" Keisha was surprised that June had brought it up, not to mention that Lizzie remembered that day. They had dedicated their new home with style. "Actually, I can probably use my dress from back then for your Robin Hood presentation, Kale."

"Mom, don't go to the library without me," Lizzie said. "If you're planning to go today, you have to wait till after school."

Keisha put her hands in the air in surrender, then returned them to the steering wheel. "I guess I'm not allowed to go anywhere today."

June smiled evilly. "You can go grocery shopping on your own. I don't think any of us want to go."

"Thank you, oh merciful benefactor."

As usual, they barely made it to school on time, but they made it.

When Keisha returned home, Jordan's car was politely parked on his side of the driveway. The neighborhood appeared peaceful, treetops waving in the wind. Funny how little Jordan had bugged her recently. He must not have dared prank her while she stayed home for work and kept watch over her house.

That was changing today though. After a quick breakfast, she got in her car with her phone and her purse.

Christina Aguilera's song "Fighter" kept her company for the first third of the ride. Up next, Taylor Swift slung out threats to her ex in the song "Picture to Burn." Keisha grew weary of the vibrant anger, however, and manually selected the next song, Tim McGraw's "My Little Girl." Maybe not all men were bad. Maybe some knew at least how to treat their daughters right—in songs anyway.

She walked to the office at last, feeling peaceful.

"I wonder, do you get paid to lie in a hammock at home and sip Slurpees?" Shawna greeted her and scooted her office chair back on its wheels, allowing a full view of her collection of giraffe photographs. George and some of the pictures were missing.

"No way. Boss wouldn't pay me unless I was completely relaxed." Keisha grinned.

Shawna raised her eyebrows. "Girl, I don't think I want to know your definition of relaxed."

"Think Mallorca. How's it been here out of the sun?"

"I've been hoping you would drop by to see us lowly workers. You know, so I could say goodbye."

Keisha stumble-fell into her seat. "Goodbye?"

"Yes. Our foster son is coming tomorrow, and I want to be there for him full-time. I'm quitting."

"You're what?" Keisha squeaked. "I didn't realize foster care would mean—"

"Troy earns enough money for all of us." Shawna tapped her fingers on the table and looked embarrassed. "The boy needs me, and I can't get a deal like yours where I only work while he's in school." She lowered her voice. "I'm glad you finally came. I was afraid I'd miss you."

Keisha gulped. "Is today your last day?"

"Yeah. But you can always visit me at my home. If you ever feel like it."

Keisha opened her mouth, closed it, and nodded. "Maybe I will." She tried to hide her dismay. Shawna had made casual invitations to visit before, and Keisha had her address, but for some reason she never dropped by. Even now, she wasn't sure she would. Her life was plenty busy, after all. "I'm happy for you. I wish you the best of luck with your new family."

"Thanks. It's been good working with you." Shawna's eyes brimmed for a moment. Then her lips quirked. "The days you showed up, that is."

Keisha forced a smile. Her trips to the office would be a lot fewer from now on if she had no Shawna to look forward to.

It was with a heavy heart that she left that day to pick up the children. Selfishly, she wanted Shawna to be at the office whenever she came in to work.

Her phone played through her favorite songs while the twins and Lizzie and Frayden scrambled in, Carl and Kale bickering over the middle seat.

"Mom, look what I got." Lizzie spoke proudly, holding up her math test with a big red "100" circled at the top. Her hair was in crooked pigtails. Evidently the girl at school didn't know how to part hair.

"That's wonderful, Lizzie. You just keep it up, and one day you'll be richer than all of us."

"She's such a smarty-pants," Frayden complained from his usual spot in the back. Keisha frowned, but the twins' increasing loudness required her more immediate attention.

"Settle down, boys. Kale gets the middle seat. Carl can have it the next time."

"Can we go for a drive after we get home?" Carl asked, miraculously settling down and buckling up in the window seat. "I want the middle seat again as soon's possible."

Doing good on those S's, Keisha congratulated him in her mind. "Sure. Lizzie, you wanted to go to the library today, right?"

Her daughter brightened. "Yes, please."

"I'll come too," Kale said quickly. Then he leaned close to Carl and whispered, "When you get to sit in the middle for the library and I don't, that means I'll be in the middle again tomorrow when we go to school."

Carl hit him with his fist. "Mom, don't let him come to the library! He's cheating."

"I'm not cheating. I'm right," Kale said, punching him back.

"Don't hit each other," Keisha commanded just as Carl shoved his brother.

"But I want the middle when—" Carl began, but Kale cut him off with another punch. Carl howled and attacked in turn.

"Boys! Do you want to grow up to be like your father?" Keisha exclaimed, provoked.

The fistfight stopped immediately.

Keisha took a moment to check her temper. "You'll take turns, and you'll be nice about it, and you'll be *grateful* no one else is fighting for the middle seat. Just think of how long you would have to wait if Lizzie and Frayden took turns with you, as well."

"And June." Lizzie giggled. "What if she wanted a ride after all, and she wanted the middle seat?"

"We have two middle seats," Frayden said in annoyance. "Why do they have to fight about it anyway?"

Keisha could tell the moment he realized he had suggested one of them come to the back and destroy his peaceful haven of a row of seats all to himself. His eyes widened in horror.

Carl scoffed. "We want the *middle* middle seat. The one in the back isn't middle."

Keisha parked in front of their home with some relief. "Okay, everyone out. Those going to the library will put their backpacks in the house and come back. Boys, we'll find some more Robin Hood and cowboy books, okay?"

Her phone started playing Carrie Underwood's "Before He Cheats." Noticing Jordan Taylor standing on his front porch, Keisha turned the music up as loud as she could through the car's speakers.

Frayden disappeared inside under the noise of Carrie's revenge. Lizzie and the twins threw their backpacks in the hallway and ran back out. Keisha waved them into the van, watching her neighbor on the sly.

His face scrunched up in disapproval, but all he did was stand there. What was wrong with him? It was hard to yell at someone who wasn't yelling first or who hadn't done something awful just now, but for once, she would have liked an excuse to yell. Her best and only friend was leaving work, and the only adult interaction Keisha was likely to have now was clashes with the man before her.

She glared daggers at Jordan while Carrie sang out about the damage she was doing to her ex's vehicle.

Jordan gulped, turned around, and entered his house.

How strange. He should have yelled about the noise. She felt a moment of guilt for wanting to antagonize him. When he made her mad, she was mad. If there was a certain triumph in besting him, there was nothing wrong with that, but she needn't use him on purpose to vent her feelings about other things.

He must be having an off day. She should probably find her earplugs before nighttime in case he decided to get revenge through another sound war.

***

THE NEXT MORNING DRAGGED like a limping turtle. Keisha propped her chin against her hand and stared at the laptop screen in front of her. She swung her legs, then got up and went to the kitchen to open the window.

A breeze brought in the smell of flowers and made the lace curtains flutter in her face. Mornings were cooler now, not unlike September in North Dakota.

September. That was the month Henry had gone to jail. Her insides clenched. It was also the month he had been let out, after only a year for domestic abuse. She had been too timid in court, not speaking out much about her years of abuse, not requesting a restraining order. Fortunately he'd never contacted her even after parole must have run out.

She jumped at the sound of a ringtone, then rolled her eyes at herself. The phone was ringing next door through the open window to the Taylors.

"Hello?" Jordan began, but it wasn't long before he raised his voice. "Again? You can't keep letting this happen. Why don't you—"

How unpleasant. He was chewing out someone the way he always did her.

"Do you have any idea where—"

Keisha closed the window on his words. She was tired of Jordan and bad memories. He hadn't even properly fought with her for over two weeks. Agitated, she grabbed her car keys and left the house for the grocery store.

Once there, it didn't take long to fill up the cart. She threw a pack of hot dogs on top of it all, barely looking at the package.

She had been so messed up inside when she and the children moved to Missouri. Then her determination had firmed, and for three glorious liberating years, she had found herself actively engaged in battle with Jordan. His outbursts and tricks had given her someone to unleash her fury on, a well-deserved vent for her pain as well as a distraction from her battered feelings.

Jordan was at once terribly similar and wonderfully different from her ex.

"Did you find everything you needed, ma'am?" the cashier asked.

"Yes, thank you." The word "ma'am" stirred her mind. The last people who had called her "ma'am" had been those missionaries on the street: Johnson and Sorensen with something that wasn't an "O". They had given her a card, hadn't they? She had left it in her pocket. Her pants had probably been washed at least twice since then, which meant the card was gone and her pocket probably full of lint.

Oh, well. Rattling her cart outside, she approached her van but caught sight of a small lone figure wandering the sidewalk.

She frowned and tried to get a better look. The girl looked like Jordan's seven-year-old. She had the same blond curls.

"Imogene!" she called, but either it wasn't her or the traffic was too heavy for her to hear. "Imogene?"

She left her cart by the van and hurried to catch up. If it was the youngest Taylor, she couldn't let her roam around like this, no matter what her dad's thoughts on safety might be. Keisha had seen her wander before, seemingly on her own, near the library and by the city center and once by the movie theater.

"Imogene," she called, catching up to her by a crosswalk as the light turned red on the other side of the street.

The girl turned and looked at her. Her eyes were blue and round, her cheeks were chubby, and her mouth was set in a natural pout that had little to do with her mood and everything to do with baby fat.

"It *is* you. What are you doing here? Are you okay?"

She nodded.

"Well, listen, you can't stroll around like this. Is your dad nearby?"

Imogene just looked at her.

"I'll call him, okay?" Keisha took out her phone and paused. Then, for the first time in her life, she dialed Jordan's number on her cell.

It rang and rang and went to voicemail. Keisha frowned but began to speak. "Jordan, I have Imogene here on the corner of 5th Street and Main." Did it sound like she was making a ransom call? She cleared her throat. "If you don't answer, I'll just take her home."

She ended the call. Imogene was still staring up at her.

"You're pretty," said Imogene.

"Oh." Keisha chuckled. "Thanks. Do you want me to take you home?"

The girl brightened. "Yes, please." She thrust her warm hand into hers, making Keisha blink at the display of trust.

They returned to the parking lot, Keisha keeping her steps short and slow. Her heart hurt for the girl. What had made her take to the streets today? Her dad? Or Samuel with his drugs? Maybe even sweet Selima, who repeatedly set the example by walking away from school. Finally there was Solomon. Keisha didn't know anything about him except that he liked to make faces at her children. He seemed like a nice, healthy nine-year-old boy.

Imogene jumped over an oil puddle. "Julie's mom is pretty too."

"Is Julie in your class?" Keisha asked.

"Yeah." Imogene skipped to the car. "I like pretty moms."

Well, she seemed happy enough at the moment.

Keisha let her in behind the driver's seat. "Buckle up and give me a minute to put away the groceries. Then we'll be on our way."

Jordan probably wasn't even worried about his girl. Nevertheless, Keisha would take her home.

***

Jordan returned to the school for the third time and drove in a new direction, his fingers hard on the steering wheel and his eyes scouring the streets.

Where could she be? Why couldn't those people keep track of her?

Imogene had been such a happy toddler before her mom died. Could she still remember her? Was it her mom she went looking for when she wandered?

He cursed, feeling pressure to go faster but resisting it out of fear that he would miss seeing his little girl, wherever she was. It had been thirty-five minutes since they realized she was gone. Should he have gone farther in the direction of the library before he turned back to try this direction?

Someone honked behind him, and his grip tightened when he recognized Keisha's van. This wasn't a time for pranks.

She honked again, two more times, three. He gritted his teeth and slowed just before the intersection. Keisha pulled up next to the curb and rolled down her window.

Jordan's window was already down. He scowled and yelled, "What? I don't have time right now!"

"I just thought you might like to know I have your daughter in my car," she called back, her expression tight with disapproval. "You know, your youngest, Imogene? Remember her?"

Jordan caught his breath and made a very quick, very illegal U-turn in the intersection, coming around to park nose to nose with the van. Keisha's face paled as his vehicle came to a stop.

He cut the engine and jumped out. Imogene was barely out of the other car before he reached her and caught her in a tight embrace. Her weight was comforting, and her hair tickled his face.

"You have got to stop doing that, Imogene." His voice was hoarse. He held her for another bit before he stood. "Come on."

He started toward the truck with her. They had nearly reached it when Keisha's voice called out behind him, "Oh, yeah, I'm just the lady who saved your daughter from the world!"

He stumbled. How could he have forgotten about his neighbor? Emotions swirled through him, from gratitude to confusion to annoyance, his inner kettle firing up. Couldn't she let him regain his composure after facing the fear of losing his daughter?

He let Imogene inside and reached for his own door but stopped. Keisha was right. He *had* feared for Imogene's life, and if not for Keisha, his girl would still be lost.

He swallowed, sending fire down his throat. All he wanted to do was take his daughter home, but he couldn't leave without expressing gratitude to his enemy—that was, his neighbor—and Imogene's rescuer.

Feeling like his feet were weighed down with concrete, he turned to his neighbor.

She looked shocked. Because he was about to thank her? How satisfied would she look once he had done so? His heart still pounded from the scare of Imogene's disappearance, and Keisha had never seemed more arrogant than she did in that moment.

"Thank you," he began, forcing the words out through his teeth, "for . . ."

Keisha's mouth slid open.

". . . finding . . ." The words were excruciating. Wildfire burned in his chest. As much as Keisha deserved his thanks, he didn't know if he could express it to her.

Silence stretched taut between them. Something changed in her expression. She pulled back a little at the same time Jordan did, possibly coming to the same conclusion as he: if he left his sentence incomplete, he wouldn't have thanked her. Leaving it this way would prove he didn't mean what he had started to say. Could they both pretend he had never tried to say it?

Only one more word. He summoned his willpower, his strength, his breath, just as Keisha shook her head and turned toward her car.

". . . her."

As soon as the word left his lips, Jordan slammed his car door behind him and pulled away from the curb, narrowly avoiding another vehicle as he forgot to check the road. He drove on, feeling steam coming out of his ears.

He had done it. He had thanked her. He had been polite, sort of, to his nemesis in a moment when his emotions were all tangled up.

Accomplishment. There was nothing sweet about it, yet it was gratifying.

***

Keisha spun around at the word "her," her heart pounding, only to see the door slam and the truck pull away and drive out of sight.

How—why? The sight of him hugging his daughter—almost crying. The moment had lasted forever as she stood nailed to the spot, seeing his concern and relief and love for the girl. It seemed he *had* worried about her.

Then he had started to leave. In her confusion, Keisha felt like she had to say something in parting, and of course with Jordan, what came out was always more along the lines of "You jerk!" than "Have a nice day."

Why hadn't he yelled at her?

She tried to take a breath, but her chest remained cramped as though something pressed on her.

Why in *heaven's* name had he *thanked* her? In all their history of hating each other, what possessed him to do such an absurd thing?

Imogene, the answer came to her. He loved her, with the kind of love fathers showed in country songs, the kind of love she had hoped her husband would have for his own children.

Her cheeks felt cold. She reached up to warm them and found tears.

Jordan loved his children. How had she not known that all this time? Since her ex, had she seen only what she expected to see?

No. She blinked away the moisture from her lashes. He yelled at her children. He had been rude to her since the day she moved in. He may be a better father than she realized, but that didn't make him a saint.

She walked slowly back to her car.

Again in her mind's eye she saw Jordan hugging Imogene. The heart-aching image faded, and she remembered the conflict in his eyes when he tried to thank her. He had said the words as though he was having his teeth pulled out, yes, and his heartstrings too.

Her lips twitched. She deserved his anger this time, and she had it. He would wake up tomorrow as angry as he'd ever been with Keisha, thinking she had forced him to thank her in front of Imogene, and he would come after her like he used to, with the worst pranks he could think up.

Imogene was going home with a father who loved her, and Keisha was about to be inundated with pranks from her neighbor once more.

Grinning, she hopped in her car. "Bring it on, Mr. Taylor!"

She didn't stop driving until she reached the city center. There, she parked and walked under a warm sun to the art boutique. The smell of corn tortillas wafted in from the next-door restaurant as she entered.

The pictures greeted her as usual. Landscape graphics, wildlife, and—people.

She picked up the print of the boy with his mouth open, his eyes wide and round. It looked like he would recover from his surprise in another moment and burst out laughing at the joke. At the moment, Keisha felt she knew exactly what the joke was.

She bought the black and white print and took it home to hang up, celebrating the battles to come.

Chapter 7

"Hey June, what are you doing here?"

June turned around on the sunny street to see Dina from her class at school run over. Her parents and sister stayed behind, pointing at something through a shop window.

"Hi, Dina. Are you guys shopping?"

"Window shopping. My family doesn't know how to buy things." She rolled her eyes. "Where're your parents?"

A breeze blew through June's hair and rustled a bit of trash on the sidewalk. "My mom's probably home. I'm running an errand."

"You're so cool," Dina said in admiration.

June smiled, charmed. "Thanks. I try."

"Dina, we're going inside. Come on," her sister called.

"I'll see you tomorrow," June said.

Dina brightened as if June had promised her a Christmas present. "See you." She turned and ran off to join her family.

They looked like a happy bunch. June wondered if Dina knew what she had. Mom, Dad, and siblings.

She set her jaw. The Johansen family was perfect as it was. Sure, there were times she wanted to punch Frayden. But then she'd remember how hard she had worked to keep him safe from that kind of harm, and she felt terrible for wanting to hurt him.

That was why there was no way she would let anyone in her family come into contact with *him*. Especially not Mom. No one was visiting anyone.

She pulled a stamped envelope from her backpack. Her cool gaze fixed on the address, written in her own handwriting, as she sent the receiver a telepathic warning.

She turned to the post office and pushed the door open.

***

WHEN KEISHA PICKED UP the children, she was almost bouncing. Jordan hated her, which meant she knew what to expect from him. Except when it came to Imogene. His love for her seemed genuine, which meant he was—different—from what Keisha had thought up till now.

That was good news for his children, but it didn't change how much he hated *her*.

She glanced through the rearview mirror at Lizzie, whose hair had been teased into two braids and clumsily pinned in a circle on top of her head. Best not to ask her about that while the others were around.

"Mommy, where's France?" Carl asked, leaning forward and putting his little fingers on the edge of her seat.

Keisha turned off the main road, the car humming beneath her. "It's in Europe."

"Oh." Carl looked disappointed. "That's far away. Anna said France has really good food. We wanted to go try it."

"The best," Kale put in. "She said 'the best.' We told her *your* food's the best, but she didn't believe us. Can we go to France and eat their food so we can show her?"

"Probably not this year, but thanks for the compliment," Keisha said with a smile. Of course, her children rarely ate food she hadn't cooked, so it was ridiculous to be pleased when they had little to compare it to. Even so, she would take the praise.

"Frayden, I haven't seen your soccer uniform in the laundry for a while," she said, meeting his eyes in the rearview mirror.

He sighed, rolled his eyes, and looked out the window.

"I haven't noticed any terrible smells from your backpack, either, but the uniform really does need to be washed now and again."

"Mom, I'm not taking soccer anymore."

She started in surprise. "What do you mean, you're not taking soccer? You've stopped going to practice?"

He turned back with an accusing look. "Soccer's for pansies. I hate it. Now, *football, that* would be something."

"I see," she said after a tense moment and guided the van into the driveway. At least eighty-five percent of the world would disagree with him about the "pansies" comment, but who were they to convince her ten-year-old? "Are there any football teams for kids your age?"

"Mom, *I'm not a kid*. And no, I don't know of any." Before the car stopped moving, he was out, running into the house and slamming the door.

Keisha sat still, counting in her mind, until she heard a second slam from somewhere upstairs. He was in his room now.

Lizzie and the twins looked uncomfortable as they headed inside. Keisha got out slowly, thinking through the talk she needed to have with Frayden even as she decided to wait until they had both cooled down. Talking to him right now would only light the fuse on both of their tempers.

"If you don't want to play soccer, that's okay with me. I won't force you to do it," she practiced under her breath. "But you should have told me instead of running around and skipping practice that I've paid for. And then there's that thing with name-calling. I don't want to hear you call others 'pansies,' 'smart-alecks,' or anything else like that."

She went inside and looked around. "Carl, where's Lizzie?"

"Upstairs," Carl answered without taking his eyes off the yoyo Kale was trying to tame.

Keisha took the stairs. Lizzie's door was closed, so she gave it a soft knock.

"Come in," Lizzie called.

Keisha entered and found her daughter sprawled on the floor with a book. The room was cool and fresh, with pale yellow walls Lizzie had helped paint a couple of years ago. A forest picture from an old calendar and two drawings from Carl and Kale hung on the walls. Keisha always thought it sweet that Lizzie would hang up the drawings. Of course, Lizzie was one of the sweetest people she knew.

Keisha sat on the bed. Lizzie looked up from the floor with a question in her eyes and used her finger to mark her spot in the book she was reading.

Keisha smiled. "You're a beautiful girl, you know that? Who does your hair at school?"

If she hadn't been watching closely, she might not have seen Lizzie start. Guiltily. "I—I do."

She blinked. That wasn't what she had expected. "That must be hard, to do it on yourself." She tried to think of what else to say. "Would you like me to do your hair?"

Lizzie's eyes brightened. "Would you?" she cried. Then, almost as quickly as her face had brightened, her expression turned downcast and anxious.

"Would you?" she repeated with a frown. "I know you like messy hair."

That was news to Keisha. "I do?"

"Yeah. You always ruffle June's hair, and you say you like it that way. Both of you like it. It's okay, you don't have to do my hair. It doesn't have to look nice."

Keisha thought fast. "I like June's hair messy partly because *she* likes it that way. It's her style because she wants it to be. If you want your hair to look nice, that's *your* style, and I'd love to see you with cute hairdos. I'd be happy to help put it up any way you like it."

"Really?" Lizzie's eyes shone with unshed tears.

Keisha jerked at the sight. She hadn't imagined Lizzie would be so affected. Apparently she had gone to school with her hair the way she thought her mom wanted it and had secretly tried to put it up while she was away from home.

"Really," she said. "How about now? Or are you too busy?"

"I'm not busy." Lizzie put her book face down on the floor and ran to her desk to open a drawer. "I have scrunchies and hairpins right here," she said eagerly, bringing them over and spilling them on the bed.

Keisha vowed to buy nicer hair decorations as soon as possible. She picked up a comb and got to work.

Thirty minutes and three hairdos later, the two of them made their way downstairs, Lizzie giggling in anticipation.

They could hear Carl and Kale sing country songs in the living room. It sounded like they had turned on the family karaoke set.

June lay on the couch with her homework, her crumpled jiujitsu uniform on the floor next to her.

"Half-time, everyone," Keisha announced. "What do you think of Lizzie's new look?"

They all looked up as Lizzie twirled into the room. Then she stopped and blushed shyly.

"You look great," June said. "That's so cute, Lizzie."

"You look really nice," Carl said into his microphone.

"I think you look *sweet*," Kale chirped up, then looked at Keisha. "'Sweet' is better than 'nice,' right? And I called it."

"Both words are perfect," Keisha reassured an irked Carl.

"It looks like a princess crown," June said. "Mom, I didn't know you could do that."

Keisha laughed. "Neither did I. It took me a bit, but I'll practice and get better at it." She looked searchingly at June. "Would you like me to do something with your hair too?"

"No thanks, I like it casual and messy." June looked thoughtful. "Thanks for asking though. Maybe someday."

"Mom, you should sing karaoke," Lizzie said suddenly, grabbing Keisha's arm and tugging her over to the television. She had probably had enough of the spotlight for now. "You haven't done it in forever, and you're so good."

"Is she?" Carl asked.

"Of course she is. I remember," Kale said, looking uncertain.

"Okay, you can go," Carl said generously and held up his microphone.

"Well, I—" Keisha began.

"You should do your number one, 'Fighter,'" June said, her eyes flashing as she leaped from the couch. "You know, by Christina Aguilera. You're so good at that one, and I love the song. It has real spirit."

"Okay, sure, but first you have to put your uniform in the laundry. Oh, and June?" she asked, halting her rush for the laundry bin. "Do you want to keep doing jiujitsu?"

"Of course I do. Why do you ask?" June's eyes widened. "You haven't lost your job, have you? If you can't pay for lessons, maybe I could . . . mow lawns for people or something—"

"No, we're fine on money," Keisha assured her. "I just need to know. I don't want you to think you have to take lessons if you don't enjoy it."

"Of course I enjoy it, Mom." June sounded like a teenager again as she walked to the laundry room. Anyone who didn't believe eye-rolling could be heard in a person's voice hadn't spent enough time with teenagers. "I've always enjoyed it." She came back without the uniform and rubbed her hands together. "Now find the song and sing it."

Lizzie laughed. "Sing it like you mean it."

Keisha did mean it. June probably understood that better than anyone. The music began, and Keisha sang, roughing up her voice, putting her all into it both for the sake of her audience and for the life they had left behind over three years and six hundred miles ago. As she belted out the song, the six hundred miles might as well have been light years.

When the song ended, Carl and Kale bounced around clapping and cheering and crashing into each other for fun. Lizzie beamed, and June looked satisfied.

Keisha turned to the couch to put a stop to the boys' shenanigans before they hurt themselves, but Kale was already plopping down on his behind with a searching expression on his little face.

"Mom, could you sing that other song," he began and broke off, his voice uncertain.

Carl plopped down, tilted his head at his brother, and then picked up where he had left off. "You used to sing something really nice and soft. It made us go to sleep."

"I think they mean Olivia Newton John," June said, watching Keisha.

"Oh. 'Hopelessly Devoted'?"

"I think that's the one. Prob'ly," Carl said.

Keisha frowned and picked up a sofa cushion that had fallen to the floor. "I'm not sure I remember it that well. It's a long time ago."

"But it's so pretty," Kale protested.

"Maybe in a few days I can sing it to you." She rubbed her forehead. "I can't believe you boys still remember that."

"We don't, not really. That's why you have to sing it again, so we'll remember."

"Okay, but not today. I need to start dinner. Keep playing, boys. I mean singing, *not* jumping. And let Lizzie and June have a turn if they want."

She turned away and bit her lip. She hadn't sung that since before the move. How in the world could she go back to singing something that required such a soft, caressing voice? It was a stark contrast to the fight songs she fed on these days, including the one she had just performed.

Her throat was scratched up from the rough songs she liked to sing and nearly as scratched up as her heart. And singing had to come from the heart.

On her way to the kitchen, June's hand caught her elbow.

"You don't have to sing it, Mom." June's normally blue eyes shone piercingly gray as they held Keisha's. "They'll forget again soon. You don't have to."

June let go and walked away.

Keisha stared. For some reason she didn't understand, the comforting words from her thirteen-year-old daughter disturbed her more than anything else.

***

"SING IT AGAIN," IMOGENE commanded. She sat up in bed, the soft covers pulled up to her lap, while Jordan sat on the edge of her bouncy mattress.

He shared a look with Solomon who lay back in his own bed against the other wall. After six months of having her own room last year, Imogene had insisted on sharing a room with one of her siblings again. Never mind that their grand house already had several empty bedrooms. Solomon had said he didn't mind, but he was getting older, and Jordan would have to give him his own room again soon. They couldn't always give in to Imogene's requests, though it was hard to refuse since she was the baby of the family. It was doubly hard because she didn't have a mom. It was triply hard because he had worried once more about losing Imogene today. His heart couldn't seem to stop pounding at the memory of her disappearance from school.

He started "Twinkle, Twinkle, Little Star" again, and Imogene joined in, clapping her hands to the beat. They added the nonsense verse Alicia had come up with before she got sick. Alicia had added nonsense verses to most of the songs she sang to the children.

How could Jordan ever fill the hole she had left behind?

He sang every song Imogene asked for until she finally burrowed down, her eyelids closing. She gave a soft sigh and murmured something. Jordan kissed her forehead, then stood. Solomon yawned in his bed.

"Good night," Jordan whispered to him.

"Good night," Solomon said through another yawn.

Jordan walked over to the light switch, turned it off, and shut the door behind him.

He went downstairs, where the lamp above the dining table shone in the otherwise dark room. He sank down at the table and put his head in his hands.

How could he make Imogene understand that she needed to stay put at the school?

The front door creaked open. Samuel's steps sounded, but he didn't bother to turn on any lights. Nor did Jordan bother to raise his head. It felt better where it was, lowered toward the table.

The steps stopped. "Dad?"

"Mm," he grumbled and slowly looked up. Samuel was frowning, his white T-shirt making him easier to see in the dark.

"You okay?"

Jordan sent him a hollow look. "How do you make a girl stop wandering?"

Samuel came over and sat down across from him. "Imogene? Or Selima?"

"Today, it was Imogene."

"How far did she go?"

He thought back to the voice message from Keisha he had eventually listened to. "Near Walmart. Keisha found her and picked her up." Now that he was past his shock, he was glad he had thanked her. Not that he had sounded as sincere as he should have been.

"Hm." Samuel looked at the table. He was probably deciding who to comment on, Imogene or Keisha. "Dad. Will you help me?"

Jordan's mouth went dry, and his heart sped up. "With what?" The shadows across his son's face deepened. Was Samuel finally coming to him about—

Samuel's lips tightened. "It's not the drugs."

"Oh." Jordan tried not to show his disappointment, but Samuel's next statement made his heart rise.

"I didn't take them that often, although I wanted the others to think I did. It was cool. It was an escape. But—Mom—I'd think of her, and I couldn't take them, can't take them most of the time."

Jordan stared at him, holding his breath.

"I'm not addicted, Dad. But I'm tempted all the same. I know where and how to get those things. I know they can help me forget."

"You don't want to forget your mom, do you?" Jordan exclaimed before he could stop himself.

Samuel pressed his lips together and shook his head. "Just the pain." Jordan grabbed his hand. For a moment Samuel's lips trembled, and Jordan held on tighter, feeling his son's pain like a blow to the stomach.

Samuel took a breath, and his tension seemed to fade. He continued, "But now, forgetting doesn't seem as important as it used to. Things have changed, with what the missionaries tell us."

So Samuel felt it too? A hope that there was an afterlife and that there was a purpose to this life—that they would be okay until they were reunited with Alicia in paradise or the Celestial Kingdom or wherever it was? The missionaries had talked in their second lesson about the Celestial Kingdom, a heaven where people would be with their families forever.

"I want to stay clean for Mom," Samuel said. "Only, I don't know what to do about my friends. It'll be awkward seeing them in the halls at school if I stop hanging with them."

Jordan would have loved to tell him to quit the drugs and those friends, but if someone were to tell him to stop drinking or to hang with a different crowd than those he chose, he would tell them to butt out. It was a huge thing already that Samuel wanted to quit. Just as wonderful was the fact that he hadn't been into the drugs much.

Jordan scooted his chair forward so he could more fully face his son. "Tell me about those guys."

Samuel played with his hands for a while. "I don't really want to. I guess I don't have anything to say about them."

Jordan leaned back. "If they're not worth talking about, maybe they're not . . ." He let his voice trail off, remembering that he couldn't just wade in and tell him what to do.

"We're really not friends," Samuel concluded.

The two of them sat in silence again. Jordan's emotions seesawed between hope for a change in Samuel's life, pain over his predicament, and worry that Jordan would somehow make things worse with something he said or did. It was a three-sided seesaw. Did those exist?

Samuel looked up slowly, a light in his eyes. "There *is* one of them I'd like to talk about. He wants out too, at least in his good moments. But he's in deep. He's been using for a while, and I don't know if he can stop."

Jordan leaned his arms on the table, eager to listen to anything Samuel was willing to discuss. "Tell me about him."

Chapter 8

WHAT WAS THE MAN waiting for? Days had passed since the incident with Imogene, and Jordan hadn't retaliated. Frayden was surly every day and wouldn't talk about soccer, and in the morning, Keisha's temper swelled within her like a snake waiting to spring free and strike as she tried to get everything ready for the day.

For a minute, she was annoyed with the twins' chatter and constant requests for more of this and that on their sandwiches. They always asked for the same thing. Didn't they realize she had their instructions memorized?

The snake within her rattled until she put herself in her place with the silent question, *What's your greatest treasure?*

Her annoyance with the children chipped away bit by bit. As she handed the twins their lunchboxes, she was able to force a light tone. "You guys are the best, you know that?" She ruffled the twins' hair. "All of you." Her gaze included Lizzie and June, and she tried to include Frayden, but as soon as she met his eyes, he pushed away from the wall and left the house.

Give it a few days, she told herself and counted to ten in her mind.

She needed something to distract her from her negative feelings. An exciting gnawing in her stomach warned her of Jordan's impending revenge. Maybe he had done something awful to her yard or her house during the night.

Rejuvenated at the idea, she sat down with Lizzie and put her golden hair in a braided crown that resembled what she had done the first night they experimented but took less time to do.

"You look gorgeous," she told Lizzie with a real smile and smoothed down a loose strand. "My pretty, smart girl. Now let's go."

As they filed outside, Keisha's gaze went to the Taylors, excluding Samuel, flocking around their car. Actually, it went straight to Jordan who stood arguing with Solomon.

"Until you're old enough, you don't get to sit in the front," he was saying.

Something swooped in Keisha's stomach. This was the Jordan who had hugged Imogene like *she* was his greatest treasure.

He pointed at the back seat. "In!"

Keisha's stomach settled. This was the Jordan she knew. She sauntered forward. "Let me know if you want any more artwork on your car," she greeted.

His mouth pulled into a thin, tight line, but he said nothing as he got in his car.

She stared while he left. Then, slowly, she got in the van.

All the way to the elementary school, she racked her brain for an explanation to his behavior.

"Goodbye, kids. Be good," she called to Frayden, Lizzie, and the twins as they headed to their red school building.

She drove on, squinting at the sun through her windshield.

Maybe Jordan had realized she enjoyed sparring with him. If "enjoyed" was the right word.

At the middle school, June jumped out, pressed a pair of sunglasses over her eyes, and swaggered several steps like a movie star.

"Bye, June. I love you."

She bit her lip, watching the stream of students. Maybe—maybe he expected her to go crazy wondering what schemes he was thinking up. That would make sense. There must be a big one on the way. In the meantime, he might know she was getting jumpy, expecting to find herself the victim of another prank any moment.

She shook her head. *Nice going, Jordan. I'm not falling for that.*

She returned home, checked out the backyard to see if Jordan had done anything to it, and promptly remembered that she kept forgetting to ask June and Frayden to mow the lawn. She'd better do it herself this time.

She moved two balls, a Superman figure, and the mini plastic slide out of the grass, then clanked the lawn mower out of the shed and pulled the string hard.

It sputtered and roared to life, eating the tops off the grass. Keisha walked along, feeling the vibration of the machine under her hands. Until it stopped.

She let go of the handlebar, pushed it in again, and pulled the string. "Come on. You wanna leave the yard looking like Cruella DeVil's head?" she muttered, giving it another vicious tug. "I know you have enough gas."

"Looks like it's broken down," Jordan's voice cut in. Keisha jerked her head up and found him watching from the other side of the hedge. "I could, uh, send Samuel over later today. He could finish mowing for you. With our machine."

Her eyebrows lifted, and her heart sped up in anticipation. Here it was at last, his next scheme. "Right," she said. "I'm gonna fall for *that* one."

He stiffened. "I was just suggesting—"

"That I let you men in here and watch you trash the place? I don't think so. Why don't you let me use your lawn mower instead?"

He frowned. "I was just thinking. With a grown man and a seventeen-year-old boy next door, it seems wrong that you should mow your own lawn."

"Ha! You set this up, didn't you?" She leaned over the mower in his direction and received a whiff of cut grass. "How did you know the lawn mower was broken and hadn't run out of gas? I'll tell you how: you broke it yourself. You destroyed it, and now you're trying to get in here and vandalize the rest of my property." The scamp!

He drew himself up, glowering. "Can't you drop your suspicion for once? Here I am, offering out of the goodness of my heart—"

She choked. "Considering our history, suspicion is the only wise feeling for me to have for you, *Mister* Taylor. And you'd better stop whatever you're planning next, because *I am on to you.*" She wheeled around and strode into her house.

Inside, she threw herself on the couch and burst out laughing. "He's back," she said out loud, chuckling and leaning her head back. Jordan was finally back to his pranks.

Or was he? She frowned at the unwelcome thought. Was it possible he had been telling the truth? That he hadn't tampered with the lawn mower? She pursed her lips. If so, he must still be trying to get her to let down her guard before he unleashed whatever scheme he was working on. How annoying.

She went to get her laptop. For the next several hours, she worked on spreadsheets and dreamed of battles to come. She thought up a number of ways to irk Jordan so he would break and return fire for fire out in the open. No more of this lame, secretive waiting around.

She put her work aside and got up slowly, stretching, she imagined, in a catlike manner. "It's nothing personal, Jordan," she whispered, putting her hands behind her back as she looked out her open kitchen window at the Taylors' window which was likewise open, leaving the house vulnerable. "Just think of it as an experiment."

Hopefully Google would have a simple, inexpensive recipe for a stink-bomb. This would be full-blown, unlike the cherry-scented explosion she had hoped to set off back when she rescued June's sling. The Johansen family would suffer a bit in the aftermath of the stink-bomb, but not as much as those in the designated house would, and it was a sacrifice she was willing to make.

The phone rang, and she started guiltily. When she reached for her cell phone, the name of the children's elementary school flashed across the screen. Unsure why the school would call her, especially at this time of day, she picked up.

"Hello?"

***

KEISHA WALKED SO FAST through the elementary school that she was breathless by the time she pushed the door open to the office.

Frayden slouched in a cushioned chair against the wall.

She rushed over to him. "What happened?"

He looked away from her, the sulky expression all too familiar, just as another door opened and Principal Woods stepped from his room, his gray suit immaculate. "Mrs. Johansen, Frayden, please come in."

Keisha wanted to hear Frayden's side of the story first. "Frayden, tell me—" she began, but he moved around her and entered the office. She had no choice but to follow.

He took a seat, and Keisha sat beside him and across from Principal Woods. Frayden still wouldn't look at her, so she turned to the principal. "Tell me again why we're here."

"It's like we told you on the phone, Mrs. Johansen. Your son is bullying other students. The teachers have tried to get him to be kinder, but what they saw today was more than a snarky comment made in class. He shoved a younger student into the wall and kicked his backpack around. We don't tolerate that kind of behavior at Aspire Elementary."

Keisha stared at him. Frayden could be difficult, but he'd never acted like that. "Are you sure that's what happened?"

"Mrs. Johansen, two teachers witnessed the occurrence."

"Faculty can't always be trusted when it comes to things like this," she forged on, her heart pounding at the thought that maybe the *other* child had been after *Frayden*. "In my time, I've seen teachers punish the victims of bullying. They'd pick up a kid who'd been shoved into a locker and give him detention for that. They even—"

"Mom, I did it. All right?" Frayden interrupted, sitting up in his seat with a scowl.

She opened her mouth and gaped at him. "You did what, exactly?"

"I pushed the kid, and I pulled off his backpack, and I stepped on it."

"But why?"

"Because I felt like it!" He pushed a hand through his hair, sounding exasperated, as though he couldn't believe she didn't get it.

"That doesn't make sense, Frayden. Was he mean to you?"

"No, Mom." He rolled his eyes. "It doesn't have to make sense."

"He threatened you." Her heart lurched. "Did he threaten you? Or was someone else mean to you?"

"Mom, there's no reason why I did it. Do we have to talk about it? Let's just get to the punishment already."

"Frayden, there has to be more to it than that."

"There isn't," he insisted, leaning forward. "It's just how I am."

She flinched. "No, it's not. That's how your dad is, Frayden." The words left her mouth faster than her brain could catch up to what she was saying. "But it's not *you*, and you don't have to be like him. You're my son now, not his."

"How's *that* any better?" he spat out, shocking her more than anything else in this conversation had. "Oh, I'm your son. That means I should behave, does it? What about you? You're always running around screaming at Jordan Taylor and being rude to his kids and—and I heard you the other day talking to Lizzie. You made her think there was only one way she could have her hair, and that was how *you* wanted it, like you're controlling her life. What am I supposed to think? Is that how you want me to be?"

Keisha reared back, her heart beating painfully, her mouth still open with the things she had meant to say. Frayden's face was set in angry lines like the ones she had often seen on his father, but his dark red-brown hair and piercing blue eyes made him almost an exact copy of his mom. And here he was telling her he had done nothing more than follow her example.

She tried to draw in a breath. It felt as though her insides had been ripped apart. Her chest heaved with a noise like a shiver as she stared at him and he stared back in defiance.

He was right.

She had thought fighting with Jordan proved her strength. Instead, she had been a poor example. Had she in her own way been as bad a parent as her ex? The thought made her want to throw up.

She closed her mouth and gritted her teeth to keep any unwelcome noise from escaping. Turning to the principal, she wished for all the world that he would give her a helpful lecture as well as punishment.

He cleared his throat, his gaze settling somewhere below her eyes. "Frayden will go to detention for a week. Is that fine with you, Mrs. Johansen?"

Where was the punishment for her? The advice? She swallowed and nodded. "Detention. Right."

Principal Woods shook hands with her as though she were a perfectly responsible grownup. The meeting was over.

She went out to the hall with Frayden and stood beside him, watching the clock. In five minutes, school would be out. In five long minutes they would find the others and drive home. She dropped her gaze from the clock.

Nice linoleum floors.

"You're right," she said.

Frayden looked up, startled out of his scowl for a moment. "What?" He looked suspicious.

"I've been awful. I was rude. Am rude. All the time. It's uncalled for." She gave him a pleading look. "Frayden, I'm a mom who's trying. Sometimes I need to be pointed in the right direction. I already talked to Lizzie about the hair thing. She pointed me in the right direction by letting me know her thoughts. You did the same thing just now, telling me what I can do better." She paused. "Thank you."

He frowned and looked away. "Yeah, Mom." His voice dripped with sarcasm. "You can tell me I'm right, but saying you've been rude doesn't change anything if you don't do something about it."

She swallowed. "You're right again." She took a deep breath. "Which is why I *am* going to change things. I'll make amends with Jordan. In fact, as soon as we get home, I'll march over to his house and talk to him." Her mind spun with the idea, but it didn't matter how hard it would be. She had to change her example and Frayden's behavior at all costs.

"'March'?" Frayden's eyebrows lifted in disdain. "You're still at war, Mom."

Oops. She lowered her voice. "I'll tiptoe over and whisper my apologies."

He wasn't amused. "I don't wanna be there, Mom. You'll only yell at him."

"No, I promise I won't." She raised her voice in desperation. "I'll apologize and I'll behave. Really!"

"Whatever."

"I will. Just wait and see. I'll be nicer from now on." She held his gaze, finding the strength to put some of her Mom firmness back in her voice. "And so will you. That means no more bullying, and you'll make an apology to the other boy before the end of the"—no way could she learn to get along with Jordan by the end of the week—"semester," she decided on.

Frayden had the decency to look down at the floor, though she couldn't tell whether he felt guilty or not.

The bell rang. Both of them pushed away from the wall and went to the car to wait for Lizzie and the twins.

When the three of them arrived and climbed in, the two boys greeted her with their usual flood of energy.

"Mom, you switched around our lunches," Carl said.

"Yeah, mine had more jelly than peanut butter."

"And mine had too much peanut."

Keisha tried to draw her mouth into a smile. "Did you switch them back?"

"Yeah, after three bites."

"I took five bites."

"That's not fair. Then you got more."

"No, cos my bites are smaller than yours."

"*How* small? Show me with your hands."

"How's it going, Lizzie?" Keisha asked her quiet girl as they drove home.

"Fine." She looked up from her book with a smile and touched her crown of braided hair. "I really like it."

"I'm glad." The words were painful in Keisha's throat. She would have to face Jordan soon. Was she driving slower than normal? With a glance at the speedometer, she forced herself back up to the speed limit.

Her gut clenched when their house loomed up before them.

As soon as she parked, Carl grabbed Kale's hand and the two of them ran into the house to play.

Lizzie kept her nose in her book as she walked, disappearing inside as well.

"Frayden, I—"

He slammed his car door behind him.

"I'm going to do it now," Keisha called out the window.

The front door shut behind him.

She took a shuddering breath. The Taylor's car was parked beside hers. They were already home. He was home.

"I'm going to talk to him just like I said." Now, before she lost her courage.

Frayden didn't believe her. He thought she was lying about making amends or that she would lose her temper while trying, which was—likely.

He hadn't stayed to listen. She was alone, a fact that made her already impossible task harder. But she had to restore Frayden's faith in her. There was no other way. She had to learn to get along with Jordan, and that meant starting with an apology.

Squeezing a breath into her lungs, she walked to the Taylors' front door, feeling like she was on death row.

Jordan had knocked on her door so many times, but Keisha had never stood on his porch with the intent to talk to him. It was strange to think about.

She raised a trembling hand to the door.

This wouldn't do.

She steeled her hand but felt her stomach drop out at the same time.

Impatient with herself, she shook her head and knocked, slightly harder than she meant to.

She froze, realizing he might think she was angry based on her firm knock. He hadn't even opened the door yet, and already she had been rude. Maybe one of his kids would open the door and think—

It opened. Jordan Taylor moved forward but stopped dead on seeing her.

Her hand was still raised. Did it look like she was trying to slap him? Quickly she let it fall to her side.

In another moment she realized she was supposed to talk. She was the one who had come to his house with something to say, and now she had to say it.

"Jordan." Her voice sounded rusty. The day's events rushed over her, and she cringed at the memory of how she had attacked him over the issue of the lawn mower. He might still be mad about it. Was he upset that she had seen through his scheme? *Had* it been a scheme? His icy gray eyes weren't easy to read.

"I'm here to a—apologize." Was this how he had felt when he thanked her for helping Imogene? No wonder he had sounded like he was dying.

His eyebrows shot up all the way to his hairline, making him look nearly as stunned as she had been that day. "For what?" His voice was cautious. "Accusing me of tampering with the lawn mower?"

A flash of annoyance gripped her. Would he make her spell it out for him and beg?

No, she couldn't get annoyed. Guiltily she looked toward the top floor of her house. She deserved to beg. Frayden was right. He was probably up in his room right now, not even watching. He had no faith in her.

She looked at Jordan again. "No." He frowned. "Oh, I mean yes. I mean, I'm sor—sor—ry about my accusation. And about everything else. Everything from these past three years. I've been a beast."

Now he looked truly stunned.

Though she could sympathize with his astonishment, it was on the tip of her tongue to say, "Well, don't look so surprised."

The retort in her mind was like a punch to her stomach. She really *did* have problems.

She looked at her house again, just a quick glance, and back at him, thoroughly humbled. His eyes, puzzled, seemed to have followed her gaze.

"I want to make amends." Was that really her voice? It wasn't supposed to squeak except when she did it on purpose to entertain her children. "In fact—"

Frayden didn't think she could apologize. He probably wouldn't believe it when she told him she had. She was failing him. He was slipping from her fingers, not wanting to be his dad's son, maybe, but certainly not wanting to be his mom's son either.

"I'd like to invite you to lunch. On Monday. At La Bianca." She named a restaurant Shawna had mentioned a couple of times. "If you like Italian. If you don't, you can choose another place, and wherever it is, I'll pay—"

"You're inviting me to lunch?" he asked, looking incredulous as he put his hand on the doorknob. Whether it was for support or because he was getting ready to slam the door, she couldn't tell.

"Yes. So I can apologize some more. So I . . . just—"

"Keisha." He leaned forward, making her tense. "What is it you want to accomplish by having lunch with me?"

She closed her mouth and tried to think. The words came slowly. "I want to prove—*show*," she corrected the somewhat aggressive term, "that I can spend time with you without being rude. I want to wipe away these three years and stop being mean to you."

He lowered his gaze. She followed his eyes and realized she was wringing her hands. Clasping her hands tight, she stopped their movement.

He cleared his throat. "Do you really want to do this?"

She nodded.

He fixed his gaze on a point beyond her left shoulder. There was a strange light in his eyes. "I'm having lunch with Samuel that day. Between his classes."

"Oh." Was that it then? "Okay." She turned away but stopped. A noise sounded behind her. A sharp intake of breath. Or maybe she imagined it. Her thoughts were darting all over the place like a nervous rabbit.

An apology on the doorstep would get her nowhere with Frayden. It wouldn't be enough to make her a good person and a shining example to her children. She needed to get along with Jordan, and for that, she must spend time with him. On neutral ground.

With a shaky breath, she turned back. Jordan was leaning forward in the doorway, his gray eyes intense.

"Dinner?" Keisha squeaked, gripping her hands until they went numb. She felt horribly small and vulnerable as she stood before him, he on his doorstep and she below it and several inches shorter than him to begin with. Oh, how she hated feeling small. She had vowed never to feel that way again with a man, so she straightened and raised her chin. She might be in a humbled position, but it was *not* a vulnerable one.

His gaze sharpened. "What time?"

"S-six-thirty," she gasped, beginning to wish she could slouch again. It would make her breath come easier.

Slowly he shook his head. Her heart fell.

"Let's take separate cars and meet over there, shall we?"

Her eyes widened, and her heart climbed back up the slope of hope. She nodded breathlessly. She had never imagined being in the same car as him.

"Monday. Six-thirty. La Bianca," he summed up in a stilted manner.

"That's right." Feeling began to return to her fingers.

"Monday. Six-thirty," he repeated in wonder, turning, but not all the way, as though he didn't trust her enough to turn his back.

She was about to move away, and he had started to close the door, when he halted and mumbled, "See you." *Then* he closed the door.

Keisha stared at the spot where he had been. Awe held her spellbound.

He had tried to be polite, as he had possibly tried for the last few weeks. Why?

It was unheard of. It was—well, it would certainly help her in her goal of making non-enemies.

Pushing out her breath, she went home.

Frayden lounged on one of the living room couches. He hadn't gone upstairs then. That was a step better than what she had feared.

Her trembling legs carried her in his direction. She braced her hands against the top of the couch and tried to catch her breath. He didn't so much as look up. She stayed in her position, waiting for him to ask what had happened while simultaneously waiting for the fog in her head to clear.

Finally he raised his head and looked at her. She could tell he tried to keep his face free of expression, but his eyes asked the question his voice was too stubborn to ask. This was as much interest as he was willing to show. She would take it.

"I asked him to dinner." Strange. She sounded so calm all of a sudden.

Frayden's eyes grew to the size of saucers. "You did *what*? No. You're lying."

"I'm not lying," she said more strongly. "I may not have been a model mom, but I'm trying to be better, and I would never lie to you."

"He's coming here? What about his kids? Did you invite them too?" Frayden looked horrified.

"No, it's just him and me. We're eating out." She took a moment to think over the logistics. "I'll make a big dinner the night before so you can warm up leftovers."

"*You're* going to dinner with Jordan Taylor," he said in disbelief.

"Jordan Taylor?" Lizzie squealed, dropping her book on the stairs on her way down. "Why?"

"So I can make things right between us again. Well, not again. I guess things were never—"

"But you hate him," Carl exclaimed from just outside the open glass door as he peeked into the room together with his brother.

"No, I don't. Well, not anymore."

"What's up?" June came in from the hallway, sliding her backpack off her shoulders.

"*Mom's eating dinner with Jordan Taylor,*" Kale screamed before his twin could yell the news. Then he turned to Carl. "Beat ya to it."

June frowned and turned to Keisha. "What did he just say?"

"It's true." Keisha felt like an animal at the zoo. Cornered, caged, and stared at. "I—"

"No, seriously," June interrupted. "What did he say? His voice was so high-pitched I couldn't make it out."

"Oh." Keisha laughed nervously while Lizzie repeated the news to her sister. Keisha took a deep breath. "I want to show him, and you, that I can be nice."

"*To Jordan?*" June was flabbergasted.

"Listen, June, I've been a bad example to all of you. I've been awful to him all these years. I've been—rude. I've been mean. I've been—"

"Wanna borrow my thesaurus?" June drawled, earning a laugh from Keisha.

Her laughter died quickly though. She had to let the children know she was serious about this. "And I've been terrible to you guys."

June furrowed her brow. "How's that?"

"I've been an embarrassing mom. I mean, come on, don't tell me all that yelling and sneaking around and those petty plots of revenge weren't getting to you." She winced at the word "petty." She had enjoyed those pranks, and seeing them as a thing of the past made her heart twinge. But she had to go through with this. "Really, I've been acting like a five-year-old," she concluded.

Carl turned to Kale and spread the fingers wide on one hand. "I was five years old last year," he said wisely, as though he was glad to have passed *that* immature age.

"The point is," Keisha continued, "I'm going to behave from now on and treat the Taylors with respect."

June scoffed. "This is crazy, Mom. This is just crazy."

But Keisha was still waiting for Frayden's reaction.

Chapter 9

"Dad, can I—"

"Sure." Jordan waved his hand at Solomon, not waiting for the end of his sentence. Or not hearing it. He gave the pot another stir and breathed in the warm, spicy smell of stew.

"Great." Solomon left the kitchen with a smile just as Samuel walked in.

"Hey Dad, where's—"

He waved his hand. "Out front." Samuel was asking about Selima, right? It was hard to focus on the now when his thoughts kept swirling around two days ago.

Samuel looked out the window. "Cool. I'll catch her later."

Jordan looked at the oven clock. It was Sunday afternoon, and tomorrow was dinner with Keisha. Dinner. With *Keisha*. His defenses had risen all over again when she got mad at his offer of mowing the lawn. Oh, how he'd wanted to let go of his new decision and return to normal. Despite his moments of regret these last few years, despite his desire to get to know her better, his habits of complaining and taking revenge were hard to overcome. Battling her was so much more enjoyable than trying to be nice.

Until she dropped that bomb on him: knocking on his door, apologizing, her face pale, her eyes darting. Why did she keep looking back at her house? For strength?

Samuel's hand grabbed the ladle from him. "It's gonna burn if you don't stir it."

Jordan watched for a minute. How did he tell his kids about tomorrow's plans? "It's done anyway. Time to eat. Call the others to the table, all right? I'll just take out the trash."

The kitchen garbage was overflowing, topped with potato and carrot peels. Jordan pulled out the bag, tied it, and carried it around the corner to the living room and down through the hall.

He stepped outside, the door closing behind him. A small pile of weeds lay in front of the flowerbed, but Selima wasn't there. She was on the Johansens' side, kneeling on the lawn with the twins. Jordan's step hitched. The children had never been enemies, but he didn't usually see them together like this.

"See, isn't it fun to pat it back down?" Selima asked, taking a chunk of grass and roots and putting it in a small hole in the ground.

Kale—Jordan was pretty sure it was Kale—watched with a shovel clutched in his hand. Carl had a matching shovel and a tilt to his head. Three chunks of earthy grass lay beside him, and Jordan realized what had happened. The twins were having fun digging up their lawn.

He grinned. That would have been a worthy prank if—

No. He pinned down the thought. Pranks were over and done with.

"Carl! Kale! Dinnertime!" Keisha's clear voice rang out from her kitchen window.

Jordan hurried to the trash can and threw in the bag. When he turned back to his house, Selima was returning to her side, and the twins were running across their lawn, leaving their little shovels behind.

Kale caught sight of Jordan, and his eyes widened.

Carl slowed when his twin did and looked over to see what had caught his attention. His eyes grew round, and he elbowed Kale and whispered something.

Kale nodded and kept staring at Jordan. His little legs carried him up the porch, but he had yet to turn his head. His eyes were full of curiosity.

So her kids knew. Jordan needed to tell his. He would, as soon as—

"Watch out," he called just as Kale hit his front door and his head bounced back. Distracted at last from Jordan, the boy rubbed his cheek and opened the door, then ran in, followed by a laughing Carl.

Selima had spun around at Jordan's call. "What is it?"

"Uh, nothing. Time for dinner."

He followed her in. In a few minutes, dinner was on the table and everyone was seated.

Jordan looked across the table. "You say it, Solomon."

"Okay." Solomon folded his hands and started to pray out loud.

Jordan bowed his head and tried to listen. The missionaries had asked them to pray often: mornings, evenings, and at mealtimes. At first, Jordan had considered saying all the prayers and not letting his kids do it. He didn't want them *too* caught up in this religion, to the point of getting brainwashed. But the first time he let Selima pray out loud, it had brought a good feeling into the room. And after all, didn't he want what the missionaries had to rub off on his kids?

After the prayer, Jordan watched while they ate in relative silence. Imogene played with her peas. Solomon slurped his soup.

Jordan couldn't keep the news from them any longer. He cleared his throat. "I'm having dinner with Keisha tomorrow."

Selima choked on a laugh. "What are you planning to do?" Her eyes sparkled with humor as she reached for one of the store-bought dinner rolls.

"Talk to her."

Selima raised her eyes to the ceiling. "If you crash her family dinner, she won't thank you for it."

"Better bring a white flag," said Samuel and raised a cup to his lips. "If you want her to hear you out on any of your demands."

"I'm not making demands. We're eating out," said Jordan.

Movements slowed around him. He met the confused gazes of his children. "Keisha apologized for fighting me." Which made no sense. He had done as much fighting as she had. Worse, *he* was the one who started it all. "She invited me to dinner."

Splash.

Selima had let go of her roll, and it had landed right in her glass of water. Samuel's mouth fell open. Solomon clapped a hand to his mouth in a fit of giggles, watching the roll gather water. Imogene looked at Jordan, then returned to eating her peas.

"Why?" asked Selima.

"I don't know." The more he said, the more unbelievable it sounded. The kids' reactions weren't encouraging. Whatever Keisha's reasons, she hadn't suddenly taken a liking to him, had she? He had entertained that thought earlier, but it was beginning to feel impossible.

Still, he hadn't dreamed his interaction with her. That part was real.

He continued to mull it over while he got ready for bed a few hours later.

Keisha wouldn't have abased herself for an apology if she hadn't meant it. There had been something very raw in her expression.

He started to smile as he plumped up his pillow. Could it be she had noticed his efforts to stop fighting? Did she feel bad that she had kept up her end of the feud while he did nothing?

That didn't seem a strong enough reason for her to act as she had. His movements slowed as he remembered again her glances toward her home. Had she made a bet with one of her children, or something?

He shook his head and got into bed. Either way, she must mean to go through with making peace. He would see her tomorrow, away from the battlefield, in a public place where they would have to behave themselves. He hoped they *could* behave. His heart picked up speed as he tried to imagine the upcoming dinner. Keisha hadn't just apologized. She had asked to spend time with him.

He smiled into the darkness.

***

MOM WAS TRYING TO make peace with Jordan? June shook her head in class that Monday and pretended to take notes from her teacher's lecture. It made no sense. Besides, June liked him where he was—firmly in enemy land and a great source of entertainment.

She broke the tip of her pencil and cursed quietly. How was she to protect Mom when she opened herself up to new threats? June could write herself blue in the face to protect her from one danger, but now she was making herself vulnerable to another?

So long as Mom wasn't too emotionally set on this newest scheme, she would probably be all right. After all, there was no way Jordan would become friends just because Mom suddenly took a notion to make it happen. The only danger would be if they somehow did make friends, leaving him open to later hurt her in a way he couldn't in his current role as pesky neighbor.

She threw her broken pencil on the floor and reached for another, then looked up to find the teacher staring at her.

"Sorry," she said, though she wasn't sorry at all. Picking up her first pencil, she sent a speculative look at Selima three rows away.

***

AFTER-SCHOOL SHOPPING. WHOEVER INVENTED such a thing should be grounded till doomsday.

At least it had distracted her from nerves over tonight's dinner.

Keisha staggered through the doorway and collapsed inside, weighed down by the bags in her arms. Carl and Kale tugged on each side of her, giggling.

"Come on, Mom. We have to show everyone our costumes. Get up, Mom."

"I thought it was only girls who were supposed to spend hours trying on clothes," she whined, getting up and dragging the bags into the kitchen.

Carl grabbed a brown vest from one of the bags, but Keisha caught the other end of it as he tried to run off.

"We have to get the labels off first. June Bug, wanna help?"

June sighed, but she came over and pulled a pair of scissors from the drawer. Her forehead was wrinkled.

"What's got you so preoccupied?" Keisha's stomach churned as she asked the question. Whatever it was, it couldn't possibly be as worrisome as tonight's plans with Jordan.

"I'm trying to count something," June said. "I think it's been seven days in a row Selima's come to her classes. On time. I wonder what's going on with the Taylors." Her puzzled look changed to a grin. "I'm also surprised you waited till the week of the twins' presentation to buy their clothes. I don't know what's going on with *you* either."

"I was waiting for the fifty percent off sale," Keisha defended herself. "It didn't start until today."

The labels and stickers were soon disposed of, and the boys ran to get dressed and rushed back to the living room, raising their arms so everyone could see them. Lizzie, who had spent a lot of time in her room recently, came downstairs to see.

"How did you even find that hat?" June asked, her eyes dancing as she inspected the Robin Hood hat Kale wore.

"Now, *that's* a good question. I'm telling you, June Bug, it was a true miracle, and it took ninety-seven stores for us to find it."

Carl squinted at her. "I can count to thirty, and we didn't go to that many. At all."

"Hold on, bud, you can count to more than that." Keisha wondered briefly if something had gone awry in his early education. "What comes after thirty?"

Carl looked pained. "I can't start from there. I have to start from the beginning. One, two, three . . ."

"Did all ninety-seven stores have fifty percent off sales?" June drawled.

Keisha blinked. "What? Oh." She shook her head and imagined June Johansen, twenty-four years old and starting her career as a lawyer.

"You guys look so cool." Lizzie giggled. "I wish I could see your presentation."

". . . twelve, thirteen . . ."

"Mom, show them your clothes," Kale said over his brother's voice.

Keisha tried to ignore the butterflies in her stomach. "Actually I have to go now. You're doing good, Kale." She would have to teach him how to count starting from a higher number, but now wasn't the time. "Take good care of each other, guys. Remember to shut the microwave after you use it. And use a lid when you heat up the food. Don't eat in the living room, and don't turn on the TV until after you've eaten, if at all—"

"Mom, just go." June pushed her toward the entrance.

"Thirty-one!" Carl tried to do a somersault and ended up splat on the floor, blinking.

"Oh, and here I thought you didn't like the idea of me spending time with Jordan for a small hour." Keisha feigned hurt.

"Well, if you go on like that, I'd rather you go babble to him. Tell him to clean his shoes and wipe his nose," June called out the door, making Keisha laugh and then break off to look fearfully toward the Taylor home. If Jordan had heard that, he would think she was making fun of him.

Feeling like a thief in the night, she slid into her car and pulled out of the driveway, breathing a sigh once the parked truck behind her was out of sight.

She arrived at La Bianca and sat down a half hour before the appointed time. It was best this way. It would have been awkward for the two of them to get in their cars at the same time and drive side by side, and since she had been the one to invite him, she ought to be here first.

She tugged at her sleeves and crossed her feet under her chair. A lot of women in her situation might have panicked and spent all day trying to figure out what to wear so that the meeting would seem casual but friendly and so that she would look nice but also look as though she hadn't spent a lot of time thinking about what she ought to wear. Keisha thought the best way to look like she hadn't obsessed about what to wear was to not have obsessed about it. So it wasn't her clothes that made her nervous.

She wore what she usually wore when she picked up the children: dark jeans and a shirt that was more of a blouse than a T-shirt. Jordan had seen her in clothes like that often enough, and it would be foolish to dress better than that tonight. Unless he was dressed up. That would be a disaster. She tugged at her neckline, feeling a cold sweat build. But again, she really didn't care about the clothes—

Someone stepped up and pulled out the chair opposite her. Jordan Taylor plopped into the seat, likewise dressed the same casual way she always saw him. His red collared shirt accentuated his brown hair and would have made him stand out as an easy target—if she were still battling him.

He was twenty minutes early.

"You're early," she said. Her heart sped up, and her foot started tapping. Her test had begun, but it wasn't supposed to have started quite so soon.

"So are you. I saw you had left. There didn't seem to be much point in letting you stew over here while I had nothing to do anyway."

"Oh." Was she supposed to thank him?

A waiter came over, seeing that Keisha's party was complete, and handed them their menus. Both of them murmured thank-yous and scanned the sheets. Keisha's foot stopped moving. For the most part.

"I'll have the, um, Rustica." She chose what looked least difficult to pronounce and clenched her hands in her lap to still their shaking. What was she doing sitting at the same table as her archenemy, thinking she could behave? Her eyes were probably round and dilating. If she didn't get her act together, others would probably think the man in front of her was some sort of terrorist sitting there with a pistol hidden in his coat.

Now, *that* would be a creative way to get him hauled off to jail.

No, she told herself firmly. She mustn't think along those lines any-more.

"La Rustica for the lady," the waiter said, writing it down. "How about soups?"

Her eyes flew back to the menu. "Minestrone." She knew how to pronounce that for sure.

He made another note. "And salad?"

"Uh, that's okay. No salad for me."

"What kind of pasta would the lady like?"

How many different things did she have to order? "Rosata."

"Rosata sauce. What kind of noodles?" he persisted.

"Fettuccine," she said forcefully. "And that's it. I don't need anything else."

He raised his eyebrows. "No drink?"

Her cheeks burned on the instant. She was so used to cooking, she'd just about forgotten how to order in restaurants. Now Jordan was sitting there listening to her fumbling. This was the most embarrassing day of her life.

"Water's good," she said without looking at the drinks section.

"And what would the gentleman like?"

"The same she's having."

Keisha blinked and looked across the table at him. "You don't have to choose the same. It's fine if you pick something more expensive than what I got." She had no idea how much her food cost anyway. She had been too busy avoiding the Italian words she didn't know how to say.

"I'll have what you're having," he said again, "only I'd like ale instead of water."

Icy anger straightened her spine. She wanted to kill him right then and there. Not only had he evaded the entire awkward process of painstakingly ordering something from every category on the menu, he also had the audacity to order alcohol!

Not that he could know what those drinks meant to her. She forced herself to calm down. She was here to behave. No getting fired up over anything he did now.

The waiter left. Keisha stared at Jordan and tried to think of something to say. "So. Would you like for me to grovel and apologize while we wait for the food?"

He opened his mouth as though to laugh, but then he paused. "You're serious, aren't you? You really think I'd make you do that?"

"It might make you feel better. And keep me from slipping into insult mode."

Jordan unfolded his napkin rather dramatically. "Miss Johansen, if you really want to 'erase' these past three years, we'll have to pretend this is the first time we've seen each other. We have no history of any kind. We're two business associates meeting for a casual meal."

She felt a small smile on her lips. "I can play pretend." Suddenly she wanted to bite her tongue. She couldn't kid around with him and say silly things the way she did with her children. He would scoff at her childish words and make fun.

Jordan's lips quirked up in a half smile, but that was it. "Great. Now, Miss Johansen, have you ever eaten here before?"

Once again, she felt her face heat. "No, Mr. Taylor. You can probably tell."

"I was just wondering how you came to suggest the place."

"I heard about it from a friend at work."

He nodded and shrugged. "Eating at home is a great habit, but it has to be hard to cook all the time. Especially for a large family. I hear you have five kids?"

She raised her eyebrows and smirked. "Who told you that? The mail-man?"

He choked on a snort, making her hide a smile behind her hand. His gray eyes shone with a humor much more relaxed than the amusement they held whenever he bested her.

She hesitated for a moment before lowering her voice. "By the way, how's Samuel? I mean, how was he? You had lunch together today."

Jordan stiffened. "Samuel's fine."

"I'm sorry for that too," she said, then hurried on at his confused expression. "I mean, not sorry you had lunch, but sorry about any time I've thrown him and his problems in your face." She was pretty sure she had done that a few times, but apparently Jordan *was* trying to help his son, and she knew he cared about Imogene.

Jordan studied her as if he were trying to read her mind. She straightened and tried to look as sincere as possible.

The food arrived, saving her from further scrutiny. She grabbed her spoon and shoveled piping hot soup in her mouth, then dropped the utensil and reached for the water to cool her tongue.

So much for a reprieve from their conversation. Would it be more of a feat to sit silently through dinner with him, or to talk to him throughout the meal without doing or saying anything stupid?

She made a quick decision. In spite of her indignation a moment ago, things had gone surprisingly well so far. "What about you, Mr. Taylor? Do you cook or do you eat out?" It was a safe question she already knew the answer to. His car was always in the driveway around dinnertime, and she rarely saw the pizza delivery truck at his place.

"I cook. Sometimes Selima cooks. She's better at it than I am."

Keisha bit her lip, thinking of the quiet young woman. Selima had been outside reworking the flowerbed this week. Keisha was starting to wonder if it wasn't her domain rather than her dad's. She felt a pang in her chest. Jordan might have goaded Keisha the day she ran over the plants, but she had never meant to hurt his daughter. "What kind of flowers does she like?"

"Huh? Oh. Begonias. Zinnias. Those two and just about any other kind."

"Does she get them as flowers and then plant them, or does she plant seeds?"

"Anything is good. She can start them indoors if it's fall," he said deliberately and picked up his fork.

She ate in relief, sensing he could tell what she wanted to do and found it acceptable. Remembering the ruined flowerbed in front of his home with her second twinge of guilt that evening, she reflected on some of the monster pranks she had done. Her heart pounded as she imagined how she would feel now if Frayden had seen her run over those flowers.

"Can I ask you a question, Mr. Taylor?"

"*May* I," he corrected, making her lips twitch in annoyance before she stopped herself. He was trying to be funny. "I'm just teasing," he said quickly. "And maybe we should switch to first names."

"That sounds like a good idea." She leaned back in her chair. "In fact, I was wondering about some of the names in your family. 'Samuel' and 'Solomon' are names from the Bible, aren't they? And even 'Jordan.' Wasn't there someone—no, there was a river. The Jordan River."

"That's correct, though I doubt that's why my parents named me that." He looked at her with interest as if waiting to see where this would lead.

"Well." She frowned. "Why is it you've given your boys names from the Bible, but not the girls?"

He blinked. "There aren't a lot of girls' names in the Bible."

She shrugged off his response. "There are enough. You only have two girls."

"So, I liked 'Selima' and 'Imogene' better than Bathsheba and Bilhah. There are some pretty crazy names in there."

She pursed her lips. "It just seems sexist if you ask me. Separate naming systems. The boys have Bible names, and the girls sound like some sort of rock star or princess."

He stared at her. "You have got to be kidding me. You're not serious, are you? You're bothered by my kids' names?"

"No, no, of course not," she backtracked, realizing all at once how preposterous, not to mention insulting, her words were. "What I mean to say is—um, you're right about girls' names in the Bible. I guess there are some interesting ones in there."

He sat back, mollified. "Have you read the Bible then?"

"In high school." That was a long time ago. "I struggled through it for the literature. It's probably the most well-known book in the world, so I felt I had to give it a try."

He smiled. "Pretty hard read, huh?"

He wasn't mocking her for having a hard time with it, was he? No. She was too suspicious. Even if he was mocking her, she would give him the benefit of the doubt. Besides, he was right. She nodded and relaxed in her seat.

"Your twins, Keisha," he said.

She started. Sure, they had decided to go back to first names, but the way he said her name sounded so different from the way he yelled it whenever he was in a rage.

"What are their names?" he asked in all innocence.

She started to smile at the game of pretense. "Carl and Kale."

"I bet they're a handful. Do they go to any extracurricular activities, you know, to get them out of the house and use up some of their energy?"

"Not yet, but it's only a matter of time. Of course, it depends on whether or not they want to do something."

Jordan's eyebrows drew together. "Why? I say just make them go. They'll thank you for it later, and even if they don't, you'll have had time off from them."

She frowned. "You make it sound like I want to get rid of them. Really, Jordan, I enjoy having them around."

"Of course you do, but you can't possibly have energy to deal with them all the time." He waved her words away.

"Ever heard of school?" she asked, raising her eyebrows.

"Never mind." His eyes darted away and back as he regrouped. "It's not just that though. Children don't know what they want. Sometimes you have to choose for them."

"We're not talking life-changing decisions like a career, Jordan." Irritation bubbled inside her. "If they think they don't want to play a sport, then I say don't make them. If they think they want to learn ballet, I say let them, as long as you can pay for it."

"But it *could* turn out to be a career choice," he insisted. "How many adults look back on their lives and wish they had taken those piano lessons or that their parents had put a violin in their hands when they were five years old? Those are the kids that grow up to be professional artists, and those who got to choose what they wanted don't stand a chance."

"*My* kids," she huffed, Frayden's rejection of soccer still a fresh wound in her heart, "will *not* be forced to do anything they don't want to."

He shook his head. "You're limiting their options, Keisha. They'll look back and wish—"

"Is that why your daughter keeps running away?" she asked, her voice going high-pitched. "Are you forcing her to dance her legs off or play the violin five hours a day? Is that what you do to your kids?"

"You think you know so much about my family." He drew himself up. "First Samuel, and now Imogene. You'd know a lot more about us if instead of spying on us all the time, you'd been friends with us."

"Spying! *You* should talk. That kitchen window of yours is open 24/7 just so you can listen in on what goes on in *my* family. Either that, or you're out in the backyard snooping, watching our lawn mower break down, or throwing beer cans into our yard."

"You're still mad about that?" he exclaimed, turning red-faced. "What about the time you flooded our basement? "

"That's an exaggeration, and I told you it was an accident." People were staring, but Keisha ignored them and focused on her target. "And have you forgotten what you did to Lizzie's doll?" The poor thing had been dressed up as a clown and clumped together with other circus toys in the middle of her front yard to prove a point about how messy it was. "She's never touched another doll after that, and she's mostly given up on stuffed animals too."

"Maybe that's because she lost her dirty bunny the same day you found the doll," he snarled.

What? Lizzie had never told her that!

Keisha pushed back her chair with a screech and leaped to her feet. "You *didn't*. She loved that bunny. That's why it was so dirty, genius, because she carried it around everywhere and couldn't live without it."

"I didn't take her bunny. I just happen to know it got lost!"

His words didn't stop her stream. "If you've forced your children to grow up without the comfort of stuffed animals, it's no wonder your family has problems."

His chair screeched louder than hers as he stood. "You read too many child psychology books. Is that what you aspire to be? A shrink that analyzes other people's kids that you have no clue about?"

"Oh, you—" She stopped cold, her clenched fists frozen midair. She had done it again. She had flown off the handle.

Ice cracked her heart. So much had been at stake this time. How could she go home and tell Frayden what had happened? How had she ever thought she could do this? She was a fiasco. Frayden would read it in her eyes before she told him. He would see it in Jordan's angry expression and stiff walk.

Her eyes filled with tears. She turned to go.

"Wait, Keisha. Wait, sit down." Jordan grabbed her arms. "Please sit, Keisha." He directed her back to her chair, where her legs conveniently seated her by collapsing beneath her.

She dropped her head on the table while he pulled his chair around and sat beside her.

"I didn't mean to—" he began.

"I couldn't even last an hour," she wailed, interrupting and raising her head. "I couldn't be good for *one, stinking* meal." Sobbing, she let her head fall back down into her arms.

"Keisha, it's okay." Jordan's voice pled with her. "Really. What are you doing this for anyway?"

"For Frayden," she sobbed out, her tears bathing her hands. "I'm a bad example to my children, and he called me out for it."

"For your children." Jordan was silent for a moment. Then a hand touched her shaking back. "Look, you did fine. Three days ago, you couldn't have sat through half a dinner with me. A couple of weeks ago, neither of us could have. Come on, we've just spent, what, fifteen minutes together before we argued? That's a huge record! We did great, and we'll keep working on it."

"We will?" She sniffed, looking up into Jordan's gray eyes. From the table behind him, a little girl watched with a curiosity like Carl and Kale's. From another table, three college age guys threw Keisha looks. She touched her hot cheeks, feeling the beginning of a headache from her crying.

"We will," Jordan said. "I'll help you. In fact, let's have dinner again a week from now at, say, Taco Bell. I'll pay this time. We'll try again, and even if we don't make it through the meal without flying at each other, maybe we can go for longer than we did today. We'll get better."

"Really?" She sounded like a child asking for reassurance, but she didn't care.

Jordan sent a glare at the college guys until they looked away. When he returned to Keisha, his expression was determined. "Of course. It's taken two of us to fight all this time. There are still two of us, but we're both trying to be nicer now. We're in this together, and we'll help each other overcome the habits we created. So, Monday of next week? Same time?"

"Okay," she said and wiped her cheeks.

He looked down at his hands. "And there's something else I've been meaning to talk to you about."

She sniffed. "What?"

"The kids and I have been meeting with some missionaries for the past few weeks. Missionaries for The Church of Jesus Christ of Latter-day Saints." He said the long name slowly.

She tensed, and her eyes darted away. Oops. How long had he known? But why did he bring it up to scold her with right after making up with her?

"They've made me rethink a few things in my life. Like the way I treated you and your family. You probably noticed I tried to tone things down. I didn't exactly try to be nice to you, except when your lawn mower broke down, maybe, but I did try to stop being mean."

He didn't know. Did he? Wait, *that* was why he had stopped responding to her barbs? And—maybe why he thanked her for picking up Imogene instead of freaking out over the fact that Keisha had his daughter in her car. Which, by the way, he rightfully could have freaked out about. She would have been scared witless if Jordan had one of her children in his car.

With a frown, she tried to remember what she had told the missionaries. Did this mean that Jordan had, in fact, been looking for God in his life?

"That's not the only thing they've done for me though," he continued. "Samuel has started to stay home and listen to the discussions. He's getting better. A lot better. About you-know-what. He's changing. Things are changing in my family."

It seemed like things were flipflopping. All of a sudden Samuel was doing "better" and Selima had stopped skipping school. Keisha's was the troubled family now, with Frayden's bullying and Lizzie's anguish and shyness in speaking up about her hair.

Jordan took a deep breath. "I think maybe you should meet with the missionaries too."

Was this a threat? Blackmail? She pulled her hand through her hair. If he had asked the young men why they came to his house, they would have told him Keisha referred them to him. Sicced them on him, really.

"I know it's a bit weird, but I was thinking maybe I could set up an appointment with them to meet you at your house. I could come too while they teach, and I can just listen and ask questions if I think of any." He gave her a nervous look. "Would you be okay with that?"

She swallowed. "Sure." *Please don't let him know what I did. Please don't let him know what I told them.*

They would recognize her when they entered the house. She was doomed.

"Great," he said, looking as though a burden had been lifted from his shoulders. Keisha figured it had been too, because she felt it descend on her own shoulders.

Jordan looked at his plate.

Keisha cleared her throat. "Maybe we should finish our food."

"You read my mind."

Watching Jordan eat peacefully beside her was one of the strangest things she had yet experienced. They didn't argue or scowl at each other for the rest of the meal. It was amazing. She was infinitely grateful he had stopped her from rushing out of the restaurant and returning home to Frayden with red eyes and her temper on fire.

They actually laughed when they went to the parking lot and got in their separate cars. Then they drove, mostly side by side, and—mostly—without racing each other until they got home.

For a brief moment it felt like they had returned to enemy territory as they got out of their cars onto their usual battlefield. This was the place where they yelled at each other and sabotaged each other's property.

However, Keisha was determined not to leave her new friendship-slash-neutral-feeling behind at La Bianca. The memories of her home turf wouldn't overwhelm her. There would be no backsliding.

Shutting her car door, she turned to see Jordan wave goodbye from the other side of his car. She raised her hand and froze. Five children's faces goggled at her from her kitchen window, Carl and Kale's squished against the glass.

Slowly, she waved and went inside.

As she stepped into the living room, the children scrambled out of the kitchen and stared at her.

"How did it go?" Frayden asked without a trace of sarcasm.

She smiled at him. "We're going to have dinner together again next week."

The children were speechless. Most of them anyway.

"Did you throw your food at him?" Kale wanted to know.

Keisha coughed. "No, I was very nice."

"Did he . . ." Carl paused and thought. "Did he spill his water on you? Or pull your chair away so you fell? Or"—he gasped with dread—"did he eat all your food?"

"Carl, he was very nice."

"Yeah, but what did he *do*?" he insisted in a whine.

"Ate his food and drank his . . . drink." She tried not to sound disgusted at the memory of the alcohol he had ordered. "Where are your pajamas?"

June still looked dumbstruck when the phone rang. Lizzie answered and then held it out to Keisha. "It's for you." Then she whispered to everyone else, "It's Jordan Taylor!"

Of course they all crowded around to listen in as Keisha put the phone to her ear, her heart pounding in her chest. "Hello?"

"Hi, Keisha. Um, I contacted the missionaries. They have time on Thursday any time between ten and two o'clock. Or if Thursday doesn't work—"

"I can do Thursday if it's at ten." Better get it over with as soon as possible. The twins' presentations would be that afternoon. Good thing Jordan's work from home seemed to be flexible.

"Ten? All right. I'll tell them, and I can come over a few minutes before. If you're okay with me being there."

"Yes, yes, you just come over." The twins' eyes looked ready to roll out of their heads. Keisha ran a hand across her hair. "Maybe they can focus on you if I don't know what to say to them."

"Great. I'll see you then. Bye." *Click.*

Keisha looked around the room. The twins were still staring. Frayden seemed intrigued, Lizzie's button-nose wrinkled, and June looked puzzled.

Keisha held up her hands and spoke before anyone else could. "Who wants ice cream?"

Chapter 10

June couldn't believe it. Dad still wasn't angry. She had sent him two rude letters, but he wasn't mad in his letter today. Instead, he seemed excited to hear from her.

She walked slowly from the dojo, trying to wrap her mind around it. The sky was cloudy, and the air was cool.

He kept writing the same things. It was his fault. He was sorry about how he had treated them. He had changed.

June would never consider believing it if it wasn't for the fact that she remembered some good times with him. There was the evening they all sat in the living room, the twins and Lizzie snuggled up with Mom while Mom read a story. Dad had sat on the couch between June and Frayden and smiled at them all. At least once he had tucked her into bed without his usual annoyance. And there were cheerful evenings when he brought home dinner for all of them and was happy with the world.

She pressed her lips tight. She had already tried to keep their family together. Before he went to jail, before Mom got divorced, June did everything she could think of. She picked up after the others. She cleaned up spills. Most of all, she kept him from hurting the others.

Families were meant to stay together. She had always known that. Wasn't everyone born knowing that? The movies showed it. Even when parents got divorced, sometimes they needed to get back together. June had hated it when Dad hit Mom, she had hated it when he got in a temper, but she had thought if they could just get past that, if they could just have more of the good times, maybe they'd be okay. There must have been a reason Mom married him. He must have been good once.

If he had changed back to that person now, what did that mean for them?

A group of older teenage boys filled the sidewalk up ahead. They were loud and smelled funny. Like alcohol? There was something else, too, though. A bit of discomfort ran down her back, but she kept going, watching for them to make room.

If Dad had really changed—

She bit her lip.

Was it possible he and Mom should—

She shook her head. There was no way. No way they ought to get back together unless she was one hundred percent certain, no, *two* hundred percent certain that Dad had really changed.

If she could somehow find that out, then maybe he and Mom should get together again. Just like in the movies.

The guys kept walking toward her, none of them moving aside. Her spine stiffened, but she stepped down on the road and let them pass, then returned to the sidewalk.

She humphed, then grinned. Just so long as Mom didn't do anything stupid like start to date Jordan. Last night would have sounded like a date to someone else, but it had just been dinner. Just a friend thing.

Not that there was anything wrong with Jordan, but June needed time to think things through.

"Samuel! Hey, Samuel," one of the teenagers yelled, making her spin around.

The group waved and shouted at someone across the street. June started. It was Samuel Taylor. He looked like he had just left the hardware store.

"Dude, where have you been?" one of the guys yelled.

"Come on, join us," another invited.

Samuel stared at the group. His gaze met June's for a moment, and her pulse sped up. Then he looked away. "I'm running an errand for my Dad."

"Forget your dad. Come on, let's have some fun."

June tried to control her pulse. It was almost like Samuel was protecting her, not drawing the others' attention to the girl behind them.

One of the guys punched another on the shoulder. "Come on, Cole, don't you want him to come with us?"

Cole didn't look like he wanted much of anything. His eyes were sunken in his pale face, and he hadn't said much. That was probably why his friend picked on him.

Finally Cole shrugged. "If he doesn't want to hang out with us, let him leave."

"Yeah, we'll have fun without him," the tallest guy said and raised his voice. "You just go home to your boring old dad and see if we'll let you hang out with us next time."

Without another word, Samuel walked away. June turned and slowly did the same.

She didn't like those guys. She knew Samuel did things he shouldn't. Those guys were proof of that. But maybe he was trying to change.

And if he could change, maybe Dad could too.

***

"I'LL GET THE MAIL," June said first thing Thursday morning.

"Thanks, June." Keisha rinsed off the sandwich knives and pulled the dishwasher open. Her hands shook a little. The day had arrived sooner than she expected.

"Mom, I still don't get what missionaries are," Carl said. "Will you talk to them about God?"

"I think so." She handed Lizzie her lunchbox.

"Mom, why did Frayden get to have ice cream with us this week?" Kale asked peevishly. "I thought he got detention at school. Doesn't that mean he's done something bad? So why did he get ice cream?"

"Yeah, there would have been more for me if he hadn't," Carl exclaimed as he accepted his lunchbox.

Keisha picked up her car keys and tried to rake through her still uncombed hair with her free hand. "There's no reason to go around punishing him with all sorts of things."

"But it's not fair. There was one day I had to go to bed without ice cream, and the others all got it, but I had been bad, so I didn't."

"When was that?"

"Ten years ago or something."

"Kale, you're six years old."

"Yeah, and I still remember!"

"Stop being jealous of Frayden," she told them as everyone filed out to the car. Now that her own conscience concerning her behavior toward

Jordan was somewhat appeased, she had started to talk more to Frayden about bullying at school, but he didn't respond well. She had a feeling he would do better if she continued to behave herself. "That's bad, too, you know. Complaining about someone else's good fortune. There's a story about it."

"A story?"

"Tell us."

She turned on the ignition and backed out of the driveway, trying frantically to remember what had popped into her mind. "Right, there was a man with two sons. One of the sons said, 'Dad, I want everything that's going to be mine when you're dead, and I want it now.'"

"He said that?" Kale asked in shock.

"Did his dad hit him?" Carl asked.

"No. He was sad, but he gave it to his son, and the boy went out and traveled and spent all the money on stupid things. When there was nothing left, he realized he had no friends to play with and no food to eat. He was hungry, and he got scared that he would starve. He knew his dad had food, but he felt so bad about what he had done that he didn't want to go back.

"But then he got *really* hungry, and he said, 'I don't want to starve. I'll go back and I'll work for my dad and do everything he tells me to and do a lot of chores, and he'll pay me so I can eat.'

"But when he got home, his dad ran to him and hugged him. He had been so worried that his son might get hurt or die, and he was so happy to see him even though he had done bad things. The dad said, 'Tonight we'll have a great meal and all your favorite ice cream, son.'"

Frayden snorted from the backseat.

"Then the other son came over and said, 'That's not fair. Why does he get to have his favorite ice cream when he took your money?'

"And the dad said, 'He's still my son. I love him, and I don't want him to starve, no matter what he's done.'"

Kale looked up, waiting.

"The end."

"Cool story," he said.

"Yeah. Who made it up?" Carl asked.

Keisha knitted her brows. "I think it was Confucius." A vague recollection of the New Testament came to mind. "Or Jesus?"

"We're here," said Kale. "Don't forget to bring our clothes, Mom."

"I won't forget. After all the time we spent finding those costumes, I definitely won't miss this."

The car was considerably quieter after she left the elementary school behind. In a few minutes, June stirred in her seat. "I don't think it was Confucius. We read some of his things in class last year."

"Huh. Maybe I'll Google it."

"Are you nervous? About today?"

Keisha let out a loud breath. "Yeah. I mean, can you see me talking religion with anyone?"

"No, I meant about Jordan coming over." June's eyes glinted. "He's actually going to be in our house."

"Oh. Yeah, it's a strange thought. He's not so bad though," Keisha hurried to add. "I think it'll be all right."

"At least you're on your home turf." June smirked and got out of the car. "He can't get you there. Enemy ground, you know."

"The war's over, June Bug," Keisha called to her retreating back. "The war's over," she muttered to herself as June disappeared into the throng of students milling toward the school doors.

She shook her head. Last Monday at La Bianca had been a miracle, even if they had both stepped on a few landmines. Hopefully today would lead them further in the right direction. Hopefully it wouldn't lead to another battle.

"Just the missionaries," she mumbled and turned the car toward home. "I guess I deserved that one."

***

THE DOORBELL RANG FIVE minutes before the missionaries' scheduled visit.

Keisha opened the door and started in surprise to see Jordan. Really, it hadn't sounded at all like him. It wasn't his customary way of punching the doorbell over and over or trying to knock down the door. He also wasn't launching into his usual tirade. Instead he stood there, rolling back and forth on the balls of his feet and looking anxious.

It couldn't be a prank, could it? He wasn't this good of an actor. Although there was the time he fooled her in his hazmat suit—

He stopped moving and gave her a weird look. She stared back at him.

"Oh! Come in," she said, remembering she was supposed to be the host.

It felt like she was rehearsing a play as she opened the door wide and motioned for him to enter, then led him through the hall and into the living room.

"It's strange to think about." Jordan broke the silence, looking around. "As well as we've gotten to know each other these three years, I've never been invited in since you moved here."

"Had you been in here before we came?" she asked, half politely, half curiously.

"Yes. I knew the Japanese lady who lived here. She loved having tea parties and invited us over now and then. Selima would sit on the floor right there and pour tea for everyone. She loved it."

Keisha imagined the scene with the quiet Selima delicately pouring tea. The mental image made her smile before she remembered anew her duties as hostess. "Would you like something to drink? We have water." Her voice came out flat on the second sentence. They had milk too, and soda somewhere, but she was saving the soda for Friday, and she didn't like putting herself in this position of serving Jordan.

"Uh, that would be great," he said, half sounding as though he were asking a question. "Thanks."

She opened her mouth but wasn't sure what she wanted to say. "Just a minute," she mumbled and made her escape into the kitchen.

They were friends in the making now. He had been so nice at La Bianca too. She sighed. He deserved more effort at civility from her.

Of course, there was still a small chance he hadn't called off the war. She took two glasses from the cupboard and held one below the water dispenser in the fridge. If her suspicions the last few weeks proved true and he wanted to catch her off guard with his next attack, now would be the time to do it, after he had showed so much compassion last Monday. For a moment she imagined that no missionaries were coming today. He had made it up, and he would laugh to himself while she waited for them to show up.

If this turned out to be a prank, she would never, ever trust him again.

Actually, what *would* she do then? She still had to be the adult and show Frayden and the rest of her children that she could be civil to Jordan. She had to stop torturing herself with these doubts. Everything would be fine.

When she returned to the living room, Jordan had his back to her. He looked up at the wall at the first CG Keisha had ever bought, a graphic of children playing in a creek.

"What's this?" His forehead wrinkled.

What a perfect topic! She put down two cups of water and stepped over beside him. "It's a computer graphic. It looks like a mix between a painting and a photograph, doesn't it? The whole thing was produced digitally. I love the effect. I have a few more upstairs, and my newest is right there." She pointed at the boy with the "O"-shaped mouth and waited for Jordan's reaction.

"I guess they're kind of cool," he replied, "but . . ."

"But?" she prompted, her shoulders dropping when he didn't share her enthusiasm. Of course, they had never shared much of anything besides a driveway, and that had created problems of its own.

"Seems like portraits are usually a picture of yourself, or one of your kids, or an ancestor. Someone you know or relate to. You like looking at these digital pictures of strangers?"

"I do. It's a different kind of portrait." She squirmed, feeling suddenly childish in her opinion, but steeled herself. "It's like people-watching without the people realizing I'm doing it and getting embarrassed. Or embarrassing me."

"Is there a story?" he asked, raising an eyebrow in amusement.

"Not really. Just people stopping and asking, 'What are you staring at?' I tried to pretend to be an artist a couple of times." She made her voice high-pitched. "'Oh, I just love your face. I was thinking, That's something I'd like to paint.'" She looked at the colorful CG. "They didn't usually buy it. Just looked uncomfortable and walked away. One guy gave me an earful."

Jordan blinked. "You watched a guy because you liked his face?"

"Don't say it like that. Mostly it was girls, but you know, I tried not to discriminate." She felt herself go hot, but she kind of wanted to laugh at the same time.

The doorbell rang.

Here goes, she thought and went to answer. Was it possible for her to signal to the missionaries to pretend they had never seen her before?

She swung the door open and paused. Two young women stood on the doorstep, one in a floral dress and one in a green skirt and white blouse. They wore nametags like the ones Keisha had seen the day she met the missionaries. Keisha had, for a fact, never seen these women before.

"You're women," she said, cutting short their greetings. They gave her a puzzled look, and her hand flew to her mouth. "Sorry. I mean, you're women missionaries. I didn't realize you would be."

"Have you met the elders, then?" asked the one in the dress.

"The what?"

"The men missionaries," the young woman clarified. "We're referred to as sisters."

Jordan stepped up next to Keisha. "Hi. I thought—never mind. Please come in."

"Oh, thank you." The visitors followed them through the hall. "I'm Sister Miyagi, from Hawaii," said the one in the dress. "And this is Sister Cole, from Virginia."

Keisha beckoned them to the couch. "I'm Keisha."

The women took a seat and smiled. "How often have you had missionaries visit?"

"Never," said Keisha. "But Jordan wanted me to give it a try."

"So your husband has taken lessons?"

Keisha's eyes flew wide open, and Jordan choked as though someone had rammed him in the stomach.

"She's my neighbor." Jordan's voice was hoarse.

The doorbell rang. "Let me get that," Keisha said and ran from the room like a coward.

She opened the door and found herself staring at the young men she had given Jordan's contact info.

"Hello. You must be Keisha. I'm Elder Sørensen," said the first of them, as if he didn't remember her.

"And I'm Elder Johnson." The other man shook her hand. "Is Jordan here already?"

How many people had Jordan invited? She managed a nod. "Please come in."

On their entry in the living room, Jordan and the sister missionaries stood.

"Sister Cole! Sister Miyagi," exclaimed Elder Johnson.

"What are *you* guys doing here? I mean, you elders," Sister Cole corrected herself.

"I'm confused," said Jordan. "I invited the elders here, but when you sisters came, I thought they must have sent you in their place."

"Oh no, we were just in the area knocking on doors. If you have an appointment with them, we can leave," said Sister Miyagi.

Keisha followed the exchange like a game of ping-pong, but when the Hawaiian missionary made to leave, she stepped forward. "Please stay. The more, the merrier."

That wasn't necessarily true, but she rather liked the energy of these two women.

"Well, then, it's a party." Elder Sørensen clapped his hands together. Maybe his energy wasn't so bad either. Just so long as he didn't recognize her and tell Jordan about their first meeting. Keisha's hands began to sweat before he continued, "Do you mind if we start our lesson with a prayer?"

So much for a party. "Uh, that's fine." She looked at Jordan. He beckoned at the elder and told him, "Go ahead."

The prayer that followed included thanks and a humble request for God's Spirit to be present during the lesson. *People can ask for that?* Keisha wondered as the elder ended with Jesus's name and an "Amen."

Elder Johnson leaned forward. "Before we begin, Keisha, we'd like to know where you're at. Do you believe in God?"

Wow. The question seemed universally general for about two seconds, and then all of a sudden it felt like a very personal, private question, the answer to which might reveal a lot about her. To Jordan who was sitting there listening. And to the four young people.

"I don't know." She fought the urge to squirm on the couch. "I guess he might exist, like in the clockmaker theory. He made us and then lets us do our own thing."

"He did create us," the elder said earnestly, "but he's also involved in our lives. Have you read about the prophets in the Bible?"

At least she had a quick answer for that. "Yes. Moses. Daniel. Those guys, right?"

"That's right. God spoke to prophets back then, as well as to normal people who believed in him. He still speaks to us today. He's our Heavenly Father, and he loves all of us more perfectly than any earthly father does. Do you believe that's true?"

She cleared her throat. "I guess it's possible." She had heard him described as a father before, but she didn't remember hearing the word 'loving' in connection with him. More loving than her own father wasn't too much of a stretch. "But he doesn't speak to me," she said, hoping to draw a laugh at the ridiculousness of the idea.

Sister Miyagi spoke up, her eyes bright. "God speaks to everyone who seeks him. Not necessarily with words. Sometimes it's a feeling, but he speaks to us and answers our prayers, including yours."

"Why?" It sounded too good to be true, though Keisha wouldn't mind some divine assistance.

Elder Sørensen answered. "He wants to communicate with his children. Through prophets and the Spirit, he teaches us about Jesus so we can come to him and have eternal life."

"The Spirit is the feeling Sister Miyagi was talking about," Sister Cole added. "When I pray and feel comfort, or I get a thought that begins to solve the problem I'm struggling with, that's the Spirit guiding me."

Keisha liked how the missionaries let each other take turns speaking. The sister missionaries weren't even supposed to be here, yet the elders accepted their comments as part of the lesson. Those boys were good-natured and much more respectful than she would have guessed.

"You might have found that in the Bible, people often rejected the prophets," said Elder Johnson. "When Jesus came, they even rejected him. The world fell into apostasy, meaning there were no prophets, and without that direct line to God, people became confused about the doctrine and created many different churches that were sometimes at odds about Jesus's teachings."

Elder Sørensen's face became a study as he looked at Keisha. "Have we m—"

"Are you saying we're lost without prophets?" she rushed to ask, cutting him off.

"We didn't have the fulness of the gospel of Jesus Christ on the earth or someone with priesthood authority from God to lead his church for many centuries," said Elder Johnson. "But that changed about two hundred years ago. Sisters, do you want to share about Joseph Smith?"

Keisha was again surprised that they were willing to share the lesson like that, but she turned her full attention on the sisters as they talked about a fourteen-year-old farm boy with a serious mind who fervently wanted to know which church was true. After much study and as he prayed in a secluded place, Heavenly Father and Jesus appeared to him.

She couldn't tear her gaze from the young people as they talked about God restoring his church through Joseph and calling him to be the first prophet in the "latter days," the last period of time before Jesus's Second Coming. There was a light in the missionaries' eyes and in their smiles and even in the room. Keisha's mind whirled with all these new ideas while they introduced *The Book of Mormon: Another Testament of Jesus Christ* as a companion to the Bible.

Elder Sørensen held up the blue book. "You can find out if this is true by reading the Book of Mormon and praying to God. Will you study it and ask God if it's true?"

"Sure." Keisha waved on the invitation. She wanted to hear more.

The elder wasn't done. "Keisha, when God answers your payer and you know all this is true, will you follow the example of your Savior Jesus Christ and be baptized?"

She caught her breath, delight sparking inside her. They would let her do such a special thing? She didn't know exactly what it was, but everything felt good, and she was excited about the idea of saying a prayer and feeling the Spirit. "Sure!"

Jordan made a gurgling noise.

"But tell me more. What do the prophets tell you today?"

Elder Johnson smiled at her. "One of the things they tell us, as you'll also see over and over in the scriptures, is that we need to be baptized and make covenants with God. We're holding a baptismal service on October 10th. Will you be baptized on that date?"

"Yes, yes." Keisha nodded with impatience and looked over at her wall calendar, trying for a moment to combine her newfound excitement with practicality. "That's in about three weeks. Now what else does God need us to do?"

Every time the missionaries tried to end, she found a way to keep them talking. She simply wouldn't let them go. It didn't matter that she had never been into religion, never wanted to talk to the two men that stopped her on the street, and never thought of the Bible as much more than classic literature. All she knew was that the rawness left behind by Frayden's bullying situation and her anxiety about dealing with it was being smoothed over. Something as sweet as icing on a cake covered those feelings as she learned about the God she had probably always believed existed but never really thought about.

The only bad part was when she learned more of the details about baptism.

"Only men have this priesthood?" she asked, feeling her defenses rise. "Why?"

"Men and women both have priesthood power," said Sister Miyagi, "but there are some things God only asks one gender to do. Baptizing is one of them."

Keisha looked at each of the missionaries in suspicion. "Women aren't oppressed in this religion, are they?"

"Far from it," said Sister Miyagi. "God loves his daughters as much as his sons."

Keisha would have to be baptized by a man. Unsure how she felt about that, she tucked away the information for now. Everything else appealed to her in some way or other.

Sister Cole checked her watch for the fifth time. "We have to leave and meet with someone else."

Elder Johnson stood. "When can we meet with you again, Keisha and Jordan?"

"I don't think I'll be able to sit in on another lesson with Keisha," Jordan said, "but I'll see you today at six, when my children are home. Better make it a *short* lesson." He gave Keisha a sideways glance.

"We'll do that," said the elder. "In that case, Keisha, would you like to have the sister missionaries teach you going forward?"

They set an appointment for the sisters to come to her home on Sunday after church. Keisha's heart beat in anticipation. What would her children think about all this?

"Jordan, will you come to church too?" Elder Sørensen asked.

"All right." His answer was slow and reluctant. They must have asked him before, if he had met with them for several weeks. Strange that he didn't want to go, when he felt they had changed his family's life for the better and that Keisha needed to meet them.

After a closing prayer, she saw everyone to the door. Elder Johnson turned around with one last smile, and then his eyes widened at her. "Of course! You're the woman who asked us to visit Jordan. Thank you so much, Keisha."

She just about turned to stone. Both elders shook her hand, the sisters gave her hugs, and then they left.

With a gulp, she turned to Jordan.

He leaned against the wall, looking weary, confused, and suspicious. "You asked them what? When?"

"I, uh." Her voice was rusty. "I met them in the streets one day. I didn't want to talk to them, but they kept pestering me, so I gave them your address and told them to talk to you instead."

He gave her a blank stare. Unfortunately, a bit of his usual anger began to seep through.

"Please don't hate them because of me," she said. He had seemed to like them, and she found what they said fascinating and wonderful. She could hardly ask him not to be mad at her though.

Slowly, he shook his head. "I didn't know you would take to them like that."

She licked her lips. "Me neither." It was like she had just spent two hours inside a ray of sunshine—excluding some of the heat, but including all of the light. Maybe this was what she had been missing in life: not someone to fight with, like she had fought with Jordan, but a loving God and his Spirit.

"I guess I shouldn't blame you for pranking me when we were both in prank mode." He sounded like he was forcing the words, but as he looked at her, the tension melted away. His lips quirked, and suddenly he gave a chuckle. "Besides, we've come full circle on the missionary thing."

"That's true." Relief swamped her.

"We *are* done with the war, right?"

"Of course." No way would she restart it.

"Good." He smiled and walked outside. "I'll see you around."

As recently as Monday when they came home from that dinner, they hadn't known how to say a polite "goodbye" or "see you" to each other. Now he had said the words almost as though he said them to her every day. And he had forgiven her.

One thing she knew for sure. Miracles did happen.

Chapter 11

"Cowboys roamed the Wild West a lot, two hundred years ago," Carl's brash voice reported to his audience of classmates and parents. "The Wild West is part of the U.S., and there used to not be a lot of people here, just a lot of horses and cows. The cowboys rode the horses and made the cows move from place to place by yelling"—he put his hands to his mouth—"YIP-YIP-YIPPEE!"

Some of the parents nearly fell out of their seats at the unexpected volume. His classmates all laughed and tried to imitate the yell.

"They wore little stars like these on their shoes." He held up his boot and touched a plastic spur. "Because they were sharp and when the horses didn't want to go, they touched the horses gently with their shoes, and then the horses went."

He had decided on the "gently" part all by himself. Keisha remembered how worried he had been when he heard about the sharp spurs digging into the horses' sides. In the end, he had brightened with the blissful decision that nobody kicked very hard.

"A lot of the girls wore dresses, but some of them didn't have to. You can see that my mom's wearing cowboy clothes too, but mine are smaller and a little bit cooler." He sneaked a glance at her. "But just a little bit," he hurried to say.

Cute, was all she could think. Her little boy was cute.

"The cowboys sang funny songs to their cows and horses, and they wore these bandannas"—he held up the red one around his neck—"so that they wouldn't get dust in their eyes. And they helped people to not be afraid of living in the Wild West, so here we all are today," he finished grandly.

"Are there any questions?" his teacher asked the room.

A little girl jumped up from her seat and raised her hand. "What did they eat?"

Carl puffed himself up. "They ate cows' hearts and the top layer of their lassoes and sushi," he said importantly.

Mrs. May shook her head while the adults laughed. "That's a creative answer, but they ate mostly the same things we do today, Julia. Potatoes, bread, meat, and vegetables. Thank you, Carl. Now it's Kale's turn."

Under applause, Keisha hurried to the corner of the room where she had left her things. Taking off her hat, she put her pretty, old-fashioned dress on over the top of her head, rolled up the legs of her jeans so they couldn't be seen underneath the calico, and changed her boots for dainty shoes.

"That's my mom," Kale told the audience while she grabbed a rolled-up poster and walked back to join him in front of the blackboard.

"I'm ready," she said.

Kale put his hands behind his back. "In the twelfth century in England," his light voice peeped, "there were two kinds of people, the Normans and the Saxons. The Normans were the bad guys, and they controlled the Saxons."

He looked so cute in his feathered hat and green tunic.

"One of the Normans was a prince who taxed the people. Taxing is bad. It means taking money, and it wasn't even illegal, 'cause he was a prince. Then a guy named Robin Hood came and took the money from him and gave it back to the poor people. Then the king came back, and he was a Norman too, but he was also a good guy, so he put the prince in timeout and decided that all the Normans and the Saxons had to be friends. The end. Oh, wait!" he cried as Keisha waved the poster in her hand. "Mom and I are going to show you what England looked like in the twelfth century."

They unrolled the poster and each held on to a side.

"This is where Robin Hood lived. It's the Sherwood Forest." Kale pointed, but he stood in front of the map so half the class couldn't see.

"And Maid Marion lived over here." He pointed into the ocean, stating a "fact" he and Keisha hadn't discussed or practiced. "Oh, and women wore clothes like what my mom's wearing. Nice dresses. They didn't like it, I think, 'cause my mom doesn't like to wear a dress very often. Now, the end."

"Very well done. Any questions?"

"Yeah. What was it like in the Sherwood Forest?" a boy asked without raising his hand.

Kale's eyes went huge, and he waved his hands. "It was glorious. There were flowers and birds and trees and so much fruit. There was, like, apple trees and fruit trees and peach trees and peanut trees and banana—"

"Thank you, Kale, that was great."

Grinning with pride, he took a seat under applause. Keisha sat down beside him and enjoyed the rest of the presentations, though to her mind, none compared to her own sons' presentations.

At the end of class, after the bell rang, a tall man with a black beard came over. "I'm Wayne's dad." He nodded toward a boy who was skipping in circles around his mom. "Wayne's good friends with your boys. He's been asking if he can go visit them after school sometime and play."

Kale tugged on her arm. "Can he, Mom? Can he?"

Keisha nodded. "I'm sure that would be fine. Maybe I can arrange something with your wife." She walked over with Wayne's dad to get acquainted with the mom and the towheaded boy. The twins were quick to join them, and by the time they decided on a playdate for next Tuesday, all three boys were yelling like hooligans.

Keisha grabbed the twins' hands, ushering them out of the classroom. They left the building and made it to the car just in time for Lizzie to arrive.

Lizzie grinned when she saw them. "You guys look great. Mom, you're just like Elizabeth Swann again. Well, except for the jeans."

Keisha looked down. Her pants' legs had unrolled themselves and now showed under the hem of her violet dress.

"Mom, what in the world are you?" Frayden called as he came over. "It's like the worst of both worlds."

Kale gave an excited gasp. "Mom, you should wear both costumes at the same time."

"Yeah, it'll look so funny," Carl exclaimed.

"Well, since all four of you have something to say about my double costume . . ." Keisha dropped her plastic bag on the ground and exchanged the slippers on her feet for the trendy cowgirl boots. Laughing, the twins pulled her bandanna from the bag and made her tie it around her neck. Finally she put on her cowboy hat, ignoring the stares of elementary schoolers and parents and thoroughly enjoying the mortified look on Frayden's face.

"Mom, get in the car," he pleaded in a shrill whisper.

If he were mad at her, he would have run to hide in the car, she was sure of it. He thought this was funny.

She struck a pose, cocking a hip and resting her hand on it. "All raight, y'all get in the cahr. Don't stend here lookin' like a bunch a cauws."

Frayden and Lizzie cracked up at the same time, bringing a huge smile to Keisha's face.

"Yip-yip-yippee," both twins yelled, yee-hawing their way into the van.

The car was warm and full of laughter on the way home. For once, Frayden involved himself in the twins' discussions without making snide comments.

"Robin Hood could step on Spiderman and squish him," Kale heatedly told Frayden. "Hey, Mom, we're home."

"Thanks for telling me, pal," she said and turned off the engine.

"They got home before us again." Carl frowned at the three younger Taylors and their dad as they all milled out of the truck beside him.

"That's because they missed out on Mom's cowgal performance," Frayden said with a shrug.

Keisha stepped outside and shut her door. All as one, Imogene, Solomon, and Selima stopped and stared.

She looked down at her bandanna and dress. It wasn't *that* strange an outfit. The Taylors sneaked looks at their dad as he came around to their side of the car.

Jordan gave a weird, startled jerk. Then he stared until annoyance bubbled up inside her. He was definitely overreacting.

Maybe he realized he was making her angry, because he looked away quickly, and Keisha felt her ire fade.

"Did Halloween come early?" Selima asked, a smile slipping on and off her face.

Jordan looked up, worry and apology in his face.

Keisha put a hand to her hat and leaned against the van. "Trick or treat," she drawled.

Jordan relaxed visibly. "No more tricks, please." His voice came out in a groan, but the corners of his eyes crinkled with humor.

Imogene giggled and pulled at his sleeve. "Look." She pointed at Carl and Kale as they raced inside in their costumes. "Dad, do we have dress-up clothes?"

The smile that spread on Frayden's face on seeing that no one blew up at each other was priceless. The smile reached his light blue eyes. Keisha sighed with contentment. "I'll see y'all around," she drawled vaguely and followed her children inside.

For the next while, she couldn't keep the smile off her face. Entertaining Frayden with her costume act was an unexpected success of the day. Her spirits remained high while she kept the twins busy until June turned up.

June's arrival was announced by a quiet opening of the door; a long pause that made Keisha begin to wonder if she had imagined it; and then an equally cautious shutting of the door.

Her eyebrows knitted in confusion. Half expecting to see June wounded and dragging herself inside, she got up from the couch, peeling off Carl and Kale and their picture books, just as June appeared, tiptoeing her way inside and looking around with narrowed eyes.

Keisha looked her over in relief. No gaping wounds anyway.

"Is the house still standing?" June whispered.

Keisha frowned, more puzzled than ever.

"How did it go today?" June continued.

Finally it clicked. The missionaries and Jordan Taylor.

"I decided to be baptized." The words were out of Keisha's mouth before she could think.

"Y—" June choked. "You what?"

She had wondered how to go about telling the children. It was a relief to get it out right away.

"Mom?" June's voice had returned to normal volume, and it sounded like there might be a lecture on the way.

Keisha found herself smiling though. "June, I felt really good today. I felt *so* good listening to the missionaries. Whatever they ask me to do, I believe it's good for me." Even if the baptism had to be performed by a man. She might still need some time to think that over, but for now, she wanted to choose faith. "So I said yes."

Turning, she found Frayden staring goggle-eyed at her from the other couch.

"You're weird," he whispered as though speaking quietly would keep it a secret. Then he turned back to his iPad.

The twins looked unsure about what was going on, but after a moment, Carl decided to give her a bright toothy smile that could have blinded toothpaste commercial-makers. Kale quickly did the same.

"Wha—okay, that's not relevant." June closed her eyes and appeared to push away the news with her hands. She opened her eyes again. "Was Jordan Taylor inside this house?"

Keisha looked back toward the others. Frayden twisted around, then quickly looked away.

"Of course," Keisha answered.

June gave an incredulous laugh.

"Jord'n Taylor doesn't b'long in our house," a small voice squeaked out while its owner bounced on the couch.

"Carl," Keisha exclaimed and paused. She didn't know how to reprove him without being hypocritical or confusing him after the countless times she had started bad talk about the Taylors.

"Mom," June said. "I'm not trying to be mean. I just can't see it. I can't imagine him being here."

"I don't believe he came," Frayden said flatly.

Hurt washed over Keisha. "Frayden. June, you weren't here, but Frayden, you saw the Taylors earlier today when we got home. Things were friendly, right? Weren't they?"

Frayden gave her a mean look. "You can't expect me to believe he was here inside our house with you *and* missionaries. I wasn't here to see that, remember? And I wasn't at your dinner." Keisha froze. "Why should I believe you and Jordan ate together without getting mad? I've seen you within ten feet of each other without saying anything nasty for two minutes today. Yeah, congratulations, pat yourself on the back. That's not proof."

According to the principal, Frayden hadn't been seen bullying students this week, but Keisha felt like she was getting first-hand experience in the damage he could do to someone with words alone.

"*Frayden, leave Mom alone,*" June snapped with so much venom that Keisha started. June's face was red and her eyes fiery. "Why do you even care? Mom doesn't need to be nice to anyone that acts like such a swine."

Frayden's eyes flew wide open in indignation. "Who's acting the—"

"Enough." Keisha's voice rang out even though she was a blink away from crying. "We need to speak nicely about everyone, including those outside this family. I haven't been the best example of that, but—"

"Mom, you haven't done anything wrong," June protested. "You—ohh, that's *it*." Dumping her jiujitsu uniform on the floor, she stalked off toward the stairs.

"You're so awful," Frayden exclaimed. Whether he was addressing June or Keisha, Keisha had no idea. He too ran off.

The stairs thundered as though they were attacked by elephants. Then two doors slammed, one after the other.

Another door opened with a creak from upstairs. "Is something wrong?" Lizzie called out.

The twins came alive. Jumping off the couch, they raced toward her room, calling, "Lizzie, let's play. Can we come in your room?"

The door closed, muffling the twins' noises.

Keisha took a deep breath, roiling her emotions through her body. Her children didn't believe in the progress she had made with Jordan. Frayden's accusations tore at her, and June, even in her defense, had only added fuel to the fire.

Her breath didn't dispel her frustration. She strode to the kitchen and jerked open the refrigerator to start dinner. If only she'd thought to ask the missionaries for tips on keeping peace in the family. Surely God had some things to say about it that he might have passed on through his prophet.

***

"Alcohol?" Jordan burst out laughing. "I'm not allowed to drink alcohol?" Wouldn't Keisha just love that? Keisha in her dress—

"The Word of Wisdom prohibits alcohol, drugs, wine, coffee, tea, and tobacco," said Elder Johnson, sitting in the armchair opposite him.

The part about drugs sounded good. Jordan sneaked a glance at Samuel on the other side of Solomon. "What's the point of this Word of Wisdom?"

"We're blessed with a lot of things for keeping it. For starters, we avoid addictions, and we're healthier."

"Wine can be healthy," Jordan protested.

Brother Pudin, a church member the elders had invited to join today together with his wife, spoke up. "Do you know the Bible stories? There was the group of young men who refused to eat the king's rich food and drink his wine based on what God had told them to avoid. They ended up being healthier than the king's other servants. The Jews themselves were commanded not to eat pork, among other things. God has given different health codes at different periods in the history of the earth. He always knows what's best for us."

"He wants us to be healthy," Jordan tried out the words. "What about sweets?"

"This is more than a health code," Sister Pudin said, "although it's definitely good for us to treat the bodies he created well. Obeying his law helps us have clear minds and be more receptive to feeling the Spirit."

"Jordan," said the elder from Denmark. "Are you willing to live the Word of Wisdom?"

He shook his head. "Part of it," he amended. "What else does God command us?"

The missionaries exchanged glances.

"There's the Law of Chastity," said Brother Pudin.

"The what?"

Elder Johnson frowned at Brother Pudin but explained, "We should only have an intimate relationship with the person we're married to."

Jordan stared at him, the gears in his brain turning. "You live this law?" He didn't see himself breaking it. It would be an affront to his wife to live with a different woman without committing to marriage. Even Keisha—he cut off the thought. Why did everything keep coming back to her? With an effort, he pulled his mind back to his family.

Actually, it might be nice if the Law of Chastity were a teaching in his family. He'd never have to worry about Selima being betrayed by a boyfriend after they were intimate. But wasn't it overly restrictive to make such a rule for his children?

"We do," said Elder Sørensen. "However, I think we should leave the commandments behind for a bit and go back to talking about faith."

They sure spent a lot of time talking about faith and Jesus Christ, but Jordan didn't protest. He let them talk for another five minutes, his thoughts drifting to a certain pirate dress while Selima took over asking questions in her sweet voice.

After they left, Selima picked up the commandment pamphlets from the table. "Dad, can I take these to my room and read them?"

Several scenarios ran through his head, making him frown. She would keep them under her pillow. She would study them until they were frayed. Jordan was happy to bring some of this religion into his home, but not the whole thing. "Bring them back out here in the morning. In case anyone else wants to read them."

"Okay." She hugged them to her chest and took the stairs.

"Come on, Imogene. It's bedtime." Jordan held out his hand to Imogene on the couch.

She took it and hopped up. "Did we have visitors when I was small?"

She *was* small, but Jordan didn't tell her that. "On occasion. Do you like having visitors?"

She scrunched up her face. "I thought they were going to read a bedtime story, but they didn't."

His chest rumbled. "Maybe we'll ask them to next time. Brush your teeth, and I'll read you one."

Half an hour later, Imogene was in bed. Jordan went to his studio and sat down, images running through his mind. Keisha in her soft faded dress patterned with tiny purple flowers, holding a three-year-old boy with a pirate eye patch across his eye. Imaginary cannons firing as they dedicated their new home. He opened and closed his computer files.

"Are you making a new one?"

Jerking at the voice, he looked up. Samuel loomed over him, tall, his frame filling out, his shoulders stretching his shirt. The knowing grin on his face made Jordan look away. "No." He stared again at the screen before him. "Do you remember the day they moved in?"

Samuel rolled his eyes. "I wasn't there, but you've pretty much immortalized the scene."

"Yeah," he said absentmindedly. Seeing her today in the dress she had worn then had thrown him off.

"How does it feel now that you're dating her?"

Jordan shook his head. "I'm not dating her." He heard the regret in his own voice. Samuel raised his eyebrows. "Even if I am, *she's* not dating *me*."

"Hm." Samuel took a seat in the other chair. "Get a move on. You finally have a chance."

Jordan didn't say anything to that. After a long silence, he turned to his son. The boy's smile was gone.

"Go ahead," Samuel said. "Ask."

Jordan looked at him for a minute, hoping he could go about this the right way again. "How's it working out leaving your friends?"

Samuel laid his hands flat on the table. "Not very well. I think I'm confusing them. Someone from the group will see me and tell me to come hang out. I come up with excuses not to go, but you know, we'll keep running into each other. They'll wonder what's up with me."

"You have to tell them. Tell them you can't hang out with them anymore because you won't do drugs."

Samuel's gaze could have bored holes in the wooden table. "How am I supposed to do that?" His voice was angry, but his hands trembled, revealing the true feeling behind his question. It was fear, and no one could blame him for it.

Even so, Jordan squared his shoulders. "Do you know what it means to be strong?" Honestly, it was an elusive term. Jordan knew he himself must be strong for going on without his wife, but mostly he just felt weak without her.

Samuel frowned at him before he set his jaw. "Tell me."

Jordan looked him in the eyes. "If you do this, you'll find out."

It didn't take long. Samuel's shoulders went back, and his expression changed. Determination, even excitement, entered his eyes.

Jordan felt stronger just looking at him. Whatever the result, Samuel would see it through.

Chapter 12

"How does fifteen dollars sound?"

"Great." June smiled at the woman who had agreed to let her mow her lawn. After knocking on ten doors, this was only the second yes she had gotten.

"Let me show you where our lawn mower is." The woman proceeded across the lawn, and June followed her to a shed in the backyard. "If you want to come again next week around the same time, just knock and let me know before you begin."

"Sounds good."

The woman pulled her mower out. "Thanks for doing this."

June took over and gripped the handlebars. "I'm glad to help." She pulled the string until the machine started, and her neighbor returned inside.

Turning the mower, June rolled it along while the air filled with sweet smells.

She had gotten the idea when Mom shocked her with her question about continuing jiujitsu. It wasn't a bad idea to be earning money. Not if she wanted to test the waters. Not if she wanted to find out just how much he had changed. In order to see it for herself, she needed money for transportation.

Mom isn't going anywhere, she had told him.

His temper used to explode over the tiniest things, but somehow her unfriendly letters hadn't made him angry. He seemed happy someone responded. When she told him Mom would *not* make the visit, he had asked if maybe she would.

She. June. He hadn't wanted her around for years.

She didn't trust him with her mom yet. But now she had a way to find out if maybe she could.

***

Keisha was counting on Sunday to lift her spirits, and it didn't disappoint. Except for a couple of half-hearted whines from Frayden in the morning about having to dress up, no one complained. The twins looked all business as they smoothed down each other's shirts and picked off imaginary lint. Their solemnity lasted for half the car ride to church.

It was fifteen minutes in the opposite direction from school. She had passed the building before, with its tan bricks and white spire, but today she parked in front of it while red leaves blew through the parking lot.

The hallway of the church featured paintings of Jesus and of scriptural stories, but when they entered the assembly room, it was simple, without paintings or stained-glass windows. It felt friendly. People greeted each other while someone played the piano in the front.

"Keisha." Sisters Cole and Miyagi came over smiling. "It's good to see you. Jordan called and said he couldn't make it after all. Hi there, Carl. Or are you Kale?"

Keisha felt a rush of disappointment. Jordan had promised to come, and while she didn't exactly crave his presence, it was annoying that he had broken his word.

"Good morning, Sister Evans." The missionaries greeted a woman around Keisha's age. "We'd like you to meet our friend, Keisha. Keisha, Sister Evans."

"You can call me Abigail," the woman said and shook hands. "Would you like to sit with us? My husband will be here with our children soon. I just had a meeting before church."

"Sure," Keisha answered and followed her into the pew. Lizzie was close on her heels, followed by the others. As they sat down, a tall man arrived on the other side with three children in tow. He gave Abigail Evans a kiss, scooped up a toddler, and placed the boy in her lap.

"This is Adam," Abigail said to Keisha. "Adam, this is Keisha. The missionaries just introduced us."

"Nice to meet you. Please let us know if you need anything." He shook her hand and proceeded to pull things from a large bag and hand them to his children: coloring books, a picture book of a scripture story, and snacks.

So that was how parents kept their children occupied during church. The sister missionaries, Keisha noticed, had sat down behind her and were talking to someone else. There were a number of other families in the room. Keisha watched them as the meeting began with announcements, a hymn, and a prayer. While a few parents hushed their children here and there, no one seemed overly concerned at the noise.

Then came time for the sacrament: partaking of bread and water in remembrance of Jesus. The room was nearly silent while four young boys carried trays to each row of congregants. Keisha relaxed in her seat. Now was a perfect time to reflect on—

"Mom, how do prayers make it to God?" Carl whispered.

"Mom, is that brown bread? Brown bread is *weird*," Kale commented.

"What'll you wear when you're baptized? Do they make dress-up swimsuits?"

"Who are those people sitting up there?"

She didn't know the answer to half their questions. Sister Evans began to answer, seemingly under the illusion that if she reverently whispered the answers, it would put an end to the flow of questions.

Keisha resigned herself to a non-silent reflection time. It soon ended anyway. Still, she managed to listen as three different people gave talks, none of them in clerical robes. Keisha leaned toward Abigail to ask a question of her own. "Are all the speakers ministers?"

Abigail shook her head. "The bishop and his counselors call on members of the ward to give talks. They pick a scripture or a theme for us to focus on, and then we'll prepare something."

"You mean they might ask *you* to speak?"

Her eyes twinkled. "Yes. All of us have experiences and thoughts to share. Giving a talk always makes me nervous, but I love the inspiration I get while I prepare it."

When the meeting ended, Abigail stood up. "I can show your children the way to their classes if you like. Unless they'd rather stay with you this first—"

"Come on, let's go!" Carl yelled, and he and Kale ran after the Evans children.

"Doesn't look like there's a problem," said Brother Evans.

After taking Lizzie, Frayden, and June to their respective classes, Keisha was guided to Relief Society, a women's class. She quickly forgot the names of the five women on her row after introductions, but she sat in growing awe and appreciation as a woman conducted the meeting, another began the lesson, and those in the room participated. Someone brought up the question of how they could make their prayers meaningful, and the women tried to give helpful answers, sharing their own struggles, thoughts, and experiences.

They were helping each other. Keisha liked it.

Even if they couldn't baptize others, they sure didn't seem like a down-trodden group. Nothing like she had felt in her marriage. If the division of priesthood responsibilities led to inequality, she saw no sign of it.

After one last prayer—how many did that make?—class was disbanded. Keisha went looking for her children in a hallway full of children and parents reuniting.

There. Twenty feet ahead stood Frayden, talking with four boys his age, his hands in his pockets. He had made friends already. Keisha's heart squeezed. She hadn't realized how much she had wanted to see him hang out with children his age. There was no sign of the bullying Principal Woods had witnessed two weeks ago.

"Mom! Look what we got." Carl and Kale rushed at Keisha and waved crayon-desecrated papers at her, pointing and explaining what each was about. Lizzie followed behind with a picture of a grand, white building.

"Look, this is a temple," Kale said. "Oh, Lizzie has one too. That's where families become forever, see? They go in there and then they come out—boom!—stuck together with power from high. Isn't it cool?"

"It's very cool." Keisha mussed his hair and stole another glance at Frayden. He was enjoying himself. She could tell.

"Mom, can we take Wayne to church next time? We'll show him all the places and teach him all the songs." Carl puffed out his chest.

"Let's wait and see how Tuesday's playdate goes, okay?" Frayden left the other boys and came over, and Keisha tried to pretend she hadn't been spying on him. "Hey, Frayden. How was church?"

His mouth twisted. "I still think you're weird for choosing this."

He would never admit he had had a good time, but she had seen it for herself, and the sight was priceless. It made her happy enough to joke around, so she pretended to be offended. "Well, ex*cuse* me."

Frayden laughed, and Keisha's mouth fell open. June came up from behind and stopped, watching Frayden curiously. "Sorry, Mom," Frayden said with a rare smile, and everything took on a whole new dimension of surprise.

Keisha barely managed to close her mouth. If this was her reward for making friends with Jordan, it was worth every ounce of discomfort it had cost. She might just thank him when they met tomorrow for dinner.

***

The next afternoon, Keisha stepped back with her hands covered in raw meat, her gaze catching on the dining table and the three grocery bags on it. She groaned. "June?" A crash from the living room made her jump. "Carl and Kale, I told you not to use that spindly chair in your game. Pick it up and steer your soldiers around it, please," she called. "June, didn't I ask you to put away the groceries when I walked in? It's been an hour, and some of those need to go in the fridge."

The timer beeped. Leaving the meatballs she had just formed, she scrubbed her hands clean and took the polka-dot dishtowel off the cookie sheet of newly risen rolls.

"Rraarr, rraahr," Carl roared. Some of the twins' dinosaurs must have sneaked into their game of soldiers.

"Psssh, tchu-psssh." Kale imitated the sounds of sword-fighting. "And then, the general hits the rex—"

"June? The groceries?" Keisha repeated and threw a glance at her other timer.

"Okay," June called back.

"Aaah, I got you," Kale yelled.

"Guys, not so loud." Keisha looked around for the egg she had cracked into a glass earlier. When she found it, she dug through the utensil drawer for a brush.

"And then he jumps on the mountain. Help! Help!"

Crash.

Keisha jumped, and her hand struck the ceiling of the drawer. "Boys, stop using that chair in your game." She withdrew her scraped hand and the brush and began to glaze the rolls. "June, are you coming? Frayden, can you come help me clean up in here?"

"Pssh. Take that."

Keisha sighed and opened the oven, shielding her face against the heat. She put the rolls in, shut the door, and looked at the flour-covered counter. Then she walked out to the living room.

Two of Carl and Kale's dinosaurs battled with a soldier on one of the rungs of a small chair, making it tip precariously at their violent movements. Lizzie must have gone to her room to do homework. Frayden lay on his stomach on the floor fiddling with a broken radio from an old emergency kit, and June lay on her back on the couch, giggling and reading aloud a passage to Frayden from a biography on Amelia Earhart.

For a moment, Keisha's heart swelled. It was wonderful to see this kind of camaraderie between Frayden and June. She tucked away her joy, though, knowing she needed to get dinner ready before she left for her own dinner with Jordan.

"Boys, move your game to the other side of the table, okay? Away from that chair. June, would you go put away the groceries, please?" she repeated in her most patient voice while the twins kept playing. "June? Frayden?"

"That's cool," Frayden said in response to June's passage and, under cover of the twins' voices, he returned his attention to the radio. June continued her reading in silence.

Keisha started to tap her foot. "Is anyone listening to me?"

"Okay," June said without looking up.

Keisha rolled her eyes. "Frayden, did you give your teacher the field trip permission slip?"

"Tchu-psssh. This is *my* castle."

"What? Oh, yeah." Frayden inspected a screwdriver.

Keisha raised her hands in the air with a huff. "Does that mean you gave it to your teacher? The slip that I signed? Frayden? June!"

June nodded on the couch and kept reading.

Keisha spun to face the wall. "I can't get them to listen to me," she exclaimed, waving her hands at the white wall. "It's like I don't exist. Do you ever feel like that?"

A crash sounded behind her.

Keisha shook her head. "How will I get everything done? The groceries need putting away, the floor needs vacuuming, the counters need wiping, and we have new piles of laundry. What about you? Will *you* vacuum for me?"

Behind her, Carl and Kale's voices became more subdued.

"Then once you're done with the floors, please go set the table. Also, do you have any papers I need to sign? I don't want to get a phone call and have to come over to the school to sign something the day it's due."

She felt rather than saw her children gather behind her.

"Mom?" June's voice was puzzled.

"I'm not through," Keisha told the wall. She might as well take the opportunity to get a few more things off her chest. "Don't talk with food in your mouth. It's bad manners. That's enough screen time. You need to go outside and play something real. Are you listening to me? Ohhh, getting you to talk is like pulling teeth!"

The rest of the room had been silent for long enough. She turned around to face the four children who stared at her. Carl and Kale's heads were tilted in opposite directions from each other, June's nose was scrunched up, and Frayden's eyebrows had disappeared under his too-long hair.

Keisha clapped her hands together, and her children jumped. "All right, Frayden, I request a full report on your permission slip."

"What? Oh, right. I gave it to my teacher."

"Great. And June. The groceries." She gave her daughter a pointed look.

June slapped her forehead. "I totally forgot." She grabbed the bags from the table and disappeared into the kitchen.

Keisha looked at the twins. She walked across the living room, picked up the chair, and carried it to the TV corner. Then she faced the boys with her hands on her hips.

"We're not s'posed to play with that," Carl concluded.

"I think we forgot," Kale said.

Keisha picked up a dark blue cushion. "You can use this as a hill in your game."

Carl nodded solemnly. "Okay."

She had gone only a few steps before Kale let out a loud "Rawr" and jump-attacked the cushion, starting a wrestling match with his brother. At least they weren't fighting across the hard wooden chair and getting hurt.

She returned to the kitchen just as one of her timers rang.

"Mom." June laughed while she put perishables in the fridge. "Lizzie would have enjoyed that scene if she'd been down here. You, talking to a wall."

Keisha shook her head. "I've done crazier things. I think."

June picked up a bag of cans and took it to the pantry. "One would think you were making a point."

"Hi, Lizzie." Keisha smiled as her youngest daughter came down the stairs. "Okay, all I need to do now is clean the kitchen"—an insurmountable task if ever there was one—"and cook everything." She put a sheet of meatballs beside the rolls in the oven and was about to set the last timer when her gaze caught on the oven clock. "Uh-oh. Time to backtrack."

"What?" June popped out of the pantry.

"I have to go, and the food isn't ready."

"That's okay. You said it just has to cook, right? For how long?"

"You guys can't handle the oven. It's not safe."

June scoffed. "What's the big deal? It's not like you've never let me touch the oven."

"June, that's when I'm around. I won't be here, you know." She threw a desperate glance at the kitchen and tried not to imagine everything going up in flames.

"So? If something goes wrong, we'll call for help. If I can't remember the three-digit emergency number, I'm sure the *neighbor kids* can help." She laughed sarcastically.

"June, that's not helping."

"Mom, you just prepared food for us, and now you'll let it stay raw until you come back? Just because you're afraid we can't handle the oven? What a waste. Don't you think you're just a little over-protective?"

Keisha blew out her breath. "Okay, maybe. But be really careful. Take the rolls out when the first timer rings, okay? When the second one rings—" she hurried to set it—"take out the meatballs, and do *not* forget to turn off the oven."

"Aw, Mom, can't we keep it on a bit longer so I can burn my science experiment in the oven?" Frayden put in his two cents from the living room.

June sent a livid stare his way. "We won't do anything immature, Mom. I'll watch the *little* children."

"I'll watch the twins," Lizzie offered.

"We'll watch TV," Carl yelled out in glee. "That'll keep us from doing any damage," he added sagely.

"Okay, but not during dinner. And don't eat anything—"

"In the living room. We know, Mom." June rolled her eyes. "What time are you supposed to meet Jordan? I'm just asking because it looks like you're going to be late."

Keisha looked at the clock, squeaked, and ran to get her purse.

***

JORDAN STARED OUT THE window at Taco Bell's parking lot, clicking his fingers on the table. Two visits. They had only had two good visits: dinner together and the missionary lesson at her house, during which he had just about been invisible. What if she had decided she no longer wanted to work on being friends? Was his chance with her over before it had begun?

The woman of his thoughts appeared and plopped down opposite him, her thick red-brown hair spilling over her shoulders like a lively waterfall. Jordan's pent-up breath left him in a whoosh. "I was beginning to wonder if you had stood me up."

She coughed. "Excuse me? This isn't a date, right?"

"No, sorry, I didn't mean that," he backtracked, although he wished it *was* a date.

"No, *I'm* sorry." She looked serious. "I didn't mean to be late."

"It's all good." He waved away her apology.

She watched him for a minute. Trying to be discreet about it, he straightened. Just for good measure, he puffed out his chest. Wouldn't hurt, would it?

Keisha broke into a glowing smile.

Jordan sucked in his breath, and his voice came out pinched. "Are you ready to order?"

"Yep." She sprang from her seat and pranced to the counter. He followed, trying to calm his pulse as they ordered food. Then he turned to her and started to speak at the same time she did. Both of them shut their mouths.

He shoved his hands in his pockets and raised his eyebrows. "What made you smile a minute ago?"

"Huh? Oh." The smile returned, brightening her blue eyes. "I was happy I didn't get mad. A few weeks ago, I would have tensed up when you waved away my words. I would have thought it patronizing. But it wasn't. It was friendly. It's getting easier not to fight."

He grinned. "It is, isn't it?"

"Not that I want to jinx it." A worry line appeared in her forehead.

"No, I know what you mean." An employee called out his number, and Jordan took his tray and turned back to her. "I'm not even tempted to be mean today. I guess an old dog *can* learn new tricks."

Her eyebrows came down. "Old?"

Uh-oh. "Um, I meant me." Keisha was a few years younger than him, right? Fortunately another employee handed over Keisha's food, and her annoyance seemed to fade as they returned to their seats.

With a deep sigh, she picked up her taco, looking enamored with the thing. Was this the way to her heart? Food she didn't have to cook? Would she ever look at him that way? He tried to rein in his thoughts, but his three-year crush had been buried for too long, and he found himself studying her face. There was a tiny scrunch down the side of her nose, and he found the asymmetry adorable, especially—

She looked up, and his gaze dived to his plate. Had she caught him staring? He couldn't afford to make her mad. "I'll go wash my hands." He leapt from his seat as though it were on fire.

The bathroom provided a nice reprieve. The water from the faucet helped cool him down. Keisha wanted to make things work, even if those "things" were different from what Jordan hoped for. She wouldn't get mad if she could help it. He remembered how she had cried the last time she got mad, and how comforted she was when he promised they would work on it.

He left the bathroom, shoulders back and confidence restored.

Keisha was on the phone as he approached their table. Apparently she had wasted no time finding someone else to talk to.

"Just tell me, June," she insisted. "Did you turn off the oven?"

Jordan sat down. Keisha looked up at him and then lowered her head as if in apology.

A moment later, she rolled her eyes in a look of exasperation. "All the same, will you *please* go check? I don't want the house to burn down."

Jordan could have told her the house wouldn't burn down if the oven was on for a few extra hours. However, he couldn't blame her for being a worried mom. June Johansen seemed old enough to be left in charge at home, but to his knowledge, she didn't have much experience being the boss.

Keisha's eyes widened. Jordan could hear June's voice speaking quickly and sounding panicked. His own heart began to pound.

"June, calm down," Keisha exclaimed. "Turn off the oven, take your brothers and sister out front, call 911 . . ."

Jordan's heart raced at those words.

"June, get—"

The sound of laughter replaced the stream of words on the other end of the phone. *"I'm kidding, Mom."* Jordan could hear what she said now. *"Everything's fine. The oven's off. I told you I remembered turning it off."*

Keisha clenched the phone in a white-knuckled grip. "June. Bug. Johansen."

June Bug?

"Bye, Mom," June's voice said merrily, and the call seemed to end.

Jordan couldn't help it. He choked.

"What?" Keisha snapped.

He cleared his throat twice. "Is 'bug' her middle name?"

She blinked. Then she began to smile. "Right. See, in our family, we like to name the girls after insects. 'Lizzie' is actually short for 'lystropod,' the Latin name for a praying mantis."

Jordan started to laugh and then froze, mid-grin. Was she serious?

She burst out laughing, and he followed her lead.

"I *thought* you were kidding." He wiped tears from his eyes. "But I didn't want to offend you, just in case."

"I'm sorry." She chuckled. "I criticized you for being sexist the other day based on your children's names. I'm not that big of a hypocrite, Jordan. I may be mean, but I'm not *that* bad."

"You're not mean, you're cu—ah, I'm gullible." He had almost called her 'cute' to her face, something he seriously doubted would go over well at this point.

"Bug isn't part of June's name." Keisha seemed not to have noticed his slip. "And lystropod—well, it popped into my mind. I don't know if it's a real word, but it sounded like it could be the Latin name of some insect or other."

"Yeah, it fooled me." Jordan shook his head. "Can't help you out on 'lystropod' either. My Latin's rusty."

Their conversation stayed friendly as they ate. Jordan soon finished his last taco and chuckled again at the thought of Keisha pretending to name her oldest daughter after an insect. Being friends with Keisha was great. And this was only the beginning.

She picked up a tray. "Thanks for doing this." She sounded a little shy, which made his hopes rise. Maybe she did feel something around him.

She turned to go.

"Wait." He put his hand on her wrist but snatched it back when she frowned at him. "I, uh, was wondering if you would join me for my lesson with the missionaries tomorrow. I'm supposed to meet them at the church so they can give me a tour, and I've never been there, and I think you might enjoy the lesson more than me, and, well, you'd be doing me a favor. I don't want my children along. Would you mind joining? We'd leave at six-thirty."

She blinked repeatedly. Confusion warred with, dared he hope, interest. What was going on in that mind of hers?

"I can do that," she said.

"Great." His smile felt as warm as toast. She smiled back, a little more tentative, and Jordan tried to rein himself in. Hopefully she was interested in more than just the spiritual lesson tomorrow.

Chapter 13

Keisha had a funny but good feeling in her stomach the next day. Being friends with Jordan wasn't half bad. She must have been craving adult company without realizing it. Speaking of which, she ought to visit Shawna soon. It would be exciting to meet her foster son.

She sang along to a fight song as she drove to pick up the children. Then she turned on an audio version of the Book of Mormon, returning to the account of Nephi and his shockingly contentious older brothers. It was hard to fit scripture study into her day, but she wanted to read at least part of the book before she got baptized.

Maybe after that she would read the Bible again. Her thoughts strayed to the near argument with Jordan about his son's names during their first dinner together. Last night's dinner had been so much easier. It had been fun to tease Jordan. His icy gray eyes danced when she did. That wasn't the man who played awful pranks. That was the man who—had dated and attracted his wife?

Keisha had a coughing fit over the steering wheel. She certainly wasn't considering him in *that* light. He had yelled at her children too often. Made her mad too much. He *drank,* for heaven's sake. She pulled up to the curb and tried to stop coughing. Even if he had been nice to look at across the table last night, that didn't make up for behaviors she wouldn't tolerate in her home.

June got in the car, throwing her a look.

"I'm fine, June. Let's go get the others."

"Okay." Fortunately June didn't ask any questions. "I'm gonna fix our lawn mower today."

Keisha glanced at her. "That'll be great, but you do know we're okay on money, right? You don't have to mow for the neighbors."

"I know, but I like earning something."

They picked up the others from the elementary school, including Wayne, who was coming to visit today.

Back home, Keisha watched the boys on and off, helped out with homework, and fixed dinner. She had to tell Carl no when he held up a stuffed animal dragon, saying it wanted to lick the soup that was bubbling on the stove. Kale stood beside him, holding a ladle behind his back that he probably hoped to use as soon as the dragon got permission, and Wayne just looked really hopeful as he watched her cook.

"Kale, dear, would you put the ladle back in the drawer?"

He looked up at her with a great, big pout.

"That doesn't work on me, bud."

He pouted deeper and put away the ladle.

"Rawr!" Carl pushed the dragon into his face, Kale squealed, and all three boys ran laughing from the room.

Tinkering noises sounded from out front. If June managed to repair the lawn mower, it would be a miracle.

Keisha was about to get started on the dishes when she realized the boys' shrieks had changed tone.

"Mo-om," Carl yelled.

"It's *ours*," Kale shouted.

Dropping the cutting board in the sink, she ran to the living room just as Wayne burst into tears. "What's wrong?"

"He wants my favorite train. He can't play with that," Carl said.

"Of course he can. Wayne is your guest." Where were her children's manners? "You need to be nice to him."

"But it's ours."

"If you can't share the trains, then play with something else." Or maybe she should make him share his toy, not to mention apologize.

"We're better than him," Kale announced.

Keisha's eyes widened. "Kale."

"That should do it," Jordan's voice rang out, and he walked into her living room as though it were his, his hands black and oily. Keisha gaped.

"We are, aren't we?" Carl frowned. "You've said we're better than the Taylor kids." Jordan froze, and Keisha's insides heated as memories of her most thoughtless moments stirred. "Aren't we better than him?" Carl pointed at his friend, who caught his breath in a gulp.

June appeared next to Jordan. "It works now?" She pulled a tool from his hands and added it to the two she already held. "Let's go try it."

"You're not—" Keisha felt pulled in several directions at once. Poor Wayne was being abused, and she had to correct her sons without making them feel like they were worth less. Meanwhile Jordan must be totally insulted at what he had just heard. She swallowed. "You're not *better* than anyone."

"But you used to say that. I remember you said it," Carl said again.

June paused and frowned at the scene as though she had just noticed how tense it was.

"I was wrong."

Something went terribly wrong at her words. Carl's expression changed from indignant stubbornness to a confused vulnerability Keisha had worn for years on her own face.

"What are we, then?" Kale sounded lost, even on the verge of crying.

She dropped to her knees and grabbed his shoulder, praying with fervor for inspiration in what to say. The most natural words in the world came to mind, and she put her other hand on Wayne's shoulder. The little visitor looked up at her with wet eyes.

"You're amazing," she said. "You, Kale and Carl, are amazing, and so are you, Wayne. Don't you remember that song we sang at church last Sunday? All of you are children of God. That includes Wayne, and it includes the Taylors." She squeezed their shoulders. "I don't have favorites, and I don't think God does either. None of his children are 'better' than others. He loves us all, so we should love everyone too."

Carl narrowed his eyes in thought. "Wait. That means Wayne's my brother. *Right?*" His voice screeched in sudden excitement.

Kale's eyes sparked, and he turned to Wayne. "You're my brother," he said and hugged the boy.

"I am?" Wayne's eyes lit up, and he returned the squashing hug.

"Yes. And you can play with my favorite train—for *five minutes*," Kale offered generously.

"Yaaay," Wayne yelled, and the three of them began to zoom their trains around.

Keisha watched, emotions tumbling. She had said the right thing, and Carl's conclusion and Kale's action amazed her.

But she had been a terror when she was enemies with Jordan. She had placed her family above everyone and been callous about others. It was no wonder Frayden had become a bully or the twins resorted to selfishness when Wayne asked for something they didn't want to give him.

She sneaked a look at Jordan. He was staring at her in a way she couldn't, and didn't dare, interpret. "I didn't mean what I used to say about your children."

He nodded. "I know."

Her chest felt tight. "I'll see you later."

She escaped up the stairs, an oddity since this was her home and he was the one intruding, even if June appeared to be involved in that. Keisha needed a minute in a place where no one besides herself could make her feel bad.

***

ADMIRATION. PURE ADMIRATION, JUST like he had felt that first day she strode into her backyard with her entourage of little pirates. No, more than he felt then. How could he have wasted so much time being enemies with her?

"Hel-lo-oh." Keisha's daughter June waved her hand in front of his face. "Can we go check on the lawn mower?"

He blinked. He was staring up the stairs in the direction Keisha had disappeared. Her twins and their friend played loudly behind him. With an effort, he tore his gaze away and turned to June. "What?"

She put her hands on her hips and said, "Outside."

It seemed to take him ages to follow the bossy girl out the door. She kept checking over her shoulder, and he kept looking back at the stairs, although what he hoped to see, he didn't know. A glance of Keisha returning? It wouldn't be a bad thing to see.

Chapter 14

"So, I don't really get it." June interrupted Keisha's musings as they sat down at the dining table half an hour later. "Tell me again how come you're going to dinner with Jordan *two* days in a row?"

Keisha swallowed the wrong way and coughed. "I went to dinner with him yesterday, but I'm not eating with him tonight. I'm eating with you guys. See? Oh, we forgot to pray."

June was not to be deterred. As soon as everyone said "Amen," she asked, "Then what are you doing with him tonight?"

"He has a lesson with the missionaries at the church. He finally agreed to let them give him a tour of the building." Strange how he had taken lessons from them for so long and yet had never come to church. "He doesn't want his kids there though. He asked me to come along instead."

"*Really.*" June's eyebrows were raised. "He wants to be alone with you."

"What? *No*, June Bug. The missionaries are there, and he wants support or—"

"It's just a lesson, June," Frayden broke in. "Take it easy."

June pressed her lips together and said no more.

***

June waited for five minutes after Mom left before she gathered the others.

"What are we doing?" Lizzie asked, looking confused.

"We're going to talk to the Taylors. Come on." June opened the door and strode outside, only checking once to make sure everyone followed her.

She walked right up to the Taylors' door and knocked three times. The hollow sound was followed by silence. Then someone came to the door and opened it.

Selima stood in the doorway. She jerked in surprise.

"Hey," said June. "Is everyone here? I mean, except your dad. We need to talk."

Selima stared. Her glossy brown hair hung over her shoulders, but she didn't look as elegant and sad as she normally did. She looked curious.

"I'll get them," she finally said.

June stepped back with a small sigh and waited while Selima called them to come out.

Perfect. In a minute everyone was outside. June looked over the group, some of them sitting in the cool grass, some of them on the front porch, everyone looking at her with curiosity.

She needed their cooperation, so she assumed her most confident stance. "I called you here because *your* dad and *our* mom are getting friendly, and I don't think it'll last."

"What?" Samuel's face went from curious to shocked.

She gave him a piercing glare. "It won't last. They've been enemies for three years. Do you remember all the things they've done to each other?"

Lizzie started to smile. "They did do some crazy things. Remember the fake mafia incident?"

"And the day they went berserk with the fire extinguishers." Frayden giggled.

The Johansens looked at each other with humor in their eyes. But the Taylors looked at each other and completely cracked up. When they kept laughing, June had the distinct feeling she was missing something.

"Is your dad in love with our mom?" she asked abruptly.

Imogene looked thrilled. Samuel, Selima, and Solomon exchanged looks again and snickered.

"So what if he is?" Frayden asked, crossing his arms.

June frowned. Frayden almost seemed to *want* Mom to date Jordan.

Well, that wasn't happening. She put her hands on her hips. "Sooner or later, Mom and Jordan will blow up in each other's faces, and this'll all be over."

Samuel leaned forward on the concrete step. "What do you propose we do?"

"End it now."

Nearly everyone gasped at that. Imogene looked up, her mouth forming a pout.

June forged ahead. "The longer they're friends before they blow up, the worse it'll hurt when it ends."

Selima inched forward. "What if it *will* last?"

"It won't. But we can test it," she conceded with a shrug. "If we try to end it and can't, then fine." *Not fine.* Mom needed to be free in case Dad had changed. "If it does end, then it wasn't meant to be."

Everyone looked at each other, sibling to sibling to enemy neighbors.

"What's your plan?" Samuel asked.

They discussed June's idea for several minutes. Then she checked her watch and stood. "Are we good?"

"I like Keisha," Selima said in a quiet voice.

"So do I," June said sharply.

"*We* agree with you, June," Carl said, and Kale nodded with enthusiasm. "We should do it."

"We can give it a try." Samuel got to his feet.

"All right," Selima mumbled.

June watched the Taylors leave, her heart starting up a march over what she was about to do. She waited until they were halfway to their house before she called out, "Samuel?"

He stopped and let his siblings pass.

She wasn't used to talking to high school seniors. Her voice shook a little as she prepared to ask for a favor. "Can I talk to you?"

***

KEISHA HAD GOTTEN IN Jordan's truck almost without thinking about it and had settled into the comfy, worn passenger seat. Strange. A few hours ago, driving together had seemed like a big deal. Now, though it felt odd to sit buckled up beside him, she had other things on her mind.

She listened to the humming of the car on the road and finally spoke. "I'm sorry about my mean comments about your children."

Jordan gave her a wan smile and ran a hand through his hair. "That's fine. Just fine. You handled it well."

He seemed distracted. She wasn't sure if he had really forgiven her, but she let it go so she could focus on the other things that tortured her.

"I know you're all for the missionaries and church and everything," Jordan said, "but I'm still not too interested in doing all the things they ask. I didn't want my kids to come along and pressure me, and I hope you won't pressure me either."

She nodded to show she heard him and stared out the windshield. What was it Frayden had said back at the principal's office? She was always running around screaming at Jordan Taylor. She was controlling Lizzie and her hairstyles. She frowned. Did he know of any other problems circulating in her family?

"So thanks for coming. I felt like I could count on you to listen to the lesson without trying to force me into anything."

"Mm." This was what she had tried to explain to June: the perfectly innocent reason he wanted her along.

"I also don't want the kids along because I'm afraid they'll get brainwashed if they're exposed to too much of this stuff. Obviously I don't want them getting forced into something that's not right for them either." He laughed nervously.

Keisha's mind went in circles while Jordan kept talking. The problem was her, wasn't it? "How is *that* any better?" Frayden had exclaimed when she told him he wasn't his father's son, but hers. She had been a bully. She had put down Jordan and his kids and made her own children think the Taylors were inferior.

She had changed though. She needed to have Jordan come visit while her children were home so they could see it for themselves. However, the thought scared her. One misstep, one argument, could mess things up.

She sighed at the memory of emptied gas tanks and painted rooftops, a graveyard of buried pranks. They had seemed so innocent at the time. So fulfilling. Now she and Jordan were literally becoming Christians, learning the teachings of a religion that emphasized loving others—even if he was reluctant to join.

The thought of the missionaries, as well as her copy of the scriptures at home, made her smile as Jordan parked in front of the peaceful church building. The missionaries had recently taught that her sins would be washed away when she was baptized. She couldn't wait for that moment.

Jordan let out a breath and turned to her. "Thanks again for coming."

Her smile was beginning to feel painful.

He started to smile back. Then he frowned. "Are you okay?"

Keisha's smile vanished. "I am a horrible mom!" she wailed. Bursting out sobbing, she put her elbows on the dashboard and hid her face in her arms.

She had no idea how long she cried. A couple of times, she felt a cautious hand on her arm, but the hand retreated.

Finally she looked up, hiccupping. Jordan sat biting his lip, his face white. A wave of shame rushed over her for making him uncomfortable.

"What happened?" he asked, hoarse.

"You know what happened. You were there during that scene with the twins today." She took a deep breath. "And Frayden's been a bully at school, and Lizzie thought she had to do her hair in secret because I approve of June's messy hair. I alienated my own daughter!"

Jordan put his hand on her arm, and the weight of it sent a comforting warmth through her. "Keisha." His tone made her look up into his eyes, which looked darker than normal. "Your children care about you a great deal. I've seen them look at you with adoration. Just like Imogene would look at her mom. You're not a horrible mom."

She clenched her teeth and shook her head. It hurt to look at him while she felt so vulnerable. "But I keep making dumb mistakes."

He slid his hand down to the crook of her elbow, sending an unfamiliar tingle through her. "So what? 'Sometimes we make mistakes, and sometimes the kids make mistakes, but mistakes can be fixed.' That's what Alicia told me after a rough day once."

"Alicia?"

"My wife. See, we teach our kids, and we have a lot of influence over them, but they still make their own decisions, you know? And when we've done wrong, it can be fixed. But we're not totally to blame for our mistakes, either, because we're not perfect. So don't—don't get too upset."

She stared at him. "Is that verbatim?"

His brow furrowed. "Is what verbatim?"

"What your wife said about mistakes."

"Yes."

For the life of her, she couldn't imagine her ex ever remembering and quoting anything significant she had said to him. Nor did she remember saying much of significance to him. It was hard to share confidences with someone you were afraid of.

No, she thought firmly. She had said things of worth to him. It was just hard to believe that when she had so often been belittled.

Of course, she had gotten divorced, while Jordan had never wanted to separate from his late wife, to her knowledge. Never had she seen such a soft look in his eyes as when he talked about her. She had to ask. "What happened to Alicia?"

He swallowed. "Aggressive leukemia."

It had hurt him. At the moment, Keisha couldn't imagine Alicia had meant any less to him than Imogene did, and she had seen his love for his daughter firsthand. She was awed that he had even shared his wife's name with her. "How long did she battle it?"

"For two years after we found out about it." He looked away, but then his lips quirked. "I think she would approve of what you did the other day."

"What? Making Lizzie unhappy?"

"Giving Selima flower seeds. She seemed pleased."

Keisha's shoulders relaxed. She wasn't all mistakes, not with her own family, nor with Jordan's. She just needed a reminder. "Selima's a sweet girl," she said and paused as someone walked up to the church door and unlocked it. She wiped the traces of tears from her face. "It looks like the missionaries are here."

***

AN HOUR AND A half later, Keisha closed the front door behind her and tried to keep her happy bouncing steps quiet. The lesson had been wonderful, as always. The missionaries had focused on how prayer and church attendance helped people receive personal revelation. Then in the car, Jordan had asked about the next step in her plan for them to be friends. She actually got butterflies in her stomach when she realized how much he was doing to help her prove their friendship to Frayden. When she blurted out her idea to have him and his family come over, not only did he agree, but he asked her to go rock climbing with him to use up a coupon before it expired. "Might as well make sure we can stay friendly in a variety of situations," was his reasoning.

It would be fun—and helpful, of course—to do something with him besides eat dinner or talk with the missionaries. Maybe she should invite him to an activity too after this.

Her home was quiet, but when she entered the living room, her children were waiting up for her. Well, mostly up.

"Someone looks tired," she said to the twins, who were nodding off with a battalion of military action figures between them on the couch cushion.

Lizzie and Frayden looked relaxed, each of them reading a library book, though Keisha wouldn't have found Frayden's explosion-packed graphic novel relaxing.

Beside them, June laid down a Rubik's Cube and got off the couch, stretching. "Mom, you know what I miss? Music."

"Music?" Keisha was puzzled.

"Yep. Christina Aguilera. You know, my favorite song? Let's get out the karaoke set so you can sing it."

"Sing what?"

"Hate Song number One. 'Fighter,'" June said, already kneeling in front of the TV and looking for the microphone. Lizzie looked up in anticipation, and Kale bounced once on the couch before his eyes drooped shut.

"You gotta sing it with feeling, just like last time. It's so cool the way you—"

"I don't feel like singing that right now, June Bug," Keisha interrupted, wondering why her happy feeling had gone away.

June looked surprised. "But Mom, if you—"

"I don't want to. Not tonight. I'm sorry, June." Keisha picked up Kale, big as he was, and cuddled him against her chest. She tugged on Carl's hand until the sleepy boy stood up. "Come on. It's bedtime."

She turned away from June's determined look and headed for the stairs.

Chapter 15

Mail, breakfast, school lunch, chatter. Keisha's morning hour went by in a blur, the routine familiar until the children rushed outside for school and stumbled over each other.

"Ew!"

"Ouch!"

"Ugh!"

"Aaah," Carl and Kale laugh-screamed as they bumped into their older siblings and fell down the sides of the porch.

"Guys?" Keisha asked, stepping outside.

Trash was strewn across the porch and partially across the lawn. June stared at it in silent shock, and Lizzie wiped her hands off on the grass in disgust.

Keisha reached for one of the torn trash bags that lay partially filled on the porch. Her hand trembled as she realized it wasn't the kind of trash bag she used in her house. It was one Jordan used.

"Mom, I swear I took out the trash last night," Frayden whined. "I swear I did."

She waved her free hand, feeling dizzy. "Get in the car."

June bit her lip. "Should we help clean it?"

"No. I'll take care of it when I get back." Keisha's tone was curt.

No one said much of anything on the way to school. Or if they did, she didn't hear them. She felt far away as she struggled to concentrate on the road and to keep her eyes from blurring.

***

Jordan worked for three hours straight after dropping the kids off at school. Things were going well, with customers asking for more and sharing his freelance info with friends. He loved this week's balance between mathematically perfect architecture and more creative projects. Things in his family had improved as well. Neither of his daughters had skipped out on classes for several weeks.

He got up to pour himself a beer and take a turn through his backyard. When he stepped outside, the air was frisky and a breeze cooled his face. A flash of black caught his eyes, and he looked at the hedge separating his yard from Keisha's.

His hedge was black.

Why was his hedge black?

He stepped closer to inspect it. Dropping his beer in the grass, he bent and touched his fingers to some of the dark leaves and sniffed. The smell was unmistakable. One corner of his mouth turned up, the other down, and he let his hand drop away from the spray-painted hedge.

***

At one o'clock sharp, the doorbell rang. Keisha opened the door and looked for signs of guilt in Jordan's eyes.

He wasn't smiling as he stared back at her. "Ready?" he asked.

"Yes."

She kept a watchful eye out as they walked to his car and got in. No booby traps. No pranks. Not yet anyway.

"You say you've rock climbed a couple of times before?" he asked, starting the engine and giving her a sideways glance.

"Yep."

He seemed to relax a little. "Great. How long ago?"

"Oh, before I ever got married. I used to go with some friends in high school, just a handful of times." She hadn't thought about them in ages. Life had been more enjoyable back then than she generally remembered. Maybe she had let Henry discolor her memories of the past.

Jordan smiled. "In that case, tonight should be a piece of cake for you."

When they arrived at the center, Keisha paused in the middle of unbuckling. She hadn't even worried about being in the same car as Jordan.

This was only the second time they had driven together, and already it felt natural.

Rock climbing turned out to be fun. Somehow she trusted Jordan not to sabotage her equipment or let her get hurt. He did tease her toward the end though.

"I hope I don't drop you," he called up to her with false concern.

"You won't drop me." She rolled her eyes and braced her heels against the wall, walking slowly downward as he gave her more rope.

"I really hope I don't. The knot's coming undone."

"I'm not scared, Jordan," she called back. "You can let me down faster."

"Faster? I'm already losing control of the rope."

"Faster!"

"But it's slipping!"

"No, it's not."

"Oh no."

"I hear fake panic."

"Hold on—"

She screamed with laughter as she dropped for a couple of seconds and then stopped, suspended in midair.

"Sorry," Jordan called up, his voice full of amusement.

She just kicked her heels. A part of her wished he would do it again.

Maybe it was the reminder of her high school days, but this almost felt like a date. She studied Jordan as they finished and returned their equipment. She hadn't always read people right in her school days, but she thought she knew better what to look for now. That square jaw and those gray eyes had radiated indignation time and time again when she had goaded him, but there was something mild in his gaze she hadn't noticed before. None of the lines in his face spoke of the self-importance she had eventually learned to read in Henry's face.

"Why are you staring at me?"

She blinked and followed him outside. Of course this wasn't a date, but it didn't hurt to make sure she understood the man she spent time with. "Have you ever gotten thrown out of one of these places?"

"No. Why?"

"Because I don't think they like it if you pretend you're in trouble and it turns out to be a false alarm."

"That's why I didn't get loud." His mouth quirked. "And I guess that's why you weren't scared. You've always been the better actor of the two of us anyway."

"How so?" she asked, opening her car door and pausing when she realized he had followed her there and been about to open it for her. Chivalry? That was unexpected.

He cleared his throat and returned to his side of the car. "Um. Well," he began when they were both inside. "You and your pirate costume . . ." He shot her an uneasy look and started to drive.

"What are you talking about?"

His gaze flickered. "That dress you wore the other day."

She only remembered one dress she had worn recently, besides at church. "The one I used for Carl and Kale's presentation? I *did* use it as a pirate dress once." Did he remember that?

He looked like he wanted to talk about something else, anything else. She watched as he searched for a way out.

It rolled in between them as he steered the car around a corner.

Keisha looked down at the unopened beer can and lost her train of thought. Her teeth clenched, and claustrophobia closed in on her. She was locked in a car with a drinker and his beer. She was locked—

Forcing herself to take a breath, she said, "When are you going to throw that away?"

"What?"

"That beer can." She gritted her teeth. This was Jordan. He never scared her even when he drank. But it did make her mad when he did.

"Oh. When I've drunk it." He waved a hand.

"Why? Don't you want to join the church?" It was such a perfect solution. If he joined, he would give up drinking. Not to mention, the church of Jesus Christ already felt precious to Keisha.

Jordan frowned. "Why should I? That church has some good teachings that helped my family, but we're doing well now. I don't need to change my lifestyle."

She braced her hands against her seat. "But what if there's more? Even more positive changes when you join?"

"So what, is this a church for greedy people?" His question was brusque. "I'm satisfied with what I have."

"It isn't just about getting a few blessings, Jordan." She swallowed. "Haven't you listened to what the missionaries say? It's the church God himself leads through prophets and apostles like in the old days."

"Does he want to force us all to join it? If he loves us, why would he be so controlling and make us follow all these rules and this overly specific church? And you, do you just take the missionaries' word for it that it's his church?"

"No, I don't." She bristled. "I know they've told you to pray about it and pay attention to your feelings, just like they've told me. I know it's true because I've felt the Spirit tell me several times already." It made it hard to be mad about some priesthood responsibilities being available only to men. Every time she felt the Spirit, her heart was further softened toward something she never would have agreed to before.

"Well, I haven't felt it."

"Have you prayed?"

"It doesn't matter."

"You're making excuses." He looked annoyed at her words, but Keisha was more annoyed, so she pressed on. "You don't want to find out because you don't want to have to give up alcohol."

He answered with sarcasm. "And isn't it perfect for you who never liked alcohol in the first place that you found a church that prohibits it? Anyway, I'm not addicted, if that's what you think. I could stop if I needed to."

"So why don't you?"

He huffed. "Because there's no reason to. Drinking isn't a problem for me or for those around me. I rarely get drunk enough to be unaware of what I'm doing. I've never lost control and done anything I regretted afterward. Plus, I'm not like you, Keisha. You agree to be baptized during your first missionary lesson, and you change on a dime and try to end the feud by spending time with me. *I* tried to end the feud, but I didn't change that drastically. I just stopped playing pranks and tried not to be outright rude. It's admirable how you change so quickly when you decide on something, but it's not me."

Painful silence ruled as he arrived at their homes and parked.

"Um." Jordan cleared his throat. "I'm out of town part of next week, but I'll see you later. We're still coming to your baptism."

She opened her car door and spoke through clenched teeth. "I look forward to seeing you there." She didn't look back as she closed the door.

***

HER HEART ACHED WHEN Jordan and his family were again not at church that Sunday. He couldn't know what he was missing. She tried to push aside her disappointment and made an effort to focus on the lessons and the Spirit.

She also rescheduled her baptism so that it would be right before church next week. Let Jordan come to *that* if he wanted.

Work sped up that week, and her children knew how to keep her busy. The day after Jordan returned to the neighborhood, she found chalk lines separating her side of the driveway from his, one section with her name and a "ladies first" warning, the other section with his name. Angrily she scrubbed away the chalk. For some reason, Jordan was returning to his old ways. Was he testing her resolve to remain nice to him? She hated the thought. She couldn't trust him if he would do such an underhanded thing.

That Saturday, she got in her car and tried to forget about her neighbor.

Her fingers tapped on the steering wheel. She was finally going to visit Shawna. Hopefully she would be home, and her son too. Hopefully she had free time tomorrow and would accept Keisha's invitation.

She pulled up outside a tan brick building. Briskly she shut the car door behind her and headed to the door, where she rang the bell.

A noise like a fire engine's siren echoed through the house in front of her. Keisha chuckled. Shawna had her own sense of humor.

A man opened the door, looking a little out of breath.

Keisha's smile faded. "Is Shawna here?" she asked, hating how hesitant her voice had become.

"Yes, she's out back. Come on in, and I'll go get her."

She followed him into the living room, a little surprised that he invited her in just like that. "I'm Keisha. Shawna and I worked together until recently."

He halted and looked at her with a genuine smile. "Keisha! She'll be happy to see you. I know you two are friends. Make yourself comfortable, and my wife will be here in a moment."

He left the room. Keisha ignored the soft couch he had indicated and looked around.

Worn but clean furniture rested on the carpet. Most of the shelves hosted books, but a basketball lay on a bottom shelf next to a pile of children's novels.

A shelf against the wall held portraits of Shawna and her husband. One picture showed the two of them together with the newest addition to the family, a boy of twelve or thirteen years. Also, not surprisingly, a photograph of a giraffe hung nearby.

She laughed softly and moved toward the family photograph, but her gaze snagged on a framed page full of words, titled "THE FAMILY: A PROCLAMATION TO THE WORLD."

Curious, she read the first line and stopped, perplexed. It was a statement by the church she had spent the last month studying.

With growing astonishment, she read on. There were truths she had heard from church and the missionaries and truths she hadn't yet heard. The paper defined the family, described the foundation on which it was most successful, and proclaimed parents' shared responsibilities, right down to issuing a warning to those who—like Henry Johansen—abused their spouse or children. It was bold, simple, and covered a broad range of principles.

She wiped her eyes and caught sight of three identical books on a shelf, all titled *The Book of Mormon*.

A door slid open behind her and then slid shut again. "Keisha!" She turned to see Shawna. "You actually visited me. You picked the perfect time too. Must have been spying on us. Now I can introduce you to Thomas." She came closer and suddenly stopped. "Are you all right?"

Keisha looked her in the eyes. "Shawna. Are you a member of The Church of Jesus Christ of Latter-day Saints?"

Shawna stiffened, and her gaze moved to the copies of the Book of Mormon and back. Several emotions moved across her face. Defensiveness. Shame. Uncertainty.

"Yes. I am."

Keisha stared at her. After all the explanations she had run through her head . . . She had imagined it would be easy enough to invite Shawna—that her friend would just shrug and agree to come—but she had wanted to try to explain to her how important this was, maybe to see if Shawna might be interested in talking to the missionaries.

A chuckle began in the back of her throat. "I was going to invite you to my baptism tomorrow."

Now it was Shawna's turn to stare. "Really? Into what church?"

Keisha found herself smiling as she said the long name again. "The Church of Jesus Christ of Latter-day Saints."

Shawna seemed to sag. "How did that happen?"

"I met some missionaries. I know the gospel of Jesus Christ is true, and I wanted you to—wait." She cocked her head. "I've attended church the last two weeks. How come I didn't see you?"

"When Tom came here, he was sick. My husband I both caught the virus and stayed home with him. That's why I said you picked the perfect time to visit. We're finally past the contagious stage."

Keisha started to laugh. "Shawna, I can't believe this. I can't believe neither of us knew."

Shawna's smile came out. She hugged Keisha. "I'm sorry."

"For what?"

The shame returned to Shawna's face. "I never told you. I always felt like I ought to try to talk to you about church, but I got nervous. If you had at least known I was a member, I could have supported you when you first started learning about it. Some missionary I am," she muttered.

"You were nervous about telling me?"

"Yes. I didn't want to compromise our friendship. Plus, we're always kidding around and being sarcastic. I wasn't sure how to talk about this and make it clear I wasn't joking."

The joking part made sense, although Keisha didn't see how talking about church would have compromised their friendship. "Shawna, I'm just happy to know now. You can come to my baptism, then, can't you?"

"When is it?"

"Tomorrow, an hour before church."

"I'll definitely be there. *We'll* be there. Keisha." Shawna's eyes sparkled. "Would you like to meet Thomas?"

Thomas was obviously already a welcome family member in Shawna's home. Watching him play soccer with his dad in the backyard was the perfect ending to the visit. Thomas looked like a happy boy, but according to Shawna, he had gone through some rough things in the foster care system. Hopefully he would find healing here.

As Keisha drove home, she felt refreshed and peaceful. In less than twenty-four hours, she would be washed clean of her sins. Her best friend was already a member of the Church of Jesus Christ and would probably be at her side every Sunday from now on. Funny that she had known Shawna for so long but had never known about her religion or met her family.

The car vibrated beneath her as she pulled into the driveway. Jordan's car was in its place, and there were no chalk marks on the ground. Whatever else was going on, at least some things had gotten better.

She opened her door and put her feet down, then felt a sticky resistance when she took her first step.

Large clumps of chewing gum stuck to the asphalt and the bottom of her shoe.

Keisha's anger sparked.

Chapter 16

Would he still come?

Keisha tugged at her white jumpsuit and stopped pacing to greet Wayne's parents. "Thank you for coming."

"Thank you for inviting us," Wayne's dad said. "We've never been to something like this."

Neither had Jordan, and based on his tricks this week, he wasn't likely to come today.

The Primary room, where the children met on Sundays, was filling up with friends and members Keisha hoped to get to know better. Shawna had at last been introduced to the children she had only heard stories about. Wayne ran about with the twins, who had apparently talked their mouths off about church all week. His parents planned to leave him with Keisha's family after the baptism and pick him up from their home afterward.

Ahead of her, Frayden straightened as he looked beyond Keisha.

She pivoted toward the entrance. Jordan's family walked in the door, Selima and Imogene in cute dresses, Samuel in dark jeans and a T-shirt, Solomon in slacks and a blue shirt, and Jordan—in a black three-piece suit, with his hair newly cut. How strange. He had dressed up for her.

She blinked and shook herself. Of course he hadn't. He had dressed up for church, and he didn't look too happy about it. His collar appeared to choke him as he adjusted it.

Their gazes met, and he zeroed in on her as though she were the cure to his discomfort. Her nervousness spiked at his approach.

He stopped in front of her, and she had to look up to maintain eye contact. Her tongue felt thick as she said, "Thank you for coming."

"Thank you for inviting us," he rumbled, his voice deeper than usual.

Selima came forward shyly. "Congratulations, Keisha. Where do you want us to sit?"

The question gave her a reprieve, a reason to turn away from Jordan. "They're keeping the front rows for close friends and family. I—I think that would be you."

Jordan's eyebrows rose, but when someone stepped up to the microphone to start the meeting, his family took the seats she had suggested, and Keisha's sat beside them.

Keisha would be the first to be baptized in her family, but she hoped the children would follow her example. Lizzie, for one, had said she wanted to be baptized after she finished reading the Book of Mormon. She was already halfway through in spite of the old-fashioned language. June seemed to take what they learned about the gospel of Jesus in stride, but she wasn't in a hurry to act on it like Keisha. Keisha held June's hand tightly during the brief talks given by some of the members she had gotten to know already. Excitement made her blood race when she was asked to stand.

Someone led her through the bathroom and out to the font that had been filled with water beforehand. She stepped in, moving through the warm water to meet Brother Evans, Abigail's husband from her first Sunday here. If it had to be a man who baptized her, at least she had gotten to pick who it was. Brother Evans wore his own white jumpsuit. Guests crowded in front of the baptismal font, her children closest so they could see.

As directed, she put a hand on Brother Evans' arm for balance. He held up one hand and spoke the words of the ordinance. She closed her eyes as he lowered her into the water, immersing her fully. Warmth flooded her, along with a certainty that this was real. This man had priesthood authority to perform this baptism that cleansed her from her wrongs and cemented her promise to follow Jesus. Christ had paid the price for her previous sins and those to come. He would help her lead a better life from now on.

She felt pure as she rose from the waters. The white walls of the room seemed to shine. Her children looked beautiful. Everyone looked beautiful, though they also blurred behind a sheen of tears.

Sniffling, she returned to the restroom and changed her clothes. When she came out of her stall, Sister Miyagi gave her a hug, and Sister Cole held up a blow-drier.

As the sisters helped her, Keisha's tears stopped, but her emotions continued to swell. The smile on her face felt like it planned to stay all day.

When she returned to the Primary room, the pianist stopped playing, the sister missionaries spoke, and someone said a closing prayer. People came over to congratulate her, and then, little by little, they trickled from the room and moved toward the sacrament meeting room for church.

She and her children walked there with Shawna, and Jordan's family followed and took their seats on the row behind them.

Ha. Her plan to get him to go to church by scheduling her baptism before sacrament meeting had worked.

"Jordan," someone exclaimed, and Keisha turned around to find a woman with a sharp nose leaning forward to talk to him. "You're here. Welcome! Justin, look." She nudged her husband. "Jordan's at church. What happened?"

"Sister Pudin." With a deer-in-the-headlights look, Jordan gestured at Keisha. "My neighbor just got baptized."

Sister Pudin looked at her, then looked at Jordan with a speculative gleam, and then looked back again. A huge smile overtook her mouth, drawing an answering smile from Keisha. "That's you? Congratulations!"

"Thank you."

"My husband and I have joined some of the missionaries' visits with your neighbor here," the woman explained. "Jordan's great, but it's been impossible getting him to come to church."

"Jordan?" Shawna asked a few seats down from Keisha. Carl, Wayne, and Kale sat between them. "As in, Keisha's neighbor? As in—"

"Yes, that's him." There was no way for Keisha to talk to Shawna without Jordan overhearing her. "I'll fill you in on it later."

A voice rang through the microphone, and Shawna faced forward. Keisha followed suit, ready for the concluding part of her baptism.

Minutes into the meeting, the bishop called her up to receive the Gift of the Holy Ghost. Heart beating fast, she stood, made her way past her children, and walked to the front. All eyes were on her, except for a few babbling toddlers and their distracted parents.

The bishop stepped from the stand and indicated a chair. With a gulp, she sat down. The elders and two other men joined the bishop, one of them holding a microphone. They laid their hands on her head. She folded her hands tightly in her lap and closed her eyes.

"Sister Keisha Johansen," the bishop began and proceeded to confirm her as a member of the church. He gave her the Gift of the Holy Ghost, then continued on with what sounded like a personal, non-scripted blessing.

Her hands clenched with her emotions and then relaxed. Beautiful words assured her Heavenly Father loved her, and she felt that. Her heart had never seemed so malleable. For a moment, it worried her. She had been strong when her heart was callused.

I am your strength, the words popped into her mind just before the bishop said, "Keisha, remember that God is your strength. He will help you in your role as a mother in Israel and as his beloved child. In the name of Jesus Christ, amen."

Tears filled her eyes anew, and she stood up to shake hands with the bishop as a new, confirmed member of God's church.

***

Jordan had a lot to think about.

Selima seemed different when they stepped outside Monday morning and got in the car. She was her usual sweet self, yes, but there was something more firm, more purposeful, in her face than he was used to.

He didn't know for sure what was going on with her these days, but he had a pretty good idea.

As he worked on his computer that day, his thoughts went in circles. They circled to Keisha, who had seemed so innocent during sacrament meeting and yet had given him distrustful looks during Sunday School. How could she look so sweet and good when she was back to pranking him? Yet even that wasn't what bothered him most today.

The problem was, he had sort of enjoyed church the day before. Of course, he already knew this religion wasn't a bad thing. It had helped Samuel decide to stop getting in trouble, helped Selima stop skipping school, and helped himself make peace with Keisha. For a time anyway. Still, too much of a good thing could be dangerous. If he let himself and the kids get in too deep, it might yet turn out to be too fanatical for them.

His family didn't have to change *that* much. He liked them the way they were now, with just a little bit of religion in their lives. Samuel could drop drugs but drink alcohol again once he reached the legal age. Jordan could pray to God and feel good without going to church every week.

Yet Selima wanted more than this.

He had felt his heart soften towards church yesterday when Keisha received the Gift of the Holy Ghost. Quickly, though, he reached for his philosophy of light religion. He would rather have felt like a stranger in a public building he didn't have to return to. No weekly church for him.

He was still thinking about it when he picked up his three youngest children.

Imogene yawned in her seat between Selima and Solomon. "Daddy, can I play with the twins when I get home?"

"What twins?"

She yawned again. "Carl and Kale."

He frowned. "Imogene, you need a nap. After that, you can play with them if they want to. You guys can mingle with the Johansen kids. I don't mind." He hadn't seen them do anything together much, but maybe his family's upcoming visit at her home this Thursday would change that. In spite of everything, he still hoped to be friends with Keisha.

"Police car," Solomon announced gravely when a siren started up nearby.

Jordan looked in the rearview mirror to figure out whether he should change lanes. What he hadn't expected was to see the police car coming right at him, flashing its lights.

He pulled up and watched the cruiser park behind him. An officer walked up to his window with brisk steps. Jordan rolled down his window.

"Sir, have you had a drink today?" the officer asked.

"What?"

"Have you had a drink today? Alcohol?"

"No."

"Please recite the alphabet to me."

"W-what?"

The officer put a hand on his belt, drawing Jordan's gaze to his gun. Jordan started on the alphabet.

The policeman nodded and interrupted partway through. "There's a piece of paper stuck to your back window. Says 'Drunk driver.' Do you know anything about that?"

Jordan swiveled to look. Sure enough, now that he looked for it, he could see a piece of paper on the back.

His children looked stunned. Imogene clutched her seatbelt in her hands, her mouth open as she stared at the policeman.

"It's . . . a practical joke," Jordan choked out, feeling his face grow red. "I think my neighbor did it. She doesn't like that I drink."

"I see. I don't smell it on you, but let's make sure, shall we? Please come out and stand on your right leg."

Once the policeman's embarrassing alcohol tests were finally over, Jordan couldn't get back in the car and home fast enough. His fists clenched on the steering wheel, and his children were dead silent. The paper he had ripped off the back of the car lay crumpled on the floor of the passenger seat, not quite out of sight.

"Here." He screeched to a stop in front of their house. "You got the house key, Selima?"

She nodded as she and the other two got out.

"I'm going out on some errands." He pulled away and stepped on the gas.

***

June grabbed her seatbelt at the sound of tires screeching. Mom was pulling into the driveway, but she, too, paused and watched Jordan let his children out of his car in front of the curb. Then he tore off and disappeared down the street in his truck.

"What in the world?" Mom asked out loud. Then she shook her head and parked. "I guess it's none of our business."

June unbuckled and hopped out. Selima wouldn't meet her eyes as she walked by. Solomon followed, looking at the ground. Imogene looked over at the twins for a moment but followed the other two.

June couldn't ask them what was going on. Mom might get suspicious. And what if it had to do with her plan? She smiled at the idea, feeling better right away. Jordan had looked angry when he drove away. If someone had played a prank and he thought it was Mom who did it, he might finally do something to get back at her. Then Mom would get mad and get revenge.

June skipped to the front door and stumbled, barely avoiding a banana peel on the porch. It must be a prank from one of her siblings. With a quick look over her shoulder, she hurried inside and waited in the hallway to hear Mom's reaction.

Frayden walked around the peel, but when he entered, he leaned over and said in a low voice, "It won't work."

Annoyance rose inside June. He was wrong. They could keep Mom and Jordan from dating. They could make them mad at each other again. A twinge of guilt rose, too, but she pushed it down. She just had to find out if Dad had become nicer. She needed to buy time before she could go see him in person. There was a reason Mom had married him, and if he was that person again, Mom might want to try to be a family with him. She couldn't do that if she was dating Jordan.

Lizzie stopped on the porch and tilted her head at the peel. "Should we throw that away?"

Mom picked it up. "What on earth?" She looked over at the Taylors' home, her eyes calculating.

"I think it was Jordan that did it," Kale said, and June pinched her lips together.

Mom stared at him. "Are you sure, Kale?"

June held her breath while Kale shifted from foot to foot. He was too obvious. Would he ruin it all?

"I'm glad you didn't trip," he said quickly. Then he grabbed Carl's arm and ran inside, past June.

Mom shook her head and walked to the large trash can.

June let out her breath. Mom wasn't anywhere close to mad. They would have to try harder.

***

JORDAN'S EMOTIONS BOILED AS he pressed on the gas. How dare she! He knew alcohol bothered Keisha, but that didn't give her the right to do this sort of thing to him.

Did she hate him? Why in the world had she restarted the feud? He had attended her baptism and she had agreed to come to his next missionary lesson at the church, and yet here she was getting him pulled over and embarrassing him in front of his kids.

By the time he returned home, he was ready to take the bull by the horn. He glared at the van parked on its side of the driveway. Oh, he would talk to her. Right after he checked on the kids, he would talk to her. Seething, he strode to his house and opened the door.

"Dad," Selima said brightly and held up a chocolate cake. "Look what Keisha gave us."

***

Carl and Kale were loud that evening, screaming and chasing each other through the living room no matter how often Keisha told them to take their noise elsewhere. June stopped her ears with her hands and retreated to the backyard. Frayden was nowhere to be seen, probably up in his room, and Lizzie did her homework on the couch, unbothered by the noise.

"Quiet, please, Carl and Kale," Keisha said again. "Go play in your room. You'd think you'd be drowsy after all that dinner you ate."

She pulled out a few ingredients for tomorrow's dessert, plugged her ears to help herself think, and then grabbed her cell phone and headed to the basement.

When the door closed behind her, she breathed easier. It got even better once she made it to the bottom of the stairs. The muffling of the shrieks from upstairs was heaven to her ears.

The twins were definitely out of control today, their energy overwhelming. Unbidden, the memory of Jordan telling her they should have extracurricular activities came to mind.

No, she could deal with them. They weren't like this every day, and sending them off to activities just to keep them busy would feel like she was giving up and passing on the responsibility to someone else. She should be able to make them behave on her own. Her own mom hadn't felt the need to expend too much energy watching Keisha, but Keisha was determined to give her children her all.

Of course it would be nice to do it with the help of a husband. A mom and dad teaching their children together— even going to church together and praying together. What a beautiful scenario. It sounded like the ideal family she'd read about in the Family Proclamation on Shawna's wall.

She shook her head. It had been a long time since she had believed the support of a spouse would be part of her life.

The screams continued, and Frayden yelled something, but there were no crashes. Nothing was broken yet.

Keisha unlocked her cell phone. She had to tell her parents sooner or later about her baptism, and now seemed like a good time. With the children still awake and potentially due for an accident or a quarrel soon, she could plead the fifth and cut the conversation short if her news upset her mom badly enough.

The phone had barely rung once before Mom picked up.

"Keisha, you never call! Something's wrong. What happened?"

Keisha frowned. "Nothing's wrong."

"Yes, it is," Mom insisted. "You have news of some kind."

"Well, if I do, isn't it perfectly normal to call when a big change comes into your life?" Keisha asked, trying not to be offended. Mom didn't need to rub it in that she rarely called. It wouldn't motivate her to call more often.

Mom gasped. "A man! You got a man in your life? Please tell me he's not—"

"No! No, Mom, there's no man." Why on earth would she think *that*? Keisha was a middle-aged mom, long past the years when she had looked for a husband.

"But you just said—"

"Mom, I got baptized," Keisha exclaimed angrily. "I'm a member of—hold on. Are you laughing?"

"Keisha, you have to let me tease you sometimes," Mom gasped between spurts of laughter. "And you needn't act so shocked about the idea of finding a man. It could happen. Now, what did you say?"

"I got baptized," Keisha said in a sour tone.

"You what?"

She made an effort to push back her temper. "I became a member of The Church of Jesus Christ of Latter-day Saints."

"When?"

"Yesterday."

There was silence on the line for about five seconds.

"Keisha, I don't believe this. Why would you wait to tell us until *after* the fact? No, don't answer that, I know exactly why, it's because you don't tell us things. You should have let us know as soon as you started studying this religion."

"Mom, it went so fast," Keisha began, then hesitated. It probably wouldn't inspire confidence if she mentioned that she had studied the gospel of Jesus Christ for less than a month.

"I just bet it did. That's your problem, Keisha. You don't trust us with the important things in your life. You don't trust us! And now you're probably stuck in some horrid cult. If you want attention, just call us more often. We'll *give* you attention. There's no reason to do anything drastic like this."

"I'm not—"

"Wait till I tell your father you've become a nun. And why? Aren't we already Christians, more or less? Weddings and funerals at church—what else do we need? Why did you need to get baptized into some obscure church?"

The word "nun" made Keisha choke. "Mom, I'm not—"

"What did you say the name of that church was?"

She repeated the name of the church.

"Well, that's just lovely." Mom's voice dripped with sarcasm. "Call us when you're ready to talk. I keep thinking you never tell us anything, and now *this.* Well, I hope you'll take care of yourself, Keisha, and don't get yourself into any more trouble. Mind you, *I will be in touch.*"

Keisha drew breath to speak and realized her mom had hung up.

She hadn't needed an excuse to end the conversation after all. It was a long time since Mom had been that upset. Of course the news had been startling, but really, it was hard for her to confide in her parents.

It was just like Mom to come to a crazy conclusion. "I'm looking for attention, Mom? Really?" she muttered.

At least the dreaded phone call was over. Feeling exhausted but hopeful, she looked at the ceiling. The noise upstairs had abated, leaving just the occasional shout and laugh. The sound of running feet had slowed.

Good. She would tiptoe upstairs, whisper-ask if the coast was clear, and let the boys attack her. Smiling, she grabbed two cans of peaches and started up the stairs.

Halfway up, her right foot stuck.

She raised it slowly and with effort. Gooey gum connected her sock to the step. When she jerked her leg to free it, her knee hit a wire.

A four-legged reptile dropped down in front of her. With a scream, she jerked backwards, flailed her arms, and just managed to catch hold of the banister. The cans of peaches went tumbling down the stairs, their crashes pounding in her ears.

Silence fell as she stared down at the lizard in front of her. Letting go of the banister with one hand, she placed the hand over her thudding heart. She wasn't afraid of lizards, but its sudden fall from nowhere had nearly given her a heart attack.

The lizard didn't move.

She didn't move.

The lizard didn't move.

Her eyes narrowed.

She reached down and picked up the toy lizard. It looked so real.

And someone big and burly had gone to the trouble of finding it, buying it, and sneaking into her house to put it in the basement.

Red seeped into her vision. Their truce was a farce and had been for the last week, but had she been the one to break it? No! She had done everything she could to maintain peace, only to be attacked by a lizard.

She banged her foot onto the next step up, testing for booby traps. When nothing happened, she banged her other foot one step higher, and then she stormed up the stairs, ignoring the stickiness under her right foot. Dropping the lizard, she ran into the hallway and pulled on her shoes with ripping movements.

The doorbell rang. She straightened, a thick lock of russet hair in her face, and flung the door open.

Jordan the Perpetrator stood on the other side with a confused expression. Well, she would wipe that right off his face, along with—

"Thanks for the cake," he said, handing her a clean plastic platter. Keisha's hands took it while she tried to look through the hair that still covered one eye. She gave the tiniest cast of her head, trying to free up her vision discreetly in front of the blasted man. Wait, what had he just said?

Jordan shifted from one foot to the other. "Um, it was good. Thanks."

He stepped away and moved toward his own house, his hands in his pockets.

In addition to being half blinded by her hair, Keisha must have gone half deaf. What cake? Why did he give her a platter?

A strangled noise made her turn around.

"You baked him a *cake*?" June asked incredulously. "Okay, I get the whole 'be nice to your neighbor' thing, but don't get too chummy, okay?" She turned on her heel and stormed off.

Keisha stared at the empty hallway. "What about the lizard?"

Chapter 17

She was still confused when she drove everyone home from school the next day. She shook her head as she watched June drag the lawn mower toward a neighbor's house. Then she went to the kitchen and knelt in front of the cupboard where she had put the cake platter from Jordan beside an identical one the day before. She was sure she only owned one of those.

When she opened the cupboard now, there was only one.

Great. She must have dreamed it. Although—she shut the cupboard, waited three seconds, and opened it again. Nope, there was still just the one. Try as she might, she couldn't conjure a second platter.

She *must* have dreamed it.

That made a lot more sense than reality anyway, because she didn't remember baking a cake recently, and she certainly didn't remember giving it to the Taylors.

Humming, she shut the cupboard one last time and left the kitchen, trying to pretend to herself that she wasn't crazy.

Her step faltered when she saw the dining table. A bouquet of flowers and a gift-wrapped box lay in the middle of the white tablecloth.

Cautiously, she approached the table. She reached out and touched the bundle of flowers. Some of them looked like they were from Jordan's yard. Her heart sped up. Some of them were from her own.

Her heart returned to normal speed. She would have to thank the twins for the flowers but tell them not to pick the neighbors' plants in the future. Only, it was strange that they'd leave her a gift with a note on top.

She picked up the small, white note and read the typed words: *To Keisha. I love you. From Jordan.*

Her mind whirled. She held out a hand as if that could stop her thoughts from going anywhere with this. Then, biting the inside of her cheek, she forced herself to unwrap the present. A delicious smell drifted up to her as she removed the paper and revealed a box of chocolates.

"Jordan," she breathed. Was all this really from him? "Don't play games." One could only take so much confusion.

She took the lid off the box and peered in. A third of the chocolates were missing.

It welled up in her, bubbling up in her stomach, tickling her throat. She started to laugh, and then she couldn't stop. Bending over, she clung to the edge of the table, unable to bear her own weight for a minute.

When the sob-laughs stopped tearing her throat, she breathed in deep. Looking around covertly, she picked up the offerings and went upstairs, where she stashed the evidence in her room. Good thing the children hadn't seen those presents. Where were they anyway?

Going back down, she followed the sounds of their yells to the open kitchen window. Carl, Kale and Imogene played outside, running back and forth between their two front yards as though they were the best of friends.

Feeling the beginnings of a headache, Keisha massaged the sides of her head.

Selima was outside, too, on her knees on the sidewalk. She must be working on the flowers. Keisha felt a flash of guilt, but she pushed it away. She had repented and been baptized. She was no longer the woman who destroyed others' flowers or threw cherry bombs at them. So she stepped outside.

Her chubby cheeks red, Imogene yelled, "Keisha, Keisha, look!" She put her hands in the grass, leaned forward, and brought her feet up in the air before tumbling forward and coming to rest on her back.

"I can roll over too, Mom. I can roll over better," Carl shouted and repeated Imogene's performance. Kale tried too, but he tumbled onto his side before his feet made it into the air.

Keisha felt a pang of joy. The children had never been enemies like she and Jordan were. Now, more than ever, she was grateful for that fact. The three of them seemed to forget her in their eagerness to best each other, so she walked over to Selima and stopped a respectful few feet away, clearing her throat. "How are the flowers doing?" Red, pink, and yellow dotted the soil. It seemed they could both survive and flourish after having a car squash them.

Selima looked up, her brown eyes liquid soft. "They're doing good. So are the ones I'm growing indoors. I like the kinds you got me."

Keisha let out her breath. "That's great. You know, I wasn't really thinking the day I ran these over." She shifted her weight. "Um, I'd offer to help, but I'm not great with flowers."

"That's okay." Selima patted the soil and wiped dirt from her hand. "Dad doesn't work on them much either. It's something I do by myself, and I like it that way. There are other things I can do with Dad and the others."

"What kinds of things do you do with them for fun?"

"Card games, swimming, rock climbing. Rock climbing's a family favorite." Selima's eyes began to sparkle. "He used to do that with Mom too, just the two of them. And they'd go bowling—Mom was really good at that—and rollerblading."

"While they were dating, or after they got married?" Keisha tried to remember whether she and Henry had done anything fun together after they got married.

"I remember them doing it. Dad beat Mom at bowling the last time they played." Selima's smile slipped away, and Keisha wondered how often she talked about her mom or let herself remember those days.

A door slammed, and both of them looked up. Samuel came down the stairs of his front porch and continued toward the driveway before he caught sight of them.

"Oh. Hi." He ducked his head as though he were embarrassed. Selima looked at him, then at Keisha, and then she lowered her gaze and returned her attention to the plants.

Keisha was pretty sure she had just been dismissed. "I'll see you later," she mumbled.

"Uh-huh," Selima said without looking at her.

Unfortunately the moment Keisha returned inside, she remembered the strange gifts hidden away in her room.

To Keisha. I love you. From Jordan.

It was a crazy joke. Funny too. That partially eaten box of chocolates—she hoped Jordan had meant it as a joke rather than as a way to offend her. After all, she was supposed to be attending another of his missionary lessons tonight.

Somehow by the time dinner was over that day, she looked forward to going with Jordan to his lesson at the church. It didn't matter that she had sobbed in his car the last time they went, or that she didn't know where she stood with him right now with all these pranks and—romantic gestures? No, *jokes*. It had been a joke.

It didn't matter. Jordan had been nice at church last Sunday. He was sure to behave himself during their time there with the missionaries, and Keisha looked forward to feeling the Spirit again.

I love you. From Jordan.

Annoyed, she shook her head. It was a joke, but he ought to know that receiving such words from anyone was enough to play havoc with a woman's emotions.

Kale climbed onto the tall chair at the kitchen counter and put his hands on her cheeks. "Your face is warm. And it's red." He sounded delighted. "I can make my face red too."

He sucked in a deep breath and held it, fish-lips unmoving and his chest out. Slowly, his face began to change color.

Keisha reached out, ready to press on his cheeks if she had to. "Please breathe, Kale. I like your face best when you breathe."

He let out a whoosh. "Okay." Then he jumped to the floor. "Carl! Let's play dinosaurs!"

Keisha left the kitchen and grabbed her things. Purse swinging in her grip, she headed for the door. If she didn't clear the air with Jordan on their way to the lesson, tonight would be the strangest missionary lesson she had had. He needed to explain himself.

Something on the door caught her eyes as she shut it behind her. She stopped and read the scrawled note.

`Please don't come tonight. I can go on my own.`
`-Jordan`

Her heart sank. She closed her eyes but continued to see the message before her, etched in her mind as though it had been carved with a knife. Funny this was handwritten, and the love note typed. She swallowed. The handwritten note felt more real.

***

WHEN JORDAN OPENED HIS front door, he saw Keisha's close behind her as she retreated to her house. Had she forgotten something? He turned toward her home, but a note on his door made him pause.

As he read the short message, frustration welled up in him. Things had been going so well. At least until a week ago. Why was she backing out now and cancelling their plans?

He tore the note off and went to his car alone.

***

JORDAN'S FAMILY WAS SUPPOSED to visit today. The thing was, Keisha didn't know if they still planned to come. Not since Jordan had canceled on her the evening before. She *could* go ask, now that both families were home from school, but the risk felt too great. She was still crushed from the night before.

Instead, she trimmed the maple tree in the front yard. The scent of grass filled the air as she picked at the tree. Snapping the branches off with the sharp blades felt good. The thicker the branch, the better.

Satisfied, she secured the clippers and paused at the sight of Jordan standing outside. He looked in her direction with a puzzled frown.

Deciding to ignore him, she walked to the side of her house and turned on the water to the hose she had unwound and laid out earlier. She would leave it on for a few minutes, enough to really get the ground wet in a patch that held a couple of plants from one of Frayden's class projects.

Then she went inside. Her steps echoed in the hallway, and a splashing noise from the kitchen told her someone must be using the sink. She put the clippers away in the basement. When she returned, the water was still running.

"June, would you turn off the water?" she asked.

No answer came.

"Or Frayden. Or someone," she mumbled, going to the kitchen.

She jumped. Jordan stood outside the open kitchen window, watching the end of her garden hose that hung through the window and fed water into the sink.

He cleared his throat, looking amused. "Are you watering your sink?"

She opened her mouth to scold him, but seeing the sink was almost filled, she rushed over to grab the hose. In a flash, it turned upward in her hands and sprayed the ceiling.

"Whoa, let me take that outside," Jordan said and grabbed hold of the hose.

Keisha flinched but held on, and suddenly she got it full in her face, cold water drenching her head.

Then the sink was being watered again and Keisha stood dripping, gasping for breath.

"S-sorry," Jordan's voice said.

Water started running down the side of the sink to the floor. Keisha shrieked and jerked the hose, which turned on Jordan and then back to her, drenching her for a second time with its shocking cold. Jordan's hand grabbed hers on the hose, which shot upward only to spray the ceiling and send more water cascading down over her, then finally, finally, into the overflowing sink.

She gasped as droplets slid through the hair in her face and water moved down her clothes and onto the floor.

Jordan looked like he was about to say something, but Keisha didn't let him. Letting go of the hose, she rushed into the hall.

She met him at the corner of her house. He was carrying the hose. Keisha ran up to him, put a hand above his on the hose, and turned it on him full force, putting the fingers of her other hand against the nozzle to make the spray stronger.

Jordan sputtered. "Keish," he managed. "Wait. Really!" he exclaimed, spitting.

The water went wild as they both tried to point it away from themselves and at the other person with a vengeance. Keisha choked and turned the hose on his body. Jordan yelled and turned it on her legs, making her yelp and jump. She twisted it away from herself and gave him another deluge.

Jordan spread his legs and pressed his back against her, gripping her arm with the hose so she couldn't control the direction of the water. She pulled back hard, turning his solid frame in a slow circle with her.

There was only one direction to go. Keisha fell to the ground like a stone, the hose in her grip following and jerking at Jordan's hands so he fell to his knees and got the brunt of the water in his face again.

He let go, fell over the hose that encircled them, and got up at a run. Keisha got on her feet and followed, likewise tripping over the hose. She dragged it with her, laughing and keeping it aimed at Jordan until he appeared with his own garden hose, water splashing out of the end. She staggered to a stop. Following her earlier example, he plugged the opening with his fingers and sent a strong spray at her. She shrieked but, instead of retreating, ran sideways, getting at him from another angle.

Oh, she had missed this. It was like the day they went after each other with the fire extinguishers. She pursued him with wild abandon, dodged to little avail, her throat growing hoarse and her lungs burning as she sprinted and braked and turned. Jordan's face was familiar and hilarious, drenched as he was, and Keisha's heart swelled with the joy of a battle against the only person who would ever play this kind of game with her.

Someone laughed. Kale ran past her, squealing when he got splashed. Samuel, Selima, and June watched at the edge of the lawn, and several of the other children ran around, joining in the fun.

Leaving them to their devices, Keisha laughed and screamed and ran. In a rare moment of success, she got behind Jordan and hit him in the back with a spray of water. He turned around and filled up her mouth, laughing while she swallowed half the liquid and spat out the rest of it, trying to aim for him with her eyes closed.

When she opened her eyes, he was running toward her. She stumbled backward and fell in the grass.

Merciless, Jordan ran straight up to her and sent water down on her.

Shielding her eyes with her arm, Keisha hooked an ankle around his foot and jerked. He seemed to catch his balance, but when she looked up, his direction was changing. He must have overcorrected, because now he was swaying forward instead of backward, and his flailing hands didn't seem to have the power to stop him.

She shut her eyes just before he crashed down, and everything got heavy and warm.

His breath was fast in her face, his arms curling around her as if to protect her from the fall. *His* fall. It was a little late for that. Her eyes sprang open.

Jordan looked stunned and out of breath. His eyes looked deep into hers, deeper than she thought anyone could go. Slowly, he pushed up on his knees, removing some of his weight from her.

"Are you okay?" His voice was a rumble of thunder, a note of worry, and the darkening of a solar eclipse all at the same time.

Keisha pulled breath into her lungs, embarrassed at the heat she felt. Now wasn't the time for poetry. "I will be if you lose fifty pounds."

Jordan chuckled, though his face remained an interesting shade of red. She didn't dare guess at the shade of her own face. He got off and held out his hand.

Keisha grabbed hold and let him pull her up. Then she looked down at the ground. Their two hoses faced opposite directions in the grass, peacefully watering the lawn. She touched one of them with her foot. "That's what you get for planting my hose in my kitchen sink."

"I didn't put that hose in your kitchen." Jordan's breath was starting to slow. "I came over to ask why you had put it there, and to find out why you stood me up yesterday."

"Stood you up?" She gathered her thick wet hair together at the nape of her neck. "The only thing we were supposed to do together yesterday was the missionary lesson, and you canceled on me."

"No, I didn't. You wrote a note telling me you weren't going to come," he growled, and a shadow fell across his face.

She frowned, feeling the burning in her cheeks fade. "I did not."

"Keisha." He sighed. "I saw you slip into your home right after you put the note on my door. The note just so happened to be signed 'Keisha.' It doesn't take a genius to figure out who it was from."

"Or to figure out who was throwing wads of gum and lizards at me," she retorted.

"Wads of—what?" He half laughed.

She didn't find it funny. "I'm getting tired of this, Jordan. The gum and the trash, after we made peace? I don't understand—"

"Nor do I. I'm just trying to figure out why you decided not to come yesterday. Your note—"

"Enough games, Jordan. We can't *both* have gotten notes last night about you going to the lesson alone."

He started to open his mouth, then stopped.

She blinked. "Can we?"

Jordan stared at her.

In tandem, they turned and looked at their children. Some of them were dripping from running around during the fight and getting caught by the sprays of water. Solomon was dry and shielded a camera in his hands. Frayden looked satisfied, Lizzie relieved, and the others nervous.

"I wrote a note to Mom that said it was from you," Frayden volunteered. "I thought you'd come over and ask why she didn't show up, and then the two of you'd figure out what's been going on."

"'What's been going on'?" Jordan repeated. "You mean, I'd find out why Keisha spray painted my hedge?"

"What? Why would I spray paint your hedge?" she countered.

"That's kind of what I was hoping to find out," he said and raised his eyebrows. "You had some reason to restart our feud?"

"I didn't spray paint anything," she said, miffed.

"It was all our idea," Carl blurted out. "I mean, not me and Kale, but everyone's idea." He scratched his head. "It was June's idea first."

Keisha frowned. "June?"

"We were trying to make you not date. Right?" Kale turned to his siblings for confirmation.

June lifted her chin. "You guys went from being archenemies to dating. We didn't think it was right. I don't think it'll work out. We wanted to help you realize you were on the wrong track. So we thought if we did the kind of things you did in your feud, you'd realize you don't want to get along, and you'd start fighting again. Things would get back to normal."

"Well, something like that," Samuel said, looking less than supportive of June's speech.

Disbelief swirled through Keisha, making her stomach clench. "That means, when we found that garbage strewn all over our front yard—"

"It was me," June interrupted. "Only I didn't think about animals getting into it. I didn't mean for it to become a mess you'd have to clean up." She sounded truly sorry—about the mess, not the deception.

"Who did the spray paint?" Jordan asked, turning to his oldest son.

"Me and Selima together," he said.

"*Selima*?" Jordan and Keisha asked at the same time, but they were given no time to process the news.

"The banana peel was us!" Carl broke in, jumping up and down beside Kale. "And so was the gum in our driveway, Mom, but I don't know if you found that."

"Oh, I did," she assured him.

"You used gum?" Lizzie asked worriedly. "I used gum too. And a lizard."

"That lizard nearly scared me senseless," Keisha exclaimed, pressing a hand to her chest as she remembered the shock it gave her. "I was ready to run over and have it out with you, Jordan, but then you showed up with—wait, who made the cake?"

"What do you mean, 'who made the cake'?" Jordan asked incredulously.

"Did it have too much salt in in it or something? How was that one a prank?" Keisha asked.

"I made it," Selima said in a small voice. "Solomon and I felt terrible after the police stopped you, Dad."

"Yeah, I went too far with that one." Samuel looked down. "I didn't think the police would get involved."

"I started feeling bad about our pranks," Selima continued, "and for trying to end your new . . . friendship. I wasn't sure about it to begin with anyway, and I do like you, Keisha. So I thought"—she turned back to Jordan—"maybe if I made you a cake and pretended it was from Keisha, it'd make things better. I hadn't thought of how you'd believe the platter was hers and you'd go return it. I got Lizzie to steal it back for me afterward."

Jordan stared at her and then turned to Keisha. "Why didn't you tell me that platter wasn't yours?"

"I was too surprised. Like I said, I was about to rush over and talk to you about that lizard and everything else that had happened, and then you showed up and thanked me."

"What's this lizard you keep talking about?"

"It's a toy, but it doesn't *look* like a toy at *all*." She stopped and cleared her throat. "It fell on me on the basement stair."

For a moment, amusement reappeared on his face. "And you thought I'd done that."

"I wrote the note from Keisha telling you she wouldn't come last night," Samuel confessed to his dad. "I kind of went along with the pranks because I thought it would test your relationship. Sorry."

So there *were* two notes. And a cake. Keisha put a hand to her head. "Did anyone else 'feel bad'? Because I distinctly remember some presents turning up on my table."

"*We* felt bad," Kale piped up. "We felt bad about the chewing gum, and it's okay if you're nice to each other, so we wanted to do something nice from Jordan. Imogene said you'd know it was our handwriting, so we typed the note and printed it out."

"What were the presents?" Jordan asked, raising his eyebrows.

Keisha opened her mouth and began to laugh. The words wouldn't come. Pretty soon, she doubled over in laughter.

She surfaced long enough to say, "Flowers picked from your yard and, and mine—"

Lizzie pursed her lips and shook her head. "The twins asked me to pick flowers for you. I picked them from a field."

"We added even more to make it extra pretty," Carl explained.

Keisha doubled over again. "And chocolate," she gasped. "I wondered why I'd been given a gift-wrapped box with a third of the chocolates eaten."

"It's because the chocolates are really good, Mom," Kale told her. "And we bought them with our own money, so we wanted to have some of it."

Jordan roared with laughter. Keisha wiped her streaming eyes, warming at their shared amusement. Maybe this was what had made their sparring the last three years so fun: seeing and spurring his sense of humor. It matched hers.

At last Jordan quieted, but his eyes continued to dance.

"So are things okay?" Selima asked tentatively.

"You definitely passed the test," Samuel said in a joking voice. "You both got pranked, but I don't think you ever went after the other person."

Keisha sighed. Her children would need a serious talking to, and so would Jordan's.

Selima's bottom lip quivered. "Keisha, I'm sorry."

The next moment, the girl threw her arms around her. Keisha's heart jumped into her throat. She was wet, but Selima didn't seem to care. Slowly, Keisha lowered her arms to hug her back.

Solomon dropped his camera and hugged Keisha. "I'm sorry too." There was shame in his muffled voice as he spoke into her clothes.

The thought of scolding anyone got stuck somewhere between Keisha's mind and her throat.

"So am I, Mom," Lizzie cried out and joined them, and Carl and Kale threw themselves into the group hug as well.

"I'm sorry," Samuel said in a low voice.

Though overwhelmed with the group hug and apologies, Keisha looked at Samuel and held out a hand. He didn't hesitate to move in and join the circle.

***

Jordan stared as nearly everyone milled around Keisha. That was possibly the first hug Samuel had given anyone since Alicia died. Meanwhile, Selima looked at home in Keisha's arms. What was up with his children?

Soon, the only ones left on the outskirts were Frayden, who stared up at Jordan with hero-worship in his eyes, and June, whose face was stony. Was this the girl who had asked him for help with fixing the lawn mower only last week?

Jordan cleared his throat. "Isn't anyone sorry for *me*?"

Frayden stepped closer and looked up at him, his face shining with admiration. He didn't look about to hug Jordan, so Jordan reached down and tousled his hair. Frayden's face broke into a grin.

"Sorry, Dad," Samuel said, his voice wobbling as he let go of Keisha and came over to give Jordan a quick hug. "I guess I did some mean things to you in the name of the feud."

Imogene came over and smiled up at Jordan. He looked at the dwindling circle, his heart aching at the sight of Selima still clinging to Keisha.

"So who put that hose in Keisha's kitchen?" he asked, embarrassed at the gruffness in his voice.

"I did," June said simply and looked from one wet figure to another.

When Keisha was given breathing space at last, she stepped back and looked around at his family. "Are you all still planning to come visit our place? How about you come over in two hours? In *dry* clothes. I'll have dinner in the oven by then. Bring your chairs, please, because we don't have enough for all of us."

Jordan's heart settled into an erratic rhythm as he gazed at her. Samuel was right. Both of them had been pranked this week, but neither had returned fire. *Keisha* hadn't returned fire. And he was free, at last, to try to pursue a relationship with her.

That couldn't go fast enough for him. "We'll be there," he said and began to shoo his children home.

Chapter 18

Keisha and her children didn't dress up, but it felt like they did when they were ready two hours later, squeaky clean from showers and wearing fresh changes of clothes.

That's what happens when you precede a dinner invitation with a water fight, she concluded sagely to herself. She drew a comb through Kale's wet hair while he sat in front of her like an angel, his feet dangling five inches above the floor from his chair. The smell of homemade pizza came from the kitchen where Keisha had thrown the food in the oven and left things a mess so she could make her children presentable.

Frayden drew her gaze as he leaned against the counter. Keisha cleared her throat. "Frayden, we're getting close to the end of the semester." It was a dangerous topic, but it was time for them to get through this. "Are you ready to make your apology to that boy? I can try to set up a meeting, and if you want me to be there, I'm happy to—or of course, if you *don't* want me there, which is more likely—"

"Mom, I've already apologized."

She blinked. "What?"

Kale laughed. "Mom, you're combing the air." He grabbed the comb from her hand and pulled it through his hair himself.

"When?" Keisha asked Frayden.

"Last Sunday."

She frowned. "Sunday? But you didn't have school—"

"The kid's at church," Frayden interrupted, looking at the wall. "It was kinda awkward in Primary that first time we came. I don't know why his older brother didn't kick my butt. Both of them just acted friendly." He looked at Keisha. "I started to think maybe I could get away with not bringing it up, but then I decided to apologize last week. It was better that way."

Keisha's surprise hadn't abated by the time the doorbell rang. "That's wonderful. Frayden—"

"Let me guess, you're proud of me? Or"—his smug expression gave way to a frown—"were you going to tell me never to be mean again? I don't plan to be. I've learned my lesson."

She heard the front door open as one of her children let in the neighbors. "I'm proud of you." She hugged Frayden's head and turned toward the hallway.

The Taylors walked in, carrying their chairs. Several of them had wet hair as well. Jordan's was heavy with water and tapered into wet points beneath the ears. Keisha averted her gaze. What was she doing, tracing the path of water in his hair? June followed behind the Taylors, her face soft and relaxed.

Keisha relaxed too. "Welcome. Leave your chairs at the dining table. We'll have the smaller children at the low table. It'll be a bit before dinner's out of the oven, so I—" She looked at the sofa where Lizzie had laid out an assortment of games at her request. "I thought we could play something." Had she assumed too much?

"Ooo," Selima exclaimed and headed straight for the picture of the boy with his round mouth. "Samuel, look."

"Oh, nice."

"I like it, I like it," Imogene squealed, clapping her hands.

Her mouth slightly open, Keisha watched the Taylor children flock around the picture and compliment it.

Jordan looked annoyed. "Did you all hear Keisha? We're going to play a game."

"No worries. Let them look." Keisha joined the children. "Isn't it great? I can't get over his expression. It's a CG. I have several more."

"What's a CG?" Selima asked.

She started to explain. The Taylors asked her questions and pointed out different things in the picture with artistic skill. It was enchanting.

"That's enough, kids," Jordan growled.

"But Dad." Samuel grinned. "You should come take a look."

If only Jordan had shown this much interest in the CGs the first day he came to her house. "Let me just show them the other two we have in the living room," Keisha told him.

The children oohed and aahed over the pictures. When Keisha turned her head, Jordan was looking daggers at them, but his eyes widened at her, and he schooled his face into gentler features.

June smirked. "Looks like Mom's found people that are as crazy as her about these pictures. Does anyone want to play Memory?"

They pulled out the game, the children setting it up together as though they'd gotten along all their lives. Keisha shook her head in wonder. Of course, the two groups had conspired together against her and Jordan. They'd know how to get along, with that history.

The faint sound of boiling water drew her attention. "Go ahead and get started without me. I have to take care of something in the kitchen."

Lizzie jumped up and followed her. "Can I pour in the pasta?"

"Sure."

Keisha let her pour and watched to make sure she turned down the heat after putting the lid back on the pot.

"Thanks, Lizzie. Now go play with the others. I'll come as soon as I've cleaned up in here."

Lizzie scurried off.

"I can help clean," said a voice quite different from that of any of her children, and Keisha jumped as Jordan entered. "What do you need?" The low timbre of his voice was at once strong and intimate.

"Um. Thanks. If you'll wipe down the counter . . ."

How strange. Jordan was in her kitchen, washing the countertop while she moved around and put the remnants of toppings in the fridge. Henry had always wanted the house clean, but he hated to clean it himself when the mess was, according to him, her fault. She tightened her lips and pushed away the memory. It was Jordan who was here, a smell of shampoo emanating from his damp hair.

She swallowed. Jordan's presence seemed to fill the small kitchen. Had he always been so—arresting? He rinsed out his rag and left it in the sink. Strange as the thought sounded in her head, there was something romantic and impressive about him completing so neatly the small job he had volunteered for. What made it even worse was the way he turned and stood looking at her.

"Are you done yet?" June stood in the doorway, her hands on her hips. She entered the kitchen and looked around for something to do. "Seriously, there are two of you, and you're still a bunch of slow pokes. What else needs to be done?"

"Uh, nothing." Keisha threw a glance at the timer. The pasta wasn't even half ready. "We're done. Thanks, Jordan."

"You're welcome," he rumbled.

June followed close behind, practically herding them to the living room.

They joined the game of Memory, trying to match pairs of baby animals to each other. The children were already halfway through the game, leaving the adults at a disadvantage.

"There's no way either of us can win," Jordan said with a glance at Samuel's stack of matches.

Keisha rolled her shoulders as though preparing for a race. "I may not be able to catch up, but at least I can beat you."

Jordan gripped the edge of the coffee table. "Oh, the game is on!"

June and Selima rolled their eyes at each other.

No matter how hard Keisha tried, Jordan kept catching up to her on his turn. At last there were only six cards left on the table. Keisha and Jordan were tied, but it was Keisha's turn, and if she got one match now, she would probably get all three and beat Jordan. If not, Solomon was sure to win the last three.

Keisha turned over a card and looked at the baby otter. She smiled in relief. Its twin was over on the left. She moved her hand that way but frowned. There were two cards, one above the other, and she couldn't remember which was the otter.

"Come on, Mom you can do it," June urged.

Jordan seemed to be holding his breath.

Keisha turned over the top card, revealing a bunny.

"Oh! You lost!" Lizzie cried out.

"She's still tied with Dad," Samuel said, hooting.

"No!" Imogene yelled. "No, Mom, you picked wrong!"

Keisha's heart hopped into her throat, and her eyes flew to Jordan.

"Mom isn't Imogene's Mom," Kale whispered.

Jordan stared at his daughter as though he'd never seen her before. Everyone else was frozen. Imogene continued to protest into the silence, leaning over the table to point. "The other one's over here. I remember."

Samuel was pale, and Selima looked shocked. But it was June who began to speak in a pained voice. "Imogene—"

The little girl flipped over the bottom card. "Look, Keisha. The other otter's here."

Hearing her call Keisha by her name again helped dissolve the shock in the room.

Jordan cleared his throat. "Yeah, Keisha, you picked wrong," he drawled.

Keisha let air flow back into her lungs. "Well, aren't you lucky I did?"

Solomon turned over the correct cards and ended the game. The kitchen timer went off, and Keisha got to her feet. "Pizza's ready, and pasta too. Let's eat."

The mood returned to normal as they set the table and said a prayer over the food. They had grown comfortable with each other over the game, and dinner, fortunately, went by without a hitch.

"I'd like to invite you all to dinner at our house next week," Jordan said, making Keisha pause with her napkin halfway to her mouth. Jordan sent his children a stern look. "That is, *if* my children will behave."

"That would be great," Keisha said, the words half foreign in her mouth. Her efforts to prove her new friendship to Frayden were exceeding her wildest dreams.

Jordan smiled at her, which for some reason made her heart beat faster. "Samuel, let's do the dishes," he said.

Even after the dishes were done, the Taylor children didn't seem eager to leave. Keisha had an inkling that once they were home, Jordan would have a talk with them to make sure they didn't start any more trouble between now and the upcoming visit. Reluctantly, they filed out the door, sneaking glances at their dad. He followed with a stern expression but turned and sent one last smile at Keisha.

It struck her that she wasn't afraid for his children. However he chose to discipline them, he would never hurt them.

She paused at the entrance. When had that become clear to her? And how? Men were jerks. She couldn't trust them. Wasn't that what she had told herself for years?

Someone tugged on her sleeve.

"Mom? Are you in there?" June asked.

Keisha blinked. She was staring at the empty front porch. The neighbors had gone home, and she was alone with her children.

She turned around slowly and returned to the living room.

Carl and Kale giggled and pushed each other. Lizzie elbowed them until they looked up at Keisha and hushed. Frayden started to sneak up the stairs, but Keisha cleared her throat, and he froze in his tracks.

She crossed her arms over her chest. "It was pretty cozy tonight. They're easy to get along with, aren't they?"

"Yeah," several voices murmured.

"Does anyone have anything to say?" Her eyes rested on each of them in turn. They were silent.

Finally, June gave an exaggerated sigh. "Jordan was waaay too helpful."

Keisha raised her eyebrows but didn't comment. "Do we like the Taylors?"

"We think they're fun," Kale said.

"They're pretty nice," June relented, her voice softening.

"And no one will restart the neighbor feud again, right? Can I trust that there'll be no more pranks on either me *or* Jordan?"

An uneven chorus of "Yes"s sounded.

Keisha looked around at them. Her lips lifted. "You know what, guys? You're doing a great job making friends with them. I'm proud of you."

"Can we stay up late and play, then?" Kale asked, bouncing up and down. "Since we were good tonight?"

"No."

He stopped bouncing, his expression falling into sadness. Keisha struggled with laughter. "It's bedtime," she said and led the way.

"Mom, is Imogene allowed to call you 'Mom'?" Kale asked as he started up the stairs.

"She doesn't have a mom," Carl told him before Keisha could think up an answer. "She has to get to say Mom to someone."

"Oh. That makes sense."

It was a relief that Kale accepted the simple explanation.

The children had barely been put to bed when the phone rang.

Gingerly, Keisha made her way downstairs. She was starting to feel sore from running around during the water fight.

She picked up and asked, "Hello?"

"Hi, Keisha," said Jordan's voice. "I had an idea for tomorrow. I mean, for our weekly get-together."

Right. As though they hadn't gotten together at her house, at missionary lessons, and at church. He still expected to meet and eat together? Her heart fluttered. She couldn't remember committing to "weekly get-togethers," but she supposed she could live with that.

"I thought we could do something fun again rather than just a meal," he said over the phone.

"Sure." She tried to take control of her heartbeat and the conversation. "It'll be a way to celebrate the end of the children's start-up feud."

He chuckled. "That's a good way to think of it."

"How about we make it my treat?" she asked. "You took us rock climbing last time. I've heard that's one of your family traditions. It's time for a Johansen tradition. I'll take you to the movies."

"Really?"

"Yes. What are they playing right now? Oh, yeah." She named a comedy.

Jordan chuckled. "They're not playing that one anymore."

"Oh yes, they are. You just have to know the right place," she said mysteriously. Her mysterious voice sounded a lot like her "thinking Great" voice.

"Okay." He sounded surprised but pleased. "Let's do that."

She nodded. "See y—"

"And Keisha, thanks. For forgiving us and letting us come over after you and I found out how our kids had conspired against us."

She shook her head. "No problem. See—"

"And I'm sorry I didn't come over to ask why you bailed on the missionary lesson."

"Oh. That's fine, Jordan, really. You don't need to apologize." It had been excruciating for both of them the first time they apologized to each other. Now the apologies flowed. "I'll see—"

"Mom?" A hoarse whisper announced Carl's arrival before his head peeped around the corner. "I'm just getting a drink of water, Mom. I'm not staying up late," he said in the same whisper. Hopefully he wasn't getting sick.

"Will you let me know what time we're leaving for the movie tomorrow?" Jordan's voice asked.

"Sure. I might go with an early afternoon showing or—"

Carl edged along toward the kitchen, pressing his body against the wall on the way. It looked like he was pretending to be a spy. Maybe that was why he had made his voice hoarse.

A small hand appeared at the corner from which he had come, and Kale's head popped into sight.

"Sorry, Mom. I'm thirsty," he whispered. "I promise I'm not staying up late." He held up his fingers in some sort of scout's honor gesture and sneaked after his twin.

"Everything okay?" Jordan asked through the phone. "Afternoon would work fine."

"Sounds good. And your children were great at my place today. I didn't mind postponing the game to look at CGs."

Jordan was silent for a moment.

Keisha was just getting ready again to tell him "See you" when he said, "Keisha?"

"Yeah?"

"What did the note say?"

What note?

"You know, the note your twins wrote to go with the flowers and the half-eaten chocolate. What did it say?"

"Good night, Mom." Carl's whisper was louder this time as he left the kitchen. He and Kale gave up on sneaking around and ran barefoot across the floor to hug Keisha.

"Good night, Jordan," Keisha said quickly and hung up. Then she bent down and kissed the twins good night.

Chapter 19

She had invited him to a movie, but why? Did she think of it as a date? Jordan resisted the urge to rub his suddenly itchy hands on his pants during the drive. "I checked last night. The movie's no longer in theaters."

Keisha laughed and moved an errant lock of hair from her face. "Just think of me as your time travel guide."

She was playful today, giving away nothing until she made a sudden turn and parked.

Jordan looked up at the building in front of them and slapped his forehead. "The dollar movie! Of course."

"Yeah, they're good at showing movies here that people think are no longer showing," Keisha teased as they got out.

He liked this side of her. "Have your kids already seen it?"

"Yes. We saw it here last week."

Was she short on money or just frugal, going to the dollar theater? Of course, she did have to provide for five children on her own.

A buttery smell welcomed him when they entered, and Jordan's stomach rumbled. Unfortunately, Keisha walked past the snack area.

He stopped. "How about I get us some popcorn?"

She considered him for a moment and smiled. "No thanks. My family doesn't buy snacks at the movies."

Now he felt awful. She *was* struggling financially. "I'll get us some."

Keisha caught his arm and looked him in the eyes, her blue ones sparkling with amusement. "That's nice of you, but I've got us covered."

"What?"

"We're doing this the Johansen way," she said, leaving the snack area without another glance.

His stomach fell as it realized its fate for the evening. However, with Keisha's hand on his arm and her usual determination in her eyes, he decided to let her lead him away. Stubborn Keisha. His inner voice was less grumbly than it might have been.

Like Keisha, he had seen the movie already, but it was no less funny the second time. He laughed along with her on the comedic parts and wondered what to do when it looked like she was trying not to cry in a couple of sad places. The movie had half his attention, but the other half of his mind was stuck on whether he could put his arm around her shoulders or not.

She probably wasn't ready for that. She wouldn't be ready until she accepted the fact that he didn't care to join her church or stop drinking.

Still, she had come a long way. Three months ago, he would never have imagined they might be friends like this. Maybe he could move closer while she laughed her head off at—

She turned to look at him, her smile brilliant with humor. Jordan jerked and faced forward. He started as her warm hand pressed into his, and his mind went spinning in circles. Heart thudding, he opened his hand in response to the pressure of hers.

She moved her hand away, leaving something in his palm.

Jordan looked down at the candy in his hand. "Where'd this come from?"

A smile played at her mouth as she watched the screen. "Home."

"I don't believe this. You let me think I wasn't allowed to eat anything." She shook with laughter and mischief.

Exasperating woman. He looked heavenward before he took the wrapper off his candy.

A few minutes later, Keisha's hand delivered several caramels into his.

Throughout the movie, she handed over candy. She had some herself too. Each portion was divided up evenly, and every time she gave him some, the pressure of her hand was warm and soft.

Man, this was one good movie date.

The movie was at its climax when Keisha once again pressed his hand open. This time Jordan held on when she started to pull away. She tugged again, in vain, and then turned to him with a look of surprise that he could barely discern in the dark room.

"What are you doing?" she whispered.

He leaned toward her. "What, don't you ever do this with your family at the movies?"

She shook her head.

He shrugged. "Maybe it's time for a new tradition."

She frowned, looking down at their hands and back up at him. He moved their hands a little closer to her, hoping she'd feel more comfortable that way. Slowly, her palm relaxed, and she looked up at the movie screen. A light blush touched her cheek, and the corners of her lips turned upward.

The characters in the movie kissed. Keisha's eyebrows flew upward, and her blush deepened. Laughter rumbled in Jordan's throat. If he didn't miss his guess, she had forgotten about the more romantic parts of this comedy when she made the invitation.

He popped the candy in his mouth with his other hand. They held hands until the end of the movie and the beginning of the music and rolling credits.

"So this is the Johansen way?" he asked when they made their way outside afterward. "Smuggling candy indoors. Is that allowed?"

She looked uncomfortable. "I don't know. I guess they want us to spend money on their snacks, but come on, who doesn't keep candy in their purse? Nothing wrong with eating whatever you happen to have with you."

"Right, I should start carrying candy around in my purse too," he said with a snort. Keisha's laughter rang out, and his chest expanded with sweet victory.

Their talk on the way home was enjoyable, but he sensed that she felt a new awareness around him. It didn't show in her words, but it showed in her posture and her eyes. She seemed unsure whether to raise or lower her defenses.

Maybe that was why he felt the need to at last ask for forgiveness for the three years of enmity he had caused.

Keisha turned off the ignition and reached for her door.

"I need to apologize," Jordan blurted out.

She looked back at him with a curious expression. "*Now* what are we apologizing for?"

"Not we." He had to be clear about this. "Me. For starting our neighbor feud."

Now she frowned. "Did you start it?"

"Don't you remember?" The beginning of it all was etched in his mind.

She shrugged. "I think we both started it."

"No," he insisted. "Remember the day you moved in? You were doing some sort of initiation ceremony to start off you and your kids' lives in your new house. You were Elizabeth Swann, and they were all pirates." He gazed at her, wishing he hadn't messed up that day, and Keisha gazed back.

***

SHE REMEMBERED, ALL RIGHT. Her hand dropped from the door handle as she thought of that day. She had arrived at her new home only months after her broken spirit decided it would never be broken again.

"This'll be our paradise," she told her anxious children, opening her arms wide and twirling around as if life was ever so carefree as they stood in the spacious living room with all their stuff. "Come on. We have to start things off right in our home. Let's dedicate the place."

They came to life, squealing and clapping as she pulled dress-up clothes from their luggage. Nearly everyone got to dress as pirates, but there were no pirate clothes for her, not even an eye patch, after Lizzie and the three-year-old twins claimed the accessories. Their wooden swords were also much too small for an adult.

In the end, she put on a pretty, old-fashioned dress and told them she was Elizabeth Swann from Pirates of the Caribbean.

They went to the backyard, June bringing her best slingshot and Frayden a mini-cannon. It was a metal case he had covered with aluminum foil for a school project.

"Are you ready, June?" Keisha asked, sweeping Kale into her arms and resting him on her hip to end his squabbling with his twin.

"Ready," June said in determination.

"All right." Keisha raised her voice. "Fire!" Frayden banged a drumstick on his cannon, making the metal emit an echoing boom, and June shot her slingshot off into the only tree in the yard.

"Fire," June echoed loudly.

"Fire," Lizzie and Frayden yelled, and the twins joined in a half second late while Frayden boomed his cannon again and again and June shot another rock at the tree.

"I remember that clearly," Keisha said.

"So you remember me breaking up the party," Jordan said with regret.

"What's the meaning of all this?" a man's voice roared from the neighboring yard. "Stop your noise and let other people live, why don't you?"

Keisha whipped around to look at him, her heart pounding against her chest, flashbacks of Henry's tirades bombarding her. Her children shrank away from the man's shout. Fire, strong and angry, rose inside her.

"You, sir, are disrupting our ceremony," she said haughtily, putting on an act for her children. It was better to make them think they were still playing a game.

Apparently it worked, because Kale chose that moment to bounce in her arms, point his wooden sword, and yell, "Fire!"

Inspired, Carl raised his own sword and ran toward the neighbor behind the hedge, yelling, "Fire, fire!"

Keisha snatched him up quicker than thought.

"You're disrupting my day. And your two-year-olds are out of control," the man said viciously.

"Three-year-olds," she snapped and looked away. "Ignore the rude man, children."

That got him more fired up. "Where's your husband? Let me speak to him."

The words struck, breaking a dam inside her and letting loose a flash-flood of anger. She stood two inches taller and looked down her nose at him in fury.

"You just stay away from my family," she yelled, and then she turned on her heel and ushered her children inside.

She shook her head. "I was so mad at you. But I don't remember you actually starting the feud."

Jordan's brow creased. "I got us off on the wrong foot from the beginning. I'm not sure who played the first prank, but after that, we'd both yell at each other whenever we met. I think within the week, we'd started sneaking around and leaving 'surprises' and traps for each other. It was my fault we hated each other from the start, so the feud is my fault."

"Hm." She shrugged noncommittally. In spite of her fury that day, she couldn't put all the blame on him. "It took two to fight."

Jordan looked away for a moment before he caught her gaze. "You know what my problem was? When I saw you with your children, I couldn't help but admire you. It felt like a betrayal of my wife's memory."

Keisha's eyes widened. He *admired* her on that first day? That was impossible.

"So I covered it up by being rude." He set his jaw. "I'm more sorry than you know."

Her emotions whirled, but one thing she knew for sure: she wanted him to stop apologizing and feeling remorse. Leaning over, she put her hand on his sleeve. "Jordan, I forgive you. Okay? It's water under the bridge. I promise."

He stared at her. She blinked and withdrew her arm, growing nervous as she remembered the movie hand-holding. It had sent currents running through her.

She cleared her throat. "What's done is done. I don't bear a grudge." At last she opened her car door.

"Keisha." His voice stopped her again, and she was struck not for the first time by how gently he could say her name when he wasn't yelling. "I'm glad you decided to change things between us. I'll have to thank Frayden someday."

She nodded slowly. Jordan looked at her in a way she wasn't used to, but the image of his beer can rolled into her mind, and she dropped her eyes. Her goals were to be friends with Jordan, to keep her children happy and safe, and to stay true to God, who had already enriched her life. No matter how fun the hose fight had been, no matter how sweet the handholding today, she wouldn't fall for someone who drank alcohol. They were friends only.

She swallowed and got out. "See you later."

When she entered the house, June was there reaching for the door with a stubborn expression. Behind her, Frayden reached for June as though to hold her back. Both of them stopped as Keisha shut the door and tilted her head at them.

"What were you doing in the car?" both children asked together. Frayden sounded elated. June, angry.

"Chatting," she answered and picked her way through the hall. "Why?"
Frayden's face fell.

June gave Keisha a sharp glance. After a moment, her face softened, and she shrugged and walked away.

***

SHE HAD FORGIVEN HIM. She had really, truly forgiven him. Jordan smiled to himself when he took the kids to church that Sunday. He watched Keisha in wonder during sacrament meeting, only slightly dismayed to have played into the missionaries' wishes by coming to church for the second week in a row. His children wanted to be here, after all, and he didn't mind attending. But he didn't *need* it.

Was this what it felt like to be forgiven? His heart pumped strong and fierce. He and Keisha had both changed and moved on. Things were finally starting to head toward love. If not before, then during the movie he and Keisha watched, she had realized they were dating. And she hadn't pulled away. Things could only get better from here. He didn't need to join a religion to be with her.

"What would Jesus say?" the speaker at the podium asked, breaking into his thoughts. "When I thought of it that way, I knew I couldn't let my temper get away from me. I tried—"

What would Jesus say?

The question buzzed like a firefly, and several scripture passages sprang to mind. Jordan scowled. Jesus did repeatedly command people to be baptized, but nowhere was it recorded that entailed committing to go to church every week, nor that one would have to stop drinking alcohol.

Was Jordan willfully disobeying Jesus when he refused to commit to specific rules and be baptized?

The thought made him uncomfortable. Yet if Keisha could forgive him, surely God could do the same without a ceremony. If Keisha could learn to love him without forcing him to make additional changes in his life, so could God.

Besides, Jordan was willing to keep some of the commandments the missionaries had taught him. The law of chastity he would keep for sure. It would be an affront to his wife's memory to live with another woman without honorably committing to be with her through marriage. Not to mention that if he and Keisha made it to that point, it would be crazy to spend a night together without commitment, what with all the children in both their families.

That made him pause. Could he provide for nine children? What would that look like?

Man, he was getting ahead of himself. Even so, it didn't hurt to think ahead. He had felt a tug toward Keisha for three years, and things were finally changing.

He bowed his head and said a prayer of thanks. God had helped him stop pranking Keisha, and he had no doubt it was divine intervention that had caused Frayden to speak up, making Keisha stop her part of the feud.

What would Jesus say?

His scowl returned in full force.

Beside him, Imogene reached up and shoved her fingers into his cheeks. "Dad, you need to smile," she whispered and raised his cheeks, forcing his lips up.

***

June punched the air and followed up with a high kick. It felt strange to do jiujitsu on a Sunday in the backyard, but she needed something to release her frustrations.

Jordan wasn't a bad guy, but Mom wasn't available. Not yet anyway. He couldn't stare at her in church, and he couldn't talk to her in the car so long that they might end up kissing.

One week. She needed one week before she knew which way to let things go.

She punched, blocked, and punched, then lowered her hands while her breathing slowed. Jordan couldn't mess things up too much in a week. Mom would be all right. June was overreacting.

She was probably just nervous about the weekend.

She tensed and clenched her jaw. No, she wasn't nervous. Nervous meant fear. Fear meant weakness, and June didn't have any of that. She was confident, she was strong, and she was ready. She knew exactly what she was doing.

Chapter 20

Jordan pushed away from his computer, stretched, and got a beer from the fridge.

The crisp fall air and a sweet smell of grass drifted through the open kitchen window, and he could hear the kids playing in the yard. This was too good an afternoon to waste indoors. He walked out to the front porch and sat down.

Imogene and Carl were making a bridge with their arms for Kale to walk under at a crouch. His impish daughter giggled and lowered her arms at just the right time to destroy Kale's passage.

"Hey," Kale protested.

"Sorry." Imogene laughed. "We'll do it right this time. Try again."

But once she had coaxed him into walking under their arms again, she and Carl laughed and let the bridge collapse anew.

Jordan took a gulp from his can and kept the taste on his tongue for as long as he could. Back when he first started drinking, he hadn't loved the flavor, but now it was hard to imagine giving it up, and he sure didn't care for people telling him he should.

One of Lizzie's books lay in the grass, but the girl herself was running around with Samuel, Solomon and Frayden, kicking a soccer ball between their two front lawns and trying not to hit the twins and Imogene too often.

Little clangs from the kitchen next door mingled with the savory smells of whatever Keisha was cooking. Curry, if he didn't miss his guess. Jordan stretched out his legs and watched the twins now collapse a bridge over Imogene's head.

He tensed as the soccer ball flew past him and hit his door, then bounced back and stopped beside him.

"I got it!" Lizzie yelled, French-braided hair flying behind her as she ran over.

"Look!" Carl and Kale yelled. "There's a mouse!"

"Where?" Imogene yelled. "I didn't see it. Where did it go?"

The soccer-playing boys crowded over to look at where the twins were pointing.

Lizzie reached the front porch. Her gaze shifted from the ball to Jordan's hands.

She jerked to a stop, and all color fled her face.

Jordan frowned and looked down. His hands were curled around his beer can. He looked back up.

The girl in front of him didn't move. Though her chest heaved from running, she seemed to force her breathing to quiet. Her eyes were wide as she stared.

It was the beer. It had to be. Jordan's throat felt tight. Somehow, he needed to get her out of her shock. "Here." He reached for the ball.

Lizzie sprang back with a cry. "S-sorry," she stuttered.

What was wrong with her? Jordan looked up at her, willing her to know he wouldn't hurt her. The girl tensed as if to run. Desperate to stop and reassure her, he exclaimed, "Lizzie."

For a split second, she looked up at him, and he got the full brunt of the terror in her eyes. It was as though he had grown horns. Under her gaze, he felt like a monster, and he was pinned to the spot, knowing anything he did or said could scare her even more.

Then she whipped around and ran inside her house.

Jordan let out a wounded noise. He couldn't go after her—it would only make things worse—but he scrambled to his feet, unable to stay still. None of the others had noticed. They were busy looking around for some rodent or other.

He retreated inside his own house, shutting the door and hurrying to the kitchen on rubbery legs, putting distance between him and the girl. He had scared Lizzie. She was terrified—of alcohol? Of men who drank? Her mom hated alcohol. Why hadn't he realized it was such a big deal? Why hadn't he cared?

He looked around wildly, caught sight of the sink, and turned his can upside down above it.

The liquid spilled out until there were only drops left. He shook it, but it wasn't enough. Backing up, he opened the garbage can and threw it in. That wasn't enough either. The memory of Lizzie's gaze seared him. Was it Keisha's ex-husband who had taught her to be afraid?

He grabbed the top of the liner in the garbage can and pulled it out, tying a knot. But then what? He couldn't take it out of the house. He couldn't bear to see Lizzie or expose her to the sight of him if she were to come back out.

He backed away again and turned and took the stairs. Bypassing the kids' rooms, he went to his own and shut the door.

Since his wife's death, he rarely spent time in here beyond the obligatory hours of sleep. Now, though, it seemed there was nowhere else to go.

With a groan, he fell to his knees and clasped his hands. "I didn't mean to scare her. I promise. I'm not a monster."

Why did she have to get so scared?

"Look, I'm sorry." Was he praying? It seemed that way. The little prayers he had said, sometimes in annoyance, in order to follow the missionaries' advice, had been vastly different from this. "I don't want her to be afraid of me. Please, please make her not be afraid of me. Please make this feeling go away."

Her scared eyes bored into his mind.

"I'll stop drinking. Okay? I'll change. For Lizzie. And for Keisha. And for you, God. I'll do anything. Just please help me stop feeling this guilt."

It roiled in his stomach, guilt and injustice and pain.

"Please, Father. I can't bear this feeling. I know I'm being selfish thinking about myself, but I can't bear this. I'll try to make things right. Just please take this feeling away from me now."

He breathed hard. He had done nothing evil, but he was no longer interested in trying to excuse himself. He needed to have Lizzie's look of horror erased. He needed to not have it directed at him. He clenched and unclenched his hands and eventually felt the wetness of tears on his cheeks.

Slowly, his breathing came easier. The weight on his heart began to lighten. It felt good simply to breathe, in and out, in and out.

He got up off his stiff knees and sat back on his heels to lean against the door.

The light feeling grew. He saw in his mind's eye a scared Lizzie, but then he saw her running and laughing and smiling. He didn't feel so bad anymore. He didn't feel like a terror.

His head hurt but in a way that felt good. He stopped feeling sick. In fact, he felt lighter than he usually did, and warm inside. The warmth spread, and as he said a wordless prayer, it felt even better. Then an overwhelming feeling of love came out of nowhere and covered him like a blanket.

It surprised him. He couldn't stop the tears. Instead, he put his head in his hands and let them flow.

Hunched over on the floor, in his room where he had felt so alone these past several years, he felt happier than he ever remembered being.

***

June scraped her dinner plate clean and watched Mom's food grow cold while she was stuck on the phone. Her nerves thrummed. She was so close to finding out the fate of her family.

"This week?" Mom asked, looking shocked.

June frowned and stood. Picking up her plate, she came over to Mom by the counter and, with her most charming grin, put her ear close to the phone. It worked. Mom smiled back and didn't move away.

Jordan's voice was on the line. June had heard Mom comfort Lizzie earlier. Something about being scared of Jordan drinking. Yet Mom wasn't yelling at him.

Jordan sounded emotional. "You can tell anyone who might need to know that I'm going to keep the Word of Wisdom. And all those other laws. If God comes out next year and tells us through his prophets that we're not to drink water anymore, I'll keep that commandment too." Mom laughed, a sound of disbelief mixed with humor, and June put down her plate, feeling suddenly weak. Jordan's voice softened. "It's worth it. For him, it's worth it."

Was he talking about God? Something had changed, something huge.

"Jordan, we'll be there," Mom said.

"Thank you. There's so much I should have done differently." Jordan's voice was tight. "Thank you, Keisha. I'll see you soon."

Mom hung up. June stepped back, getting a clear view of her stunned expression as she announced, "Jordan's getting baptized."

"What?" Lizzie cried.

"Yes!" Frayden pumped his fist in the air.

June blinked. Then she began to smile. "That's so good." After all, Jordan was a good guy. She was happy he wanted in on the things they'd all been learning.

"Shoot," Lizzie said. "I thought I'd get baptized before him, but I want to finish the Book of Mormon first."

"Congradderlations to Jordan!" Carl raised his fork in the air, and Kale met his fork with his own, starting a fencing match.

"When's he getting baptized?" June asked.

"Saturday morning."

Dread filled June.

"That's fast," Frayden said.

"But Mom!" June straightened as her plans flashed before her eyes. "That's my sleepover."

Mom blinked. "Right. Sorry, June. You'll have to tell the girls you can't be there."

There was no way she could postpone this. It had to be now, before Mom and Jordan got closer. Things could really speed up between them now that Jordan had made up his mind. Besides, there was Imogene. Her slip-up when the Taylors visited had showed that people were getting attached. That girl had too much power. She could sway Mom before Mom even knew what hit her.

June flattened her hands against the dining table. "No, Mom, I can't miss this. We've planned it for a long time."

"Hey, we're excited about Jordan getting baptized, right?" Mom touched her hair. "I'm sorry it conflicts with your schedule, June, but I want us all there to support Jordan."

Frayden spoke up, his voice annoyingly sage. "Lizzie, remember this when you have a sleepover: always put family before friends."

Lizzie turned to him. "But Jordan's not—"

"Jordan's getting baptized, Jordan's getting baptized," Frayden sang, and the twins grabbed his hands and danced around with him, chorusing the words.

"Mom, does this mean he'll stop drinking?" Lizzie asked while the boys continued their dance.

"It does." Mom smiled at her. "He's going to try to do all the things God asks of us."

This had to stop. June drew herself up and summoned her firmest, most stubborn voice as she talked over her siblings. "Mom, make him reschedule. He could get baptized on Sunday just as well. *You* did it on a Sunday, and it's only a day later."

"June, I can't—"

"Just tell him to do it on another day," June exploded and ran from the room.

***

JORDAN WAS AMAZED AT how different he felt. A line of communication had opened, and he couldn't seem to stop speaking to God over and over that day. "Thank you for this," and "I should have done that" were his mantra. He said a full, earnest prayer that evening, thanking God for making his presence felt and vowing he would try to live worthy of his love.

All the excuses he had had for not joining this church, all his thoughts about not needing to come close to God had disappeared. Why *wouldn't* he want to be close to God? He had intentionally kept his family at a distance from religion, but no more. Nothing could be better for them than the full light of Christ.

The next day, he managed to approach Lizzie outside and apologize. He hadn't thought it possible to talk to her so soon, but there was no fear in her eyes when she saw him. God had taken away his feeling of horror *and* Lizzie's terror. It made him want to sing, although he couldn't remember any hymns. Maybe he'd have to start memorizing something, unless God was okay listening to country.

God probably did enjoy country music, now that Jordan thought about it. He wasn't a God who looked down on people and forced them to follow a bunch of specifications. He was a Father who loved his children and who had to be proud of the creative things they made: art, music, and more.

The answer to Jordan's prayer in his room replaced his perspective on life and splashed it with color. Jesus's death and resurrection, the creation of this world, and the people around him meant so much more than he used to think.

His actions in the last few months stabbed his conscience though. He had thought his regrets regarding Keisha had ended with the feud, but now he realized how proud he had been even after they started making friends. He had expected her to conform to him and his ways. He had hoped to date her, possibly even marry her, and yet had never once considered giving up the alcohol she hated. Was that love? His stubbornness indicated he didn't love her anywhere near as much as himself.

If their relationship was to become something more, then rather than wait for Keisha to accept him, he needed to do something about himself and make sure he was ready to care for her the way she deserved. He needed to change.

Baptism would be a start, washing away his sins up till now, but he'd have to work to change from then on too.

***

KEISHA FELT UNGROUNDED, AS though the floor had been removed from underneath her. In one swift phone call, Jordan had removed all the barriers she kept putting up. Her stomach bubbled with a mixture of excitement and uncertainty as she herded her children to the Taylors' door that Thursday evening.

This wasn't about proving herself to Frayden any longer. It was something more.

Frayden was bright and cheerful as he whistled a tune. June seemed to have made peace with Jordan's timing despite her initial anger. If she wasn't smiling, at least she wasn't frowning.

Lizzie raised her hand to knock, but before she could, the door opened, creaking inward to reveal an empty hallway with the lights turned off.

Well, empty apart from the rows of shoes and light jackets that peppered it. Keisha doubted they were usually this neatly lined up.

A giggle sounded behind the door.

Fighting a smile, Keisha stepped inside. "Hello?"

The giggle grew.

"Hello?" Jordan's confused voice echoed from a different room.

Carl and Kale rushed past Keisha. "Mom, she's behind the door," they yelled, reaching for it, but just then a screeching yell halted them all, and Solomon jumped off the stairs and landed in front of them. Keisha clapped a hand to her mouth, stifling the urge to laugh.

"Kids, what are you doing?" Jordan asked, appearing in the doorway with a spatula. Keisha felt a rush on seeing him. "Why are the lights off? Hey, welcome. Whoa."

Imogene ran giggling out from behind the door and into the living room, and the twins and Lizzie and even June ran after her.

Keisha couldn't contain her joy. "Congratulations," she exclaimed and threw her arms around Jordan.

He stiffened for a moment in obvious surprise. Then he hugged her back until she feared he wouldn't let go.

Solomon let out another howl, and Jordan released Keisha and clapped his hands to his ears. "Tone it down, Solomon. Come on in, Keisha."

He took her hand and led her inside. Keisha's heart pounded at the thought of letting the children see, yet she didn't want to drop his hand. He was through with alcohol. He was about to embrace the church of Jesus Christ. What she had started to think and feel on some of their dates, she could now allow herself to feel.

Jordan let go and backed away the tiniest bit toward the kitchen. "We're still cooking." He didn't seem to want to leave her side. "We have jigsaw puzzles if you want to—"

"Come on, we'll give you a tour of the house," Solomon said, grabbing Keisha's wrist and tugging her away from his dad.

The Taylors' house was similar to the Johansens' on the inside, but the kitchen's location was a bit off and the wall of the living room was a dark wood rather than white plaster. Keisha had found that out the first time she sneaked in on a revenge mission.

Imogene led the way—right up to the wall, where she stood and smoothed her hand over it. "This is our wall."

"I see," Keisha said. There were nails up higher where Imogene couldn't reach, but no pictures hung on them.

"As you can see, we don't have a lot of pictures. Clearly, this place needs a woman's touch," Samuel said, hands in his pockets as he looked at the bare wood.

Keisha's cheeks warmed.

"This way," said Solomon, continuing on with the tour. "Here's our washer and dryer. Bathroom's right there if anyone needs to use it."

"Do you only have one?" Carl asked, intrigued.

"No, there's another upstairs," Imogene piped up.

"If we only had one bathroom," Kale said, looking at Carl as possibilities flew through his mind, "we could lock ourselves in and no one could use it all day. Wouldn't that be funny?"

"I don't know." Carl frowned. "I feel bad when I have to wait for the restroom. The others—"

"We'd just have to go in the backyard," Lizzie said.

"Or in the front yard," June said with a wicked grin.

"Or we'd come next door and ask you guys if we could use yours," Frayden told Samuel.

"You wouldn't want to be stuck in the bathroom all day," Imogene told the twins. "It'd be *bo*-ring."

Carl's eyes widened with a new idea. "No, it wouldn't. We'd bring all our best games in, and we'd bring our stuffed animals and have them swim in the tub—"

"No one's locking themselves in the bathroom," Keisha said, realizing she needed to put a stop to the idea before it became too exciting.

"This is Dad's study." Samuel swept a hand at the cozy room. A computer sat on a smooth desk, and a plush-backed rolling chair was pushed against it, but there were other things in the room too: a bookshelf with toys and books for several different age groups and a comic book lying open on the carpeted floor. "We're all usually allowed in here while he works," Samuel said.

"If no one can lock themselves in, then anyone can walk in on them while they're using the toilet," Lizzie whispered, making Keisha's mouth tug.

"I just bet he put all his papers away and locked them in the drawers," Solomon mumbled and tried one of the drawers. It rattled but didn't pull out. He shrugged and then grinned from ear to ear. "But maybe we can show you some things on his computer."

"I don't think—" Keisha began as the Taylor siblings pulled out the rolling chair and pushed her into it.

Samuel raised his voice and bellowed, "Dad, would you come type in your password?"

Imogene wrinkled her nose at the open comic book and bent to pick it off the floor. "I think Daddy wanted the room to be nice when you came." She took the offending object to the bookshelf. Laying it down carefully, she grabbed both hands full of railroad tracks and stuffed animals. Trailing toys behind her as she crossed to the Johansens, she held what hadn't fallen from her arms out toward the twins and Lizzie, her face bright. "I like to play in here. Wanna look at my toys?"

A voice from the doorway made Keisha's head jerk in that direction.

"That's my work computer," Jordan said quietly, leaning against the doorway with his arms crossed against his chest. "There's absolutely *no reason* for me to log in while the Johansens are here."

Samuel appeared to be fighting laughter, but Keisha's palms began to sweat. She cleared her throat and joked, "You know, back when we were still feuding, I used to dream about sneaking over and going through your computer to uncover your illegal activities."

"A-ha-he-huh-huh," Jordan said. Or at least that was what it sounded like.

Now who was nervous? But why?

"Why, Dad?" Imogene said, dropping the rest of her toys on the floor. "They should see the pic—"

"Not today, Imogene," he interrupted, flushing.

The little girl's face darkened.

"Dad, quick," Selima's voice called from somewhere. "It's boiling hard."

Jordan looked hassled. "Why don't we all go back to the living room?"

Samuel's hands hung loose as he walked to the doorway and leaned in. "Someday she'll have to know your secrets," he said in a voice that carried beyond Jordan.

"I want my mom!"

Startled, everyone looked at Imogene, whose eyes had filled with tears. With a sob, the girl ran from the room.

Jordan grabbed Solomon. "Go help your sister in the kitchen."

"What? I don't know how to cook."

"Just do what she tells you. It'll be fine." Jordan ran off after Imogene.

Solomon rushed to the kitchen. Keisha and the others returned to the living room in silence. Samuel cleared his throat and pulled out a jigsaw puzzle, not looking at anyone in particular.

"Yes, let's work on this," Keisha forced herself to say. "Come on, guys. That's a cute picture."

Several minutes later, Jordan came back with Imogene. The girl reached out for Keisha, and before she could stop to think about it, Keisha took her in her lap. The sweet, heavy weight made her heart fill. Imogene turned around and began picking out puzzle pieces. Keisha kept her steady with an arm around her waist.

June's jaw clenched while she focused on the puzzle. She was unhappy about something. Maybe she was thinking about the sleepover. June scowled up at Jordan. Keisha followed her glance and then grew warm under Jordan's stare. "Uh, do you need any help with dinner prep?" she asked.

He ducked his head. "No. I'm glad you're sitting with Imogene."

He blushed, but Keisha blushed harder.

***

Jordan leaned against the door with a sigh after the Johansens left. Bone-weary, he dragged himself away and called out, "Bedtime" in a voice that sounded exhausted even to him.

Fortunately, Imogene didn't require much of his time before she snuggled under the covers and went to sleep. Would that she had been this easy to deal with earlier.

He made his way downstairs and tightened his lips when he saw Samuel. "My office," he barked out. "Now."

Samuel followed him meekly. Once inside, Jordan whirled around to face him. "What was that today? Showing Keisha my computer and everything?"

Samuel kept his hands in his pockets. "We just wanted to push you along a little."

"What have you told Imogene? She's clearly decided I'm going to marry Keisha. What if that doesn't end up happening?"

Samuel lowered his gaze. "I'm sorry. I didn't realize she had taken it to heart like that."

Jordan held up his hands. "I don't need an extra push from you kids. Things are going fine. I'm dating Keisha."

"Does *she* know that?"

"I don't know, but you can't rush it. Keisha may make split-moment decisions that change her life, but I'm not like that. I take my time, and I bumble along. I'm sorry if I'm a mess." A mess whose children thought he needed help with dating.

Samuel stared at him. "Man, you must have it bad for her if you're getting down on yourself like that. Dad, you're doing fine. In a lot of things. I'm excited about your baptism."

Jordan sighed and rubbed the back of his neck, his anger leaving and exhaustion returning. Samuel knew how to calm him. "So am I."

"I was thinking. I'd like to be baptized too one of these days."

"Really?" Jordan raised his head. "You know that means committing to that Word of Wisdom, right?"

"Among other things. I'm cool with it."

Jordan felt his spirits rise. "Let's work toward that then." The room seemed lighter than it had a moment ago. "Are your friends still giving you trouble?"

"They've actually started to ignore me when they see me. It's easier than I thought it would be after I told them I was done. Except they don't like it when they see me talk to Cole. Then they threaten to beat me up." Samuel gave a ghost of a smile. "And I can't seem to help him."

"Does he want to try going to addiction recovery meetings?"

"I don't know. I haven't asked."

"Ask," Jordan said. "And go with him if he says yes. If he says no, you and I can go. It could give us an idea of how to help."

Samuel nodded, thoughts flashing through his eyes. Jordan held still. This seemed like one of those times he needed to let him think.

"Can we talk to his parents?"

Jordan blinked. "What?"

There was a new light in Samuel's eyes. "You should have seen him when I mentioned your advice from one of our talks together. I can't stop thinking about it. He was shocked to hear that you and I talk. I think if you and I could go with him to talk to his parents—if only they'll react the right way and not freak out." He bit his lip. "If they can get involved, I think it'll help."

Jordan's heart swelled. He felt a great respect for his son, along with a haunting wish that they could improve things for his friend. With a lump in his throat, he put his hand on Samuel's shoulder. "If your friend agrees to that, I'll go."

Chapter 21

The Saturday morning of Jordan's baptism dawned bright. Keisha called upstairs several times for everyone to get up, and then she pulled cereal bowls from the cupboard while scrolling through the songs on her playlist. She wanted to listen to something spiritual on the way to the baptism. It might help calm her heart, which beat fast at the thought of seeing Jordan today.

She was already dressed, which was risky, but hopefully she could avoid stains. Jordan wouldn't think she had dressed up for him, would he? Just because her dress *happened* to be new. The green color went well with her russet-colored hair, and the white flowers and flowy length put her in mind of fancy dinners and dances.

"Mom, will I feel the Spirit when Jordan gets the Gift of the Holy Ghost?" Lizzie asked, appearing at the bottom of the stairs in her yellow pajamas. "I felt it when you got it."

"You did?" Keisha came over and gave her a hug. "Then you likely will today too." She ought to find a time to interview her children about their experience at her baptismal service. It might do all of them good, including her, and would help them prepare for their own baptisms.

"This is early," Frayden muttered, stumbling to the cupboard and pulling out all the sugary cereals Keisha had left in there on purpose.

"Where's everyone else?" Keisha headed for the stairs but was waylaid by the twins, who came bouncing down, tugging back and forth on a pile of clothes. When one twin tried to go on Keisha's right and the other on her left, she gripped the clothes that pushed against her. "Whoa, whoa, hold it. What's going on?"

Carl looked up as though he'd just now noticed her. "Kale says they're his clothes, but I think they're mine and those are his."

"Well, don't tear your Sunday clothes. Look at this. Who wants this nice shirt? Wow, it looks so nice. Who wants it?"

"Me, me," both of them shouted, forgetting how eager they had been to pawn that shirt off on the other person.

"Okay, go eat your breakfast while I figure out how to divide up these clothes." She shook out the shirts.

"Think Great, Mom," Carl told her.

"Do it like Solomon did," Lizzie said, holding a dripping spoonful of cereal above her bowl.

"Solomon Taylor or Solomon from the Bible?" Frayden grinned.

"Bible. Cut the shirts and the pants in two."

"Who's he?" asked Kale and picked out his favorite pieces from the cereal box.

"He was a very wise person," Lizzie answered.

"Did Solomon think Great too?"

"Where's June?" Keisha asked.

"Can you do my hair, Mom?" Lizzie looked hopeful.

"And leave mine be?" Frayden pleaded.

Keisha opened her mouth only to be interrupted.

"We're done eating, Mom."

"Already, Carl?" She turned and looked at his bowl. It wasn't empty.

"Yeah. I can't eat very much right now, but if you bring snacks to the baptism, I'll eat them. Especially if it's gummy worms."

She shook her head. "If you're hungry, keep eating. If you're done, go upstairs and get changed."

Carl and Kale scrambled from the table. Keisha watched them disappear and then looked at the clothes she was still holding. With a sigh, she set off after them.

"Where are our clothes?" Carl howled.

"We left them downstairs."

They barreled into Keisha, and she had to fight to keep her balance.

"I have your clothes right here," she panted, steadying herself on the banister. "Take them and go back to your rooms."

"Mom, where's June?" Frayden yelled from the living room.

"I'm getting her," Keisha called back.

"I'm coming up too. June, you better not be sick." Frayden's steps sounded on the stairs behind her.

Keisha walked down the hall to her oldest daughter's room. When she put her hand on the doorknob, she felt it. Dread to the pit of her stomach.

Pushing open the door, she stepped inside. "June?" She stared into the darkness. Until the light came on.

"Is she sick?" Frayden asked at the door, his hand next to the light switch.

Keisha felt sick. She approached the bed and asked the empty covers, "Where is she?" Pulling the covers back made no difference. June wasn't there.

"Why isn't she here?" Frayden asked, coming closer.

Carl and Kale ran into the room and jumped up on the bed. They hadn't gotten changed, but Keisha didn't care. She looked around. Had June even slept here last night?

Lizzie tiptoed inside, her wide eyes asking a question. Carl and Kale bounced on the bed until they tumbled off.

"The sleepover," Keisha said. "There was that sleepover. But who—" She brushed her hands over her face, remembering only the names of a few friends who were going. "Who was it with?"

"Is this secret?" Carl asked. He and Kale pulled a shoebox from under the bed, the lid off. "Why does she have papers down here?"

Frayden leaned in to look. "They're letters."

Keisha grabbed the top three or four sheets and turned them over in her hand. She prepared to tell the twins not to look through June's private things while she shuffled through the pages, looking for a hint. Surely June would have left a note.

The words on the first envelope she came across struck her, sending her reeling: Henry Johansen.

"Isn't that Dad's name?" Lizzie whispered.

Keisha's hands sped up, flying through the small stack and handing several pages to Lizzie to read. Her stomach clenched tighter and tighter, her former husband's handwriting and words making her hands shake. Words like "sorry" and "can't wait" sprang out at her like little monsters pecking her face. *Can't wait for what?*

"'I'm preparing the house for your arrival,'" she read in a croak. Her eyes skimmed the letter. "She was planning to visit him this weekend." How could that be?

"But Daddy's mean, isn't he?" Carl exclaimed in the silence that followed. "Why would June go to him?"

Keisha got to her feet, feeling like she was made of wood. Each step on the stairs was painful. Likewise in the hall. Her children followed her outside, their voices strangely distant.

A deep laugh broke through her trance. "Are your kids wearing pajamas to my baptism?" Jordan asked.

Keisha stopped. Jordan and his children were on the other side of the driveway. She couldn't look at them.

"Jordan." She closed her eyes, her anguish complete. "I'm sorry."

She walked to her car and reached for the door. Lizzie slid right up in front of her and put her back against the car, covering the handle. "Mom, no. You can't drive. You'll get in an accident."

Keisha stared at her in shock. "Lizzie," she said in a voice she barely recognized. "Get away from that door."

"No. You're trauma—traumatic—" She struggled for the right word but kept her hands firmly planted behind her. "You're upset right now, and something will go wrong, I know it."

Keisha tried to get to the handle behind her, the uselessness of this sudden fight riling her. "Lizzie, there is nothing, *including* careless driving, that will stop me from going up there and *ripping* Henry's throat out. Do you understand me?"

"What's going on?" Jordan asked, stepping closer, his voice tentative.

Carl turned to him, wide-eyed. "June ran away."

"June's gone," Kale echoed, sounding lost.

"What? Did she go to her dad's place?"

Keisha whirled around and stared, along with everyone else, at Samuel. The young man flushed.

"What do you know of this?" Keisha asked, with no time to lose.

He swallowed. "She asked me some weeks ago if I would drive her up there in a month. She was going to pay me what she earned mowing lawns. I didn't feel good about it, so I said no, and I thought she gave up on the idea. It felt like a half-baked plan. She was embarrassed and asked me not to mention it to anyone, and I thought she decided not to do it."

Keisha turned back to her car and her daughter that was in the way.

"Please," Lizzie insisted, but she wasn't looking at her mom.

"I'll drive," Jordan answered.

Keisha whirled back to face him again. "What?"

He watched Lizzie. "Will you feel better about that?"

She nodded, her back still braced against the car.

Frustration tore at Keisha's insides. Each minute wasted was another minute June was in danger. "Jordan, you can't," she said tersely. "Your baptism—"

"Oh, yeah. Right. I'm scheduled to make a covenant to help my neighbor and do what Christ would do." Jordan's voice was sarcastic to the extreme. "What'll it mean if I ignore your situation to go get baptized?" He wrenched his car door open and jerked his head at her. "I can get baptized later, Keisha. Come on."

"Mom." Frayden's choked voice stopped her. His face was scrunched up, and he didn't bother to stop the tears that welled up in his eyes. "I don't want you to go." The tears ran over, sliding down his cheeks.

She put her hands on his shoulders. "I need to go, Frayden, and I need to go now," she said in a low voice, tense with the need to leave but aching at her ten-year-old's agony.

"He'll hit you," he whispered while another tear welled over and reddened his cheek.

Keisha set her jaw. "No, he won't," she promised.

Frayden wiped his sleeve across his face. "Will he hurt June?"

She squeezed his shoulders, the urge to go getting stronger. "I won't let him. *We* won't let him." Frayden looked in Jordan's direction. "But we need to go now."

Frayden bit his teeth together and nodded.

In an instant, Keisha hopped into the passenger seat while Jordan barked out to the children, "Watch out for each other. Take good care of the Johansen kids. Samuel and Selima are in charge."

"Call Shawna," said Keisha. "She can help. I'll text Selima her number."

"Let the missionaries know there's no baptism today," Jordan called before he shut his door and turned on the engine. "Where are we going?"

Keisha looked down at the envelope in her hands. Only one part of the address mattered for now. "Nebraska." That was hours away.

Jordan's gaze didn't so much as flicker. "I'll head for the freeway, then."

As they pulled away, Keisha looked in the rearview mirror. The children stood forlornly behind them, more tears streaking down Frayden's face while Samuel and Selima looked at each other and then started to speak to the others.

She felt something hard in her hand as she put on her seatbelt. She looked down at her phone, which was still on Spotify. The device had left lines in her hand where it had been crushed the last few minutes. Loosening her grip, she turned on the music.

Hate Song Number One, as June liked to call it, came on. It took her an eternity to push the button that skipped past the song "Fighter."

"Undo It" was next, Carrie Underwood singing out her regrets for having gotten involved with the guy.

Skip.

"Before He Cheats."

Skip.

"Done," then "Chainsaw," both by Band Perry.

"Cowboy Casanova," a warning to the girl about the bad guy.

Jordan winced as each song came on, but he never said a word.

"Good Girl," another warning.

"Jesus, Take the Wheel."

Her finger paused above the forward skip button.

The soft beginning strains of the song changed the atmosphere in the car. When the lyrics came on, Keisha sat still, listening. The artist's beautiful voice held no anger. The storyline and the pleading chorus advanced, and Keisha didn't move for four minutes.

After the song, silence reigned for two seconds.

She and Jordan both jumped as the next angry song crashed on, but her finger found the back button, and "Jesus, Take the Wheel" made another soft entry.

Another four minutes of music passed. Then she started it over again.

She sat numb in her seat, her finger hovering over her phone, her eyes looking out the windshield, unfocused. Every time the song stopped, she pushed the back button.

After it played for the ninth or tenth time, Jordan put a restraining hand on hers. Taking his eyes off the road for a moment, he found the pause button and turned off the music.

Silence filled the car. Keisha didn't move her hand. Or her eyes. Or anything.

Jordan took his hand from hers to make a lane change. "What's the deal with June's dad?" he asked cautiously.

Keisha's phone rang in her hands. She sat still for a moment before she looked down at it.

Her mom's name on the screen disappeared as the phone stopped ringing. She felt like she was stuck in a world of molasses, the least movement and the smallest thought requiring great effort. Yet the strange thought, uncharacteristic for her, that her mom ought to know what was going on with June took hold in her mind. Fighting the molasses feeling, she clicked the button to call her back. Too tired to lift the phone to her ear, she turned it on speaker and listened to the usual storm of words that greeted her.

"Keisha, you called back! I was just leaving a message. Now, I'm not calling to say we're joining that church of yours, but I'm also not saying we're *not* joining, if you know what I mean. You've found something quite—quite amazing. I do like that plan of salvation. There are so many commandments I don't have them all memorized yet, but they're starting to make sense."

"What . . ." Keisha couldn't complete the sentence. Her mouth was too dry.

"That church, The Church of Jesus Christ of Latter-day Saints! I knew you wouldn't tell us about it, so we found these young people called missionaries—well, you probably know about them—and we have them over all the time so we can ask them everything from A to Z. Your dad wasn't present for the first two visits because he had other projects on his mind, but once he finished them, he decided to make a project of it to find out everything he can about your church with me, and he caught up quickly. The questions he asks! He already finished the Book of Mormon, and now he's reading it for the second time. *I* haven't finished it yet, and it's not all fun and games, believe *me*. Like those Nephites, I get so annoyed with them. Why do they keep going wicked when things are good?

"But no, that wasn't one of the questions I wanted to ask you. Never mind. This plan of salvation, do you believe it?"

Stunned, Keisha stared at the billboards and trees that flashed by. "Yes."

"And you believe this thing about families being eternal?"

She blinked, and the action didn't take as much effort as it would have a minute ago. "Yes."

"Do you believe Joseph Smith was a prophet?"

Something stirred in her. She couldn't believe she was sitting here sharing her testimony with her mom while miles and miles away, June was in danger. But Mom's questions got Keisha's blood pumping, and she started to feel better. "I do."

"All right. That's all I needed to know. Bye, honey—wait."

Keisha hadn't moved. She might be waking up, but she wasn't fast enough for her mom's abrupt phone manners. Only, Mom hadn't hung up yet.

"How are you doing, Keisha?" she asked. "You sound tense. Are you okay?"

Keisha couldn't believe it. *Mom* was giving her the time she needed to gather her wits.

She would take the opportunity. She swallowed. "Mom, it's June. She's gone to Henry's place."

The line was silent for a moment. "For a visit? You, um, let her?"

"No. She left during the night. I didn't know until this morning."

The silence on the other end was terrible, but Keisha didn't care if Mom judged her for realizing so late that June was gone, or even if she thought Keisha had pushed her daughter to want to leave. All that mattered was June.

"Is she okay?" Mom asked, her voice anguished.

Keisha's heart sped up in fear. "I don't know." Her voice cracked. "We're on our way to bring her back. Would you—would you pray for her?"

"Wait, are you driving right now? You should have told me! You could get in an accident driving and talking on the phone, Keisha. I'm hanging up, but I'll pray, and I'll find your dad and tell him to do the same. Keep us updated, and drive safe."

The line went dead. Keisha felt bad that her mom thought she was driving and was now worried about her safety, but she hadn't been given time to correct her.

She shook her head in awe. She had just asked her parents to pray. That was a definite first. Her parents were investigating the restored church of Jesus Christ, Jordan had just had his first exposure to Mom, and June had run away.

Jordan gave her a sideways glance but asked no questions. His truck ate up the miles on the freeway, and neither he nor Keisha spoke.

Chapter 22

Families were meant to stay together. June knew it, felt it in her bones, along with a burden of duty that had grown heavy the last few weeks. By now she almost wished she could have ignored it, but there had been good memories with Dad. If he was back to who he had once been, then he ought to be with them.

With a tired sigh and her bag of overnight stuff, she stepped off the last bus, ready to find out what she needed to know.

She hadn't slept much on her trip. All night long she had traveled by FlixBus, followed by various city busses, and now it was close to noon. The sun was bright but a cold wind blew, and everywhere was wet.

As she got closer to her dad's address, the lawns looked more unkempt and the streets were filled with trash. Not the nicest of places to live, but she wouldn't judge him too soon. She hadn't even seen him yet.

Soon, she reached his door and tilted her head back. The house was big enough for their family. It was a dirty white with a brown tiled roof. Through the scrawny door, she heard movement inside. She raised her hand and knocked.

Quick heavy footsteps approached, and the door swung open.

June looked up at Henry Johansen, her dad and the man she had once thought she was through with. "I'm here."

"Right." He moved aside to let her enter. She did so but frowned as he strained to look in both directions outside. "Where's your mom?"

"I told you I was coming alone."

He looked down the street again. "Right," he finally repeated and closed the door.

June followed him to the living room. He hadn't so much as asked her to come in.

She studied him. He was built much like Jordan, actually, although his stomach hung out more. Both of them were burly, but Dad had a hard lined face with glinting eyes that didn't smile.

He swept a hand over the living room as if to say she should make herself comfortable. He wasn't ignoring her, then. That was a start.

"Any plans for today?" she asked, keeping her voice casual.

"Yeah, I'm working on something in my room. It'll take a while. Treat the place nicely, all right?"

"Of course," she mumbled as he left.

She inspected the living room. It was a little empty but clean.

Walking to the kitchen, she took another look around. It was clean here too. One of the things he had hated when they lived with him was messes. Mom knew how to keep house, but Dad still got mad when anyone left out toys or drew on the grown-ups' books with crayons or dropped food on the floor.

She opened the fridge, and her gaze zeroed in on the six-pack of beers on the middle shelf. A couple of open cans stood in the door.

She didn't blink. Dad was rapidly failing his test. If he was still drinking, there was no hope left. He had promised in his letters that he had stopped drinking.

She thought back to the bus schedule and imagined leaving.

Just like that? After two minutes in his home?

She hadn't come to take a peek and then leave. She needed to be thorough, to grab this chance to find out as much as possible.

The air from the fridge cooled her. She took out the open cans, shook them to feel how much was left, and poured them into the sink. Then she rinsed them with hot water to get rid of the smell.

It took her a minute to find the garbage can. She stepped on the foot pedal to open it and threw the cans on top of the contents: several crushed cans and a pizza box.

Then she got to work on the six unopened ones.

***

JORDAN FELT KEISHA BESIDE him bracing her feet against the floor of the car as if urging it onward. They were an hour's drive from the place, and they had spoken little besides when he had to ask her for the address.

He exited the freeway and drove through a small city, the reduced speed aggravating. On entering a country road, he sped up.

Ten minutes later, his truck stalled.

Jordan felt each shock as it sputtered to a stop. Impatient, he turned off the engine and ran to the back of the truck.

The first gas can he grabbed nearly flew from his hands. He hadn't expected it to be so light. Was there anything in it?

He shook it, then threw it back in the bed and grabbed another.

"Can I help?" Keisha appeared beside him, her voice rusty.

He picked up the third and last can, baffled. Where was the splashing? The weight? The liquid? "It's empty."

"Take another one. We need to get going."

He dropped it and raised his hands. "They're all empty."

She looked at him and then at the cans in the truck. A line appeared between her brows. "When was the last time you checked them?"

"I don't check them." Did anyone do that? "I bought them all filled up a few years ago for emergencies, but I've never used them. I don't understand this."

A nervous giggle erupted beside him. He turned to look at Keisha. Tears filled her eyes as she started to laugh hysterically. She collapsed against the truck and sank down to sit on the ground.

His lungs tight with worry, Jordan slowly sat down beside her, watching.

She put her head in her hands and let out her breath in something between a laugh and a sob. "It's my fault."

"How?"

"I stole it to get back at you for taking my gas. It was a long time ago." She hiccupped. "I dug my own grave."

Jordan's stomach churned. He had stolen her gas months ago, and here was the punishment for them both. He had never imagined such a consequence. They were too far from both the gas station and their destination for it to make sense to walk.

He pulled out his phone, smacking his elbow against the tire behind him and holding back a curse. A quick call to his car insurance told him it would be at least half an hour before someone would be by with gas. He thanked the agent and dropped the phone to his side.

Fields of shrubs stretched out on both sides of the road. Jordan stared at the distraught woman beside him. She seemed halfway gone, a shadow of the woman he had lived next to and energetically clashed with the past several years. Never had he felt he knew so little about her. He'd received hints about what kind of a man her ex was, but she'd never talked about it. Frayden's reaction when she left had been chilling.

"Do you want to tell me about June's dad?" he asked quietly.

Keisha breathed in deep and raised her face, leaning against the vehicle behind her. "He was abusive. It began around the time June was born. He would grab me and shake me when he got mad."

A combination of fire and ice crawled through Jordan's veins.

"He was usually drunk when he did that. I hated the drinking."

So did Jordan in that moment.

"The first time he hit me was while I was pregnant with Frayden. After that, it got worse."

It hurt to breathe. Whatever he had imagined, it wasn't this. He had never thought anyone would hit Keisha. She wasn't the sort to take it. His hands clenched into fists that shook against his legs.

Keisha looked at the sky. "He'd attack when he was sober too. I think the drinking was what got him started, but later on it didn't matter if he was drunk or not. He got mad when the kids were noisy, he got mad when something was dirty, and he got mad when I didn't read his mind and do whatever he wanted."

She gripped a strand of her hair and held it tight as though she meant to pull it out. "I was scared. I didn't know how to deal with it. I lived with it. For ten years, I lived with it. I kept thinking we'd be okay. As long as he didn't touch the kids, I could stretch it out for them. I could keep going and keep us together as a family."

Jordan stared at her. This couldn't be the woman who had put up with ten years of domestic violence. This was Keisha. This was the woman who had yelled at him to get out of her chimney, who had welcomed her children to their new home with pretend cannon fire, who had attacked him with a fire extinguisher and passed him candy during a movie. She would never have allowed anyone to lay hands on her and not have struck back.

He tried to shake away the ugly image of her cowering in front of a violent man.

"I can't imagine you getting beaten." His voice sounded like it had been scraped across gravel.

She snorted in true Keisha-fashion. "I've changed. I don't let people step on me anymore." Her voice hardened, and her eyes glinted like stone. "One day, he hit Frayden. That was when I took the children and walked out. I went straight to the police station. He ended up getting sentenced to about a year in jail. We got divorced while he went through the court trials. I kept his last name only for the children's sake. If he wanted a different last name than mine, he could change his." She harrumphed. "But I didn't want to stay in the house where we'd suffered for so long, so we moved halfway across the country." Her nose wrinkled. "Apparently he's moved too. Nebraska's closer than where we used to live."

How many times had Jordan's stomach dropped during her story? He wished he could wipe away every bad thing he had ever done or said to this woman. He wished he had stopped drinking the moment he knew she disliked alcohol. Or at least the day he saw her pace after he put his beer cans in her yard. Or even the day she talked to him in the car about it.

A bitter taste harassed his mouth. "I yelled at you on your first day in your new house." He saw the scene in his mind's eye from a new horrifying perspective. "And I asked to talk to your husband. No wonder you got mad at me."

"I was so ready to hate anyone that treated me with less than respect." Keisha let out a small laugh. "I actually needed someone to be mad at. It felt good to let it out on you." She gave him a brief smile and looked down. "It wasn't fair to you. I carried on the feud just so I could relieve my feelings."

"It wasn't fair to *you*," he exclaimed, still sick over her story, but he stopped when she shook her head. His forehead creased as he thought of her oldest daughter. Determined, independent June. "Keisha." She looked up at him. "I don't understand. After all this, why would June go to him?"

Tears reappeared in her eyes. "I don't know. I can't imagine why," she said in heartbreak.

A sound came from down the road. Jordan looked over to see a blue Jeep coming their way. He sprang to his feet.

Keisha got up slowly. It occurred too late to Jordan that he should have helped her up. She watched the car, hope and urgency filling her gaze.

Then she began to jump up and down and wave like crazy.

The driver turned out to have enough gas for them to get to the nearest station. Jordan called back the insurance company to cancel his request while the newcomer poured the precious liquid into Jordan's truck. Jordan tried to pay the man, but he wouldn't hear of it. Keisha put her hand on Jordan's arm as he tried again to hand him money.

"Thank you," she told the man who had served as an angel in need. "Jordan, we need to get going."

Of course she was right. Jordan gave the man a nod of respect and got back in his truck. It was time to hit the road.

Chapter 23

June was seething. After all his promises in the letters, Dad hadn't done a single thing to welcome her.

Within minutes, she had switched from her plan of scrutinizing everything he did, trying to see through his changed, wonderful-father behavior for any sign of weakness, to instead looking for the smallest sign in his rude behavior that there was still a hope of something, anything, good. Something to indicate there could be hope for him in her life even if it was years down the road.

She hadn't found anything yet.

He popped into the living room for the third time and looked out the windows.

"Don't you want to do anything?" June asked, her voice more sarcastic than inviting. "Go find a playground, go to a museum, or walk through the neighborhood?"

He shook his head in irritation. "I wasn't planning on babysitting you."

She stared at him in accusation. "You wrote you were preparing for me to come. You said you were excited. Aren't we going to do *any*thing?"

He began to pace.

"Did you even prepare a room for me?" She had been willing to spend a night—just one—and then start her journey back on Sunday morning.

"I don't like your tone," he growled, turning around.

"I have a right"—she began, and ducked as his hand flashed out.

She came up madder than a hornet, rage steaming inside her. Violence was a no-go, *the* no-go of them all. "I've wasted enough time here." Her back straight as an iron rod, she turned toward the front door. "I'm leaving."

He stepped in front of her. "No, you're not. Not until your mom comes."

Her pulse sped up. "She's not coming." Why hadn't he listened to her the first time?

He looked out the window again. "She's taking her sweet time."

"I told you she won't come," June repeated more strongly. "She doesn't know I'm here."

That got his attention. "You didn't leave a note?"

"Why would I do that?" she scoffed. "She thinks I'm at a sleepover. Which means I need to be back tomorrow at the latest, and public transportation takes a while, so *move*."

A calculating look entered his eyes. "Oh no, you're not leaving. She'll figure it out sooner or later. She'll be out of her mind with worry, and once she realizes where you are, she'll rush over like her tail's on fire." He rubbed his hands. "You're staying until she comes."

June felt her face go pale with anger despite her best efforts. The judgment she had tried to keep in check since arriving at his home released itself as she looked into his glinting eyes. "Did you come up with all this to scare Mom?"

"I said in the letters I want her back," he insisted, raising his voice.

Her fingers curled into fists. She had been prepared to face Dad's temper but not to face this kind of plan. Mom would be terrified if June stayed. "You said you wanted your *family* back."

"What's it to you? Once she comes, she'll have to stay."

June gave him a disgusted look and stepped around him.

He grabbed her arm. "You've decided to live with me. And Keisha won't let you live here alone. She'll stay with us."

She tried to pull away, but his grip tightened painfully. "Let go."

The front door slammed open, and Mom and Jordan rushed inside in their Sunday best.

"Keisha," Dad breathed, a strange light in his eyes.

"Mom?" June's eyes opened wide. Mom was never supposed to get involved with this. "Mom!" June made to run to her, but Dad pulled her back, his grip rough.

June jerked her arm free so hard that he stumbled. Angered, he grabbed her again, and his free hand flashed toward her.

***

Keisha's heart somersaulted, and a scream of outrage tore from her throat.

Her shriek might have drowned out the sound of the slap, but there was no slap. There was only Henry landing on his back with a whoomph and a stunned expression as he looked up at his daughter.

June looked at him with revulsion, her stance in the fight mode she often adopted in jiujitsu. "You don't know me, and you don't want to." She jutted her chin in Keisha's direction. "You don't love her, and you didn't try to."

Keisha caught her up in a tight hug. She nearly melted in relief when June returned it.

Jordan stepped up to Henry, his fists raised. "I'll pummel you if you so much as move," he ground out. "Keisha? What do you want us to do?"

How she wished she had had Jordan earlier in her life. A buffer. No, someone to keep her from making the mistake of marrying Henry.

She rubbed June's back. "Nothing. We're leaving." As she had run up the porch steps, she had heard the infuriating Henry tell June that she and Keisha would live here, but he had had his way enough for a lifetime.

Hugging June close, she started toward the door.

"Keisha," Henry said, his voice intense.

He deserved nothing from her. She wanted to ignore him, this man who made her heart and soul burn with anger. She wanted to walk out of his life without looking back, proving he no longer meant anything to her.

Yet this might be the one chance she had to say something, anything, she wanted to.

For the last three and a half years, she had done everything in her power to live without fear. She turned and looked at her tormentor on the floor, Jordan standing above him. She wasn't afraid now.

Henry's clothes were in disarray, but his eyes glittered at her as though he thought he had a right to look at her. As though he thought she could still be his.

She gritted her teeth. It was time to set him straight. In as few words as possible, and then she would get out of here.

"You don't know what you missed." Her voice was low but filled with iron. "You saw your children as nuisances and your wife as someone to bend to your will." The words were distasteful on her tongue, but she had never said them to him before, and she wanted them out now. It needed to be clear what his crimes were and clear that she recognized them. "Those days are gone. The woman who let you bend her doesn't exist." She eyed his pitiful profile. "Find your happiness elsewhere."

At last she turned away. Jordan followed, putting a hand on her arm and shielding her and June from behind as they walked out.

Keisha held her head high. A euphoric sense of accomplishment mingled with the currents Jordan's hand sent through her. Keisha was walking out on Henry with June and Jordan at her side. Yet that wasn't the biggest difference between three years ago and now. The biggest difference was the confidence she had gained, her relationship with an all-powerful God, and the knowledge that her dignity was worth fighting for. She deserved safety just as her children did.

She squeezed June's shoulder before letting her climb in the truck.

When Jordan's hand left her arm, the cold reality of seeing Henry again slapped Keisha in the face like a bucket of ice water.

She took her seat and didn't draw a proper breath until Jordan pulled out. He drove quickly as though sensing her need to leave the neighborhood.

June sat safely between her and Jordan. "How did you know I was there?" June asked.

Keisha breathed through her nose. "Letters under your bed. Why did you come here? Aren't you happy at home?"

June jerked. "Of course I am."

"Then why would you run away?" Keisha stared into her daughter's blue eyes.

"I didn't. I came to find out what he was like now."

"And then what? Were you going to live with him?" Keisha's voice broke.

"What? No," June exclaimed in a tone of absolute shock. "I would never have left you."

Keisha drew a painful breath. Jordan pulled over and shot her a look of anguish. Maybe he would have reached over and touched her if June hadn't been between them. Instead, he pulled out his cell phone.

"I'll let the kids know we've found her," he said.

Keisha blinked wetness from her eyelashes and turned from her daughter to pull out her own phone. At the moment, she could barely look at her. "I need to make a call too."

It was perhaps the first time in her life she managed to be the first to speak when her mom picked up the phone.

"Mom, we've got her. She's okay. We're taking her home now." Her mom started to speak, but Keisha talked over her. "I promise I'll let you know more soon, but I have to go now. I need to speak with her."

"Hold on, let me talk to her a moment, Keisha," Mom demanded. "I need to hear her voice."

Keisha hesitated. Then she held the phone out to June. "Your grandma wants to talk to you."

June's eyes widened. *Me?* she mouthed. Tentatively, she took the phone.

Keisha could hear her mom's voice go on and on while Jordan completed his call. He wasted no time grabbing the wheel and pulling away from the curb.

June nodded and spoke a couple of times. "Yeah. Uh-huh, I'm fine. No. Okay."

She handed the phone back without saying goodbye. Obviously Mom had made her standard abrupt ending to the conversation.

Keisha looked at her daughter, really looked at her: her blue eyes; the freckles that dotted her snub nose; her tired pale cheeks; and her short blond hair that for once wasn't rubbed wild on purpose, though it probably hadn't been combed since yesterday.

"You didn't run away from home," she restated, trying to draw comfort in that fact even while she feared what she would learn in the rest of this conversation.

"Of course not." June clenched her hands on top of her seatbelt. "I went to check on things. Dad's been writing letters for months. I tore them up at first. But then I started to read them. He said he had changed and he wanted to be a family again. I didn't believe him, but eventually I thought

I'd go find out. If he was like he used to be in his good moments, then maybe I could let you see him, and we could find out if we wanted to try again to be a family."

"A family? With *him*?" Keisha's hackles rose. June had taken it upon herself to—Keisha would never have—

"I knew it wasn't likely," June rushed to say. "That's why I kept it secret. I didn't want you to get upset by any of this. I was supposed to go to his place, find out, and come back, and if I didn't think he had changed enough, you'd never have to know about it." Her fingers gripped the seatbelt. "Only then Jordan decided to get baptized the day I was supposed to be at Dad's, and that messed things up."

Keisha's mouth was dry. "You came up with a sleepover to cover up this visit."

"Yeah." June's cheeks turned red. "Sorry."

"I still don't understand. June, you should have talked to me. How did you ever think I would be willing to give this a try?"

"Mom." June's eyes were liquid. "You tried so hard to keep us together back when we were with him. You did everything you could to make it work. Families are supposed to stay together. I knew that, and I saw what you did, and so I tried too. Even though I hated when he hit you"—her frame trembled—"I tried. I'd clean up messes before he saw them if I could. I tried to remember to speak quietly when he was around. The first time he hit me—"

Keisha reeled in her seat, and the car hopped halfway into the next lane. Someone honked.

"Sorry," Jordan mumbled and brought the car back in position.

Keisha removed her hand from her heart and stared at her daughter. *"He didn't hit you,"* she hissed as though saying it would make it so.

"I'm sorry, I know you think the first time he hit any of us was the day he hit Frayden and you walked out." June spoke rapidly now. "But that's just it. When he hit me, I realized how close we were to falling apart. I just knew that if you knew he hit any of us, you would leave. Even though it would have been a relief, and I hated how he hurt you—"

"When did he hit you?" Keisha broke in, cutting short the stream of words.

June chewed on her lip. "When you were in the hospital giving birth to the twins," she whispered.

"Three years before we moved?" Keisha squeaked. "That was the *first* time?"

June tucked her head lower into her shoulders. "I couldn't let you know. And I promise, I never let him touch the others."

"June." Keisha's heart hurt as though it had been steamrolled.

"It was my goal to keep us together just like it was yours. So that's what I did. I covered things up. But Dad made it hard." June ground her teeth. "The twins were so little. Everyone was so little. You couldn't just teach them not to bother him. But whenever I saw he was mad enough to hit one of the others, I'd do or say something to get him mad at me so he'd hit me instead. I couldn't protect you, but I could protect them."

"You—" Keisha felt too sick to complete the sentence.

"I kept him from hitting the others." June's tone was matter of fact. "Until that stupid day when he hit Frayden. It was so dumb! It wasn't even Frayden he was mad at, it was me, but you were there, so I couldn't let him hit me, and I ducked, and Frayden was behind me, and—" June made a noise of disgust.

Keisha's memory of that moment leaped to mind, but it floated and blurred like a scrap piece of paper in a stream. She didn't remember what had upset Henry. She thought for sure it was Frayden he was mad at. She didn't remember where June had been standing at the time. What did it matter? Whether it was Frayden or June, she would never allow it to happen again.

"I was so mad." June's eyes were fiery. "Dad couldn't even control his temper enough to stop himself from doing the one thing that would make you leave. When you walked out, I was right there with you. I had had enough of him. I was done trying to keep the family together that he kept destroying."

A painful tension left Keisha's body. She slumped in her seat, exhausted. "June, I can't believe he was hurting you all those years."

"That's not your fault, Mom." June crossed her arms. "I kept it secret. I—I made my own decision."

Keisha felt too tired to wipe the tears that slid down her face.

"I prepared for today," June said as though hoping she could ease her mind. "I wasn't afraid to face him. I've been working harder than ever in jiujitsu. Even if he tried to hurt me, I'd know how to defend myself."

"You took jiujitsu so your father couldn't hurt you?" Keisha exclaimed.

"Not really." But June didn't meet her eyes. She stifled a tired yawn. "I've taken it for three years, Mom. We didn't get that first letter from Dad until this year."

But she had been taking it to make sure no one could hurt her again. Hadn't she?

Then again, wasn't that why Keisha had been so happy when June first started showing interest in the sport? Because then surely June would never find herself in a situation like Keisha's?

June leaned against her, exhaustion from her night of traveling and the day's depressing events shadowing her face.

Keisha put an arm around her and held her close, angry and scared and relieved all at the same time. "So you were upset about Jordan's baptism because you planned to come up here."

"Jordan was a problem," June murmured. "I like him just fine, but when you two got all cozy, I was worried. If Dad really had changed, then I wanted you to have a chance to get back together with him."

Jordan slowed to let a car cross in front of him. His suit jacket bunched up at the sleeve as he turned on the wipers and sprayed the window to get rid of some of today's dirt.

"But he didn't change," June continued. "He didn't even try. So it's over. I don't want us to ever go back."

Keisha rubbed her forehead. It still made her blood pressure spike to imagine that June had ever thought she could get them back together again. Their conversation left her with some comfort but also a distinct feeling of nausea.

"I'm sorry I restarted the feud." June's voice was earnest but sleepy. "Sorry, Jordan."

He shook his head as if to say it didn't matter.

Keisha held June tight while several more tears slid down her cheeks.

"Sorry I scared you, Mom. But it's okay now, with you and Jordan. I won't get in your way anymore." June's voice sounded more like a yawn. "You can marry him now."

Keisha stiffened, but June didn't seem to notice. She had fallen asleep.

What a thing to say! Suddenly finding her throat extremely ticklish, Keisha cleared her throat. Once. Twice.

Jordan looked over at her. "Don't worry. I don't have a ring in my pocket."

Her breath came out in a laugh. "Thank goodness for that."

He paused. "I'm sorry about what you've been through today. And in earlier years."

"Thank you." Her throat was still dry. "Thank you for helping me."

Emotions popped and crackled inside her like fireworks. The warmth and sparks she had felt when Jordan walked her to the car. The grief she had felt when she feared that June no longer wanted to live with her. The intense fear, and the equally intense frustration that came from knowing that June had taken over a decision that was Keisha's to make.

The strength she had felt when she told Henry what she needed to say.

She leaned her head against the top of June's and shut her eyes, breathing through her nose. A peaceful feeling began to ease the anxiety in her throbbing heart. June would never go back to her dad like that again. Her daughter and her family were safe.

And they were going home.

***

So that was the man who started it all. Jordan rubbed his bleary eyes and signaled to change lanes on the dark road. The image of the burly man with angry eyes filled his mind. That man had abused his wife and children. He had sent Keisha off to Missouri where she had built a home for her family and a wall around herself, where Jordan had reinforced her distrust of men and the two of them had wielded battle axes for the last few years.

Jordan's stomach twisted. The feud had been fun—and it had held regrets. Though if he wasn't mistaken, Keisha had enjoyed it. At least the parts she played.

He looked over at the passenger seats. Keisha sat leaning into June's seat, her cheek resting against the upholstery above June, who leaned into her. Both had been asleep for a while. Love and the desire to protect them both rushed his heart. Fingers tensing on the wheel with his emotions, he looked back at the road.

He had been so stubborn about refusing to give up alcohol he never thought to dig deeper into why she criticized him for it. He ran a hand across his face. Why hadn't he asked Keisha more about her ex when they stopped fighting? He would probably compare himself to Henry for a while to come.

But the nightmare was over. Keisha was done with the man, and even June seemed convinced there was no chance for him to be part of the family anymore.

In her own way, June had tried to do what she thought was best. Jordan hated the thought of her being hurt when she lived with him, yet he couldn't help but admire her spunk. Especially when he remembered how she pulled the man to the ground in self-defense.

His lips spread in a smile. Streetlamps and his headlights lit the way, and a memory popped into his mind.

He was on a road trip. Alicia and the children slept in their seats while he drove on toward their hotel.

Or was it Keisha and June who were on this road trip with him? He shook his head and tried to focus. It had been a good trip, hadn't it? He couldn't remember.

The clock on the dashboard said 2:01 as he pulled up next to Keisha's van and stopped.

For a moment, he stared at the driveway. Had he really just driven all that way? No breaks, no overnight hotel?

He turned to find Keisha blinking. She too looked surprised.

Without a word, she pushed June awake. Everyone unbuckled themselves, and Jordan made it out of his car. Keisha and June got out and all but staggered to their home.

Jordan went to his own house, his eyes blurring.

The hallway was dark and silent. He walked up the stairs, sliding his hand along the banister for support. When he reached his bedroom, he headed straight for the bed and flopped down.

"Ow!"

He rolled off the bedframe, fell to the floor, and got up on his knees, gritting his teeth in pain. Putting his elbows on the bed, he ran his hands across it. The mattress was gone. Why was the mattress gone?

He got up and went to Samuel's room, where he turned on the light. There was another empty bedframe.

With a sigh, he returned downstairs. The moment he opened the front door, Keisha stepped inside, June behind her.

"Are they in here?" Keisha asked quietly.

He shook his head. "I thought maybe they were in *your* house."

She seemed to hear something and headed for his living room. He followed slowly, letting his eyes adjust to the darkness.

Stopping in the doorway, he counted heads. Or, in some cases, feet. Whatever was visible from under the covers. The living room was invaded by blankets and bodies. Samuel was on one of the couches, Selima was under the covers with Lizzie and Imogene on Jordan's king-size mattress, Frayden and Solomon were on the floor, and a shorter double bulge under a blanket on the second mattress seemed about the right size for Carl and Kale.

On the other couch was Keisha's curly-haired friend, Shawna, sound asleep.

"You don't have to wake them if you'd rather not," Jordan said.

Keisha made no move to wake anyone up. June went to Lizzie's side. "Can I sleep here too, Mom?" she whispered.

Keisha gave a tired shrug. "I guess you wanted a sleepover."

June blinked slowly. Her mouth spread in an uncertain grin.

Jordan turned away, half wanting to laugh but too tired to do it. "I can bring another mattress down for you if you wanna sleep here with them," he told Keisha.

Her eyelids were half closed. "That'll work," she mumbled.

CHAPTER 24

A SWEET TRILL OF birds drifted into Keisha's consciousness. The trills were soon joined by the hoarse caws of crows. Her smile turned to a frown. Then a crash of horror music came to life, and she jerked up from her mattress and looked around.

Solomon sat up and reached for a cell phone. He clicked something on it, and the alarm turned off.

"Mom?" Lizzie asked sleepily.

"You're back," Kale said with a yawn.

Keisha rubbed her eyes. "I am."

Shawna sat up on the couch, stretching. Then her eyes popped open. "Keisha! And June!"

That brought the others' attentions to June. Her siblings sprang up and swarmed her with hugs and cries.

"We missed you!"

"June!"

"Why'd you go?"

"Keisha." Shawna came over and hugged her. "She's back."

Keisha nodded. "And she's staying. Shawna, thank you for your help." Her words were heartfelt.

"I got to mother eight children." Shawna waved away her words. "I'm just glad you're back. How are you doing?"

"Tired." She fought a yawn. "Are Troy and Thomas home?"

"Yes, we thought it was best for Tom to sleep there."

Keisha nodded. "You should go back to them. Really, thank you." She smiled at Shawna and looked around the room. "Come on, guys. Let's go home."

She and the children gathered their things. With a wave to the Taylors who were getting up, they trudged next door.

She was ready to fall into her own bed when the doorbell rang. Returning to the door, she opened it to Wayne and his parents.

"Oh, it's Sunday." She looked down at her wrinkled clothes. "I forgot."

"Would you rather we take Wayne home and bring him back next week?" his mom asked tentatively.

"No, we'll go to church," Keisha decided on the spot.

When they arrived at the church, the Taylors were already there, looking spic and span except for Jordan, whose eyes looked as bleary as Keisha's.

The two families sat together, with Shawna's family in front of them. Keisha dozed through the talks, waking up for a minute here and there to look around at her children before she nodded off again.

When the meeting ended, Shawna gave her arm a squeeze and left to teach a class. Keisha let her youngest children run off to their Primary classes while she walked June down the hall.

"Sister Johansen." The Young Women president stopped her with a bright smile. "Did the bishop talk to you?"

"What?"

"Oh. I thought he was supposed to meet with you today. Never mind." Her smile turned mysterious.

Now that she mentioned it, Keisha thought she had received a text or two yesterday she hadn't read yet.

"Hey, June." A brown-haired girl came up and hooked elbows with June. "Let's go."

The two of them rushed off before Keisha could collect her tired mind. She had meant to tell June she would stay with her through her Young Women class. Now she might have to change her plan. Walking into the classroom and asking June in front of her peers if she could stay was different than telling her before they walked in together.

She knew June wouldn't run off, yet she didn't like to let her out of her sight so soon.

Swallowing hard, she turned and headed toward the Relief Society room.

Someone came around the corner, nearly colliding with her. He grabbed her arms to steady them both, and she found herself looking into Jordan's face. "Keisha. How are you holding up?"

She was fine. She was completely—

Jordan's arms came around her, and he pressed her to his chest.

Keisha's eyes popped open in surprise. "Uh, I'm okay," she mumbled into his shirt. How did he know she wasn't? "What about you?"

He rubbed her upper back. "I'm tired. I'll be fine."

Emotions rolled and tumbled through her, finding release where Jordan rubbed. She sank into him, letting him continue.

After a minute, he let go. "Do you need to skip the second hour of church?"

She worked a deep breath through her body and let it out. "I think I'm okay." That hug sure had helped. "I'll go to class." She touched his arm. "Thank you, Jordan."

"Yesterday will still stop hurting." He wasn't done trying to comfort her. His gaze was concerned but earnest. "Keep looking forward."

And to the present. Gratitude washed over her for what she had now: God, a busy life with all her children, and an unexpected relationship with her neighbor.

***

It took her several days to regain her normal energy, and then her commitment to enjoy the present was tested. Her parents came to visit.

"We thought it was high time we come see our daughter and our grandchildren," Mom said after giving Keisha a bone-crushing hug. The twins watched in fascination as Dad took off his boots with the help of his shoehorn. "Now, where's June? June!" When the girl stepped forward, Mom pulled her into her arms. "No more running away now, do you hear me?"

"I didn't run away," June protested, her initial shyness melting away. She hadn't spent much time with her grandparents, but that wouldn't stop her from setting the record straight.

Keisha looked over her shoulder at the rest of the welcoming committee. Lizzie shifted her weight from one foot to the other. In a moment,

Mom swooped down on her. As most of Lizzie disappeared in her arms, her nervous expression transformed into a smile that eased Keisha's own anxiety. Lizzie would be quick to love anyone that showed her love.

"Now, Frayden," said Mom.

Frayden backed up into the living room, but Mom followed, her eyebrows rising with each step. "Come now, you get to choose between a hug and a kiss."

"Or a high five," Keisha suggested.

Mom stopped. "Do you want just a high five?" she conceded, disappointment thick in her voice.

Frayden bit his lip. "Maybe just a small hug," he said to Keisha's surprise.

Mom brightened and threw her arms around him. She didn't know how to do things small. Keisha rolled her shoulders, still feeling the effect of her own moment with Mom. It had nearly brought tears to her eyes. Sometimes she really did love her mom.

"Hello there, young man," Dad said after Mom let go of Frayden. "You've grown."

Frayden reached out, and they shook hands. It looked much more comfortable than the greeting with Mom, yet there was something in Dad's gaze as though he wished for more.

Keisha blinked. *Dad* wished for more affection, or for a closer relationship with one of his grandchildren?

"As I was saying on the phone last night," Mom began, "Missouri had far too many ice storms last year, so I hope you're all set for this upcoming winter." She beckoned at Dad, who began pulling scarves from a bag. "Just in case, we bought you all Mongolian scarves. Cashmere is the warmest wool there is, you know."

Lizzie giggled like Keisha was tempted to do but accepted her scarf and buried her hands in it.

"Thanks, Mom. We have hot cocoa and snacks for you to warm up with." Keisha pointed at the coffee table.

"Do you want marshmallows, Grandpa?" June asked, getting down to pour a cup.

The image of Selima pouring tea in this room popped into Keisha's mind, making her smile.

"Mm, I'll have some of those chocolate sprinkles," Mom said and reached for the jar.

"I'll get it." Lizzie hurried to grab a cup, eager to please.

"Thank you, dear. You can all make the trip to our baptism, right, Keisha?"

"Of course." She wouldn't miss it.

"Good, because we're not going through all that work for nothing. I mean, not that it's nothing if we can't have you there on the big day, but still, this is a lot of work." Mom frowned. "Your dad got a copy of all the scriptures combined in one, and it's a heavy book, believe you me, but we're working our way through—"

"I'm getting baptized soon too," Lizzie interrupted.

"Is that so? We're only here for a week this time around, but we'll have to come back for you."

"Jordan's getting baptized this Saturday," June said.

"Jordan?" Mom asked.

"Our neighbor," Keisha explained. He had rescheduled his baptism to next week.

Mom frowned. "Didn't you two used to butt heads?"

"Uh, yes, but that's in the past. He helped us last week to pick up June."

"Well, *that's* a change, I must say. I thought you hated men, excepting your father, of course. Now, is he getting baptized for you, or did you get baptized for him, or what was the reason? You've been making a lot of changes, Keisha, and I couldn't help but wonder if you really did have a new man in your life, but he better be—oh thank you, dear, the cocoa looks wonderful—I'll size him up at his baptism to make sure—"

"I can tell myself—" Keisha protested in irritation as Mom put the cup to her lips.

"Don't forget the whip cream, Grandma," Carl yelled, and Kale grabbed the can and sprayed. The cream hit both the top of the cup and Mom's mouth. The twins' eyes widened.

Dad snorted. His snorts turned into laughter. "Here, dear," he said, picking up a napkin. "Now, are you Carl? Kale?"

"Kale," Keisha whispered.

"I'd like to have some of that whip cream, Kale."

***

Sitting on the front row of the Primary room in his white jumpsuit, Jordan felt nervous. It could be because he was about to commit his life to God. It could be because Keisha sat two seats away, beaming. Or it could be because her parents were there.

He leaned across Solomon, feeling Mrs. Hogue's gaze bore into his back as he whispered to Keisha, "How do you ever get a word in when your mom talks?" Within minutes of Mrs. Hogue's arrival, she had cornered him. Mr. Hogue, the Johansen kids' grandpa, had eventually rescued him, only to start asking deep, philosophical questions. How was Jordan to know whether their society today could ever live the law of consecration?

Keisha shook her head. "I'm still trying to learn that myself." Her words were exasperated, but there was fondness in her gaze as she looked over her shoulder at her mom, who was settling Kale beside her.

Samuel poked Jordan on his right side. "You're up."

The room of people turned to Jordan in expectation. He stood and followed Elder Sørensen. Each step out to the hallway and into the font entry area felt like part of his journey, the journey that had led to this decision. He had been stubborn, but God was patient, and he didn't give up on his children.

Jordan entered the font, the water squelching around his waist and splashing up the wall. The bishop had suggested he choose someone from the ward to baptize him, seeing the missionaries would soon leave the area and he would have a longer-standing relationship with a member who was here to stay, but Jordan had chosen the Danish elder, remembering how struck he had been by him and his companion the day they met and how much he wanted his children to be like them.

He positioned himself with his hand on the young man's arm. Elder Sørensen raised his right arm and spoke the words of the ordinance. Jordan was lowered into the font, a hand on his back as he bent his knees and plugged his nose. The water closed over his head. Then he was raised from the water, raised as if from death, symbolically reborn, with his sins washed away. The water lapped at his waist.

Elder Sørensen had tears in his eyes. Jordan quickly looked away, but it was too late. Answering tears welled up in his own eyes. He stopped them by giving the missionary a hug and a clap on the back.

"Thank you," Elder Sørensen whispered.

Jordan was glad he had asked him to perform the ordinance.

When he returned to the Primary room after getting changed, his children surrounded him with hugs and congratulations. A number of people shook his hand and then stood around talking. Jordan turned in Keisha's direction and was instantly rewarded. She came right over.

"Jordan." She raised her arms and stopped. He held his breath until she followed through with a sweet hug that filled him from head to toe with energy.

It was a good thing he had held her last Sunday. If he hadn't, she might not have made it into his arms today.

She stepped back, giving him a clear view of her bright face. She could have lit up a halo. Her gaze went to the top of his head, and Jordan grinned. He didn't mind having wet hair around her again.

"How come you cried at your own baptism, but you're only smiling at mine?" he teased.

She raised her eyebrows. "Don't you want me to be happy?"

"Of course I do." He couldn't look away from those smiling lips. "You know, a fourteen-year-old recently told me I could marry you."

She opened her mouth and shut it. Then her signature bold look appeared. "Actually, she said *I* could marry *you*."

His smile disappeared. "What's the difference?" he exclaimed.

She shrugged. "Don't tell me you have a ring on you today."

He was going about this all wrong. "No, I thought we could start a little smaller. How about a kiss?"

Her eyes lightened in understanding, and her cheeks flushed, but it didn't stop there. Rather than look away shyly, she kept eye contact, her flush deepening. Jordan's blood rushed in his ears. She was thinking about it!

At last she looked around. "The children would hate that."

"Then how about a date next week?" He got the question out just in time. Keisha's parents were headed their way.

She tilted her head. "Maybe that can be arranged."

***

JORDAN WAS PRETTY SURE he was more nervous than Cole, the young man Samuel had introduced him to ten minutes ago. As they stood on Cole's front porch, Samuel was the only one who seemed relaxed. Cole cracked his knuckles, and Jordan repeatedly told himself not to wipe his sweaty palms. He was supposed to help inspire confidence.

"I really think asking for help would be a good thing," Samuel said with his hands in his pockets.

Cole grimaced and wiped his nose. His eyes were sunken. "There's no way my parents will know how to help. They've never been addicted. They're so innocent, they haven't even caught the signs and realized I'm using." His hoarse voice cracked. "I just need them to know what I've been doing and that I want to quit. That's all."

The look in his eyes was bleak when he mentioned quitting. Jordan's heartstrings tugged. Samuel had dodged the bullet—or rather, the messy battleaxe—of addiction. Cole didn't sound like he had much hope that he could make himself stop.

"It's up to you," Samuel conceded. "Still, I'll tell you the times I've felt strongest were when I asked someone for help instead of trying to do it all on my own."

Cole didn't answer. Wiping his runny nose, he turned on Jordan. "Can you keep my parents from freaking out?"

Jordan took several seconds to reply. "I'll do what I can."

The young man sniffled but apparently decided to make do with that. "It's now or never," he said, his hands shaking. "I've been clean since last night." He pushed the door open and led them inside.

"Mom, Dad," he called and motioned Jordan and Samuel into the living room.

"Hey, Cole." A medium-built man with a kind face lowered his cell phone and gave the visitors a curious look. A short, curly-haired woman came down the stairs and stopped beside him.

"These are my friends that I wanted you to meet," Cole said, his voice lowering to a sullen pitch by the end of the sentence. He was probably trying to cover up his nervousness. Either that, or he already regretted bringing them.

Jordan stepped forward with his hand outstretched. "Jordan."

"Uh, I'm Noah. This is Jill."

"Samuel."

Cole barely let the introductions rest as they all sat down. "We wanted to talk to you about something."

His parents shot him a nonplussed look. He took another swipe at his nose.

"Cole, dear, isn't your cold any better?" his mom asked.

"It's not a cold," he snapped.

Jordan swallowed. If Cole wouldn't follow Samuel's advice, was he going to simply blurt out the fact that he was doing drugs?

Cole cleared his throat. Samuel put a hand on his arm. Cole repeated his action. "I want to ask for your help."

Jordan's shoulders relaxed the tiniest bit.

"There's something I want to stop doing. But I don't know how. I thought maybe if you knew about it, like Jordan knows what Samuel's been involved with, it would help."

Jordan had never felt so proud—of Cole and of Samuel both. He watched the parents. Their faces were question marks. Worry slid across them, but there was no panic yet.

"I need help quitting. And wanting to quit. From something I've been doing for about a year."

"Quit what, exactly?" his dad ventured.

Cole's gaze slid back and forth between his parents and the floor. "Marijuana. More recently cocaine." His leg bounced, but he pressed a hand against it and stopped the nervous tic.

"Cocaine?" his mom faltered.

"Yeah." His eyes stayed on the floor now.

"He wants to stop," Samuel repeated. "But he needs your support."

"Of course he has that," his dad said, a touch of fierceness erasing his surprise.

Slowly, Cole's mom asked from the other couch, "How—how did you get involved?"

"And how often are you taking it?" his dad asked.

"Most days," was the mumbled answer.

Jill began to cry.

Before he could stop to think, Jordan's hand shot out and restrained Cole's leg. He felt a surge of energy in Cole and could just imagine him leaping to his feet in a fit of temper and agony over his mom's more than understandable reaction. "It'll be all right," he said. So much for keeping the parents calm. At the moment, it seemed more important to keep Cole calm.

Opposite them, Noah mirrored Jordan's movement with a comforting hand on his wife's knee.

Beneath Jordan's hand, Cole's leg relaxed by degrees. The boy let out a slow breath. "I want to quit. But I think it's too late."

Samuel clapped a hand against his back. "I know of a program that meets near here that can help."

Jordan nodded. He and Samuel had researched it together. "Would you like your parents to attend with you?"

"And me," said Samuel. "I need to learn this too."

Cole looked dubiously at his parents, his face forming a scowl.

"Let her cry, Cole. She's human." Noah rubbed his wife's back. "But we both want to help."

"It'll get ugly. I can barely stand a day off of it." Cole sounded forlorn.

"Let it get ugly before it gets better," his dad said firmly, and Jordan agreed. Cole was embarking on a huge undertaking, but he wouldn't be alone. His parents and Samuel would try to help, and if nothing else, Jordan would fill the heavens with prayers for him.

Chapter 25

Keisha laid her red coat in her lap and watched the icy road, looking for any clue as to where Jordan was taking her on their date.

"How's Frayden doing with the kids at school these days?" Jordan asked. His hair moved under the heat blowing through the vent.

"Good. He's friends with the boy he got in trouble for bullying, and I think he gained more friends through him. It's great to see." She gave Jordan a sideways glance. "Samuel told me about how the two of you are trying to help his friend, Cole."

"He did? You two don't usually talk."

"I know." Honestly, she had used to be afraid of Samuel, but that was changing. "We were both outside, so I asked how he was doing. He lit up and told me he's looking into college degrees that'll help him do work in drug rehabilitation programs. Pretty soon he was telling me about his friend and his talks with you. I'm impressed. With both of you."

Jordan ducked his head. "I'm not doing much. I'm beyond grateful Samuel's in a position to help rather than stuck in addiction himself. Cole's nowhere near as lucky." Jordan parked and got out, then came around and opened Keisha's door.

She got out and looked up at a grand brick building: the city's art museum. Anticipation built inside her.

"You like art, right?" Jordan asked. "Especially portraits."

"Yes." Suddenly her spirits fell. "I didn't think you were interested in art though. You didn't seem to care when I showed you my CGs."

He cleared his throat. "That's what I wanted to confess. You see, I'm an artist. A computer graphic designer. I do a lot of freelance digital artwork, and I make my own pieces and sell them."

It took a minute for the words to sink in. Jordan didn't wait that long before he continued.

"That first time you had a missionary lesson in your home, when I saw my CG on your wall, I—"

"What? *Your* CG?" Her breath came out in a cloud.

He scuffed his boot on the icy ground. "Yeah. I was so surprised I didn't know what to say. Then I wanted to know what drew you to it. We were just beginning to make peace, so I wasn't sure how you would take it if you knew I had made it. I thought I'd tell you later, but not with my kids there, so when we visited your home, I expressly told them not to comment on your CGs. Of course, they had a blast doing the opposite."

"They did." She shook her head in a daze. "Which one did you make? The picture of the boy with his mouth open?"

"Yes." He offered a small smile. "And the one with the people on the street."

"Are you serious?"

He looked self-conscious. "I really did mean to tell you. Your visit to our home didn't seem like the best time either. I removed the CGs of my children from the wall before you showed up. We haven't put them back up yet."

The wall had been bare, the nails empty. The Taylor children had walked Keisha right up to the wall of their living room and told her the place needed a woman's touch.

Her cheeks burned with a mixture of embarrassment and humor. Jordan's children had teased him on both visits, embarrassing him on purpose, maybe tried to draw him into a confession.

Jordan opened the back seat of his car and pulled out a rectangular package. He gave her a cautious look. "I'm sorry for keeping this from you. And I want to give you a present."

Surprised, she accepted the package. It was lighter than she expected. She removed the brown paper, revealing a framed digital portrait of the boy whose expression she had come to love. This time, instead of having his mouth opened in an "O," he was laughing. Full on laughing, his cheeks round and his eyes sparkling.

Keisha felt herself respond, her mouth spreading in an answering grin. It was impossible not to react that smile. She looked up at Jordan, whose gaze turned hopeful.

"Jordan, I love it." Impulsively, she stood on her toes and touched his face for balance. She was about to kiss his cheek, but at the last second, she paused. His face under her hand pulsed with energy. In a wink, she changed her mind and kissed him on the lips.

His expression was astounded when she returned to the ground. Then he put a hand on either side of her face and leaned in, claiming her lips.

She closed her eyes, sensations running through her like little nymphs. Joy, love, admiration. A chemistry that had used to show up only in their efforts to best each other and had been repressed through yelling and distrust. Her heart swelled, and she leaned in closer, putting away the memories. All she wanted to feel was this caressing kiss.

Slowly he pulled away, his breath uneven. "Well. That's an adventure I'd like to have again." He took her hand, looking extremely pleased, and indicated his present. "You can leave that in the car while we check out the museum."

"Are you kidding?" She hugged the portrait to her chest with one arm. "This is going in the building with us. I can't risk it getting stolen. They better allow me to carry it around."

His smile grew. "I guess we can ask."

Keisha turned to the building, her insides tingling, her gaze repeatedly drawn to her neighbor. "I can't wait to look at art with a real artist."

***

JUNE CLICKED HER PEN closed on the kitchen counter. It had been a month since her trip. A month, and already their families had gotten chummy. She shook her head at the conversation she heard through the open window. Selima was asking Mom to come to her sewing class fashion show. Of course, the bishop had called Mom to be a Young Women advisor for Selima's class at church, so they were getting to know each other better, but still. The other week, Samuel had shared his educational dreams with Mom. Were they trying to pull her into their family and set her and Jordan up again?

Not that June minded. She looked at the paragraph she had written on the inside cover of the Book of Mormon. The letters from Dad had stopped. He had no interest in reuniting if it didn't include Mom, and that wouldn't happen. Even so, June wanted to send him something. Just in case he was willing to accept something good in his life.

"Here." She handed her pen to Lizzie and turned the book around, watching as her sister bent over it to write.

She had felt some disappointment and some relief the day she found out how little Dad had changed. Mainly though, the words "I told me so" had run through her mind ever since. There was no reason to sit and cry. No reason to grind her teeth. June was a fighter. No, a defender. A defender who was trying to pull herself back to the bleachers and relinquish the decisions to the person who was really in charge of her family—Mom.

June loved her family. It didn't matter if she didn't have two parents. They were fine as they were.

But if the Taylors were to join them, she could probably live with that.

Samuel wouldn't be a bad brother. He had felt like a friend ever since she asked him to drive her to Dad's place, and that was even though he had said no. He had proved himself trustworthy when he didn't tell anyone what she had asked for.

Imogene though? June grimaced. She was still a powerful weapon when it came to pulling on Mom's heartstrings. But June supposed she could live with a somewhat spoiled, somewhat attention-demanding little sister. She'd learn to live with her. Anyway, it was a good thing she was cute.

Selima was downright sweet, but she had personality beyond that. Even if she hadn't meant it to be a rebellious act, she *had* played hooky from school the last few years. She had needed something beyond what she had, and she had tried to look for it. June appreciated that.

And then there was Solomon.

"What do you think?" Lizzie asked, putting down the pen.

June read through her paragraph for a minute. "It looks great. Come on, let's take it to Frayden."

The voices from his room were loud. June pushed the door open and walked in with Lizzie in tow. "Hey, Solomon, can you give us five minutes? I need to talk to Frayden."

Solomon groaned. It wasn't half bad. Nowhere near as lethal as Frayden's scoffs could be, but stronger than last week.

"We're in the middle of a game," Solomon complained.

"Yeah. Give *us* five minutes to make our next moves," said Frayden. "I've almost found a way into his fort."

June sniffed and laid the book and pen on top of their board game. "Lizzie and I have both written our testimonies in the Book of Mormon. I want to send it to Dad today. Are you ready to write yours?"

Frayden's face lost some of its color, making her pause. She had mentioned her idea to him a week ago. Apparently he was still unsure about it.

She left behind the army-commander attitude and gave him a softer look. She wouldn't begrudge him his problems with Dad. "He probably won't even read the book"—she tried to gentle her voice—"but if he does, it might do him some good. Maybe he'll at least read what we write about how we came to believe in God."

Solomon pretended to study the parts of the board that were still visible. Frayden hadn't yet taught him how to be obnoxious.

Frayden stared at the book she held open, his eyes sliding across the penned words.

A look of determination entered his eyes, and he took the pen. June bit down on a silent hooray.

***

FOLLOWING CHRISTMAS WAS A season of miracles. Keisha's mom complained when she and Dad had to make different visits as first Lizzie, then June, and finally Frayden were each baptized on separate weeks.

"At least you don't have to come to the Taylors' baptisms," Keisha told her as they returned to the church parking lot. Between the Taylor children and her own, the ward's baptismal font wasn't empty for long.

"Right, the Taylors," Mom said with sudden interest and no subtlety. "How very interesting he baptized both June and Frayden. How is that man?"

"Fine," Keisha said with an eye-roll.

It was a good word to describe Jordan. Her heart softened as she thought about him. He was a fine father, a fine neighbor, and a fine man, something she had long believed didn't exist. He was also a fine date, and most certainly a fine kisser. Her face grew hot, and she hurried to change the subject.

When it was time for Mom and Dad's double-baptism, Keisha packed up the children and took them on a road trip.

She bawled like a baby when each of her parents was lowered under the water but found a perverse satisfaction in knowing she was embarrassing June and Frayden. The twins watched the ordinance as though their lives depended on every detail.

"Why can't we get baptized yet?" Carl whined as they returned to their seats to wait for Keisha's parents to change into dry clothes.

"Because you don't need it yet," Keisha reminded him gently. "You have to wait until you're eight. Jesus's atonement covers your mistakes up till then without the ordinance of baptism."

"But all the others are getting baptized before us. It's not fair."

"You'll get baptized younger than anyone else in our family," Keisha said, the thought occurring to her before she even had to think Great. "Everyone else has been older than eight."

"Oh, yeah!" Carl and Kale raised their heads with identical expressions of excitement.

"That's not fair," June said but winked at Lizzie. "Why couldn't I have been baptized younger?"

"It's okay, June." Kale patted her hand. "I won't tell your friends."

***

Keisha loved her time with Jordan. She had never had someone she could truly talk to about the triumphs and trials of raising her children. Jordan filled that void, and now that he knew about Henry, she even got to talk through some of her transition period following the divorce.

In addition to dates, somehow they ended up making a habit of grocery shopping together. Both of their families went to a CG exhibition where a number of his works were featured. He and his family joined hers to see the new skate park. Another day, Jordan bought ice cream for everyone and handed it out to them while they played on their front lawns, enjoying a late spring day not long before summer break.

After finishing off her ice cream bar, Keisha ran around under the sun with the children, playing freeze-tag and doing her best not to get caught. Jordan jogged past, lowering his voice to say, "You really don't let the kids win, do you?"

"Sometimes I do," she argued, then gasped and made a beeline for the end of the Taylors' yard to escape Carl. Now wasn't the time. Her mouth spread in a grin. It was much more fun to run past Solomon and hear Carl tag him behind her.

At the edge of the lawn she stopped and turned, panting. Carl chased after someone else while June freed Solomon. Lizzie fell down on the grass and rolled around long enough to be caught. Keisha shrugged. There were enough people that were willing to let the youngest win.

Frayden approached Lizzie as if to rescue her, but instead of touching her to unfreeze her, he tickle-attacked.

A movement from Keisha's left caught her attention. Jordan stepped onto his porch. Catching her gaze, he beckoned.

She hesitated for a moment. Then, under cover of Lizzie's laughter while Kale ran to her aid and tried to tickle Frayden, Keisha followed Jordan into his house.

Her steps slowed as she walked through the living room. The wall that had been bare during her family's visit now had pictures. They were digital portraits of each of Jordan's children. Seeing the fairy tale-like images filled her with something like nostalgia.

"What did you want?" she asked, tearing her gaze from the pictures.

"I wanted to show you a few of my art pieces." Jordan looked nervous. He motioned her into the study where his computer sat on the desk and his children's toys and books were clustered mostly on their shelves.

She looked around at the walls. The only picture in this room appeared to be an actual painting. Confusion gave way to excitement. "Do you mean, on your computer?"

He pulled at the collar of his shirt. "Uh-huh."

She plopped down at the desk. "Will you show me how you make them?"

His face relaxed into a smile. "Sure." Reaching over her shoulder, he opened up his software and spent several minutes explaining it, showing her some of the things it could do.

The process was fascinating, but most of all, it fascinated her how Jordan would recreate details Keisha might never have thought to include.

"Do you have the boy with the open mouth in your files?" she had to ask.

"I do." He opened a folder and pulled up the boy with his mouth opened in an "O." Keisha felt her own mouth crack into a full smile. She wanted to laugh, she liked the picture that much, not to mention the smiling version Jordan had gifted to her.

He minimized the folder and double-clicked another, his arm brushing hers. It sent tremors through her, a rush of pleasure that had grown whenever they touched the last few months.

"I wanted to show you something else. I've made a few of you." He took a deep breath as the first image appeared.

Her mouth opened in an "O."

There she stood in full profile in her old-fashioned dress, eyes sparking, chin raised, and neck exposed.

For a full minute, she sat staring. Jordan's hand shook slightly on the computer mouse.

"You said there are more?" she asked, not taking her eyes off the picture.

With a click, the image was replaced by a second one where she stood in the same posture, only this picture included a three-year-old pirate boy with an eye patch held in her arm against her hip. A cloud of smoke billowed around them as though from the cannon they had just shot off with cries of "Fire! Fire!"

Jordan raised a hand and rubbed his neck.

"That's beautiful." Did he see her that way? Her heart thudded in her chest. "How did you remember all the details so well? It was such a long time ago."

He shook his head. "Keisha, I made this four years ago. I made the first one the day it happened. I couldn't get the image out of my mind after that scene in your backyard. I know I yelled at you and everything, but before the day was over, I had to get this out. Before the week was over, I had both images completed on my computer."

Her head whirled. He had made these back then? "Wait. Have your children seen these images?"

He nodded, reddening. "They saw this one too." He skipped to the next image.

Keisha and Jordan were sprinting around in front of their houses, aiming fire extinguishers at each other, both of them covered in carbon dioxide foam.

Jordan skipped to the next one, which showed just Keisha, extinguisher fluid in her hair and on her clothes while she determinedly ejected more stuff from the extinguisher in her hands. Her hair fluttered off the back of her neck as she ran.

Stunned, she reached for the computer mouse and clicked on. The next images showed her and Jordan running around, again in their front yards, hoses in their hands and cascades of water dripping off them.

"My kids took pictures of that fight," Jordan mumbled, "so I could make CGs off the photos."

One last click brought the first Keisha back to the screen, the Keisha that wore a dress and took on the world with a resolute air, having just ordered the firing of cannons.

She turned to look Jordan in the face. "Why?"

He took a deep breath. "The scene in your backyard that first day was beautiful. You and your five kids, starting a new life. I had no idea what you'd escaped from, but it was touching. And noisy. And I didn't think I should be so affected when I still mourned Alicia." He reached out his hand and rested it on hers. She thrilled at the look in his eyes. "After creating those two images, I thought I'd be fine. I thought I could be rude to you and prank you for the rest of my life. But the pictures didn't get my admiration out of my system." His smile grew fond. "I liked you with all your innovative tricks and the energy you put into being my enemy. By the time we had that fight with the fire extinguishers, I couldn't help immortalizing it in another picture. Some of these images from our war stuck with me so I couldn't get you out of my mind.

"When you ended the feud, I started to hope for the first time."

His hand squeezed hers. She turned her hand over to clasp his. "That's when I really got to know you," he continued. "Your determination and strength, your desire to do what's right. Your humility that lets you change your way of life in the wink of an eye. Your absolute love for your children, and finally your love for me and my family."

Tears gathered in her eyes. She did love them. She loved *him*.

"Keisha, I fell in love with you the day we met."

Her tears stopped. "What?"

"Will you marry me?"

Arguments ran through her head. "You can't have fallen in love with me that first day," she exclaimed. "I know you admitted to admiring me, but you didn't know me at all."

He frowned. "But I—"

"And we hated each other."

"Not exac—"

"*You* hated me. You—showed up disguised in a hazmat suit, made us evacuate our house for a fictional life-threatening gas problem, and planted cacti between the couch cushions. And that was only a few months after we moved in!"

"Okay, that was a fun one," he admitted. "But—"

"Jordan, your love came later," she insisted, putting her hands on her hips. "So did mine. I may have started thinking differently about you the day I saw you worry about Imogene, but I didn't fall in love that day."

He dragged a hand through his hair, looking harried. "Okay, but—"

"Mo-om," a reproving voice said from the doorway. "Are you going to answer his question or what?"

Keisha blinked and Jordan froze. At the doorway peeped, Keisha guessed, no fewer than nine children, though she couldn't see all of them. The faces of those she could see ranged between expressions of eagerness and impatience.

Hands still on her hips, Keisha looked up at Jordan. Sometime during her rebuttal, she must have stood up, leaving her face only inches from his.

She liked his eyes. They spoke of a whole list of characteristics she ought to tell him in exchange for the good things he had noticed about her. And his eyes looked straight into hers, filled with hope and panic as he waited for her answer.

"Yes."

Jordan's face cleared in a look of pure joy that made him absolutely gorgeous. Slowly, slowly, he reached for her while she moved closer in a slow-motion trance.

The children were under no such spell. That one word from Keisha brought them flooding into the room, and Keisha and Jordan were jostled and hung onto by laughing, yelling children.

"You're getting married," Carl and Kale yelled, each hugging one of them.

"I love Keisha," Imogene yelled, holding on to Keisha's leg.

"Oh, Mom. Oh, Mom," June said and sounded like she was about to cry. "Oh, *finally*." Her smile broke out like the morning sun.

"Congratulations," Selima yelled, getting in Keisha's way to hug Jordan.

Keisha couldn't even make out what Samuel or Solomon or Lizzie were saying. Frayden didn't speak, but he grabbed Lizzie's and Solomon's hands and danced around the two of them.

Jordan stubbornly continued to try to maneuver Keisha into his arms, and Keisha leaned forward and managed to put both hands on the back of his neck even with little ones holding onto her while the three-man circle pressed her closer to Jordan.

Selima grabbed the back of Solomon's shirt. "Let's go. Hey, Lizzie, come on."

"Please, tell me when I fell in love with you," Jordan said with a warm smile as he looked Keisha in the eyes.

"It happened gradually." She smiled back at him.

"We'll go with your version for now." His eyes danced.

Samuel pulled his siblings and Frayden in the direction of the door. "Go on. Shoo."

The three youngest stuck around, bouncing up and down and hugging each other and their parents.

Keisha nestled closer and pressed her cheek to Jordan's chest while his arms tightened around her. Why had she ever wasted time scolding him?

"Come on," Samuel hissed from the doorway.

Carl looked at the older boy in defiance. "Mom and Jordan are getting married," he announced happily, as if that explained why he shouldn't have to leave. Then he looked up at Keisha, and his face took on a look of horror.

"Are they going to kiss?" he squeaked.

"Ew," Kale yelled.

The twins ran from the room closely followed by Imogene, who clapped her hands to her ears.

Keisha turned her face up and kissed the man she loved.

Epilogue

"I can't believe you're already leaving," Keisha told Samuel as the family gathered out front to see him off at the end of summer, two weeks after Jordan and Keisha's wedding.

"We're proud of you, son," Jordan said. "You're going off to college." He slapped Samuel's back but appeared to struggle to keep his expression festive. Samuel slapped him back.

Men. Was that really all the goodbye they'd give each other?

Samuel turned and gave Keisha a proper goodbye hug, so she decided not to complain.

His dented blue car along the curb was weighed down with boxes. Jordan's truck took up a second curb spot. In the driveway was Keisha's van and the new neighbor's car that claimed what had used to be the Johansens' driveway.

Keisha hadn't at all minded moving into Jordan's house when they discussed their options. They had turned his empty guest bedrooms into regular bedrooms. Her children had thought it a grand adventure. They especially loved the pseudo tea party they had held their last day in the house, a scene Jordan was now working on making into a CG. With the furniture already moved out, all eleven people had sat on the bare floor and enjoyed hot cocoa served from Selima's porcelain tea set. They couldn't have left the house Keisha and her children dedicated with a pirate ceremony without having a farewell ceremony as well.

"I'll call home, at least until the homework starts to kill me," Samuel promised.

She squeezed his shoulder and let him say goodbye to his siblings—the ones he had grown up with, as well as the Johansens. Any fear she had ever felt around Samuel had been replaced with a growing feeling of closeness.

"We'll make a CG and send it to you," Carl said, bouncing in place. "Jord—Dad's been teaching us."

"When you get a girlfriend," Kale said, "send us a picture so Dad can make a CG with you two playing with fire 'stinguishers."

Selima giggled. Keisha closed her eyes in consternation. Hopefully the twins didn't think they would have to fight with a girl for three years before marrying her.

"Samuel won't have time for a girlfriend," Lizzie said. "He'll be busy studying."

"Lizzie-girl, there's more to life than school." Samuel tugged her hair and quickly let go at her glare.

"*Maybe*," she relented. "But school is still important."

"I want my older brother." Imogene stomped her foot on the ground.

"I guess I'll have to take over as the older brother," Solomon said, drawing himself up to look bigger.

Frayden shoved him. "You're younger than me, and I don't see that changing." The two of them began a shoving match, and Solomon held his own.

June picked up the last bag and squeezed it into the full backseat of Samuel's sports car. "Have fun, but not too much fun without me." Her voice was unaffected by the sadness of parting, her eyes hidden by sunglasses. Ever the cool girl, she was still taking jiujitsu.

"Imogene, he'll be back at Christmas," Lizzie said.

"Yes, and hopefully I'll have a letter to share with you all." Samuel paused. "I'm putting in my mission papers."

Keisha's heart skipped a beat. Judging by the moment's silence, everyone was surprised.

"That's wonderful!" Selima exclaimed, clasping her hands and nearly jumping up and down the way Kale and Carl so often did.

Keisha's heart filled with light while the children flocked around Samuel with more hugs and congratulations. A noise made her turn to look at Jordan. Tears welled up in his eyes as he stared at his son.

Samuel quickly turned away. "Oh man, I'm gonna go now."

"Come here." Jordan's voice was rough as he drew him in for a close hug. Then he pushed him away. "Okay, you can go now. Bye."

"See you all at Christmas," Samuel called, rushing to get in his car. Having escaped the emotional scene, he grinned as he pulled away from the curb.

Jordan, still fighting tears, buried his head in Keisha's shoulder. "I didn't think he'd *become* a missionary."

Her love for this soft-hearted man swelling, she put a calming hand on his head. She knew how much he had wanted his children to be more like the missionaries. It was why he had let them in his house in the first place.

"You and Alicia have raised a wonderful son," she said.

"Don't underestimate your own influence."

She straightened with mischief. "I take full responsibility for siccing the missionaries on you for my own revenge."

Jordan laughed and raised his head just as Samuel's car disappeared around the corner.

"Now what?" Carl asked.

Kale looked up at Keisha with a pout. "Why do people still have to go to school when they're grown up?"

"He won't have to go all his life," she assured him. "Maybe four or six more years. We've talked about how important school is. It'll help him have a good life."

"I'm never moving out, not even when I go to college," Kale declared.

"Or when you get a girlfriend," Jordan agreed, regaining control of himself. "You'll live at home while you torment her with lizards and half-eaten chocolates, and you'll never be embarrassed about living with your parents."

"That's right." Kale nodded with enthusiasm and nearly got a tennis ball in his head.

"Catch! Kale, catch!" Carl yelled belatedly.

The children scattered across the front yard, some to play, some to read, and some to tend to the flowers.

Jordan slipped his arm around Keisha's shoulders as she watched the children. "This is my favorite time of day."

She leaned into him. Moments like this were precious. Still, if she were to throw in a vote, her favorite time of day might be the evenings.

Leading up to the wedding, she had pondered keeping her blessedly flexible job—right up until she realized it wouldn't work while she mothered these nine children. There was always something to do, disasters and teenage insecurities and housework and more. She loved—and so far had survived—the daytime, with all the children's challenges and joys, but she especially loved the evenings.

She would walk through the living room past a framed copy of the Family Proclamation, the one she had first seen at Shawna's and since then adopted as part of her family motto. A very long motto.

Next, she passed CGs of all nine children and herself and Jordan on the dark mahogany wall. He had made the one of himself at her request. At her suggestion, he had also pulled the CG of his first wife out of obscurity and hung it up with the others. Keisha was starting to get to know this woman as the others shared stories about her, and she liked her very much.

Having passed the living room, she would go upstairs and help the youngest children into bed. After she and Jordan read them a few stories, they would go to their own room and kneel beside the bed to pray together. That nighttime ritual gave her something she had never had before. It brought an added measure of unity to their relationship and their family.

Jordan's arm slid from her shoulders. He turned to her with a gleam in his eyes. "I'll go get some work done. Don't forget about our date."

For the next while, Keisha got as much done as she could in the house with some help from the children, and Jordan cleaned the kitchen before working on his CGs. But at 5 p.m. sharp, they both dropped their work and got in the car, waving goodbye to the children.

For three minutes they drove, exchanging glances and smiles. Then Jordan parked behind their neighborhood.

Keisha opened her door and stepped out into the summer humidity. Jordan came around with dancing eyes and took her hand, wrapping his fingers around hers and leading the way.

They made their way across the hedge to their own backyard, Keisha giggling at the absurdity of stealing into their own home, and sneaked up to the back of the house. Jordan held the ladder he had left out after yesterday's lawn work, and Keisha climbed to the second story and crawled through the window to the attic. Jordan followed, shut the window, and picked up a covered picnic basket before he motioned to the stairs.

The muted sounds of their children yelling and laughing in the front yard became clearer when Keisha popped her head outside and climbed out onto the roof. She reached back and took the picnic basket from Jordan so he could climb out and join her.

A breeze fanned the back of her neck and made the nearby trees rustle. Sunshine glinted through the maple tree that had been hers before the move. The children's voices sounded far away below them, but she could hear that they were safe and, for the most part, happy.

"Ready for dinner, Mrs. Taylor?" Jordan asked.

"I'm ready, Mr. Taylor," she said, putting as much sweetness into addressing him as she could. She must have had success with it, judging by the way he beamed and leaned over to give her a quick kiss.

With a smile, he took the basket from her and grabbed her hand with his free one as they walked across the roof.

Keisha looked up at the bright sky. "I love this. We should have more at-home dates."

"Just remember, if someone starts crying, we're not home," Jordan said.

She just laughed. They had gone to great lengths in order to keep their location secret from the children. "It's amazing how long they can go without calling 'Mom' when they think I'm not here."

Jordan dropped her hand and took a blanket from the basket, shaking it open with a snap. "Voila," he said—and then he stopped short, staring at the spot where he had been about to lay the blanket.

"Gotcha," he said.

"What?"

"It says, 'Gotcha.'"

Keisha looked down. Her own handwriting glared up at her with large, red letters. She blinked. "I don't believe it. You haven't scrubbed it off?"

"What? I've never seen this before."

"I wrote it right after you destroyed my sheets and toilet-papered my tree. I thought you found this ages ago!"

He stared at her.

After about ten seconds, he shrugged and spread the blanket on top of the painted letters. "I guess you did." He sat down and began to set out the food.

"Did what?"

"Get me."

He laid down a few sandwiches, some cookies, and two paper plates. Then he looked up at her, his slate-gray eyes dancing.

A smile growing on her face, she sat down beside him. She began to laugh. But her eyes shone when she looked at him and said, "Yes. Yes, I did."

TERMS RELATING TO THE CHURCH OF JESUS CHRIST OF LATTER-DAY SAINTS

Explanations by the author

The Family Proclamation: In 1995, the prophet of the time was inspired to write and share with the world a statement on the family. Back then, most of the principles in the proclamation were embraced by society, and many Latter-day Saints wondered why the proclamation was needed. As the years have passed, society's values have shifted and God's definition of the family has become more pertinent. Many find comfort and clarity in the Family Proclamation.

To read the Family Proclamation, see churchofjesuschrist.org/study/scriptures/the-family-a-proclama-tion-to-the-world

The Word of Wisdom: This was a revelation given to Joseph Smith in 1833. It was introduced slowly, not as a commandment at first but as a guideline from God to benefit those who were more likely to struggle with addictive substances. It has since become a commandment and a prerequisite to enter temples, which are special places of worship. The promises associated with it are beautiful.

For more information about the Word of Wisdom, see churchofjesuschrist.org/study/manual/gospel-topics/word-of-wisdom

Dear Reader

This book was a thrill to write, especially once I decided to switch between three points of view, keeping June's voice alive in between Keisha's determined voice and Jordan's gruff one. I hope you enjoyed both the feud and the change in these families' relationship.

I would love your help in spreading the word about this book. If you're willing to rate and review Neighbor Feud on Amazon or elsewhere, it will help other romance readers know you found it worth your time.

Thank you for reading, and I can't wait to share my next novel with you!

About the Author

Annika Champenois grew up partly in Denmark, partly in Utah, and wholly in the world of books. Today she lives an exciting life, splitting her time between data analysis and giving voice to the stories that dance around in her imagination. Her books are sweet, sometimes sassy, and always clean, dedicated to brighten readers' days and make them laugh.

annikachampenois.com
facebook.com/annikachampenoisauthor
instagram.com/annikachampenois